NORYLSKA GROANS

Tales of the Veneficum

By Michael R. Fletcher & Clayton W. Snyder

This is a work of fiction. Names, characters, business, events, and incidents are the products of the author's imagination. Any resemblance to actual persons, living or dead, Dyrk Ashton or otherwise, or actual events is mostly coincidental.

Editor: Sarah Chorn
Cover Art: Clayton W. Snyder
Typography: Michael R. Fletcher

Other Books by Clayton W. Snyder

River of Thieves

Thieves' War

The Obsidian Psalm

Demons, Ink

Cold West

Other Books by Michael R. Fletcher

Ghosts of Tomorrow

Beyond Redemption

The Mirror's Truth

Swarm and Steel

A Collection of Obsessions

Smoke and Stone – City of Sacrifice #1

Ash and Bones – City of Sacrifice #2

Black Stone Heart – The Obsidian Path #1

She Dreams in Blood – The Obsidian Path #2

The Millennial Manifesto

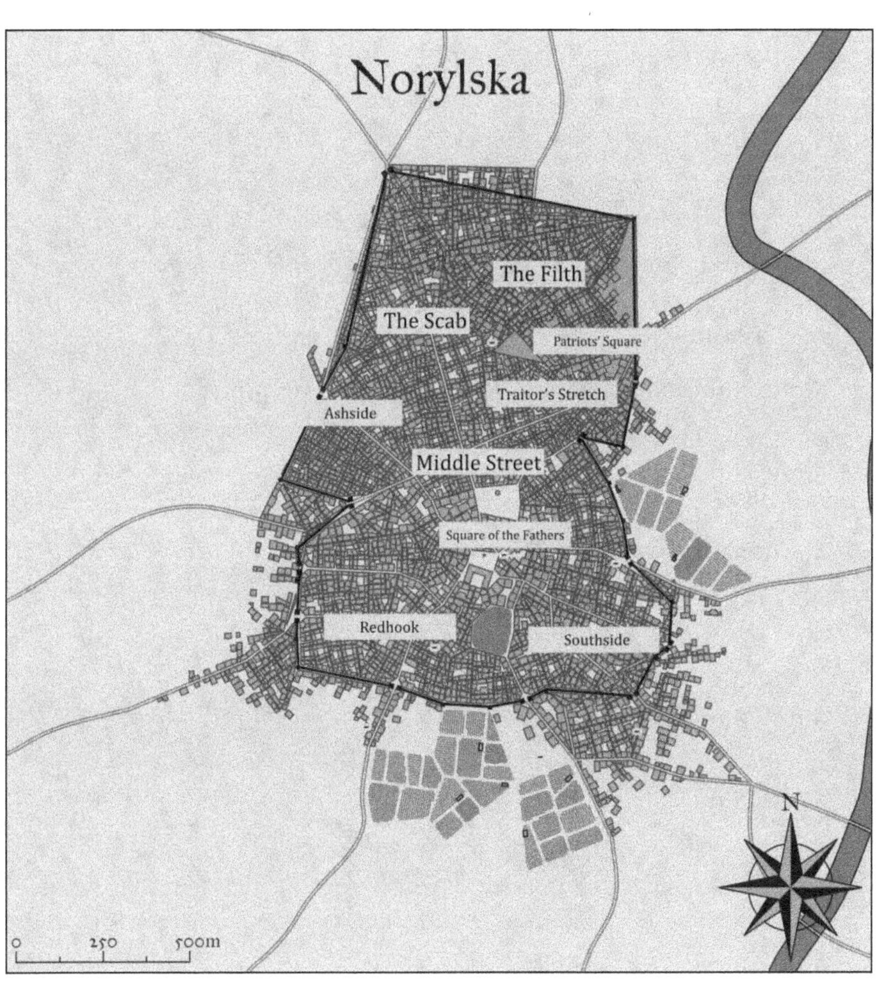

Norylska
The Filth
The Scab
Patriots' Square
Traitor's Stretch
Ashside
Middle Street
Square of the Fathers
Redhook
Southside
0   250   500m
N

Clayton:

For Shelly. Your face parts are in all the right places.

Mike:

For all the crazy people who read this stuff.

GENNDY ANTONOV – CHAPTER ONE

There are three ways to die in Norylska: The cold, the cold, and the cold.

—D Puskyn, Exile

When winter blew in, the bottom fell out.

Gen worked the fleshracks at the rendering plant on the skirts of the Filth for three years before life took a downward turn. It plummeted like a bird shot in the breast, spiraling to the ground. Day in and day out, he'd render fatty layers of the great beasts of the taiga, tearing muscle from bone with the big saws.

The Filth. If the world was an apple, the Filth was its rotting misshapen core. The district's original name had been lost along with the lives of the city planners, and now it was simply *The Filth* to anyone who lived in Norylska. At the northernmost point of the city, ringed by factories, ore refineries, and rendering plants for the megafauna that fed the country, it collected the refuse of Kievan in its streets.

Gen's job was to hang severed flaps of meat on hooks to drip onto the stone floors, driving his shoulder under a flank and heaving upward, nearly a hundred pounds of meat working against his strength and gravity. A shift in weight, a misstep, and it would pop his arm out of the socket as easily as a man rips a bone from a chicken wing.

Once hung, men with curved knives on poles worked their blades beneath the thick skin, pulling down, stripping it away and exposing the fatty layer beneath. Gen moved on to the next slab, hoisting it so the cutters could get to work.

Hung on the scales, life and death weighed out that way. The balance of risk and reward. In this case, for a paltry ten koyln a week.

What might it be like to buy a sack of potatoes and still have money left for oil, or a necklace for Irina?

He lived in the Filth his entire life, scraping for every clipped cent. What he couldn't buy, he stole. What he couldn't steal, he sometimes beat out of a more fortunate man. When he joined the militsiya, he'd only made ten koyln a week from soldiering. When he retired, his pension paid the same ten. Then, when he found work at the factory, another ten. To his parents, twenty would have been a fortune. For his parents, the state hadn't yet begun to tax them to fund the wars, and now his pension was down to five a week. Twenty in their day would have bought food, clothing, and kept a roof over their heads for months. He'd lost a quarter of his pay to the men who'd sent him to die, and all in the name of 'reconstruction'. For Gen, supporting a new family, fifteen barely stretched to make ends meet. At fifteen, a single overspent koyln could land he and Irina in the street.

He heaved another slab of flesh onto a set of hooks, metal protesting against the sturdy steel rail they hung from as the weight of the meat settled. A wave of stink rolled from the raw flesh as it stretched. The stink clung to everything like putrescent perfume. A thick, musky, gamey stench crawled into his head like a cold, and hung out until he thought he'd retch. But then, everything in Norylska stunk. The rendering plants, the oil lamps lighting streets and taverns, the runoff from the stone mines, the acrid stench of rain turned caustic by the smoke belching into the sky. Ash and grease coated every surface of this pit of a city. It clung to his fingers when he touched a doorknob, made his shoes slip on the cobbles, and sat in the back of his throat like a film waiting to be spat into the street.

The saw tore through the flank of another paracera. Inches thick in places, the skin pebbled like river stones, meat laid in thick striations beneath. The blade whirred, driven by steam superheated by coal, ripping into the side, sending a wash of gore across the surface of the cutting table. The gamey stink hit him again, even through the bandana over his face. As bad as it was, nothing stank like Irkysk. Like the war.

Nothing sounded like it, either. Or so Gen thought.

The braying howl of someone nearby snapped Gen from his thoughts. His head jerked to the left to find the source.

Misha.

He'd warned the man, again and again: keep your sleeves rolled, your apron strings short. The warnings weren't enough, the young man had nodded and smiled each time, as if Gen had just shared a joke. Gen wanted to tell him it wasn't a fucking joke, but some men just don't listen.

Gen watched as the big blade hooked Misha's shirt, rolling the tough fabric up like a stray piece of yarn, until it snagged flesh. The saw belched, thick and wet as it dug into Misha's meat.

Misha screamed, the noise a swirling mix of desolation and despair. The sound of a man who saw the end coming, but insisted he still had time. The sound of life draining away onto the snow.

Gen had heard screams like that before. He'd been the other side of the street from a whorehouse. A pimp snipped a man's balls for refusing to pay, leaving the would-be client rolling in the alley, clutching the bloody wasteland of his manhood, a crimson stain spreading between his fingers.

Now, the young man from Khozo, who, just a day before, bragged about how his girl moaned when you slapped her a little, became a red ruin. The blade unraveled flesh as easily as Gen's wife undid a knitted cord.

Misha's skin parted, tendon and muscle laid bare before the saw peeled them away. Next came bone, young and strong, but still no match for a machine made for the big beasts. It ripped and split, marrow leaking out like sap from a fresh cut board.

Misha grabbed the upper part of his arm with his free hand as the saw yanked him in, teeth on the blade catching meat and bone like the inevitable turning of a gear. His fingers scrabbled for purchase on the slick flesh, slipping on the blood.

He braced his feet against the table, halting the agonizing process for a second. His eyes bulged, tears running freely. For a moment, it seemed he might even win his battle. He opened his mouth to say something, cool relief flitting across his features amid the fires of his agony.

Then the saw lurched, internals squealing as the belt overcame resistance, and yanked Misha forward.

Arterial spray arced, spattering Gen in the face. He stepped back in reflex. It wasn't that he didn't want to help. But he'd been frozen by… something. Memory? Fascination? Death was always the same. It wasn't that. The method— the way men traversed from this place to the next, was the interesting part. No two men died the same. That feeling held him in place, and he watched. He knew the only mercy he could offer the man would be a quick blade across the throat.

A deluge of blood spilled in a wave and headed to the drains, mingling with runoff from other stations. The screaming held Gen's attention. Memory rippled briefly through his skull.

A soldier beast snatching an infantryman from the trench and tearing into the victim's torso with teeth like knives of ice.

Gen couldn't say what possessed the beasts to do that. He figured maybe, taking who a man was and trapping them mind and soul in a monster the size of a shack might make them brittle. Angry, even. Ready to take a little bit of sadistic rage out on the world.

Someone jostled him, and the memory burst, leaving him standing alone. The screaming stopped. Misha lay prone on the saw, staring to the side, eyes milky. The blade finally halted at his shoulder, standing out like a serrated wing from his back. Blood pooled beneath the man's body, the stink of voided bowels so strong it crushed the gamey odor of cut beasts.

One of the other men—Vitaly—shouldered past Gen, hook on a pole in hand.

"Gonna help?" he asked.

He snagged the kid's body with his tool, giving the corpse a shake. It made wet squelching sounds on the table but refused to break free. Vitaly grunted and waved to another man further down the line, getting a shout in return. In a moment, the other man came trotting around the corner with his own pole-hook. Together, they caught Misha's shoulders with the poles, tried to pull him up and back, grunts and curses mingling as they worked.

Gen looked around for some way to help, and found Vlad standing at his shoulder. The slight, bald man with a pate full of wrinkles wore an apologetic smile and a single stone around his neck. Memory? Skill? Personality? No, couldn't be personality. Vlad always looked as if he might deliver bad news at any moment.

Your wife has died. Your children were sold into slavery. I ate your cat. It was delicious.

He passed for a simulacrum of humanity in a place like this, one of the few men not covered in gore. He gave his sorrowful smile and gestured for Gen to follow.

They made their way across the factory floor, the plant already lurching back to life as recovery was underway. Misha wasn't the first man killed here and wouldn't be the last. The city needed heat, needed oil, needed meat.

Best not to think on it.

You couldn't forestall winter any more than you could stop a cavalry charge with a stick.

Gen nodded at a few of the men he ate lunch with and climbed the clanging metal and wood staircase behind Vlad.

"You getting time off?" A man called from his line, chunks of fat sliding past on rollers.

"Lucky bastard!" someone else shouted. The room echoed for a moment with laughter before the noise of the stairs and the immediacy of the job cut it off.

The heels of Vlad's boots made a different sound than Gen's as they climbed. Good soles, not the shit boots he could afford. Why own something you didn't need? That was a question about the wealthy all the philosophers in Kievan couldn't answer. He wondered what possessed men to take a job like supervisor in a slaughterhouse. Seemed to be more honest to at least take part in the cutting, instead of putting on airs above the floor. Man's only as good as the work of his hands, his father used to say.

He suspected the answer to both was simple: they're pricks.

Never trust a man without dirt under his nails. Or in this case, blood.

Service guarantees citizenship slipped into his head, that old propaganda chestnut the state hammered into them time and again. Property, pension, the good life. Pick up a rifle and kill some Altin Ordu, that's all they asked. On that, at least, Gen could agree. Altin Ordu needed killing.

Vlad led them through a simple door with a glass window, his name and title stenciled on it. In the office, noise from the work floor fell to muted levels. It even stunk a little less. A simple desk, with a chair on each side, stood near the opposite wall. Behind that, a shelf, various objects piled atop it. Vlad collapsed into his chair and gestured for Gen to do the same.

Gen glanced at the knickknacks on the shelf. A sketch of a plump woman, done in broad strokes. She was pretty, in her own way. A piece of wood carved to look like a Khagan tower—slender, with a cupola atop it, and words burned into the base. A paracera tooth. Gen flicked his gaze away, to the stack of papers clinging to the edge of the desk like a handful of promises, and finally sat. Vlad leaned forward, fingers interlaced, hands on the bald wood surface. He still wore that half-sorrowful smile, and Gen wondered if the stone hanging around his neck had something to do with it. Which traits might it have? Which memories?

"You've been here how long?" Vlad asked.

Gen's stomach threatened to flip. No one who ever meant to deliver good news started it with an accounting of time. "Three years, sir."

"Three years." Vlad turned in his chair, until he could look out the thick bubbled glass overlooking the factory floor. "That'd make you a junior man here, yeah?"

"Yes, sir," Gen said. Cold certainty pushed into his bowels like a worm.

"Hard times. Hard times," Vlad said. "Things aren't what they used to be. Lost two teams to a herd of paracera last month. Did you know that? Yeah, two teams. Getting harder to hunt the bastards. And then there are the exiles. Flesh carvers, you know? Eat a man alive. And now winter's coming, that cold bitch. Can't send anyone else out until the thaw hits."

He spun his chair back, leaned forward on elbows sharp as knives, and tented his fingers. He looked at Gen through the web he'd made and gave his sad smile.

Like an erection on a dog.

"You see my problem? Not enough men out there, too many men in here. I can't send you out there because, well, I don't run that business. And the men in here have been *here*. Not that you haven't, you understand. But they've had their positions longer. You have to reward loyalty like that, yeah?"

A memory, cold and nasty, hovered at the edge of Gen's thoughts. The man's words echoed those of the state, before they gave the men who bled for them the shove-off.

Vlad paused. Gen didn't know what the man expected from him.

Does he want acknowledgement? Some sort of understanding? Absolution?

Gen offered none of those things. The cold worm in his gut turned, sunk needle teeth into his spine.

He was numb, disconnected. He nodded mutely; only half-aware of the words spilling from Vlad. Irina. The baby. How would he feed them? How would he house them? Every winter was a killing winter, and without fail, when the thaw came, refuse and bodies frozen to the cobbles choked the alleys.

"You're a military man, right?" Vlad asked.

Gen nodded again.

"Good, good. You'll find something. Plenty of work for strong, willing men out there." He took a breath, licked lips cracked from the perpetual cold. "Now, don't look as if I've just stabbed your puppy. You'll be fine. You've got your pension. That pretty wife. She'll keep you warm."

For a moment, like a spark threatening to catch dry leaves, rage welled in Gen's chest, and the numbness fled. He imagined taking this man, grabbing the back of his head and smashing his skull into the worn desk until there was nothing left but splintered wood, shattered teeth, and gore.

"We'll send your things. You understand," Vlad finished.

I have no things.

The company provided lockers for the workers, but what would he keep here? A service revolver? Then he could dirty the floor with his brains when the pain of twenty years lay on him like a lead weight? Hell of a retirement plan.

Vlad gestured to the door at the far end of the room, indicating the interview had come to a close. Gen blinked once, rage receding. He stood and, without another look, trudged out of the room. The door shut with a small click behind him.

Gen took the stairs, one at a time, footfalls echoing in the empty stairwell. Shame rose in him, followed by a black wave of depression and fear threatening to overwhelm and subsume rational thought. He fumbled with the exit door, stumbling into an alley stinking of smoke and rancid fat.

He leaned against the wall; bricks cool against his back. Wind snapped through the city, stirring papers at his feet. For a moment, the world smelled of ice and rage. Memory chased its heels and smashed into him for the second time that day.

Irkysk. They fought for seven days, no sun. Only hazy light varying in intensity from hour to hour. Smoke obscured it, a black fist clenching the fiery disc as if it could quench the flame. Early on, they'd traded artillery barrages with the Altin Ordu. The shells digging great smoking holes in dirt and men, the bottom of the trench a carmine river, body parts like shoals of broken fish floating past.

Then one of their own guns misfired. The detonation took out their right flank. The enemy cavalry wheeled in to fill it, hacking with sabers, opening men like bags of suet, insides spilling out in a haruspex's wet dream.

Great soldier beasts—monsters with the minds of men, thanks to the efforts of the veneficum and their stones—tore men limb from limb or met their Altin Ordu counterparts on the field.

The cold set in. Rivers of blood froze, making footing treacherous. The dead stuck to the ground, limbs sometimes trapped at awkward angles, a nightmare forest of petrified flesh. Where soldiers were able to break or hack them free, they piled corpses as high as possible, a makeshift barricade of arrested rot where the craters left their lines open.

Still the Altin Ordu came. Pale skin and eyes. Uniforms decorated with frippery—

ribbons and medals, ropes and braids. They wore mustaches over their lips and plucked their eyebrows. Some powdered their faces before battle, others drowned themselves in perfume, until it smelled like a cathouse come calling, razor in hand.

Decadent. Iniquitous, his instructors had called them.

Gen remembered thinking they left 'deadly' off the list after a quarter of his line fell to men with lightning-fast reflexes and thin, wicked blades.

In return, Gen did what he had been trained to do. The only recourse they left him. He killed them—young and old, fat and skinny, weak and strong. If they stepped within range of his rifle, he put a round in them. When the rounds ran out, and the cavalry horses were panting and lathered with foam, and the bastards were still sliding into the trenches, he killed even more.

No gods. Only men. Save yourself.

If there were gods, this might have been avoided. Surely no beneficent deity allowed slaughter on such a scale.

Dimly, he was aware of the saber he held, blade dull and heavy. His shoulder was throbbing, body aching, weaving on his feet from lack of sleep. And still he killed. Not killing meant joining the vast pile of dead to the north.

Those days, he had youth. He had plans. No, death wasn't in it for him. Not until he had the chance to crack the bones of the earth and suck its marrow.

The stupidity of youth.

And so, he cut, a butcher with an endless supply of meat.

When it ended, warmth swaddled him like a newborn. A dripping sound accompanying it as he sank to the ground. Red obscured his vision.

The blood of others helped take the sting out of winter.

The wind kicked up again, cold battering. He looked up from the memory, saw the alley. Saw the trash at his feet. Recollection and experience littered his heart much the same way. Reality came back like a thug kicking in a door, murdering everyone inside. He'd lost his job. His income. Irina. The baby. How would he care for them? His nerves tensed, and he tasted bile.

He needed a drink.

KATYUSHKA LEONOVA – CHAPTER TWO

A veneficum is part sorcerer, part alchemist, and part psychologist. Theirs is the art of drawing memories and personality traits from people and storing them in stone. In polite society they are therapists, dedicated to helping people. They draw out painful memories and dangerous traits so their patients may lead healthy, productive lives. The stones storing dangerous and unhealthy memories and traits are destroyed.

But there is a dark side to the art. What is stored in stone can be accessed by anyone touching it. Back-alley veneficum buy or steal pleasant memories and useful personality traits from the desperate to sell to the powerful and hawk cheap stones to the poor. Bravery. Inventiveness. Compassion. What is surprising, however, is the demand for less savoury memories and traits.

—Iskusstvo Veneficum

Unable to sleep, Katyushka rose before the sun. She slipped from bed, careful not to wake Fyodor. Collecting the wool shawl from the back of a chair, she threw it over her shoulders, padding barefoot to the kitchen. Each breath plumed before her like a tiny cloud. The ancient wood floor, shellacked in varnish, grumbled and creaked with each step.

Norylska groans.

She first heard those words from a retired soldier, days before father brought them north. That was three years ago. One night in Kievan's northernmost coal mining city and she understood. Norylska was never silent. The smelting furnaces worked night and day, belching smoke and soot. A constant flow of coal wagons, hauled by massive aurochs, rumbled the streets, shaking the walls with their passing. The reducing-factories growled and screamed like rusting grinders, turning the paraceratherium and other megafauna of the ancient Taymyr Forest into the fat, oil, meat, and furs Kievan relied on. The cold shrank wood and iron, squeezing it in an icy fist. Douse the fires of the furnaces, stop every coal and meat wagon, freeze every person motionless, from the highest chancellor to the lowest prostitute, and Norylska would still moan under the crushing pressure.

Katyushka found the woodstove dead, filled with ash. The woodrack sat empty and accusing. She'd been too excited about her first day at work and forgotten to fill it. Fyodor would be angry. He hated being cold, hated waiting for his morning coffee.

Collecting the hemp sling she used to carry wood, Katyushka stepped into her boots. Somehow, they were colder than the wood floor. Her feet ached. Not bothering to lace them, she unlatched the door and stepped into the dark. The sun, far to the southeast and never much clearing the horizon this time of year, had yet to blush the sky. If there were stars above, the belched vomitus of the coal furnaces occluded them.

Huddling in her shawl, she hurried to the woodpile. Her nostrils froze closed with her third inhalation. She'd heard stories of people's lungs freezing and tearing from the cold, their teeth shattering. Every day the sootmen who cleared the streets, collecting the filthy coal-stained snow in their wagons and hauling it north to the forges and furnaces, found rigid corpses. She'd seen a few frozen dead. Most still had their teeth. She wasn't sure about the condition of their lungs.

Sheltered in a narrow alley, the woodpile was mostly snow-free. Filling the sling with wood and kindling until she struggled under the weight, Katyushka returned to the kitchen to find Fyodor slumped in one of the chairs.

Rubbing his eyes, he peered blearily up at her. "You let the stove go out."

"Sorry," Kat said, stacking the wood in the rack.

He watched, glancing toward the cold kettle with a frown of disappointment.

That stung. As the youngest lawyer at Kuznetsov and Alyokhin, it wouldn't do for him to arrive at work looking like he'd done menial labour. The partners were particular about the types they hired and not terribly picky about who they fired. Last week Fyodor told Katyushka they let a junior partner go because he went to court with mud on his shoes.

'The sacrifices we make now,' Fyodor often said, 'will pay off later.'

He had a five-year plan. The *long game*, he called it. Once he made junior partner, they'd get married and move into the southern quarter, to somewhere less embarrassing to live. In this little shack, with but one slim alley separating them from Middle Street, he could never invite senior lawyers to dinner.

They made sacrifices, both of them. Fyodor worked long hours, often returning late to shovel food into his mouth and collapse into bed. Sometimes the lawyers met at The Golden Chalice, a drinking and gambling establishment located in the legal district. He hated it. Disliked crowds and the social pressure to match his vodka intake with the other young lawyers, whom he complained outweighed him by a good twenty pounds.

'No one likes a weakling,' he'd say. 'A man is judged by how well he holds his vodka.'

And so, at the end of each week, he stumbled home drunk, pipe and cigar smoke not quite concealing the expensive perfume of the waitstaff.

She'd learned not to complain. Doing so only upset him and made things uncomfortable. Anyway, it wasn't so bad. Once he made senior partner, he wouldn't have to attend these functions every time.

Katyushka did her part too, handling the messier tasks so Fyodor wouldn't have to waste time scrubbing dirt from his fingernails every morning before work. She did the shopping in the northern markets, where the coal and butchery workers shopped, because it was cheaper. It was a long walk, hauling bags of groceries nearly an hour each way, but it meant Fyodor could afford to keep his only suit in good repair. There were nicer markets a few minutes south, with better selections of fruit and vegetables, and meat. Fyodor said the prices would beggar them.

With the fire lit, Katyushka took the bucket outside to fill it with snow to be melted and filtered for coffee.

Fyodor waited, fingers drumming impatiently on the tabletop.

"I'm going to be late tonight," he said, when she finally placed a steaming mug before him. "Alyokhin wants me as Second on the Teplov case."

"Is that the one where the neighbor's dog keeps crapping in the magistrate's garden?"

Who cares about a garden buried under two feet of snow?

Fyodor shook his head, distracted. Sipping his coffee, he grimaced. "Maybe we can splurge a *little*. Just on coffee." Pushing the hair from his eyes, he dashed her a boyish grin. "I can pick it up while I'm at work, save you the walk."

"Thanks, hon."

He bit his bottom lip, nose wrinkling, and she knew what he was going to say. They'd argued about it for weeks.

Katyushka waited.

"Do you really think," he began, hesitating, and then reconsidering his approach. "The partners... We'll be fine without..."

She hoped he was smoother in the courtroom.

"Working in the north quarter?" he asked, all doubt and concern. "All those men… *militsioners?*" he added like it was a dirty word. "Maybe it's too dangerous?"

Maybe. That word. Always that word. Half question, half suggestion. His unwillingness to be definitive was the only thing she disliked about him. By asking questions instead of making statements, he left little room for discussion.

"I'll be in the secretarial pool," she said, retreading old ground. "The most dangerous part of my day will be the walk to work."

"That's dangerous enough!"

"I make the same walk to buy groceries," she pointed out.

"You know I hate that." Fyodor's eyes changed, like the man she knew stepped back and someone altogether different took control. "You know I worry about you. If anything happened…" He gave his coffee cup a despondent look. "I'm working as hard as I can. As soon as I make junior partner, you'll never have to shop in the north end again."

"It's not that bad."

In the north, her rough clothes didn't draw the same looks of disdain they did in Norylska's southern quarter. She was just another woman shopping for her family. Not once had anyone bothered or accosted her.

Kat wanted to say that taking this secretarial job would ease the pressure on him, get them out of this border district faster, but knew he'd see that as a condemnation. Her employment was a slight to his manhood. Supporting a wife and family was a man's duty—not that they were married yet. If she lacked something, he felt it was his failure. She went to great efforts to want as little as possible.

She'd heard things were changing in the capital. So many men died during the long and bloody war with the Altin Ordu, now women were forced to take jobs. A few years ago, an employed woman would have been unthinkable. Now, in Khagan, women worked factories and assembly lines. Daughters of wealthy families worked in corporate positions, stepping in to fill vacancies left by the deaths of firstborn males. Little of that had reached Norylska. This far from the hustle and bustle of the heart of Kievan, such things were still seen as gross contradictions of the natural order.

After a quiet and uncomfortable breakfast of cold sausage and boiled potatoes, leftovers from last night's dinner, Katyushka and Fyodor left for work. Fyodor headed south to the legal district. Kat walked north.

Squat and grey, with wrought iron bars on every window and crenellations lining the roof, the Chernyshevsky Street Militsiya Bureau looked like a prison. All it lacked was an outer wall and rifle towers. The massive iron-bound oak doors were no invitation to enter. Broad-shouldered no-necked men in black militsioner greatcoats stomped in and out. Each wore a standard militsiya-issued iron-tipped cudgel, but many also wore a selection of personal equipment. Knuckle-dusters and an array of vicious, serrated blades seemed to be favourites. Officers, always from the better families, uniforms crisp and creased, wore polished revolvers.

Katyushka's uniform, never before worn, starched hard and merciless, itched and scraped as she walked. The shirt chafed at her armpits and neck. The ankle-length skirt, stiff as a board, made a grating swish with every step. She wasn't sure if it was designed by someone who'd never seen a woman, or by someone who never *wanted* to see one. Unlike the black of men's uniforms, hers was the sickly blue she'd been informed was standard to the Secretarial Pool. Heading up the steps, she saw no other similar uniforms, no other women at all. Judging by the looks from the men, eyes widening and then narrowing as they searched for some hint of curve or femininity, they hadn't seen any women recently, either. At least not in the precinct.

Shoulders hunched, Kat tried to shrink to nothing, make herself invisible. When a man with head like an anvil, cigareta clenched in angry yellow teeth, stomped through the front doors, she ducked in behind him. Inside, she found a long hall lined with plaques of wood and bronze, names carved into each one. Avoiding the centre of the hall, she stayed near the wall, reading as she walked. Militsioner Preobrazhensky – fallen in the line of duty. Militsioner Kuznetsov – missing and presumed dead. Fallen in the... Missing... On and on, hundreds of plaques.

The man at the front desk, old and bent with age, black uniform faded grey and wrinkled, watched her approach with a jaundiced eye. An equally frayed patch covered the other. With a shaking hand missing two fingers and a thumb, he lifted a crumpled cigareta to wrinkled lips, inhaled hard, and blew a cloud of smoke into her face as she arrived. Somewhat concave, his face looked as if it had been shaped by decades of smoking. Beyond him, chaos. Scores of desks, all littered with loose paper spattered with ink and hastily scrawled notes in the blunt hand of the poorly educated, were scattered at random. Cheap hand-rolled cigareta, clamped in stained teeth or used to punctuate whatever the men were yelling about, turned the air blue with smoke.

Saluting, Kat said, "Katyushka Leonova reporting for duty, sir."

He either winked or blinked at her, jamming a bent, yellowed finger under the eyepatch and rummaging around as if searching for something.

"Secretarial Pool," she added, when he said nothing.

"Didn't think y'were a door-kicker," he grunted.

An officer cleared his throat at her side. "Excuse me, ma'am." An elderly gentleman, bent at the shoulders, he wore three stars and two stripes on the ep-aulettes of his uniform. Where most men got fatter as they aged, he seemed to be going in the opposite direction. A black cigareta dangled, forgotten, in his mouth.

"Colonel," she said, starting to salute.

Catching her arm, he said, "We don't do that here."

"The textbook—"

"Is old, and this is Norylska."

Uncertain, Katyushka glanced from the officer to the old man at the desk. *Shift Sergeant*, she remembered, belatedly. He'd already gone back to shuffling crumpled papers and raining ash all over his paperwork.

"I'm Colonel Grinin." The officer studied her, looking her up and down. There was nothing vulgar about the appraisal; he might have been checking a potato for blemishes. "You might do rather well for a project that's landed in my lap." Remembering his cigareta, he inhaled hard. A lazy worm of smoke coiled from his nostrils as if exhaling demanded too much effort. "Follow."

Without waiting, he spun on a polished bootheel and strode away. He led with his forehead as if he'd ram through anyone who got in his way.

Everyone scattered from his path.

Noting the downcast eyes and concealed looks of fear on these hardened militsioners, Katyushka obediently followed.

A monstrous oak desk, no doubt hauled here from Khagan, filled most of Colonel Grinin's office. The walls were bare, devoid of family portraits or awards. An oil painting of Tsar Khromov sat propped in one corner as if someone had been distracted as they were about to hang it.

Shoving aside a pile of papers, Grini perched on the corner. Stacks of bound reports filled the chair on the far side. He drew an ornate cigareta tin from the breast pocket of his uniform, and lifted it in offering. When she shook her head, he selected one for himself, using the nub of the previous smoke to light it. Though sunken and frail with age, his eyes remained bright and alert.

Crushing the finished smoke into an overflowing ashtray, he said, "There is a project. A new project." Smoke leaked from his nose as he talked. "Orders from Khagan."

Katyushka read nothing in his expression, no hint of emotion.

"Tensions are rising in the west. The Altin Ordu army gathers on the bor-der."

"War?" she asked. "Again? So soon?" The last war, a decade-long conflict, ended two years ago. Kievan still reeled in the aftermath, the majority of the em-pire's young men buried in shallow trenches far from home.

Colonel Grinin ignored her questions. "I have been instructed to place a few women into... active duty. As a test."

A test? For what?

Not daring to ask, she said, "My training is secretarial."

"Memory stones from retired..." he inhaled, leaked smoke, "from retired officers will give you the knowledge you need. Have you ever fired a weapon?"

"Of course not."

"Have you ever been in a fight?"

Shocked, she shook her head.

"Soft, then," he said. "The veneficum will fix that."

Veneficum?

She'd never worn stones before but had heard horror stories of back-alley veneficum tearing memories and personality traits from helpless victims.

Grinin focussed on Kat and she suddenly understood why all those militsioner scampered from his path. "I want you to volunteer."

Is that an order? She didn't know how to ask.

"I'd have to discuss this with—"

"The pay is double that of a secretary."

Double? That would get her and Fyodor out of the north-end much quicker. She could really contribute!

"I'd make what the men make?" she asked.

"Don't be silly, girl."

"Right. Of course. Sorry."

"I'll assign one of my best officers to look after you. You'll be perfectly safe. I promise. This is purely for show. I've been instructed to make sure this little project succeeds."

"Why?" she blurted.

He scowled. "A good militsioner does not question a superior officer. You'll know that once you have the right stones."

The right stones. Fear shivered through her. At least if they were giving her stones, they weren't carving out parts of her personality. When she removed the stones, she'd be herself again.

Grinin spoke like she'd already volunteered. Maybe she had. Father always sounded bitter when he talked about 'volunteering' to move the family to Norylska. Maybe sometimes you were *volunteered.*

What happens if I reject the offer?

She didn't want to find out.

And double the pay!

"Should I—"

"Dismissed."

So that's what volunteering feels like.

GENNDY ANTONOV – CHAPTER THREE

Neither the militsiya nor the people care if you fail. It is neither the job of the institutions of the state nor that of your fellow comrades to support you. Instead, it is your own right, the right of every true patriot, to lift themselves up and build their own fortress amid the injustice of the world. The weak will fall away, leaving true stone behind. Only then can we begin the work of fortifying the nation.

—D Puskyn, Exile

By the time Gen started moving again, slipping from the alley behind the fleshracks on numb feet, the wind redoubled its efforts. The temperature dropped as he walked past rows of tenements, the structures brown shambles, wood slats curved from decades of exposure to the elements and poison from the factories. Residents stuffed the cracks between the boards with old rags, thick daubs of mud, and in some cases, masses of stinking fur cut from stray dogs and ever-present rats.

If you can count on one thing in this stinking city, count on rats. Animal and otherwise.

In the summer, the homes smelled of piss and decay, enhancing the already powerful stench of the rest of the Filth. One upside to winter: Ice deadened scent as easily as camphor under the nose. In the south, they said the north burned out your sense of smell. Gen thought the opposite true. You just became more attuned to the ever-present shit-stink of a city that hated you.

All over the Filth, things were the same. The war ground men to meat. The ones who survived, however, still needed to be housed. The government promised, after all, and it wouldn't do to break a promise to an army of freshly trained killers who'd cut their teeth on flesh and bone.

Over the years, the cynicism of the move became apparent to Gen. He saw the way the government kept its promises. Tenements were kept away from the gentry, where the common man wouldn't stink up the hardwood parlors. Forced into jobs no one else wanted. Soldiers paid with a pension, then levied with tax, the excuse being, in the wake of so much loss, they needed the money to rebuild.

You've given to your country, and we are grateful, but a true patriot, a hero, never stops giving, they'd say.

More likely, they needed it to line someone's pockets. The situation reminded him of those stories where a man wishes for his dead wife to return, and the malevolent spirit granting it kills his son in exchange or drags her rotting from her grave and gives her the semblance of anima. A knife where even the hilt wounds.

Horror stories, all.

He turned up the street to Hawker's Row, where the tenements ended and the businesses began. They didn't have a lot of money, but Irina liked to come here in the warmer months and window shop. She'd stand in front of the dressmaker and clasp her hands, sometimes twirling in place, imagining skirts flaring out around her. Other times, she'd lean into a jeweler's window, eyes fixed on a little stone with a particularly brilliant shine. Rare enough, that. The jewelry stores in the Filth were nearly, to a man, run by conmen. Didn't do to have real gems down here. No one could afford them, anyway.

Regardless, she'd stare, then make up stories about the jewels she liked, their reflected light sparkling in her eyes.

"Oh, that one! Look at the shine. I'll bet it was an imp's heart, once. Probably dug from its chest by a man hoping to bring it to his daughter," or "If I had that, I'd wear it on my neck all the time, and all the other women would be so envious. I'd tell them about how you loved me, and," she'd turn her head, and raise her eyebrows, a slight smirk lifting the corner of her mouth, "and how you love me."

Gen always blushed at that. He loved her heart. Strong and irrepressible, he didn't doubt she would impress the Tsar should he come calling. Her adages always made him smile. It wasn't where you lived, but who you lived with. It wasn't what you didn't have, it was what you did with what was on hand.

And yet... you've failed her.

Guilt and anxiety in a flood, filling the cracks in his soul. Despite her generosity of spirit, or maybe because of it, a part of him always considered himself unworthy of her love. Now he'd failed—he paused, leaning against the rough wood of a cobbler's shop. The sound of a hammer came from within, and he counted the strokes and sucked in a deep breath, heart slowing. Cold air, like ice on mint rushed down his throat, and it helped cool his feverish thoughts. He thought of that drink again, and pushed off the wall, leaving the cobbler behind.

Another turn, and the street widened into a plaza. Businesses bordered it on three sides, the fourth a mostly boarded up but still occupied old precinct of the local militsiya. Statues stood at the cardinal points, though the rain had long washed any discerning features from the stone. In the halcyon days before the Filth came into being and the planners had such high hopes for the glory of the Empire, it had been known as Patriot's Square. The idea was, anyone walking through might be inspired to serve the cause.

A set of gallows stood in the center of the square, the statues facing toward it like a blind jury. Snow drifted from the sky. Though the clouds hadn't completely occluded the rising sun, leaving the horizon a burning brand on

Gen's irises, the black shapes swinging in the wind broke the beauty of the distant view. The convicted turned gently, faces bloated and purple, bodies swollen with gas. Tongues and eyes protruded from purplish flesh and blue lips. The creak of the rope a mournful counterpoint to the wind. A sign had been tacked to the base; the words sketched out in black paint.

SEDITION, it read.

It should have said POOR.

Isn't that always the way? The less money, the harsher the punishment, no matter the size of the transgression. Likely, these poor souls had done nothing more than question some policy of the government's within earshot of the wrong people. Or perhaps they had the bad taste to be near starvation, stealing a crust of bread while bloated politicians feast on steaming roast.

Gen turned away as the wind picked up. His fingers and toes tingled with the first pins and needles of cold, and he hurried past the square and onto Crown Street. Here, inns and bars shouldered one another for space, some already with carriages waiting, others with beggars hoping to score a few coins and find a warm place to sleep before winter came down like a hammer on the anvil of the city.

The Bucket was a squat thing pressed between a lender and a pawn shop, narrow in the front, long in body, it glowered out at the street. Light spilled out onto the darkening lane, laughter and music following as the door did a steady trade. Gen shouldered his way in, past a bouncer with a scar running the length of his jawline. The air pushed in close and hot, the room stank of body odor, cigareta, and stale beer. Threadbare red carpet covered the floor, the walls paneled with a thin veneer of dark wood. Dirty brass accents marked the lamps and rail of the bar, a long wooden counter running along one wall. Two bartenders worked it, doling out drinks.

Gen pushed through groups of men and women gathered on the floor, most of them with the still-blackened faces and stinking clothing of miners off-shift. A row of booths crowded the opposite wall, hosting the hardcore drunks, men on the dole who had little prospect, but enough government money to ruin their livers. Some mumbled over their drinks, others stared into space or lay face-down on the small table before them, drool forming a puddle at the corner of their mouths.

He reached the bar and pulled up a miraculously empty stool. The bartender, a woman in her forties, raw red eyes colored by drug, smoke, or sorrow, and hair the color of straw pulled back in a tail, eyed him.

"Drink," she said without preamble.

A tic made her cheek jump, her lips chapped. Her sleeve pulled up as she moved, a cluster of pockmarks forming a constellation in her flesh. Probably a kroc user, then. The stuff devoured addicts from the inside, causing a variety of nervous system and muscular problems.

"Drink," she said again, tinged with impatience.

"Vodka," Gen replied. Not a hard choice in Norylska. You had vodka, brandy, vodka, pivo, vodka, and kvass.

She snorted and threw a bottle and glass in front of him. Gen nodded his thanks and dug through his wallet, coming up with the cost. After a moment's thought, he included a modest tip. He knew he shouldn't, with the job gone and the baby on the way, but he'd already sat down.

Can't dig the hole much deeper.

He popped the cork. His hand hardly shook when he poured his first measure, the scent of alcohol burning his nostrils. It smelled like the degreaser they used in the factory. He slugged the drink down and grimaced. It tasted like it, too.

Funny story, that. He tried it once—degreaser, that is. Dima, who looked like boiled leather, and was probably twice as old, had convinced him. They'd pulled extra duty, cleaning the shop for inspection. Dima swore you could get a buzz from the stuff if you filtered it through a rag. Gen vomited for an hour and ended the night with a three-day headache the old man's laughter did nothing to help. He swore off anything stronger than vodka on the spot.

The burn from the first shot faded, and Gen poured another. He stared into it for a moment, the bottom of the glass distorted through the crystal liquor.

Irina. The baby.

The thought of returning to their little home at the edge of the Filth nearly overwhelmed him, like a hook snagged between his shoulder blades. He felt it dig into his spine like knives, ripping into sinew and bone, the pain of it pushing the air from his lungs, seeking a heart poisoned by disillusion and lies. They'd promised him a life outside the militsiya. A life colored by lack of want. What he got fell so short of utopia, it caused misery to pound in his head like the drummers in the back of the lines, commissars screaming out orders.

Gen's hands shook worse than before, but he managed to get the next shot in him. Fire burned his throat, chased by ice. Numbness spread. Not total, but enough. His hands calmed; fingers stopped gripping glass to the point of shattering. He took a breath, sat back, squared his shoulders. Rubbed a hand across his face.

He'd thought once to see a veneficum about his anxiety and fear. The little things adding up, barbs on a poisonous bush, leaving him shaking and sweating in the night. But no veneficum would see him without a fee, and without a job it was just another pipe dream.

He glanced around the room again. Miners stood in clusters across the floor, throwing vodka and brandy back like water. The toll of their job wrote itself in the way they stood, half-stooped, lines etched in the face, fingers gnarled where they weren't missing, bodies twisted like trees bent by the wind.

In the booths, half the insensate drunks still wore militsiya jackets, patches relating them to one brigade or another. Likely washouts or exiles. No former soldier clung to some vaporous idea of glory like those that had never been or failed in trying.

Lounging in the darkest corners, men in faded finery reclined, with others still drunk on hope beside them. They didn't spend better than anyone else, and likely didn't smell any different, but those clinging to them like lice on a prisoner held on to the hope *this* political exile only played at exile, a prince slumming it.

Gen weighed his prospects. He could try for the mines. Miners had a short life-expectancy, but he only needed a few months' work to get on his feet. Once winter ended, the fleshracks would take him back. He stared at one former soldier, face-down in his own drool. Mercenary work wasn't an option. Not enough pay, too much risk. Perhaps if the salary were a few hundred koyln more... but no. You could not raise a family on only enough pay to drink in a night. The mines for him, then.

Kill another, or kill myself? No one aside from Irina will miss one more Filth man. And not even her if I fail again.

A ripple of discontent traveled through the bar, more felt than seen. The noise pulled him from his morose thoughts. Gen looked up in time to catch a lean man dressed like a Filth resident carrying himself like a sheathed blade, slipping in. He glad-handed people as he went, leaving a trail of sour looks and discontent. At his heels, a small brunette followed, cute in the way Gen might have liked twenty years ago, crisp blue suit marking her out.

Militsiya. Fuck. What a capper to a shitshow of a day. What's next? Firing squad?

Someone jostled his elbow as he contemplated, a cultured but friendly voice following it up.

"Sorry, friend."

Gen looked over. The man who bumped him wore a genial smile, hands open in apology. He wore a well-made suit, fingers adorned with rings, the chains of necklaces disappearing under his shirt. Face heart-shaped and dark, hair slicked back, he held out a hand.

"Let me buy you another…"

"Genndy," Gen said. "Antonov."

The man's smile grew wider as Gen took his hand and shook it. "Arkady Vetrov."

His grabbed Gen's hand with a firm, warm grip.

Arkady signaled the bartender for two more drinks, and while she readied the bottles, swung to Gen. He indicated the already half-empty bottle in front of Gen.

"Long day?"

"Yeah," Gen said. He hesitated. The liquor loosened him up some, but an unspoken rule in Norylska said troubles were only shared among friends and family. And even then, rarely.

The drinks came, and Arkady turned, leaned on the bar, elbows on the polished wood. He picked his glass up, took a sip. "Let me guess. Job let you go?"

Gen tasted his own drink. The other man had ordered brandy, a nice change from the vodka. Pleasant fire versus the cold burn of ice. "You a militsioner?" Gen asked.

Arkady laughed and shook his head. "No, just observant. You ever notice how the plants need fewer workers every year, but the men at the top get richer?" He glanced over his shoulder, in the direction of Patriot's Square, then pressed a finger to his lips and winked. "But that is just the talk of drunkards, no?"

Gen allowed himself a small smile at the temerity of the man. This close to the Square, you never knew who might be in the crowd. "Yes, drunkards and dead men," he said.

"To drunkards and dead men, then!" Arkady announced and held his cup out for Gen to clink his own glass against.

Gen lifted his drink, and someone bumped him for the second time that morning. Liquor splashed across his lips and down the front of his shirt. Turning to look, he found himself face to face with a staggering miner. The man leaned in, breath stinking like turpentine, spittle flying from his lips as he vented his frustration on the nearest target.

"Leech!" the miner declared. "Fuckin'… fuckin'… welfare cases. Ain't got enough to go around, and you shits suck it up anyway," he spat.

Tension snapped at the heels of his rant, violence threatening to break like a storm. This close, the man's breath stunk of alcohol and meat. Like burning carrion. Gen shoved him back, and the drunk stumbled into a pale, skittery youth.

The boy flinched, a kroc user mid-high, scabrous wounds tracking the length and breadth of his forearms. A blade appeared in his hand, then in the miner's belly. Blood drooled from around the knife and onto the carpet as the man staggered back with four inches of steel in his guts, fingers scrabbling at the hilt.

The bar erupted as miners attempted to get at the youth. The kid threw himself under a table to escape. The building became a melee, bodies and fists thrown together in a rain of flesh.

Fists hammered jaws and noses. Hands broke on impact. Snot and teeth littered the floor. The spatter of vomit pattered onto bare wood, acrid stink billowing from pools and joining the growing cloud of copper-scented rage. Voices bellowed curses, cries of pain. Someone wept in a corner.

Men, red-faced and too long repressed, mouths open in snarls, went at one another with anything to hand.

Bottles shattered over skulls; flesh ripped by broken glass. A crescendo of violence, the conductor the ever-present state.

Someone came at Arkady, an upraised mug in his hand, intending to smash it into the other man's skull.

Gen moved, stepping inside the man's reach, blocking it with his arms. He hooked one leg around the attacker's, and with his free hand slammed an open palm into his sternum.

The would-be assailant went down in a tangle of limbs and curses. He made to rise, but a knot of fighting men obscured him from view and the press of bodies soon trapped him.

"Gen!" Arkady shouted in warning.

Gen spun and saw another man coming at him with a knife. The drunk's lip lifted in a sneer, coat open. Instinct took over, and Gen snapped himself to the side as the man lunged, Gen trapping the knife arm with his own. He locked the man's elbow, then used his free hand to press down at the wrist.

The elbow dislocated with a sickening pop, and the knife fell from nerveless fingers.

Not enough.

Gen pressed harder, and bone snapped, elbow bending the wrong way. The man screamed and clutched his arm as Gen released him.

He grabbed the soldier's coat and spun him into another knot of brawlers, adding a boot to his ass for momentum and good measure. The soldier crashed headlong into the fracas and disappeared; his cries were those of a wounded animal.

The melee continued, though only half-heartedly as though the resounding snap of bone and resulting scream were trumpets sounding retreat. Gen tucked himself tighter against the bar, keeping Arkady to his left, eyes scanning the crowd like a man watching for bears in the taiga.

The only thing these animals understand is blood.

It was his inner voice, but his sergeant's words from the war punched into his skull like a steel stamp. The smell of copper strengthened as more blood spilled, and Gen caught sight of the little brunette and her partner making their exit, the one with the crooked smile barking something about a veneficum.

With their disappearance, tension slipped from the air like a loop of intestine from an open wound. Gen sagged against the counter, Arkady beside him, leaning on his elbows and looking out over the floor. The bar quieted, the only sounds from those still in pain or nursing their wounds with a double dose of booze.

The two stood in relative silence for a good minute before Arkady broke it.

"Nice work there. That is, I mean to say, thanks."

Gen waved it away. "Welcome."

Arkady reached inside his suit and came back with a small card between his fingers. He passed it to Gen. It held only an address embossed in heavy black lettering. Near the Square of the Fathers. South of the Filth, but still north. Shkut territory. He frowned at it.

What the hell is someone with that kind of money doing slumming it down here?

"Come see me tomorrow if you're still looking for work. I know some people."

Gen nodded absently, head still full of violence. If rich strangers wanted to pay him good money, how could he argue?

"Thanks," he said through numb lips.

Arkady finished off the last of his glass. He tipped a finger to his forehead and sauntered out the door, a blast of cold trading places with him. Outside, a blanket of white covered the ground.

Gen tapped the card against the bar counter, mind reeling. Finally, he finished his own drink, pulled his coat tight, and struck out into the cold, toward Irina, and home.

KATYUSHKA LEONOVA – CHAPTER FOUR

Memory stones are a two-edged blade. When one is worn, the wearer has access to the memories previously stored in that stone. But a memory stone never stops collecting. Any memories created while the stone is worn are also stored. When the person in question removes the stone, they lose not only the memories previously stored in the stone, but the memories created while wearing it.

— Iskusstvo Veneficum

Katyushka stepped from Colonel Grinin's office and back into the smoke and chaos of the precinct.

What have I done?

She hadn't volunteered, not really.

But the colonel certainly acted as if she had. She wanted to scream, to flee back to her kitchen. Gods above and demons below, how often had father warned her about catching the attention of the authorities?

Stay small. Everyone said it like a prayer. Secretarial pool, that was small. She thought she'd be one of many women in a comfortable shared office, typing and copying reports and gossiping during lunch. Small.

A man in crumpled slacks and rough shirt coughed for attention, a militsioner greatcoat slung casually over one shoulder. He looked out of place here, among the uniformed men. Long-limbed and broad-shouldered and ruggedly handsome the way the posters always depicted soldiers, he looked smug, all too pleased with himself.

"Katyushka Leonova?" he asked.

He knows my name.

From bad to worse. She was nothing, no one.

"Are you by any chance related to Nikhil Leonov?"

Kat's heart kicked. *Stay small. Stay small.*

"Great man," he continued. "From what I've heard. Man of virtue, and all that." He looked down at Kat, appraising. "Ah! Sorry, forgot to introduce myself. Maksim Tkatchenko." He lifted a hand as if about to offer a handshake and hesitated. "Never sure what to do these days. Shake hands with a woman?" He laughed at the absurdity. "But here you are, doing a man's job, so..." He completed the motion, stood, hand out, waiting, with a confident smirk.

Unsure what to do and feeling increasingly uncomfortable, Kat shook the hand.

"Gotta grip harder," he said. "Especially in the Filth. Here, a man would get stabbed for a weak handshake like that." He patted her on the shoulder. "We'll put it down to lack of practice, but we're going to work on it, right? Every morning until you don't shake my hand like a suka."

Kat blinked, startled at the casual cuss word.

"Yeah," he said, "you're definitely from the south. How long you been in Norylska?"

"Three years."

"Never been to the Filth though, right?"

"I shop in the northern markets," she said, defensive.

"That ain't the Filth."

"I'm not sure—" She cut herself off, trying to figure out whether she should explain how this was all a mistake or ask if it was. "Mister Tkatchenko—"

"Please," he said over top of her, "call me Maks. Everyone does." He winked. "At least those who don't call me worse." Pulling on his coat, he gestured toward the main entrance. "I'm supposed to introduce you to the department veneficum, but he's not in yet. We'll go for a drink while we wait. Lazarev—he's the veneficum—is going to give you the *stones* to do the job." Stones being a common street slang for testicles, he smirked again.

Kat ignored the vulgarity. "What kind of stones?"

"Memory stone, for sure. You need to know all the players and connections. And seriously, no one wants to bring this shit home with them." Pulling open his shirt, he displayed a green stone shot with lines of crimson hanging on a necklace too strong to be decorative. There was a second necklace with a half dozen stones, but she didn't get a good look. "I'm going to hazard a guess the cutie from the south-end doesn't have the personality for this kind of work. Lazarev will fix all that. You'll be a right old militsioner, ready to take bribes and snog silkies by the end of your second shift!"

She stared at him, appalled. This was too much!

"Relax," he said, dragging out the a. "I'm kidding."

"Mister Tkatchenko—"

"Maks."

"Maks. I think there's been a mistake. I was hired to work the secretarial pool." She made typing motions with her fingers like maybe he didn't know what secretaries did, even mimicking the lever-action of a carriage return.

He watched, amused. "Yes. Well. First," he said, "the militsiya don't make mistakes. That's the important fact. Everything always goes to plan. If the plan looks like shit and a whole pile of people end up dead or ground to chuck, that's because either some underling fucked up or that was actually the plan the whole time and you never knew the details." He fumbled at the pockets of his greatcoat until he found a dented cigareta tin. "Smoke?"

Kat shook her head.

Shrugging, he grabbed a lit cigareta from the mouth of a passing man and used it to light his own before returning it. The other, dressed in a shabby, faded uniform of a street militsioner, acted as if this was normal and continued without comment.

"Where was I?" he asked. "Right," he said without waiting for an answer. "Second." He inhaled hard, held the smoke in his lungs for a score of heartbeats and blew it out through the corner of his mouth. "Fuck. Can't remember the second thing. Anyway. The first is all that matters, right?" He gestured toward the entrance, half bowing as if to a lady of the Khagan court. "After you."

With little choice, Katyushka headed for the door. Maks trailed along behind.

"You'd look better with your hair down," he mused. "Gotta lose that nun-bun. No one in the Filth wears their hair like that. And that starched-to-the-tits secretarial uniform is doing nothing for your figure. Sorry to be blunt, but we're going to deal with some unsavory characters. The kind of men you want distracted. In the right clothes, you'll be a lot more distracting than I could ever be. Not that I'm not stunningly good looking."

Keeping her back to him so he wouldn't see the flush of tight anger, she said, "I was hired for—"

"Secretarial. Yeah. That was a miscommunication."

"The militsiya made a mistake?" she asked.

Maks laughed, a surprised bark. "You have a tongue, I'll give you that. I hope it doesn't get you killed."

After the thick stink of men and smoke, the air of the street tasted like freedom and escape.

The sun, cold and distant, hung over the south-eastern horizon. Filtered through the omnipresent haze of coal dust and furnace smoke, it turned the sky a bruised yellow like the skin around a healing bone break.

"Beautiful day, eh?" said Maks, squinting at the sun. Cigareta smoked to the butt, he flicked it into the street. When the wind stopped it short, slapping it to the ground, he grunted with disappointment.

Withdrawing another smoke from the battered case and patted down his pockets, looking for matches. Finding none, he angrily jammed the cigareta back into place. "Let's go. Time to introduce you to the Filth."

Katyushka followed him north.

Jogging to match his long-legged stride, she said, "I thought everything north of Middle Street was the Filth."

"Middle Street." Maks snorted. "Fucking great name. Lazy fuckers. Everyone south of Middle Street thinks everything north of it is the Filth. But that's only because they've never been into the *real* Filth."

The air changed. Two streets north and each breath felt like trying to choke down a putrescent meat pudding.

"You get used to it," said Maks, noting her expression. "In a couple of weeks, you won't even notice it. After two years you'll have lost your sense of smell altogether." He wrinkled his nose. "You've got that to look forward to."

With the furnaces, forges, smelting and reducing factories running day and night, coal dust blanketed all Norylska. In the south, the sootmen who shovelled and collected the blackened snow kept every lane and alley clean. Or mostly clean. Here, everyone left footprints in the slurry telling of their passing. Busier streets were relatively clear, due mostly to the constant foot traffic. Less-travelled alleys were inches-deep in ashen slush.

No one seemed to notice Maks, but everyone stared at Kat, eyes widening when they saw her uniform. If she made eye-contact, they immediately stared hard at the ground. If they saw her coming—and her starched, painfully clean pale blue secretarial uniform stood out among the drab tan and brown like a lighthouse beacon—they crossed the street. A few turned and fled.

They're afraid?

A thrill ran through her. No one had ever been afraid of her before.

"A woman, in uniform," said Maks. "and so brazenly walking the streets of the Filth. They think you're Militsiya Secret Police or something equally terrifying and untouchable. Who knew secretaries had such power!" He stopped suddenly, turning to face her. "Do you have matches?"

Kat shook her head. "I don't smoke."

He gave her a 'what the hell does that have to do with anything' look. "You should always carry matches."

"You don't."

"Cute and clever," he said. "A terrible combination. Follow."

Spinning on a well-worn bootheel, he headed into a trash-strewn laneway. Katyushka followed.

Working up her nerve, she said to his back, "This is a mistake. I'm supposed to be—"

"Secretarial. I know."

"We should go back. I don't belong here. My fiancé won't like—"

"You're engaged?" he asked, interrupting.

"Yes." It was only a slight lie.

"That's a shame."

It is? Why?

She decided she didn't care.

Maks stopped in the middle of a block of converted tenement housing. Jammed between a pawn shop and what was probably an illegal moneylender, the bar looked like something huge had sat on it. A slab of poorly carved wood looking vaguely like a tilted bucket hung above the door.

He gestured proudly at the sign. "Welcome to the Dripping Bucket. The best vodka north of Middle Street. And by 'best' I mean almost drinkable. And don't order the cognac. It's vodka with rancid corn syrup for colour and flavour. And don't drink the pivo. They brew it in the basement from horse piss and broken dreams."

"Never trust a poet," said Kat, remembering the line from *Zhiglov's Defeat*, the state-written play everyone had to see at least twenty times as a child.

"Poets make the best lovers," said Maks, pushing the door open.

Entering without waiting, he didn't hold it for her. Unsure she could find her way back to Middle Street without being robbed, raped, and murdered, she followed him in.

A band clanged away at something that might have been music, one member banging at a steel pot with a bent trumpet. Between the twin onslaughts of stench and sound, Kat felt like she hit a wall. Mismatched tables littered the room. If forethought or planning went into their placement, she couldn't discern it. The patrons, slumped at tables or on stools at the bar, hunched over their drinks like dogs guarding a bone. They had that same beaten twitchiness too, attention darting, tracking every movement. And the smell! Sour vomit, stale pivo, cheap cigareta, and—

Maks put a too familiar hand on Kat's lower back, guiding her toward an empty table with two chairs.

"Do they not go outside to urinate?" she asked taking a quick step to free herself from contact.

He thought that hilarious, roaring with good-natured laughter.

"Sit," he said. "I'll get drinks."

"I don't—"

He left without another word, weaving through tables, patting shoulders like they were good friends, laughing and joking with men who looked incapable of humour. An ugly undercurrent followed him, quiet rage and resentment. Maks dressed like these men, but he wasn't one of them. He was a militsioner, and they all knew it. They feigned acceptance because he was dangerous, because he had power.

He doesn't know.

Or maybe he didn't care. Maybe that was part of why they hated them. Maks thought he was better, *knew* it. Where men slumped, beaten and broken, terrified of losing what little they had, Maks walked tall, grinning into their dour hate.

Is he brave or stupid? she wondered. *Or both?*

The room changed. Not the smell, that was relentless, all-pervading. She wanted to raise a hand to her face, breathe through the fabric of her uniform in an attempt to filter the worst, but worried someone might take affront. Tension spread from where she sat like a pebble dropped into a pool. The nearest tables fell quiet, hard men studying her from the corners of their eyes. This wasn't like the looks she got in the market. This wasn't men admiring a woman. This was loathing choked down deep by fear.

They think I'm militsiya. Maks was right.

She wanted out. She didn't belong here.

With a start Katyushka realized she wasn't the only woman in the bar. Not only was one of the bartenders female—which would have been unimaginable a few years ago—but a third of the hunched shapes, blunt and grubby hands gripping chipped vodka glasses, were women. Shapeless in their rough clothes, just as filthy and coal dusted as the men, it was almost impossible to tell them apart.

Placing a vodka before her, Maks collapsed into the other seat. Uneven, the table wobbled. He stomped on the base to keep it from moving.

"We should go," she whispered.

"Nonsense. We just got here. You haven't even touched your drink." He gestured back toward the man behind the bar. "How will Shchukin feel if you leave without so much as tasting it? So rude!"

Katyushka darted a nervous glance at the bar and the big man behind it. Towering a full head over everyone, he looked like he was part cave bear. Focussed on cleaning a mug with a stained rag, he didn't notice her.

Accidentally, she locked gazes with one of the men crowded at the bar. Head like an iron bolt. Jaw too square, like he'd been chiselled from stone. Nose crooked, bent to one side and crushed, he looked like he entered fights face-first. A huge, scarred hand clutched a cognac glass. Hopeless eyes. He stood chatting with a well-dressed man with slicked hair and a suit out of place in this rough establishment.

Maks shook his head in mock disappointment. "Damn you are gullible." Lifting his glass, he said, "Ura!"

"It isn't even nine in the morning!"

"Yes, well, it took longer than usual to get here because you walk so damned slow." He waited; glass raised. "You know it's terribly rude to let someone drink alone."

When Kat lifted her glass, he tapped his against it, downing the vodka in one go. Sipping hers, she winced at the fire.

"Not bad," said Maks, wafting the glass under his nose. "It starts strong, with a rancid potato finish. Hints of boot-polish and..." Flaring his nostrils, he inhaled deeply. "Paint-thinner, if I'm not mistaken. Shchukin has outdone himself! Fabulous!"

Replacing her still-full drink on the table, Kat said, "Maybe we should go. The uniform—"

"Exactly the reaction I was hoping for," said Maks. "This will do wonders for my reputation. For years I've been telling my friends in the Shkut Family— they run most of the gambling, whores, and narcotics in the north-end—"

"I've heard of them," said Kat. "Everyone has."

"For years," he started again, as if she hadn't spoken, "I've been telling my friends in the Shkut Family that I have contacts in the secret police. If I had to hazard a guess, I'd say those lies are at least thirty percent responsible for my continued breathing." Taking her glass, he downed its contents and added, "My rugged good looks, quick wit, and charm are the other seventy percent."

Desperate for an escape, Katyushka tried one more time: "This is a mistake," she enunciated. "I'm not a militsioner. Not really. I'm a secretary."

Barely even that.

He stopped her with a raised hand. "This movement to add women to the work force, to see if they can handle men's work, comes from Khagan. It comes from the highest ranks and it is *not* a suggestion. This is happening. This kind of thing is a lot like sex: you can relax and let it happen, maybe even enjoy it a bit, or you can fight and struggle and afterward it's going to hurt a lot more."

"That sounds more like rape."

"You're right," he said. "Your analogy is better. Receiving orders from the militsiya brass is like getting raped. But otherwise, what I said. You can march into Colonel Grinin's office and tell him he is wrong. You can tell him that hiring women to do a man's job is stupid and call him an idiot, and I will applaud you all the way. Though from a safe distance because I'm not suicidal. After, when they load you into a wagon and haul away what might be a shapely ass—seriously can't tell in that uniform—I'll wave bye and get on with my day."

He was an asshole, but he was right. Questioning the state was always a bad idea. "I don't like you," said Kat.

"Yeah, you do. Everyone does."

Movement at the bar caught her attention, and she focussed over Maks' shoulder. Sharp words, tight and angry. One man shoved another.

"Leech!" someone roared.

A squeal of pain, blood spraying into the air.

In a heartbeat, mayhem. Thrown chairs and glasses, bottles used as clubs. Men lost teeth they couldn't spare.

The man with the crushed nose stood at the bar, watching. Calm. Dead eyes.

Knives, bright and vicious among these filthy men.

Dead-Eyes broke a man's arm. Kat saw the cold decision to do more damage. He twisted the limb until the elbow bent wrong and the victim screamed in agony.

"Much as I love a good barfight," said Maks, rising from the table and grabbing Kat's collar to haul her to her feet, "Grinin will have my ass if you get knifed."

Spinning Kat, he shoved her toward the door.

"Enough fun!" he bellowed over the ruckus. "Let's get you to the veneficum!"

GENNDY ANTONOV – CHAPTER FIVE

Family can forgive any sin. Except the sin of relation.

—D Puskyn, *Exile*

Gen's blood continued to hammer in his ears four blocks later. A fight, a job, and a brush with the law that didn't end with him being hanged, all in one night. He hadn't felt this alive since the war: Young, strong, and full of fire.

Fire's greedy. Eats the fuel that creates it, suffocates itself in a headlong rush to hedonism.

What was that from? Medyev's *Annals of the State*? Anatoly's *Blood of the Revolution*?

Vodka clouded his memory, stifling recall and the ability to retrieve it. Any other time, the inability to remember would have annoyed the hell out of him. The wind cut through his coat like teeth of ice as he trod the streets, however, so he forgave the vodka its trespass in exchange for false warmth.

Storm shutters hid windows, families getting an early start in buttoning up for the winter. Thick tarps of cured leather stretched over woodpiles, logs straining against the material as shapeless lumps. Rags hung from cracks in windowsills to keep the drafts out, tails of fabric fluttering in the wind.

Those with neither home nor shelter stood, leaned, or hunched against alley walls. The stink of infection and unwashed flesh rolled from narrow canyons of stone like a plague cloud. The dispossessed picked at scabs left behind from kroc use, others worried blackened teeth with tongues scarred by blisters. Desperation clung to the human detritus like shit on cobbles.

Still others, eyes on the lowering sky, stood wet-eyed, perhaps thinking of how they should have moved on while the taiga was still green. The rest pleaded or exposed themselves, hoping to find a willing partner, coin, and a warm bed for the night.

Gen passed a woman, shirt open to her waist, breasts laying round and heavy against a thick belly, dark nipples erect in the cold. She called to him with an accent that spoke of somewhere further south and west. He turned his attention to the street ahead.

Don't mention this part to Irina. Maybe don't mention any of this to Irina. You went for a walk.

Where?

To the park.

Which park?

The one without the naked women offering sexual favors.

He moved on, the woman's tone growing harsh, heavy tread of her feet plodding on the cobbles as she followed and harangued. Gen refused to turn. Finally, her invective ended in a string of curses. She hawked a wad of phlegm and lobbed it his way in contempt.

Another few yards and he turned the corner onto Coal Harbor. The sea lay a few miles distant, but things like facts didn't preclude the Kievan propensity for sarcasm. Soot and snow mixed and gathered in drifts. It moved in swirls and eddies like the tide, leaving a gray patina on every surface it touched, filthy fingers on a grasping lech. Rows of rough homes stood backed up to the north wall of the city, pressed against it like forlorn lovers. He shared a home with Irina here.

The thought of her, and the sight of the home they shared; clapboard grey, shingles and door slightly crooked, made the fire in his blood cool. Smoke curled from the chimney. Irina woke at dawn. She liked to see him when his shift ended, before he crawled into bed for the day. Even now, sun creeping into the sky, he would be home before the usual time. What might she think?

Failure.

He railed against the thought, anger rippling through him like a sheet in the wind. Guilt and self-loathing hung from the tails of the emotion like twin corpses.

Ah, there you are, father.

Worthless.

Trash.

Fuckup.

Bullshit. I have a job. Just not at the racks. I served my country. I provide, godsdamnit. I provide.

He lifted his chin and tramped through the snow, determined not to let melancholy and doubt show. Irina deserved better. He stomped up the porch and opened the door, the scents of baked rye and boiled cabbage greeting him like eager children. He knocked his boots clean in the entry, then kicked them off, hanging his greatcoat on the hook set in the wall.

Inside, warmth wrapped the rooms in a blanket. A fire crackled merrily in the grate lighting the small living area. Gen winterproofed their home the month before, and though it made for a few uncomfortable summer nights, they never need worry about catching an ague. An all-too common occurrence in Norlyska. Those the cold didn't kill, the flu throttled in their sleep.

He glanced at the bookshelf where they kept the few volumes they'd gathered over the years. His books were mostly philosophical screeds on the state and man's contract with it. Not that he understood most of it. But he wanted her to believe he did.

Hers, conversely, were treatises on the natural world. If it flew, crawled, or slithered, it fascinated her. Interspersed with their diverging interests were novels where heroes rescued damsels from Altin Ordu devils, and brave soldiers liberated whole cities from the 'foreign menace'.

Propaganda, but that doesn't make it less fun.

Two overstuffed armchairs sat facing the fire, a small table between them. Irina's knitting in a basket, needles poking out of a ball of yarn. Further in, through an open doorway, stood the rough table and chairs where they shared dinner. Just around the corner and down a short hall, was a commode and their bedroom, the mattress, misshapen and down-stuffed, was a luxury his pension bought in ages past.

Irina rounded the corner, peasant shirt off one shoulder, thick curls tied up in a loose bun. Full lips and laughing eyes, lines at the corners of both. She wrung a towel between long-fingered hands. Her stomach swelled only slightly, but to anyone looking, gave her away as expecting. She smiled when she saw him, and his heart soared.

In Kievan, a popular saying went: *A man might live forever on bread or vodka but will find no joy in only one.* Irina nourished him.

Home.

"Thought that was you," she said.

I failed you. I failed the baby. Throw me out. Do better. You deserve better.

A wave of self-pity threatened to suck him into an undertow of misery. He forced a smile. "Dinner smells amazing."

The pressure of her feet on his own as she climbed to kiss him. The warmth of her body pressed close. Lips tasting of sour winterberries. A favorite daily ritual of his, this moment never ceased to warm him.

They parted, and she gave a comical grimace.

"You, however, smell like the ass-end of a rancid potato. Go clean up."

A sheepish grin slipped onto his lips, acknowledgement of her wisdom.

Okay, maybe I'm still a little drunk.

The towel snapped him as he passed, and Gen chuckled. He stood over the basin and splashed water on his face until some of the fog lifted from his thoughts. Bleary eyes stared back from the man in the mirror, stubble clinging to the cliffs of his cheeks.

Courage. She loves you. Courage.

He made a brave face. It came out a snarl.

No wonder that militsioner in the Dripping Bucket hauled ass. Just a little girl who'd never seen a rough day. Worst hardship of her life, breaking a nail. Not even a worry line. One of those people whose hardest decision is whether to hire another servant or buy a new carriage.

When he returned to the kitchen, Irina stood at the stove, curls clinging to the back of her neck in the heat. A kiss planted there filled his nose with the scent of lavender from her bath. A small sound of pleasure came from deep in her throat. Without turning, she said, "Sit, and you can tell me why you were at the bar all morning."

Gen's heart dropped, threatening to roll out his feet and across the floor, where it would likely become the victim of a passing rat. He pulled his chair out, wincing as the legs scraped against the floor, then sat, hands trembling again.

This is it. This is where she tells you to get out. To never come back. You'll die in an alley, and she will find someone else. Someone younger, more handsome, smarter, wealthier, with a bigger cock.

Nonsense. No one has a bigger cock.

That second voice. Sometimes the foil to his reason, others, a cutting blade of sarcasm. The veneficum called it *the intruder.* Gen thought of it as a pain in his ass.

A steaming bowl of stew and a thick slice of rye placed before him cut the thought off. Irina pushed the crock of butter across the table then returned to the stove and made her own meal, finally settling into her chair with a grateful sigh.

Bits of cabbage, potato, and pale carrot danced in the broth as Gen stirred it absently. Outside, wind snapped at the eaves.

Irina took a small sip of the meal, then broke off a hunk of bread and dipped it in broth, carefully taking a bite and chewing.

She's waiting. Stolid. Implacable. The woman's a glacier.

She'd make good militsiya.

"The plant let me go," he blurted.

Guts clenching, his heartrate spiked. He waited for the stream of recrimination and anger.

"Oh, Gen." Then she was next to him, arms around his shoulders, kissing his hair. "Oh, Gen."

He wept, tears splashing in his soup, making his bread soggy.

Suka, the voice in his head accused. *You little bitch.*

Still, she brushed his hair with her fingers, nails gently scraping his scalp.

His breathing slowed, sobs subsiding. Calm spread like a balm as muscles he'd been clenching all night slowly unknotted. Wiping his eyes with a napkin, she took her seat again. Cleaning the tears did little for the hot flush in his face and the headache clawing its way to life behind it.

She reached out and took his hand. A quick squeeze of his fingers, a smile.

Veins of gold. What every man beneath the earth wishes for. That's what we are. Subterranean. Beneath her.

They sat by the fire in comfortable silence. Irina knitted, a bottle of kvass at her side. Needles clacked together in soothing rhythm.

The brandy he'd pulled from behind the bookcase—his special stash—burned pleasantly as it went down, easing his aching head. He stared into the flames.

Time to leap again.

He reached into a pocket and produced the card Arkady gave him, laying it on the table between them.

"What's this?" Irina asked.

"A job," Gen said.

A whistle slipped from her lips. "The same day? Well, I always said you were an impressive man."

She picked the card up, turned it over in her hands. It caught the light. It was made from impossibly clean stock, only within reach for the wealthy. She paused, reading the address, and her brows knitted together.

"No," she said.

What?

Skip-beat of the heart. "What?"

"I know this place. This is Shkut territory."

"Most of the city is someone's territory," Gen protested.

Breathe deep. Push it down. You don't have the high ground here, Gen. Calm. Calm.

She shook her head. "But this is Shkut territory, specifically. What do you know of the man who gave this to you? Will you run drugs for him, Gen? Weapons? Flesh?" she shook her head again. "I won't have it. I need you. The baby needs you."

There it was. The baby, a weapon.

Even when Gen had a point, Irina knew how to leverage guilt, wield it like a cudgel.

On the heels of that, more guilt. A cascade of self-loathing in return for unkind thoughts. Still, he pressed on, blood up, his own advice falling to the wayside.

Is it ever enough? When will it be? What more can a man do? I give my flesh and bone, day in and day out, and you sit on the fruits. Would you have my blood? Striga. Witch.

"I will *not* let you starve. I will *not* have my family in the street for the sootmen to find in the spring. I have always provided for you. This could be our chance to get out of here. Into a place deserving of you," he argued.

She looked at him a long moment. "No. You can do better," she said.

Better? I would move the earth. I would split a legion of skulls, and you want better? Fuck you.

More guilt. A pang so sharp it hurt.

You'll see, he amended.

"You'll see," Gen said, echoing the thought. His heart hammered. He hated to argue with her. "You'll see. This isn't up for discussion. I'll make every one of your dreams come true, because you deserve that much."

Because I failed you in so many other ways.

She flipped the card at him and stood. "A dead man cannot provide."

She stalked out of the room, stomping down the hall. The bedroom door slammed shut behind her.

Gen stared after her, then tore his gaze away from where she'd disappeared. Flames licked the logs in the fireplace. His heart stopped hammering, and in its place, sorrow. Behind it, like a shadow on the sun, cold determination. She would see. He survived Irkysk. This was no challenge at all.

He snuck out as soon as Irina's breathing turned regular, light snores marking her sleep, indicating it was safe to breathe again. Relatively, as these things went.

Coward.

He shook the thought off.

Would a coward be here, in this place? Doubtful.

He considered leaving her a note, perhaps a long letter reasoning out his argument for why this was good for them. In his daydreams, she saw the light of day, and welcomed his bravery with open arms. Instead, he dashed out a quick excuse.

Taking a walk. -G

Coward.

Anger hounded him. Anxiety bit at his heels. He raged silently through the streets, emotions turbulent. Eventually, it overtook him, savaging his insides. His hands shook, heart pounded.

A black curtain descended at the edge of his vision, and he paused to lean against a wall. Through the thin clapboard, someone screamed. The smack of leather on flesh. A beating, then.

His breath caught; shoulders aching as anxiety tightened around him like a bandage wound too tight.

War came on like a rabid dog.

The press of men in the trenches, sweat and liquor and fear oozing from pores. Unwashed uniforms crusted with mud, caked with shit, stained with urine. The stink of soldier-beasts stalking among the ranks, violence chained for the moment. Worse, the stink of combat. Gun smoke, cordite, and fire. Blood and bile. Sweet cut-flower rot of the man next to you who'd forgotten his helmet. He'd taken a round to the skull and now his brains dripped onto the frozen soil, bowels leaking into his trousers, weight pressed against your shoulder while you tried to sight down the barrel. The stench of a man who used to be, who was, filled your nostrils. Try as you might, you never shook it. Like remembering the worst moments of someone else's life.

Another scent came to him, snapping the memory as easily as a man breaks a brittle twig. Cedar. A hallmark of the wealthy. The poor burned whatever trash their paltry coin paid for. The rich fired wood with scents leaving their homes smelling of pleasant days. As much as was possible in Norylska, anyway. He pushed off the wall and moved on, taking in gulping lungsful of air to calm himself.

A few more minutes walking, and finally Gen stood in the frozen slush at the edge of The Square of the Fathers, stamping his feet, hands in his armpits under his greatcoat. As the sun rose, so did the temperature, forming a low fog on the cobbles.

His breath came in great white plumes. Rumor placed a great engine in Khagan, capable of moving a hundred or more people from one location to the next, without horse or auroch. He doubted as much but fancied sometimes he was that engine. Powerful, driven.

The snowfall abated, clouds parting. Pale sunlight shone on ridges and waves of ice and snow on the ground. It lent everything a ghostly glow, reminding him of stories of the deadlands his grandmother used to tell.

A figure approached in the gloaming, breath puffing out in thick clouds. The newcomer came close, and Gen's heart dropped like a rock.

The debt collector, Pyotr, smiled, a slimy thing that seemed to want to crawl around the side of his head and escape to the thicket of his hair.

Fuck. They'd find you six feet under, I swear.

"Gen," he said with false warmth. "Just the man I was looking for. I'd heard about your... misfortune at the plant."

"And?" Gen asked.

You know *they just fired me. Go on. Go on, ask for the money. Ask for the money and I'll fucking gut you right here.*

"And I just thought I'd check on my favorite client. You *are* still my favorite client, right? I wouldn't want anything to happen to... affect your ability to settle your debts, you know. Physical ailments can be so long-lasting."

Man like you wouldn't know what true violence is. But I'd be happy to show you.

Gen shook his head. "You'll get what you're owed."

Pyotr eyed him, stepped a little closer. A set of brass knuckles appeared on his fingers. Primed for violence, Gen tensed, easing weight onto his back leg, shifting his hips subtly.

Can't knock a man stupid if you don't put your hips into it.

"You want to fuck off, now," came a voice behind Gen.

Arkady stepped into sight, and Pyotr paled, hand slipping back into his coat. Arkady kept hard eyes on the other man.

"Go on. Piss off. Before I decide to let my dogs piss *on* you."

Pyotr nodded once, shot a venomous look at Gen, then disappeared into the fog rising across the square. Arkady watched him go. When the debt collector dwindled to a wisp in the distance, Arkady turned to Gen and clapped a hand on his shoulder, a grin crawling across his still-new friend's face.

"Comrade! You look cold. Walk with me."

He turned and led the way. Gen watched him for a few steps, indecision halting him. Part of him wanted to return home, lay a bouquet of apology at Irina's feet. Instead, he looked in the direction Pyotr had disappeared, and all it implied. Freedom from debt. A possible enemy. Then he hurried to catch up.

KATYUSHKA LEONOVA – CHAPTER SIX

A Grand Master Veneficum can take everything a man is, personality and memories, and store him in a stone. Should another wear that stone, a clash of personalities will result. If the personality on the stone, referred to as a parasitical personality, is stronger than the host, it will come to dominate the shared body. Often there is no clear winner and the result is insanity.

A stone containing the complete memories and personality of a human can also be placed upon an animal host. This has been most successfully used by the militsiya to create great monsters of war, dangerous men inhabiting the bodies of colossal cave bears. In the crude vernacular of the commoner, these are referred to as soldier beasts.

— Iskusstvo Veneficum

Katyushka followed Maks through the maze of the Filth. He kept up a constant stream of inane chatter; the best places to buy black market delicacies like Altin Ordu plums, pointing out homes and boarded up buildings and listing off names of officers murdered within.

"What is it like to wear a memory stone?" she interrupted, his monologue threatening to become an impenetrable Ruskyn play.

"It's like anything," he said. "There's good and bad."

"What's the good?"

"At the end of my shift, I get to take it off. The moment I do, everything I've done that day falls away. Disappears. You don't realize you're carrying a burden until it's gone."

"What burden are you carrying?"

Maks shot her a sharp side-eye. "You'll learn."

Is the job that bad?

She'd seen militsioners lounging around street posts or having pastries and sweet Darjking coffee in the market. They didn't look like they bore the terrible weight of responsibility. Most winked or cat called as she passed, proposing marriage or cruder possibilities. Always alone, she averted her eyes and hurried away, laughter following.

"What's the bad?" she asked.

"Starting your shift," he said, voice heavy. "You don't remember anything, but as you reach for that stone, some part of you is screaming not to touch it."

A tad melodramatic. "Why?"

"Bleed," he said. "Veneficum say the stones are perfect, that they trap all memories. That's bullshit. Memory is…" He waved a hand, helpless. "It's all over the place. Like sometimes you'll catch a whiff of something, and you'll get this flash of memory, but it'll be something you've never done or seen; it'll be a memory you don't remember."

A memory you don't remember?

"There's brain memory," he continued, "and there's muscle memory. But there's also bone memory. Sometimes you remember things in your bones. Pain. Real pain. Your brain doesn't get it, can't access it. Maybe it's a defensive measure, to protect you. But your bones are screaming at you not to touch the fucking stone."

"Couldn't you stop wearing the stone?"

Was it voluntary? She had no idea.

"Right," he said. "You didn't go to the akademiya. Day one, page one: The state owns your day." Maks snorted derision. "Years ago, in my first week of work, I took off my memory stone. Just for a moment. I'd found a baby someone drowned in a tub. Fucking lying on the bottom, staring up at me. Maybe I wanted off-work me to remember this. Not a fucking clue. But it never happened a second time." He looked away. "No matter how good you think your reason, never take off the memory stone mid-shift. Anyway," he said, suddenly beaming, "there are ways to make it easier. The trick is to get the right personality stones, and always put them on first. No bad bone memory tied to personality traits. When you start getting the shakes every time you reach for your memory stone—and I do mean *when*—ask the veneficum for a bravery stone. Best fucking things." He shot her an oddly vulnerable glance, eyes like wounds. "Those and confidence stones. Fucking hell I wish we were allowed to take those home."

She'd heard of stones making people funny or quick-witted, stones capable of healing debilitating phobias or social awkwardness. It was one thing to read about veneficum draining personality traits from one man so another might carry them, but the thought of wearing one was very different.

What would a conversation with Fyodor be like if I wore a bravery stone?

How many of their almost-arguments ended because she lacked the confidence to go on? He was so smart, quick and clever with words. Sometimes, he brought up some minor quirk or flaw he found annoying about her, speak like he spent weeks preparing an argument for court. Never prepared, always caught off guard, she always promised to try harder, do better.

"You being you," said Maks, "you'll have to wear personality and memory stones."

"Me being me?"

Grabbing the lapel of her jacket, he slammed her into the nearest wall, pinning her. Pedestrians, moments ago about their errands, disappeared or focussed on the ground as they shuffled past.

"What are you going to do?" demanded Maks.

So close. Breathing hot into her face. "What are you going to do?" he repeated.

Kat shoved him and he laughed, mocking.

"What are you going to do?"

He released her lapel, moving his hand to her throat. Skin on skin. Too close. Invasive.

His grip tightened.

She couldn't speak. Fear crushed her to silence.

"I'm a bad guy," he breathed into her ear. "A criminal. I'm going to hurt you."

Keeping her pinned with one hand, he slipped the other into a pocket. It reappeared adorned with a set of tarnished brass knuckle-dusters. He brandished them before her eyes, and she focussed on the brown blood crusted in the grooves.

"I'm going to knock your fucking teeth out. I'm going to fuck up that pretty face and your fiancé is going to leave you. What are you going to do?"

Kat sagged in his grip, tears spilling free.

"What are you going to—" Maks twitched, grimacing. Stepping back, pocketing the brass, he said, "Shit. Sorry. I just— That's why. You need to *remember* how to fight. You need to remember that even though you're a weak little girl, if you're mean enough, you can still fuck people up. And you need to be the kind of person willing to do so."

She shook, jittery aftershocks of terror running ragged through her muscles.

"I'm sorry," he said, looking away and wincing. "Do you really want to remember the shame of being helpless? Do you want to go home and lie in bed shaking with rage over something that happened that day? No. Wear the stones you're given. Leave it all at the precinct." He faced her. "At the end of this shift,

I'm going to hand in my stones and forget this ever happened. I'll go home and sleep like a godsdamned baby. Pure and innocent. So yeah, the memory stones are mandatory. But without the personality stones, you won't last a week."

"I would never be mean."

"You've never worn a stone. You haven't a fucking clue who you could be."

"And I would never hurt someone!" she added. "That's terrible!"

"Tell that to the man who's trying to put a knife in your ribs. When you're there, you do what you need to do."

"Stones aren't going to change who I *am*," she said.

Maks grunted an amused laugh, a little of his smugness returning. "We are our memories. When you remember being someone else, how can that not change you?"

Was that true? She didn't know.

"Let's get you back to the precinct," said Maks, setting off. "Grinin's going to have a fucking fit."

Wiping her face, Kat hurried to catch up. "Vulgarity is a sign of a shallow mind."

"And believing every fucking thing the state tells you is a sign of rampant fucking stupidity," he answered.

Back at the precinct, Maks led her inside. Once again Kat was the focus of side-eyed examination. She did her best to ignore the judging looks and ill-hidden anger.

Maks pointed out the veneficum's office. "I'll be across the street having ponchiki and coffee. Come find me when you're done."

"Don't you do any real work?"

"Not if I can help it."

Kat watched him leave, torn between wanting to follow, wanting to flee back to Fyodor and tell him he was right.

If the state says you volunteered, you volunteer.

Father's favorite saying, back before they came north. Now he didn't say much of anything. He wouldn't talk about what happened, but in a single day he went from being the Secretary of Finance for Yuryev Industrial, one of Kievan's largest arms manufacturers, to an assistant manager at a bank in Norylska. He called it *the frozen armpit of the north*, when into his vodka. Which was most nights.

The man with questions sees answers through the bars of his cell.

Where had she heard that? Was it from *Zhiglov's Defeat?*

Knowing she had no choice, Kat squared her shoulders, drew a deep breath, and approached the veneficum's door. Not giving herself a chance to reconsider, she knocked.

The door swung open and a young man, sallow face pocked with acne scars, watery green eyes peering at her through thick spectacles, blocked her entrance. He wore a spotless suit, buttoned tight, tie in the vicious Ivanov knot preferred by bankers.

"What?" he demanded.

"Are you Veneficum Lazarev?"

"Of course not."

When he didn't continue, she said, "I'm Katyushka Leonova. I was told to see the veneficum about stones."

He blinked at her. "Weren't you told to report here first thing in the morning?"

She wanted to say no, that no one gave her explicit instructions, but realized it was the wrong answer.

"Sorry," she said.

"Oh, that makes everything better!" snapped the young man.

When he stood staring at her, she said, "Should I come back later?"

"So you can waste his time *again*?"

"I didn't—"

"Enter."

He stepped aside, but just enough she had to squeeze awkwardly past him.

Flawlessly neat, the room beyond reminded Kat of her grandmother's second library, the one reserved for impressing guests. Everything perfectly placed, no detail ignored. Even the most important dignitaries knew better than to sit and risk displacing a cushion and displeasing the old lady.

Pointing at an uncomfortable looking chair, he said, "Sit. Veneficum Lazarev isn't in yet."

Didn't he just accuse me of wasting the man's time?

Kat sat, back straight, legs crossed as was proper.

The young man returned to his desk and set about rearranging neat stacks of paper with a scowl of intense concentration. Sometimes he stopped to read, eyes narrowed, lips moving slightly.

An hour passed, Kat's bum going from sore to numb and back to sore. Every time she shifted in an attempt to find a more comfortable position, the clerk shot her an annoyed look as if she'd blurted a rude question.

Finally, the clerk nodded to himself and stood. "Come," he said.

Rising with a sigh of relief, Kat followed as he crossed to the far side of the room. Knocking crisply on a second door, he somehow conveyed both annoyance and disappointment.

"You don't have to knock every damned time, Penkin," said a reedy voice.

Penkin opened the door, this time stepping aside. "Your morning appointment. *Late.*"

Kat opened her mouth to argue, to point out that she'd been sitting out here the whole time and decided against it. Better not to cause a fuss.

An elderly man stood within, his office in stark contrast to the one Kat just passed through. Dressed in a crumpled suit, sleeves rolled up, glasses perched on his bald head, he looked lost, like he'd accidentally stepped into the wrong room. Three desks, piled high with paper, sat at odd angles to the room. A fourth remained only mostly covered. It looked like he used one until it became inaccessible, and then simply had another desk brought in. A massive iron door like a bank vault filled the rear wall. Another door hung open, a long hall beyond. Had he only recently come to the office? Kat hadn't heard anything.

Though lanterns lined the walls of the windowless room, only one was lit. The old man squinted at her, remembered his glasses, and dropped them into place with a sharp nod.

"Ah, yes," he said. "Leonova, right?"

Katyushka nodded.

He turned on the young man. "That will be all, Penkin."

Once the young man left, door closed firmly behind him with one last look of wet distrust shot at Kat, the old man sighed and collapsed into the only empty chair.

"I had a couch," he said, "for patients." He waved at a long pile of stacked documentation. "I think it's under there."

Katyushka stood at parade rest, hands clasped behind her back, like she'd seen soldiers do in Preobrazhensky Square back in Khagan.

Lazarev peered up at her through his glasses. "There are two types of men who become militsioners. There are little boys who want a crusade, who want to be the state's iron fist of justice. And then there are little boys who want to wear a uniform and crack skulls and continue being the bullies they were on the playground. Neither tend to be big on expressing emotions."

"Which kind is Maksim Tkatchenko?" she asked. She couldn't picture him as either.

Lazarev's brow furrowed, but not in anger. "Hmn," he said. "However, dashing and handsome as Maks thinks he is, he is not what we are here to discuss." His lips twisted in thought. "Where was I?"

"Militsioners not big on expressing emotions," supplied Kat.

"Right. And so, I don't give them a sofa to lie on. It's easier to read someone who's standing. Angry little boys in particular. You, however, I'd offer a sofa. If I could find it."

"Because I'm a woman and, therefore, comfortable with expressing my emotions," Kat said.

"Blood and bones, no. I read everything I needed in your interaction with young Penkin."

"I hardly think—"

He silenced her with a look. "You're introverted, but not shy. Obedient, yet questioning. You're not a coward but are too smart to be brave. You're soft, but only because you're untested. You hunch your shoulders to appear smaller, weaker, but chop wood and haul groceries. Given the chance, you'd happily go the rest of your life without ever learning your potential."

She thought about that for a moment, hating that she agreed with most of it. "What kind of militsioner does that make me?"

"Well played," he said. "Wrong question though. The real question, is what kind of militsioner will you be after I've assigned you the correct combination of stones?" He examined her, shook his head. "Go on, ask the question."

"Will the stones change who I am?"

"Are you so perfect that you should never change and grow?"

Asshole. She kept the thought from her face.

Lazarev pushed back to his feet with a groan, rubbing at his lower back. As he rose, she saw a necklace of six or more polished stones beneath his shirt.

Does he make use of his own art?

It made sense. Why wouldn't he? Were there stones to help him get through the tedium of a day spent in this cramped office? Did he have a stone to help him deal with Penkin's peevish personality?

If the veneficum is willing to use stones, they must be safe.

And the old man was right. What was so amazing about being proper obedient Katyushka Leonova? What would it be like to be brave Kat, to be commanding Kat?

"Can I wear the stones home?" she asked.

Lazarev grunted a laugh. "Gods above, no. I'll get in trouble if you go back to your quietly angry boyfriend and kick his manipulative ass."

Manipulative? She let the thought go. "How did you know he's quietly angry?"

Lazarev gave her a look of sad disappointment. "Women like you always have such men. At least at your age." He gestured for her to follow; fingers bent with age. "Let's take a look in the vault and see what kind of militsioner we can make."

GENNDY ANTONOV – CHAPTER SEVEN

Wealth is never earned, only stolen.

—D. Puskyn, Exile

The manse Arkady led Gen to could've fit ten of his own home inside. The grounds, extending past that to a small pond, well-tended shrubs, and a stone path, another three or four.

"Charming," Arkady said.

"Sorry, what?" Gen replied.

"Your mouth, dear. It's open. In my experience, only carp and bumpkins have the right to gawp."

He reached over and shut Gen's mouth gently with long fingers. Gen flinched back from the touch—this sort of thing wasn't done in public between men—and a pained look crossed Arkady's face. It disappeared in a flash, and he put on a smile.

"Come. They're waiting for us."

He led the way past a well-built stone wall and up a clean path skirting a wide drive used by carriages. Light spilled from the windows in the early evening hours. Wide steps led to a colonnaded porch, a valet standing in a sheltered portion. The man glanced them up and down, eyes lingering on Gen as they approached. He addressed Arkady.

"A guest, Comrade Vetrov?"

He refused to look at Gen, nose wrinkling in distaste. He was handsome, in a conventional way, short blonde hair, bright blue eyes, trim. Arkady patted him on the cheek.

"Now, now, Sergey, love. Jealousy is ugly on you. This," and he swept an arm at Gen, "is Comrade Antonov. Get used to seeing him around."

Funny thing, a man like Arkady. Wouldn't last a minute outside these ivory towers and the shelter of the Family. Not in the open. Golubois aren't loved here. As Puskyn says, Money buys privilege, privilege buys indulgence.

Besides, it'd be real fucking stupid to call a Shkut a goluboi.

The valet nodded curtly and opened the door, sparing only a moment to glare daggers at Gen. Then they passed over the threshold, door shutting softly in their wake.

The sharp division between the world Gen inhabited and Arkady's demesne lay on the edge of a razor.

Fuck me.

Everything here was clean and white and free from the stink of shit and sweat and rancid meat. Except for what clung to Gen like a leech on the thigh.

Irina was right. I shouldn't be here.

The carpets weren't soiled, freshly scrubbed tiles gleamed in the light of gas lamps, and the air smelled of cedar and juniper. For once, his head didn't hurt, the pressure in his sinuses easing off by a fraction.

He nearly turned and fled, sure he was either the butt of some joke, or soon to be a meal for some wealthy degenerate.

A thin veneer of dark wood clung to the walls. More furniture than Gen had seen in a lifetime lined the hall and various rooms they passed. Voices echoed from ahead, and Arkady paused at a wide pair of double doors, turning to regard him.

I've seen cutters look at paracera flanks like that.

The inspection continued until Gen's hackles threatened to rise. A scowl creased his forehead and Arkady laughed.

"Yes, that'll do. Hold that."

"What?" Gen asked, taken aback.

"No, stop gawping. You've ruined it."

The noise continued unabated on the other side.

Frustration welled in Gen's chest. "What're you on about? Did you bring me here just to parade me around, mock me?"

His hands curled into fists. This was Shkut territory, but their blood spilled as easy as any other man's.

Break a few before they take me out. Probably be doing the militsiya a favor.

Arkady stepped back, glib expression gone. Steel slid over his features as easily as snow buries a hillside.

"Check your temper. You're here at my largesse. I like you, Gen, but I am still a Shkut. At a word, I can have you hanging in the fleshracks as easily as the paracera."

Panic rose in Gen's chest, fear subsuming rage.

Right on time, fuckup.

A breath, two, red tide rising, yellow at the edges of his vision. Old anxiety, threatening to drown him. His fingers and toes tingled; ears burned. After what felt like an eternity, he choked the rage back.

"Good," Arkady said, slapping Gen on the shoulder. "I need you to look angry. I need you to look dirty. The Shkut have a reputation to uphold, after all. We help the common man rise."

And line your pockets while doing it.

"Ready?" Arkady asked.

One more deep breath, out slow through his nose.

The man is clever. A pit of snakes. I'll have to watch him.

Finally, he nodded at Arkady. The other man turned and flung open the doors, smile plastered over the razor-sharp viciousness beneath.

The room turned to look, the men's' entrance grabbing attention and throttling conversation into blue-faced silence. At the edges stood a number of men and women, drinks in hand, faces etched with hard-cut looks.

Wolves in wool suits.

Closer to the center, a group of four clustered near one another. A massive divan dominated the area, and the inner circle alternately lounged or leaned against it. Like their lessers, they wore the look of chained beasts.

Arkady took Gen's arm in his own, smile widening as he threw his other out in greeting.

"Introductions are in order!" he declared, turning Gen toward a man who wouldn't have been out of place in a bear enclosure in the zoo. "This is Boris."

The man's face formed a thunderhead, and he turned away. Gen disliked him on principle.

Arkady leaned in. "We call him Stinkteeth. But never to his face. It's said he likes to eat his victims."

Gen pushed his unease back. He'd heard of battalions resorting to cannibalism during the war. Though the state had promised an investigation, none had ever been produced.

Rumors abounded the Tsar was unwilling to punish those with the fortitude to do what was needed for their country. Other rumors placed a great deal of those surviving soldiers in the militsiya.

Gen found his arm genially pumped by a tall man with broad shoulders. A set of sable robes swathed him, and stones of various sizes and colors adorned his body. He grinned, all white teeth. It put Gen in mind of a conman in the market.

"Ah, this must be the new recruit?" the newcomer asked.

"Gen Antonov, meet Dmitry Marchenko," Arkady said.

Gen nodded. The man's presence weighed on him like the shadow of the moon, making him feel small and robbing him of speech. Dmitry dropped his hand, and the feeling passed.

"Veneficum," Dmitry said, bowing.

Archaic, but fitting with the overdone robes and the bombastic personality. He glided away, and Arkady led Gen into a gap between sections of the divan. Or tried to.

Two men detached from the wall. Gen tensed.

Here it is. Blood in, blood out.

Instinct kicked in. The man on the right, whip-thin, produced a blade, lips pulling back in a grimace.

The man to his left circled, trying to get on Gen's blind side. A momentary lull, the beat of a heart waiting for rupture.

The blade man lunged. Gen stepped to the right, away from the knife. At the same time, the man behind him charged. Gen saw the opening, shoved the would-be ambusher onto his partner's weapon.

A soft grunt. Leaking hiss of pain from lips. Eyes widening.

The wounded man staggered back, hands scrabbling at the steel in his guts.

Ignore him. Break the other.

Gen took the opening. Two large steps, and inside the other man's guard. Stink of copper, sharp tang of fear.

Scything the edge of his hand into the man's throat in a sharp chop. Cartilage popping, the man wheezing, doubling, clutching his throat. On his knees, eyes bulging.

You know the price of admission.

He slammed his knee into the bridge of the choking assailant's nose. It burst like rotten fruit. Snot and blood sprayed Gen. He tasted it, the tang of death hovering.

The Altin Ordu still struggled. Hands on the side of the head, brace the hips. Twist. Sharp snap, dead weight in his arms.

The other, burbling, holding his guts in, ten inches of steel in his hand regardless. Made of hate, the Altin Ordu.

Gen stepped in, took the knife away. Like candy from a stupid child.

He opened the man from groin to gullet, a purse unstitched, treasures spilling out in purple-red lumps and translucent loops.

Another, and another.

Bleed them. Break them. Shatter them like stone. Leave them screaming in the frozen mud. Widows cursing his name.

Fuck them. He'd kill them, too. Kill and kill until the world ran red. Until the great leaking ruin of flesh behind the veneer of civilization lay exposed. The truth in the lie.

The world stretched, pulled taut with each snap of flesh on flesh. Straining against reality. Tight, like the skin of a drum.

It snapped.

Exhaustion washed over Gen. In his absence, someone painted the room red. In his hand, the brush, once bright steel, now sticky with gore. Up his arms, past his elbows. On his chest and thighs. Coating his face.

Bodies lay scattered around him. Four. No, six. The room an abattoir, and he the butcher.

He sagged, blade falling from his fingers.

Light applause.

A woman lounged against the high back of the divan; tall collar of her snow-white gown pressed into the cushion. Gorgeous would have been an insult. Flawless skin. Eyes the color of emeralds. Black hair artfully arranged in a shoulder-length cut. She quirked one eyebrow and the corner of her lip followed. She lowered her hands.

"You'll do," she said.

If Dmitry's presence occluded him like shadow, she burned like the sun. Her smile melted his insides, stirred things below the belt. He clamped down on it.

Irina. Irina. Irina.

"You look like a panicked doe. Relax, sit. You're among friends," she said.

Arkady appeared at his shoulder and gave him a little push. Gen drifted over. He hesitated over the cushion. He didn't want to dirty it by sitting.

The woman saw and winked. "I'll buy another." Gen swallowed and did as requested. A distant part of him suspected if he hadn't, the realm of possibility didn't preclude her feeding him to Boris. At the thought, his eyes drifted.

There.

The big man stood against a pillar in the room, idly swirling his drink. He glared at Gen as if he'd set fire to Boris' dog. The woman reached over and pulled Gen's face toward her. His cheek burned at her touch.

"Do you know who I am?"

Gen shook his head.

"Lia Shkut."

Fuck. The head of the Family? Gods above and devils below, Gen what have you got yourself into?

Her smiled widened. She knew he knew. "Arkady thinks you could be an asset to us. To Arkady's credit, he's rarely wrong."

Despite the carnage, panic flared again in Gen's chest. This was wading into the river with ice forming overhead. He tried to push up, but Arkady was at his shoulder again, a firm hand pressing him down.

The other Gen did that. The strong Gen. Not you, fuckup. Relax.

Gen glanced up, and Arkady gave the slightest shake of his head.

Ah fuck. Ah fuck. Trapped. They could have me arrested now. Hung.

Something echoed in his mind, like hinges on a box he hadn't seen, inevitably closing over his head, locking tight.

"Not much of a talker, is he?" Lia asked Arkady.

The other man barked a laugh. Gen suspected good humor was a requirement in the Family. "He's lugubrious enough when you grease him up a little. Hear her out, Gen."

She fished a cigareta from a silver case and lit it, smoke curling like a halo around her head.

"You have a family, is that right?"

Gen managed to find his voice. "Yes, ma'am."

She knows. How?

Arkady. After the fight yesterday. Came here and told her.

He tried to remember if they'd discussed that. Couldn't pin the thought down, hidden as it was behind a haze of alcohol and adrenaline.

"You want to provide for them? Baby on the way? What will you name it?"

"Artyom if it's a boy. Lilia if a girl," he blurted.

"Good," she purred. "Most of my men are in the family way. Providing is important. The state certainly doesn't, do they?"

"Not great, no."

"A simple job, then. We're moving some goods. I'd like you to tag along with Arkady. Observe. Maybe move a few boxes. You look like a strong man. Arkady told me you used to work the fleshracks. If we like you, we'll have other work. And if it doesn't pan out, well, you'll still get paid for this. What do you say?"

Trepidation curled in Gen's guts like a snake.

Lia noticed. "Tell you what. Speak to Dmitry. He'll help you out. And if it still doesn't feel right to you, we'll part," she dusted her hands together, "friends, who knew each other once."

Arkady squeezed Gen's shoulder, and he nodded at Lia. Her smile burst into full bloom, nearly blinding him. She turned away, addressing another man who'd appeared at her shoulder. Gen stood, trying to hide the tremor in his legs.

"You did good," Arkady said in his ear. "We'll have Irina in a house on the Row in no time."

The Row.

Only the wealthiest lived there. Gen's mind turned to gems and furs and polished marble, and his doubts fled for a time.

After the intimidating opulence of the sitting room, Dmitry's office seemed a safe haven. Warm and cozy, shelves hugged the walls, stuffed with books and papers. Glass cases lined against one wall held a dizzying array of stones, and a pair of overstuffed armchairs sat facing each other in the middle of the room.

Dmitry hunched over one case, glass cover open, rummaging through stones, muttering.

"This one for hate. This one for engineering. This one for counting grains of sand. Fear, pain, misery. Hm. Where is that?"

Finally, he came up with a triumphant shout, blood-red stone dangling from the end of a gold chain in his gloved fist. He strode across the floor and deposited it into Gen's hand.

"This will calm your nerves, bring your courage to the fore. A balm for the troubled heart. Try it on."

Hesitation. These stones were one of the things he'd always dreamed of. Of what he could accomplish with them. Now he found his courage faltering. Irina would be so pissed he'd defied her. He really should just thank them for their hospitality and go home.

With a room full of bodies, you idiot?

Put it on.

He snarled spitefully at the voice in his head and jammed the chain over his neck before his nerve failed him yet again. The instant the stone touched him, a warmth spread from it. His doubt fell away, the insistent voice little more than a murmur.

Gods, I could take on an army!

"How does it feel?" Dmitry asked.

"Good," Gen said, a smile spreading across his face. "Real good."

Dmitry nodded. "A friend brought me that one. Rumor is that it was the very stone General Patruskev had at Kyev."

I could take on an army.

The thought warmed Gen. "Thank you," he said.

Dmitry waved it away. "Lia is happy, I am happy," he replied.

The door opened, and Arkady appeared. "Lia wants me to show you to your room," he said.

A room! Irina would be so proud.

The thought of his wife should have brought more guilt—instead, only an eagerness to get to work suffused him. The stone? No matter. She'd see how wrong she'd been when he brought home mountains of cash. Likely even forgive his little stay here.

"And a bath," Arkady said.

Gen looked down at his tattered, blood-clotted clothing. He nodded in agreement. "And a bath."

"And a new suit. Something befitting a Shkut man."

The room held a four-poster bed, a drink cart, and a scattering of furniture. Arkady disappeared for a few minutes, returning with a thin man bearing a rope measure over his shoulders and a critical eye. The tailor circled Gen once, twice, and nodded.

As he took Gen's measurements, Arkady rummaged around in a dresser set against one wall. When he turned back, it was with a pair of scabbarded knives. He handed them to Gen.

Beware strangers and their gifts. Only blood comes of them.

Who was that? Pavlyv? No matter. Arkady stood, grinning, waiting. Gen pulled the first knife from its sheath. Thin and double-edged, it had been made for artery work. Between the ribs, behind the clavicle, into the carotid. Efficient, and beautiful, the blade black.

Gen set it down and pulled the other free. The length of his forearm, it held a single heavy edge, its blade black with a slight curve. The back of the knife was heavy and thick. A cutting weapon, then. Made for close, brutal work. He hefted it.

It felt like the only true home he'd ever known. Like holding Irina. Like taking a life. This was a gift worthy of an officer, not a grunt. Worthy of a beloved hero. He was not any of those things. Words failed him, and his vision misted.

He looked up at Arkady.

"Thank me later. Welcome to the Family," Arkady said, smile dazzling.

It felt good. Belonging. Being part of something bigger. Something important.

He hadn't felt that way since the war.

KATYUSHKA LEONOVA – CHAPTER EIGHT

Veneficum find their most ancient roots in the shamanic practices of the Plemya, the savage tribes who ruled these lands before the rise of the Tsars. Worshipping crude and brutal gods, these shamans routinely practiced aspects of the art now considered foul. It is one thing to move the memories and personality of a man to the body of an animal so he may better serve the state. Taking aspects and traits from animals so they may be instilled into the thoughts of men, however, is purest blasphemy. A man with the cold morality of a bone snake or the predator focus of a cave lion is a dangerous monster.

— Iskusstvo Veneficum

Collecting the oil lamp, Lazarev led Kat through the vault door at the rear of his office. Beyond, she found an armoured chamber much larger than the one they'd left. Long rows of shelves displayed neatly ordered stones sorted by colour. Too many to count, there were more stones than militsioners in all Norylska.

Noting her attention, he said, "During the war, Norylska was a militsiya outpost." He sighed, looking longingly at the shelves. "I made soldiers to terrify the world." He spoke more to himself than Katyushka. "And now I make militsioners brave enough to face svoloch street scum and help them forget their own petty sins so they can sleep at night. How the mighty have fallen." He glanced at her, flashing a crooked, apologetic thing that was probably supposed to be a smile.

Uncomfortable, Kat gestured at the rocks, each labelled in a strange and blocky script she didn't recognize. "What language is that?"

"That's the secret language of the Order of the Veneficum" Seeing her expression he laughed. "No, it's the runic language of the Plemya. Even if you could read it—and few can—it's written in a personal code."

"What do the colours mean? Do different rocks hold different traits?"

That earned a surprised look, quickly concealed. "Not quite, though some stones are better for different aspects than others. Rocks are chosen for their colour to help the veneficum remember which is which. Each master has his own system."

He's a master veneficum, and served in the war?

He was old enough, though he appeared too gentle. She'd heard stories of wartime veneficum experimenting on themselves and volunteers, pulling traits from insects, predators, and convicted murderers, building nightmare soldiers capable of any horror. She'd always assumed the stories were so much hyperbole. She couldn't imagine this kindly old man involved in such crimes.

"Like red for rage?" Kat asked, eying the long row of crimson stones.

"Well, not quite so obvious, but essentially."

Spotting a set of shelves separate from the rest, Kat asked, "What are those?"

"Leftovers from the war," he mumbled, rubbing at his chin and studying the shelves before him. "The militsiya never make mistakes, but they do occasionally forget things."

Veneficum Lazarev hung the lantern from a hook in the ceiling. Though there were many hooks, all were empty. Was this a typical Kievan cost-cutting measure, or the veneficum's preference?

He drew a pair of fine leather gloves from a pocket, sliding them on with practiced ease. Selecting a green stone, he held it up to the lamp. "This should be a good start."

"What's that?" asked Kat. "Trait or memory?"

"What would be the point of using a long-dead language written in code if I was going to explain everything?"

"Won't I know which stone is what once I put them on?"

"You'd be surprised. Personality traits are subtle beasts; you won't know bravery until tested. Memory even more so. No one walks around remembering everything they've ever done. Such things are called as needed. Donning a memory stone is no more being flooded with all the memories stored within than waking up in the morning is being flooded with your entire history."

Having woken many mornings to the memories of her mistakes and failures, stupid things said or done, Kat was less sure. She opened her mouth to ask another question, and he raised a hand to interrupt.

"You're stalling," he said. "Your questions are rooted in fear and ignorance. Not to worry. I can fix that."

Stones to fix ignorance?

Or did he mean he had stones to stop her from asking questions?

A drilled hole pierced each stone. Lazarev strung rock after rock on a necklace of heavy steel, much like the one she'd seen on Maks.

"That's not going to go with my ballroom gown," she blurted.

He sputtered laughter which turned into a lung-rattling cough. "Sorry," he managed when the fit passed. "But it has to be strong enough it can't easily be taken." He looked over his shoulder, brow crinkled with concern. "I keep forgetting you've had no training."

"There should be a stone for that," she quipped.

That earned her a tolerant smile; he'd heard the joke before.

"Everything I take for granted in a new recruit isn't there," he said. "That's good and bad."

Good and bad? What was the good part about not being remotely qualified?

"At the akademiya they'd take six months to teach you this, so here goes." He ticked points off on his fingers. "The stones are valuable. Criminals will want to take them. Keep them hidden beneath your uniform. Visible stones are a sign of wealth and power, flaunting them is common among thugs and idiots. But they're also a sign of weakness. Wearing a stone means you *need* to wear a stone. A woman such as yourself who appears not to need stones will be a more frightening opponent than one bedecked with them." Closing one eye, he squinted at his fingers. "Am I forgetting anything?"

Kat shrugged.

"Oh, yes. If you sell your state-assigned stones, you will be shot as an enemy to the state. If you lose your state-assigned stones, it will be assumed you sold them, and you will be shot as an enemy of the state."

"Hide the rocks," said Kat. "Don't lose them."

"I knew you were smarter than the typical militsioner," he said, handing her the completed necklace.

"Is this everything?" she asked.

Ignoring her question, he selected one last stone, a polished garnet, stringing it on a second chain. "This is your memory stone. The militsioner who wore this did so during his time at the akademiya." He winked. "The militsiya are quite capable of *some* forethought. It contains everything you need to know about being a militsioner. After coming to Norylska, he worked the Organized Crime Division. He knows the families involved. He knows the streets. No doubt he has informants you will remember as it becomes necessary." He held out the chain in offering.

Reaching for it, Kat hesitated.

Lazarev sighed, a long-suffering sound. Doubtless he'd encountered this sort of uncertainty a thousand times before. "If it soothes your pre-troubled conscience, he was a good militsioner, and by all reports a good man. In a way, you're lucky. Some here are barely above criminals." He shrugged an apology. "An unpleasant truth, but such men are drawn to law-enforcement."

Careful not to touch the stone, Kat accepted the chain. "What was his name? Grinin said the stone would come from a retired militsioner. How long ago did he retire? Does he have a family? Is he still alive now, will I remember being someone who is out there living his life?"

"So many questions," said Lazarev. "But as a veneficum I swore an oath. Several, actually. Part of my work here is helping militsioners through difficult times. Even with the stones, there can be traumatic experiences which need to be... digested. The relationship between veneficum and patient is strictly confidential."

Kat stared at the stone swinging on the end of its crude chain.

"I won't *become* this man, right?" she asked.

"Of course not. This stone contains only memories. There are no personality traits."

Unsure what the difference was, she licked her lips. "If our past shapes us, our memories decide who we are."

He frowned, a slight edge of annoyance slipping past the kindly demeanour. "No. *We* decide. We aren't the past. We are our choices. We are the choices we make today. Anything else is dodging responsibility. Now, if you don't mind, I have another patient to see."

Patient.

Nodding, Kat turned to exit the vault.

"My apologies if I wasn't clear," he said, collecting the lantern. "I need you to put the stone on before you leave. Please hang it about your neck and tuck it under your clothes."

Not seeing she had any choice, Kat did as instructed.

Blink.

No longer in the vault, she stood in the Veneficum's office, the chain held out in offering. She had no memory of removing it. Clothes crumpled, mouth tasting of vomit. Exhaustion dragged her down, feet aching like she'd spent the day walking. A throbbing headache pulsed behind her eyes. She knew that feeling, like she'd spent hours crying.

Lazarev accepted the necklace, hanging the chain on a hook with her name written beneath it. She couldn't remember the placard being there a moment ago.

"The other stones as well, please." He looked tired.

Removing the second necklace, Kat handed it over, confused. "What happened? Didn't the necklace work?" She half-hoped that was the case, that she couldn't be a militsioner and would have to return to her life.

"It's always like that the first time," Lazarev said, offering a kindly smile. "The day is done. You've worked your shift. It's time to go home."

The sore feet. The taste of puke. Feeling like she spent the whole day sobbing. What happened?

Panic gripped her as she realized she'd lived eight hours and had no recollection of any of them. She felt robbed. Someone stole a piece of her life!

People can't live like this!

"Not to worry," said Lazarev. "I know it's jarring. You'll get used to it. Don't wear your secretarial uniform tomorrow. That's not the kind of militsioner you're going to be."

"How should I dress?" she asked.

"Like your partner, Maksim." Brow furrowed in thought, he added, "Think of it as Filth-casual."

He ushered her to the door, out into the precinct. It was still full of militsioners, but she recognized none from the morning. Pale and haggard, eyes like wrung-out dishcloths, they looked as if they hadn't seen the sun in months. Another old man worked the front desk. He had both his eyes, but his left arm ended at the elbow.

Maks strode past, looking her up and down the way men always did. She saw no hint of recognition. He flinched from eye contact. In a heartbeat he was gone, out into the street.

What have I done?

She didn't know what to do but couldn't stay here.

Go home.

Could she find some reason not to return? Could she stay home forever?

Exhausted, Katyushka stumbled out the door.

Home. Fyodor. Comfort. Safety.

Or would it be?

He'll ask about my day.

What had she been up to? How was the secretarial pool? Had she made friends? Did the men leave her alone?

The last question asked oh so casually.

She wouldn't be able to answer.

Her day was gone, a headache and bad taste was all that remained.

Would he be angry she couldn't answer his questions? Would he think she had something to hide?

Kat stood in the street. *Zhiglov's Defeat* called the northern sky an ocean of stars. So much auroch shit. She'd been to the beach in southern Kievan, stood with her toes in the sand, watching waves crash against the shore. It was alive, a great throbbing breathing beast of water and foam. The night sky was dead and cold, a corpse.

I want to go home.

Home was Khagan, the capital, not the grotty shack she shared with Fyodor.

It's not grotty. It's fine.

It wasn't fine; it was a shithole. Fine was the house she grew up in. Fine was a bedroom larger than her entire house. Fine was cook staff, a butler, servants, and your nostrils not freezing closed every fucking time you left the house. Fine was the life she had, not the pale life she currently lived.

Standing before the Chernyshevsky Street Militsiya Bureau, the lamp-lit city looked different than it had in the morning. Not that it ever seemed large or clean, but now it felt cramped and crushed, squeezed in a winter fist. Dirty. Not the kind of unclean a quick scrub and sweep would fix, but the ground-in filth of centuries of furnaces, factories, tanneries, and fat-rendering plants working non-stop. Stained to her very bones, Norylska would *never* be clean.

The feeling passed and she sagged.

Go home before you freeze to death.

Fyodor sat at the table in the kitchen, scratching at the top with a manicured fingernail.

He is so fastidious.

Her own nails, blunt and short, were always dirty. Chopping wood, cleaning the house, doing the dishes, sorting through the sad and wrinkled vegetables in the northern markets; none of these tasks were kind to one's nails.

The woodstove throbbed heat. The woodrack beside it, empty and accusing.

"I made dinner," he said, nodding to the plate of cold chicken and gelid boiled potato sitting across from him.

Three words that could have been a gesture of kindness, weren't.

One meal. He makes one meal and now I'm a terrible girlfriend.

The flash of anger died. He was right. She should have made something before leaving for work. Filling the woodrack was her responsibility. She'd been thoughtless.

"Sorry," she said.

I'll do better.

Fyodor frowned, noting the crumpled state of her uniform. "You look awful."

Not 'how was your day' or 'are you all right'.

She wanted to apologize again. Her appearance mattered. Hell, *appearances* mattered. Her grandmother used to say that. Those rare times Fyodor took her to a company event, he studied her with a critical eye before they left. He was proud of her, wanted to show her off, and it felt good.

Or usually did.

That coin had two sides. Sometimes he pinched the flesh of her hips and his eyes changed. He never said anything, never complained, but she knew she had to shed a few pounds. Skipping meals and going hungry was a small sacrifice.

He said nothing, waiting.

"How was your day?" Kat asked.

Fyodor dove into the details of some case he was assisting on and she half-listened, nodding and making the appropriate noises, as she picked at the flavourless chicken. He was helpless in the kitchen. Strange how that was usually cute. He worked so hard. Meals were her chance to take care of him for a change.

Now, I work too.

By the time she finished the chicken he was in a better mood. Not wanting to ruin it, she ate the tasteless potatoes.

"I'm tired," she said during a brief pause in his explanation of Norylskan real-estate law.

He gave her a look of understanding and a half-smile bordering on apologetic. Attention shifting toward the empty woodrack, he said nothing.

"You look like you had a rough day," he said, not asking how it was.

After filling the woodrack from the stacked logs outside, Kat gave him a hug. He disengaged quicker than usual, hands not reaching for her ass, with an ill-concealed look of distaste.

She couldn't blame him. The secretarial uniform was anything but attractive. And whatever she'd been up to that day had done it no favours.

Kat brushed her teeth, staring at herself in the vanity mirror.

Who are you?

She knew the lines and angles of her face, the dark hair loosed from its bun for the night but felt like she was seeing it from a new angle. She was pretty, but it was meaningless. She saw herself as a man might see her, soft curves and a pleasant face, yet beneath the appreciation lay an utter lack of interest.

Crawling into bed, pulling the heavy blankets up to her neck, Kat slept.

She dreamed of blood and pain. Her hands chained over her head, she knelt on cold stone. Naked, it wasn't her body. Hard. Lean. Strangely knobbly. A man cut her, a long line down her ribs. Another well-dressed man stood behind the first. He asked questions she didn't dare answer.

She screamed and begged, and they cut her again.

They were waiting for me. They knew I was coming.

GENNDY ANTONOV – CHAPTER NINE

Shit happens, tovarich.

—Anton Petrov, Shkut bagman

Irina. Irina screaming, her mouth a black void of rage and pain. She stands over Gen, naked, breasts and belly swollen. Something moves in her womb. Fingers and toes press against her stomach from the inside, distending it. She's berating him, laying it on thick. It crushes his shoulders, piercing like a mantle of thorns, guilt and fear. Fear of being alone. Fear of the past. Fear of failure. Guilt for abandoning her.

The thing in her guts presses harder, lines radiating out from the pressure, skin thinning. First to stretch marks, then to translucent webbing, tearing, shredding her midsection. She's still screaming invective and doesn't seem to notice.

Her stomach rips wide, amniotic fluid, mucus, and blood cascading down her thighs into a wave splashing against the floor. A raging beast with matted fur forces its muzzle free, yellow eyes searching, fangs long as Gen's fingers gnashing.

It catches sight of him, the wolf's lips working like worms over its teeth.

"Get him up! Get him up! He needs more stones!"

Still Irina's words crash into him, each a cold weight. The wolf pushes free, first one long limb, then another, human hands on the ends of canine legs. It's grabbing him, shaking, pink and black lips pulled back from ice-white teeth.

"Gen!"

Sensation flooded him as he tumbled from the bed, tangled in the sheets. Cold marble of the floor. An ache in his hip where he landed. Soft linen. The smell of Arkady's aftershave, and the light of the moon streaming in through open shutters.

"Ah, you're up," Arkady said, as if this was the normal way to wake.

Gen remembered the dream, looked down. He wore a new stone, its green counterpoint to the red he'd gone to bed with.

"What is this?" he asked, holding it up.

Arkady turned from a small liquor cart in the corner, squinting. "I believe that's a stone."

Useful, and annoying.

"What kind?" Gen persisted.

Arkady picked up the glass of vodka he'd prepared, took a sip.

"Don't ask me, darling. Dmitry heard you struggling in your sleep. Came to help."

"Why?"

Arkady shrugged.

Against the light, the stone was dark and shot through with veins of gold.

The stone's not worth asking about. Later.

He shrugged and let it drop.

Arkady stood against the wall, nursing his drink. "Are you quite done playing on the floor?"

"Yeah." His mouth tasted like a cat slept in it. "Yeah, just... let me get dressed."

"Yes, do. The Family prefers its men clothed. Naked men upset the dogs."

Gen nodded. Arkady pushed away from the wall and handed him the vodka. It smelled like turpentine.

"Consider this your breakfast. We have work to do. Meet me downstairs when you're ready."

Another nod, and Arkady left as quietly as he'd come.

The suit they fitted Gen for hung over the back of a chair, gray as a thunderhead. The scrape of dry lips against each other reminded him of the vodka he'd had the night before, and he slugged back the remains of the glass in his hand.

Get to work.

The thought echoed events of the previous night, and Gen shrugged off the shiver threatening to climb his spine and lodge in his hindbrain. He dressed, splashing chill water from a pitcher in the corner over his hair and face, and left.

Dregs of the dream clung to him like cobweb.

Irina.

Shook his head, blinked it away. Enough things to worry about, without her and the guilt she brought taking up residence in his head.

She's probably worried. Likely frightened. Terrified for the baby.

Gen expected a cold knot to form in his stomach at the thought, as it so often did with his anxiety. This time, only a vague sense he should be concerned. Whatever the new stone was, it did a good job of stifling his fears, muting the extremes of worry. In their place sat rough analytical detachment.

I'll apologize later. A necklace. That's what women like. A necklace, and then, a good hard fuck. She hasn't had one of those in a while.

He grinned to himself, remembering the shape of her ass. Free from the weight of his fears, he found himself closer to the old Gen. The one Irina fell in love with.

Yeah, we both need it. She'll be grateful.

Arkady waited on the other side of the door. At the look on Gen's face, his own crooked smile crept to the corners of his mouth.

"Better mood?"

"You know how when you see a really nice ass—" Gen started, hands marking out an hourglass shape. Arkady quirked an eyebrow, and Gen cleared his throat. "The best," he replied.

Arkady led them from the manse, taking the Tsar's Way toward the east. Snow had ceased to fall sometime in the early hours. Slush foamed on the cobbles, ashen from falling soot, churned by morning traffic. Few people walked the streets yet. A couple morose militsiya, unhappy with the foot beat, two or three pensioners out to find groceries, and a few desperate whores calling out as Gen and Arkady passed, commenting on the men's shoulders or backsides,

Arkady threw one a wink, a woman skinny enough to fit between the bars of a cave bear's cage. The other shared his southern complexion and hefted her breasts in Gen's direction. He looked away, ashamed of the stirring in his trousers.

Arkady saw his blush and laughed, slapping him on the back. "Brother, it would do you well to lie with a Solostian. Curl your hair."

Gen risked a glance back, found the woman leering. Snapped his head forward. Arkady laughed until he had to place a hand on his ribs and they devolved into hiccups.

"So timid for a man who nearly described to me exactly what makes his blood flow!" he roared in amusement and made an hourglass shape with his hands.

Had I done that? Need to lay off on the vodka around this man.

"Where are we going?" Gen asked in a desperate attempt to change the subject. His tongue flicked between his lips. They felt dry as scales.

The rustle of leaves in the wind.

A poet now?

He ignored the thought. An errand strand of sensation. Probably something to do with a mixture of vodka and the day's dreams.

Arkady gestured toward the eastern quarter of the city. The buildings squat and sturdy, the sound of steel on steel and the smell of potash and charcoal thickened the air.

"Gruzdev territory," Arkady said.

A rival Family. Gen's shoulders tightened.

What's he getting me into?

Pushkyn was fond of saying *A man is never so lost as in his hometown when he takes a wrong turn. The familiar becomes sinister, the comforting harrowing.*

Deep breath. His hand crept to the knives in the sheaths against his ribs. Gen had named the big one *Ublyudok*, Bastard, in a sudden burst of inspiration and exhaustion. Probably stupid to name a knife. It was just a tool, after all. But it felt special all the same.

"Any particular reason we're crossing their border?" Gen asked. "Death-wish?"

Arkady smirked. "A little bird told me they're trying to broker a deal with the Altin Ordu. Get in on arms trading before the next war."

"Another war? When? How?"

The other man held up a hand. "One thing at a time. First, we ask questions. Besides, there's nothing they can do. We have a truce. Unless they want the full weight of the other families coming down like an avalanche, they'll hold their tongues and knives."

Smoke from the forges hung over the street as they crossed the line into the rival Family's demesne. While not as dire as the Filth, the place had its own grotty charm. Soot clung to every surface, a black patina of misery. Where carefully carved porticos and stout pillars supporting the eaves of homes and businesses once proudly stood, only pitted stone remained.

They fetched up against the door of a long low building, two men roughly the size of aurochs standing guard. Gen blinked, licked his lips. Arkady nodded to them and walked past. Whoever they were—likely Gruzdev muscle—they made no attempt to stop the Shkut from entering.

Inside, fire roared in a wide hearth. Tables stood a few feet from each other, men and women eating quietly. To the right, another door from which waitstaff came and went. Low conversation tumbled through the room like a Kievan acrobat.

Scents drifted on warm currents. Roast bear and auroch, garlic, bay leaf, and cloves. Under that, another insidious stink. Gen tensed as it slipped into his awareness. On instinct, he turned his head. An Altin Ordu. Whip-thin. Pale. Wide mustache oiled and curled at the ends. A shirt reminiscent of a sheet dyed by a blind lunatic. Striped pants. A thin blade hung from a loop over the back of the man's chair, length filigreed in silver, hilt and basket wrapped in gold. Ostentatious. In an Altin Ordu's hands, deadly. Rage warred with disgust, and his hand went to *Ublyudok*.

Meat. Fucking meat, and I am the butcher.

Arkady's thin fingers on Gen's arm. He shook his head once, dark eyes cautionary. Gen sucked in a deep breath. Let it out slow. They crossed the room, Arkady in the lead, and paused at the table.

The Altin Ordu dined with a heavy-set Gruzdev. His suit was a brighter shade than most, star tattoos on the backs of his hands, indicating rank. Gen wasn't familiar enough to know what position the man held, but every child in the Filth knew enough to hold their tongue and their fists if they ever encountered a Family man. The Gruzdev shoveled a thick rope of meat into his mouth, sopping up gravy with bread before looking up.

"Arkady. And you've brought a friend," the Family man said.

"As have you, Grigor," Arkady said, throwing a wink at the Altin Ordu.

If the gesture was meant to catch the man off-guard, Gen couldn't tell. Bright on the outside, dark on the inside, the Altin Ordu.

Arkady hooked a nearby chair and spun it, sitting so his arms were on the back. His coat fell open, revealing a service pistol in its holster. Grigor stopped chewing and leaned back in his chair. The Altin Ordu kept eating. Heat lapped at Gen's face as he struggled to keep his rage down as he recognized the meaning of the man's clothing.

A Süvari. Scum, even among scum.

The Süvari were Altin Ordu's answer to Kievan Spetznyz. Specialists in sabotage, not above committing atrocities in the name of victory. In Irkysk, a small team slipped behind Kievan lines. Poisoned a battalion's water supply. Two hundred men, vomiting blood, weeping pus into their trousers as their bodies screamed for release. In the end, the Kievan had no recourse. Moans from the sick and dying were breaking morale. They'd sent a detachment to quiet the stricken. Gen had been forced to slit the throats of his own brothers in arms to protect the fighting spirit of the army.

Some things can never be forgiven with distance or time.

He licked his lips and tore his eyes away.

"Hearing rumors, Grigor," Arkady said idly. "Rumors the militsiya would be sorely interested in." His eyes drifted over to the Altin Ordu. "Not that I would tell them, but even the Families cannot abide treason. No matter what you think of the state, to give it over to these foreign devils—"

The slap resounded through the room, the Altin Ordu's hand there and gone before anyone could react. Arkady's head rocked to the side in its wake.

What the fuck? No one's that fast. What kind of shit have those animals done?

Arkady's head turned slowly, slower than Gen believed possible. He fixed blazing pupils on the Altin Ordu. The foreigner picked up another string of meat and shoveled it into his mouth.

I will fill your mouth with shit while you die screaming.

Gen stepped forward, hand slipping inside his coat. He slid the blade free an inch, eyes fixed on the foreign bastard. Turned slightly. Wouldn't do to catch the hilt on the fabric.

The Altin Ordu caught his eye, stared. Grigor stopped chewing, his own hand creeping toward something.

We're all gonna fucking die.

Yeah, but we're gonna take that piece of shit out with us.

Glory, then.

The Altin Ordu leaned back, hand casually going for the hilt of his gaudy sword. Gen heard the ratchet of a chamber as the hammer of a pistol eased back. Likely Grigor, that one. Arkady's hand disappeared inside his suit a moment later.

The room, ready to ignite.

Faster than an old fat man and a wafter?

Let's find out.

He stepped forward, not much, a subtle shift of weight. Close enough to lunge for the foreigner's throat.

"Genndy!" Arkady's voice like the crack of a whip. "Stand down."

Gen stiffened, fever cooling. He blinked, relaxed. Slipped Bastard back into its sheath. As much as he wanted to gut these men here and now, he wanted to please his new friend more.

"In my country," the Altin Ordu said, eyes flicking back to Arkady, accent thick with glottal stops, "People like you are summarily executed."

"Like. Me," Arkady repeated, voice dead as stone. The temperature dropped palpably, despite the fire.

The Altin Ordu nodded. "Criminal scum." The words hid the insult. *Goluboi.*

Arkady's jaw muscle worked silently, bunching as he ground his teeth. Without taking his eyes from the Altin Ordu, he said, "Gen. If he raises his hand again, remove it."

And ram it up his ass.

Rage roared in Gen, a hungry inferno. The palms of his hands itched with the need to do violence, to feel a slick of blood coating them.

Arkady turned back to Grigor. "So, the rumors?"

Grigor, eyes wide as saucers, realized Arkady was speaking to him, the Shkut's voice cutting through the tension in the room like a razor through a throat. He swallowed, recovered his composure, eyes flicking to his dinner guest. Waved a hand as if to dismiss the accusation. "Rumors, only that. Petra is a guest. An ambassador to our fine nation."

"A fine nation to raise pigs in," Petra said.

Gen fixed the man with a stare. For the first time, the Altin Ordu noticed him, in the way a man is aware of a knife, but only finds his attention drawn to it once it's free of its sheath. His eyes, lined with kohl, sparkled with smug superiority.

"A soldier." He sneered. "I know your kind."

The Altin Ordu stood, wiping his hands on a napkin, carelessly tossing it aside. Grigor raised a hand, tried in vain to stop him. "Now, now," he said, mouth working like a landed fish, "this is Gruzdev territory. Any action here would be seen as an act of war!"

"Yes, war," the Altin Ordu said. The stink of the man's perfume was overpowering this close. Gen stifled the urge to gag. "I know war. You know war. I know your type. Fratricide. Patricide. Orphaner. Murderer!" The last a shout.

Steel so cold it may have been forged from ice lashed out, burned a line of fire across Gen's cheek. He hadn't seen the blade in the man's hand. Flinch, step back. Tense. Muscle quivering, heart a hammer against his ribs, threatening to tear cartilage, rip free of its moorings. Fever in his flesh. He stared at the Altin Ordu, the man holding the knife with something like contempt on his narrow face, hooked nose wrinkled in a sneer.

This one is a child. Eager to fight. Arrogant. Too stupid to realize neither are a good idea.

Beat. Breath. Beat. Breath. Rush of blood.

Arkady's voice in his ear: "You gonna do something about it, or just stand there and bleed?"

A red curtain, rust and blood, slammed over his vision. A veil of carnage. He went to work, a scythe, a thresher of men.

Snap bone, *Ublyudok* in a shoulder. Screaming. Work the other man's hand back and forth, the palm short three fingers after Bastard sheared them off. The Altin Ordu smearing blood across Gen's cheek, trying for his eyes. The knife Petra had held lay in a pool of blood with the remains of his hand.

A gunshot, the impact of a body, heavy against the boards of the floor. The stink of cordite. Another shot, then another. The door guard, one clutching the remains of his balls, blood spreading like oil in water across the front of his trousers, the other staring at the ceiling from the crater in his skull.

Distractions.

Blink.

Here, tendon. Here, cartilage. Bastard ripping them like paper.

Petra's screams the howl of a storm. His arm came away in Gen's hand, heavy, shoulder impacting the floor with a meaty *thwack*. Gen dropped it, slammed the big knife into the other, started work there.

Someone at his ear, shouting, shouting.

Let me finish my work first.

Sawing faster, this arm falling free. The Altin Ordu silent, body collapsing with the release of tension from the severed limb. The floor a red tide. Gen followed it down, thighs tight against the ribs, hacking at the neck.

Stupid. Fucking. Mustache.

The head rolled free. Another gunshot, too close. Gen's head split with pain, and he rolled off the body, clutching one ear. Arkady in his face, shouting. The world rang, but he read the man's lips.

"We have to go!"

Gen nodded and struggled to his feet, slipped once in the blood. Arkady grabbed his shoulder, hauled him up. They rushed for the back door, fire spreading from the hearth.

When did that happen?

Bodies decorated the floor like errant flower petals. Some bore the gaping wounds of pistol rounds. Others had been cut and ripped and torn. Fire blossomed, and they shouldered the back door down, smoke escaping into the alley with them. They stood, sucking fresh air in scalding gulps. Gen ached. He licked his lips, tried to blink already freezing sweat away. Blood on his tongue.

Stalking prey through the taiga, the smells of loam and fecund undergrowth.
What the fuck?

It slipped away.

They stood in the relative peace of the alley for a minute, recovering. Arkady stared at Gen, unblinking. The pistol still dangled from his hand.

He's going to kill you. Put you down like a wild dog. Way to fuck up yet again.

Gen tensed, wondering if he had the strength to slit Arkady's throat, flee back to his shack.

They'll find you. They'll find you and hang you from those gallows in the square. You and Irina. They might even cut the baby free and hang it for good measure. Failure.

The other man took a deep breath, body shuddering like a shack in a storm. He slipped the pistol into its holster, and nodded, as if confirming something to himself. A muscle in Gen's neck loosened, and some of his ache receded.

"Let's get the fuck out of here before the rest of the Family shows up," Arkady said. "Oh, and Gen, darling?"

"Yeah?"

"You ever think about seeing a veneficum? You know, for your rage problem?"

Gen snorted a manic laugh, and they fled into the night.

KATYUSHKA LEONOVA – CHAPTER TEN

The Altin Ordu oppressed are allowed once every few years to decide which members of the oppressing class will represent and oppress them from parliament.

—Tsar Ilyich Ulyanov

Katyushka woke before the sun. Ghosts of the dream chased circles through her thoughts, fading with each revolution.

Knees hard against icy stone.

Questions and pain.

A man, expressionless, with a straight razor. Each rare blink an awkward, stuttering thing. A pink tongue, pointed and wet, poked between his lips, tasted the air, then vanished. He jerked, snapped his head to the side as if to examine her from another angle.

Like a snake.

Cut.

Peel flesh.

Scream.

Stuttering blink.

Emotionless.

Fyodor farted in his sleep, a sharp *phrrp!* and the dream dissolved.

She couldn't remember him coming to bed. How long had he stayed up?

He didn't sleep on the couch.

That was a good sign. The rare times he got angry, he punished her with distance, his silence filling the house. She hated lying alone in bed fretting about him. Those were sleepless nights for her.

That wasn't a problem last night.

She'd been asleep moments after her head hit the pillow, hadn't given him a single thought.

I was tired.

It wasn't that she didn't care.

My first day at work, and he didn't even ask.

Not that she could have told him much. Her day sat on a shelf in Lazarev's vault.

Careful not to wake Fyodor, Kat slid from bed and padded into the kitchen.

After refilling the woodrack from the snow-covered pile outside, she lit the stove and cooked him a breakfast of salted porridge. Remembering the cold chicken and boiled potato from the night before, she fried pork chops and thinly sliced potatoes, leaving them wrapped in waxy paper in the icebox for dinner. Drop them in the cast iron fry pan with some butter, and he'd have a hot meal in minutes.

Today, she promised, she'd leave work on time, get home at a reasonable hour. He didn't like eating alone.

When Fyodor still hadn't risen, she crept to their shared closet.

No uniform, she remembered.

Kat chose a long wool skirt and leggings, slinging them over her shoulder. They'd itch, but her legs wouldn't freeze. Fyodor hated when she wore the leggings to bed on those truly cold nights, called them the ultimate prophylactic. Selecting a cotton undershirt, a heavier overshirt, and a bulky wool sweater, she retreated to the kitchen to dress.

Gone was yesterday's excitement.

Had she spent most of the day crying? Why had her mouth tasted of vomit when she removed the stones?

It wasn't until halfway to Chernyshevsky Street Millitsiya Bureau she realized she'd forgotten to eat, or pack anything for her lunch.

The same crumpled old man with one eye and crumpled cigareta worked the first desk. He waved her in, nodding at the veneficum's door, and returned to digging at whatever was behind the frayed eyepatch. She saw no sign of Maks, and Colonel Grinin's door remained closed and uninviting.

Go tell him this is all a terrible mistake.

She swallowed a terrified sob of self-mocking laughter. She'd need several stones of bravery before knocking on an officer's door to explain how he'd been wrong. Men hated that, even when they weren't uniformed militsioners accustomed to being obeyed by underlings.

Bravery stones. There must be one among the rocks Veneficum Lazarev gave her.

Brilliant! Wait until she had the bravery to face the man and then do so! She imagined striding into Grinin's office filled with confidence, telling him that a woman working the Organized Crime Division in the Filth was madness, and strolling out. Almost funny they were handing her the means to quit.

It's a plan.

Why hadn't she done it yesterday, once she had the stones?

What if I did?

She'd have no way of knowing.

No point in worrying about it. She'd know as soon as she put on the memory stone.

Penkin, Lazarev's skinny and rude assistant, was just as skinny and rude as he ushered her through to Lazarev's much messier office with a disapproving scowl. Grabbing a neatly folded pair of lambskin gloves off his desk, he followed her in.

She saw no sign of the veneficum. "Where's Lazarev?"

"*Veneficum* Lazarev is busy elsewhere," said Penkin.

"Slept in, eh?"

"Hardly, Miss Leonova," he said, turning the *miss* into an insult, as if she was an undesirable spinster or worse. "Come." Pulling on his gloves, he marched imperiously into the vault.

Kat followed.

His ass wiggles like a berezka dancer's.

Finding the shelf with her name, Penkin lifted the two familiar necklaces.

Maks said he put on the personality stones first.

He needed the bravery to put on the memory stone. Having no recollection of the previous day but heeding the advice, Kat accepted the traits necklace first, ducking into it, and tucking the stones beneath her shirt. They felt cold against her chest.

"Be nice if you could warm these up," she joked.

"Veneficum Lazarev dictates the temperature of these offices," said Penkin, passing her the memory stone. "I shall pass along your complaint."

"No, I didn't... It was a joke."

"Are you quite sure?"

"I... Sorry."

Apparently even her apology was a disappointment to the assistant.

He passed her the necklace with the memory stone, and she hesitated, waiting to feel the effects of the first necklace.

Nothing is happening. She felt no manly rush of bravery and confidence. *Why are confidence and bravery considered manly traits?*

She'd heard of a squad of female snipers from the war who'd been dubbed the Tsaritsas of Death. They killed so many Altin Ordu officers the enemy sent assassins of their own to kill them. She'd seen a one-woman play about the death of the last Tsaritsa. Alone, hunted through an abandoned city by snakes, lions, and cave-bears adorned with memory and personality stones, she killed hundreds before they brought her down.

Victory in Defeat, that was the play.

"By all means," said Penkin, "please, take your time."

"Sorry," she apologised again, slipping the necklace over her head.

For a moment, nothing.

Then, she remembered.

She'd put the stone on for the first time yesterday, said something to Lazarev about how she felt no different, had no memories she hadn't previously possessed. He'd gone on about how you only got slammed by traits and memories from stones made by lesser veneficum. A master of the art, he'd said, is a master of subtlety.

There was pride there, but something else too. Something terrifying she couldn't nail down. As if by wearing his stones she was inviting him into her head.

Kat had met Maks across the street, and they ate ponchiki and drank coffee and she joked about how she was getting paid double a secretary's salary for this. He said that told you how little secretaries were paid.

She remembered a day spent wandering the streets, doing absolutely nothing. It was strange. They went into districts she'd never previously visited, and she knew all the street names, never felt lost. She recognized people she'd never met; knew their names and the crimes they'd been arrested for.

"Is this it?" she had asked. "Is this the job?" This wasn't so bad.

Maks laughed and explained the first day was for acclimating to the stones. There was a period of adjustment that changed from person to person. Generally, it took hours.

Kat remembered.

She and Maks had been passing a narrow alley, strewn with refuse, piled deep with soot-caked snow, when she stopped.

I followed Kasak's tracks into an alley just like this.

No. Not her. Someone else had followed the man.

It had been a trap. Kasak knew she was trailing him. Instead of fleeing, the small-time crook stopped, turned to face her.

Not me. Not me!

Kasak grinned. "The Family wants a word."

Kat wanted to ask which Family, but already knew: the Shkut Family. She'd been looking into their business trying to find... trying to...

Men exited doors, surrounding her. Most carried crude clubs or wore knuckle-dusters. A slim man, handsome and well-dressed, stepped from the shadows. He held an officer's revolver, loose and relaxed. This wasn't the kind of man who needed bravado and threats. His southern complexion, out of place among the pale Norylskan faces, grinned welcome.

I know him! I know him!

Arkady. She couldn't remember the last name.

"Kostas, my friend," Arkady said to her. "I have some questions."

Trapped fear. A cornered animal.

They took her revolver. They took her knuckle-dusters.

They took her.

When Kat finally remembered who she was, she was kneeing in the snow puking and retching and screaming.

People crossed the street to avoid the scene. Maks ignored them.

"There you go," he said, standing over her. He made no offer of assistance. "It happens to the best of us." He barked a rueful laugh. "Even happened to me."

She wasn't sure what he meant. Did he not count himself among the 'best of us' or did he hold himself separate, above the others?

She knew the answer. This was Maks. Good old Maks. Handsome enough you wanted to forgive his foibles. Funny enough, it was easy to overlook his faults. Gods, he was so good-looking! Those slim hips and broad shoulders. That taut ass. How many nights had she rubbed one out thinking about hammering that?

I never!

"Do you know your name?" Maks asked.

She blinked, confused. There were two answers. One, she hesitated to give. "Katyushka. Katyushka Leonova."

"I mean the other one," he said. "Whose stone are you wearing?"

Kostas.

"I don't know," she lied. "Too confusing."

"It'll come," said Maks. "Sometimes it takes weeks."

Only three people knew Kostas was following Kasak.

Her partner was one of them.

"It's weird," Maks had said, looking down at her, eyes filled with pity. "You know, interesting-weird. The way we know who we are but spend surprisingly little time thinking about it. People don't walk around thinking, 'my name is Maks.'" He laughed, but it was distracted, thoughtful. "As if who we are is a background thing and not front and centre of our lives." He looked down at her. "Shouldn't that be the front and centre?"

Kat stared up at him, only half-following. *I am Kostas Malakhov. I am your partner, and I've been in love with you since the day we met four years ago.*

"I don't love you," she blurted.

Maks snorted. "Of course you do. Everyone does."

No. Everyone pretends to. It said something about the man that he didn't see the difference. Kat pushed the foreign thought away.

You can love someone for who they are and hate them for what they are.

That wasn't Kat. What did it even mean? There was no separating yourself from your actions and choices. They defined you. Anything else was prevarication.

They'd spent the rest of that day hanging out in Maks' favourite ponchiki shop. It was a dump. She knew what the coffee tasted like before it touched her lips, had eaten a thousand fried balls of sugar-dusted dough here, though she'd never set foot in the establishment.

Waves of memory and nausea had swept through Kat, periodically sending her running for the bathroom to vomit or cry. Once, she accidentally dashed into the men's room. Luckily it had been empty.

Maks smiled tolerantly through the whole thing. He offered napkins to wipe drool and spittle from her face. He made jokes about how the nun-bun was a good idea, saved her from puking in her hair.

"Tomorrow will be better," he kept saying. "The first day is always the worst."

When their shift ended, he asked if she was ready to head home.

She sat there in the dingy ponchiki shop, the buttery smell of hot pastry at odds with the greasy walls and chipped tables and realized she didn't want to go home. Fyodor would be there with his pathetic passive-aggressive anger. He'd make her feel terrible, like everything was her fault and how could she do this to him when he did so much for her?

"Can we stay for one more coffee?" she'd asked Maks.

Understanding lit his eyes, and something that might have been pain.

He nodded. "Sometimes you don't want to go back to who you really are," he said. "The stones come off and you're just shitty you again. All the things you told yourself you were going to do and say during the day are gone, forgotten. But the truth is, you're a different person now and even if you could remember what it was you wanted to say, you wouldn't say it." He looked away. "Because you're a coward."

She understood maybe half the rambling speech, but it didn't matter. Good old Maksim Tkatchenko. For all his faults, for all his bullshit and bravado, when the stones came off, he wasn't a bad man.

They only left when the ponchiki shop finally closed for the night.

Katyushka left the veneficum's office and stood on the precinct floor. Militsioners flowed around her as if she were an island in a stream. They still cast speculative glances, but her street-clothes—Why did she think of them like that?—showed no more hint as to what lay beneath than the over-starched secretarial uniform.

Too many memories crowded her mind, demanding attention, clamoring for examination. Fyodor. Maks. Kostas Malakhov, the murdered militsioner whose memory stone she now wore.

Colonel Grinin's door caught her attention. Just moments ago she'd planned to stride in with her bravery stones and whatever else she now wore, and tell him he'd made a mistake, she couldn't do this.

She hesitated.

It wasn't fear, which struck her as weird. She knew Grinin. His bark was worse than his bite. No, something else bothered her.

"If you start something, you finish it," she whispered.

You do? Says who?

"Your choices and action define you." she said.

A militsioner shot her a curious look and continued on his way.

Was she the kind of person who fled from a fight?

Yes!

No, she wasn't.

Someone cornered her in an alley. Someone tortured and killed her. They were going to fucking pay for that. Every fucking one of them.

Kat blinked in surprise. She never used such foul language!

Only three people knew where I was going.

Maks spotted her across the precinct hall and sauntered over, hands in the pockets of his open greatcoat, an unlit cigareta hanging from his mouth. She wanted to kiss him, suck on his bottom lip, slide her hands into—

No, I don't!

"Hey partner," he said. "Feeling better?"

No. No, I'm not.

"Yes," she said because in truth, she did.

"You got a light?"

Rolling her eyes, she fished for matches before remembering she didn't smoke. "No."

He gave her a strange look, snagged a cigareta from the mouth of a passing militsioner, and used it to light his own. The militsioner reclaimed his smoke. Just another day.

Without thought, Kat snatched the cirgareta from Maks, spun it in her fingers, and jammed it in her own mouth. She inhaled deep, glorying in the rush of the day's first smoke. Maks stole it back, used it to light another, which he popped into the corner of those perfect lips, and returned the cigareta to her mouth.

It was a strangely practiced move, like this happened all the time. Almost gentle. Those lips. Kiss them, breathe smoke from his lungs. Those long fingers. She wanted to lick them, taste them. Taste him. She could never tell him, never show the smallest hint of what—

Maks blinked at her, suddenly realizing what he'd done. "What the fuck? Who are—"

But she was bent double coughing and gagging so hard she thought her lungs would shred apart.

When the fit passed, he studied her, the thoughtful look out of place on his face.

"Right," he said. "Right."

He wants to ask about the memory stone.

"Are you wearing perfume?" he demanded.

"Just a little."

"Blood and bones! Militsioners don't wear perfume. We don't smell like fucking flowers."

"This is—"

He cut her off with an imperiously raised hand. "No. It's distracting. Bad enough the men have to spend the day wondering what's hidden beneath that," he waggled fingers at her clothes, "but to have to *smell* you as well? No, no. Militionsers come in three flavours." He held up three fingers, lowering them one at a time as he continued. "A drunk's armpit, corpse, and fried onions. Though some of the men have experimented with combining scents to great success. I suppose, because you're a woman and no doubt fastidious about such things, it might be permissible to smell like harsh peasant soap."

"You don't smell like an armpit."

"That's because I'm so very pretty. Now." He paused to suck hard on his cigareta. Letting the smoke leak lazily out of his mouth, he pulled it back in through his nose. "Let's get you a proper militsioner's coat."

Maks led her to yet another part of the Chernyshevsky Street Militsiya Bureau she'd never seen. A sign reading Armoury hung above a barred window. Beyond sat an elderly gentleman with ice-blue eyes, iron-grey stubble blanketing most of his face and head. He glared at them, eyes locking on Kat and then dismissing her.

"This is where we requisition additional equipment," said Maks. "All the best toys are in here, from revolvers to repeater rifles to some really fun stuff left from the war." He gestured at the man behind the bars. "Pudovkin, here, is the Keeper of the Toy Chest and acts like each attempted requisition comes out of his personal pay."

Pudovkin sneered at Maks.

"Pud, buddy," said Maks, leaning on the bars. "My lady friend here needs a militsioner-issue greatcoat."

"A woman?" Pudovkin demanded, without looking at Kat. "Why?"

"Go ask Colonel Grinin," said Maks. "We'll wait here and deal with whoever replaces you."

Pudovkin grunted annoyance. Grabbing a crutch from beside his desk, he levered himself upright. "Size?" he demanded of Maks, still refusing to look at Kat.

Maks pretended to study her with a cocked eyebrow. "We'd like something fitted. Take it in at the waist, but she'll need a little extra room up top. Sleeves should be tapered. Have it lined in something comfortable but durable." He inhaled hard on his cigareta, blew smoke from his nose. "Do I look like a fucking tailor? Just get her the smallest one you can find."

Leaning heavily on the crutch, Pudovkin shuffled to the back of the room, disappearing through a second door. His right leg ended at a stump just below the knee.

He returned moments later with a militsioner greatcoat, and handed it to Maks, stuffing it between the bars.

Maks passed the coat to Kat. "Welcome to the militsioners. Find an empty locker in the locker room and hang your old coat there. Each night, your greatcoat goes in the locker. Do not wear it home. Wearing your militsioner-issue greatcoat home will be considered theft from the state and you will be shot as a traitor."

"Do they really—"

"No. Go hang your coat and meet me in the main hall." He left without another word.

After finding the locker room and stowing her coat in an empty locker, Kat met Maks by the front entrance.

He looked her up and down. "You look like a rabbit in riot-gear."

"It's a bit big," she admitted.

"Blasphemy! You dare impugn the state's ability to properly outfit its militsioners?" He plucked at one of the shoulders, which extended well past her own. "Apparently the state wants to be able to fit two of you in that coat. Though where we'll find a second militsioner as cute as you, I have no idea"

Uncomfortable, not knowing what to say or how to react, Kat said nothing.

"We're going to take it easy today," he continued. "Like a meet and greet."

"Meet and greet," she repeated. That didn't sound so bad.

"Yeah. I've got a line on some back-alley veneficum who's been pedalling fake personality stones. Word is he has a line on some stolen militsiya surplus, stuff lifted from animals. Snakes. Cave-lions. Nasty shit."

Snakes. She remembered the man in her dream, the stuttering blink, the flick of pink tongue.

"We're gonna grab a couple of the Big Boys Club," said Maks, heading toward the far end of the precinct. "Don't expect sparkling conversation like what you get from me."

Katyushka followed Maks as he wove through desks, cracking jokes with follow militsioners, stopping to straighten one man's tie with an exaggerated show of motherly concern. They smiled. They laughed. But it was toleration rather than camaraderie.

He can't see it.

How could someone so sociable be so blind to the reactions of those around him?

Or was it that he didn't care? She couldn't imagine such self-confidence.

She remembered the way he looked at her at the end of the previous day, gaze flinching away when she tried to make eye contact. Had he already handed in his stones? Was she seeing the real Maks for the first time?

"My CI told me where the veneficum operates from," Maks said over his shoulder.

"CI?" But she knew the answer. Criminal Informant.

"In Bashenko's case it means Crusty Idiot."

Gods, will he never tire of that joke?

"This is small-time," promised Maks. "No Family connections."

No Family. This back-alley veneficum didn't belong to the Shkuts.

Shit, busting him will be doing him a favour.

If the Shkuts got the poor bastard first, they'd peel him.

Like they did me.

Maks led her through a door in the rear of the main precinct hall, past several offices, all with shutters drawn, and into a smoke-filled lounge.

The Shkuts knew I was coming. They were waiting.

Only three men knew she was going to be in that alley, and Maks was one of them.

Who were the other two?

She had no idea.

GENNDY ANTONOV — CHAPTER ELEVEN

The brutality of the Kievan man is not a flaw, as those who decry our nation love to claim, but a strength. In the face of killing cold, the threat of the state's heel on one's neck, and the predation of the corporations, a certain moral flexibility is required. Those who lack fortitude to spill blood in their own defense will soon find themselves bait for the wolf pits. Meat is meat, after all. No matter if it breathes or not.

—Leonid Yahontov, Alley Philospic

It took some time to reach the manse. Arkady insisted on taking a twisting path leading them not only through a maze of warrens in Gruzdev territory, but then shot south, into Tikhonenko territory, where willowy women with pinched faces and men wearing suits smelling as if no one had ever shit in them on a drunken night radiated disapproval at their harried flight. Finally, they turned north, back to Square of the Fathers.

Obelisk monuments stood at the corners, luminaries such as Potymken and Nybakyv frowning down in paternal concern and stony welcome. Gen breathed easier at the sight. Somewhere in the distance, dogs brayed. He tensed, but the sound soon passed, fading into the mist. The Shkut home loomed ahead. Gen muttered a silent prayer of thanks to whatever god might be listening. The fight and the run warmed him, but slowing to a walk, blood on his clothing formed a stiff layer of freezing gore, cracking softly as he moved. Sweat chilled on him, raising gooseflesh, shivers chasing waves of pimpled skin. Still wearing a wolf's grin, Arkady slapped Gen on the back.

"Fine work, comrade! Fine work! And not a fucking thing they can do about it!"

Gen clenched his jaw to keep his teeth from chattering and shot Arkady a sideways glance. "How do you figure? Didn't we just spent an hour running from them?"

Arkady waved a hand. "Oh, if they had caught us, we'd be fucked for sure. The Tsar Special, no doubt. Skirt over the head, poker up the ass. But since they haven't, they're tied tighter to a post than a penitent on flogging day."

Just get to it, you asshole.

The cold slid into Gen's joints, aching, making him surly. He sucked cold air down his throat to cool his temper. "Explain."

Arkady caught his mood. "Ah, I see. Plagued by conscience? Perhaps fear? Let me soothe your guilt. The Gruzdev can bring complaint to neither the militsiya or Lia. To do so would be admitting they harbored an Altin Ordu.

"Quick: How is an Altin Ordu like a cockroach?'"

"No idea. How is an Altin Ordu like a cockroach?" Gen asked.

"No matter how many you kill, there's always another."

Gen snorted in amusement. Sometimes the best jokes hold a kernel of truth. Then his mind circled back to the bar, setting him to brooding again.

How'd he know about the Altin Ordu? Knowledge doesn't just fall out of the sky.

They'd bent the Gruzdev over a barrel with this. He nodded. "It would open them up to scrutiny. Retribution. They'd be burning their own house down while chasing a stray match."

"Well put."

"How'd you know?" Gen asked, echoing the earlier thought.

"I have a friend. Well-placed. It's a mutually beneficial relationship."

Gen nodded. "Like the valet."

Arkady laughed as they climbed the stairs to the Shkut mansion. "No, my friend, not like the valet. He is more... a distraction." He paused, hand on the door. "Lia will want to talk to you. Take her praise. If she wishes to rebuke you, let her. Say nothing of my friend. I wish to keep him safe."

He dances around the subject.

Not that I care. Men in the field grew lonely all the time. Others simply preferred the company of other men. None of it matters. All that does is if the man beside you can gut the man against you.

Something cold and alien slithered through the back of his mind, tasting his thoughts, testing the quality of each. It approved of an idea found there and nudged it forward.

He's talking about an asset. This is mercenary, not love. Arkady is using the man. If Lia finds out, she'll take him away. This is a test. Do I betray him, or keep his secrets?

Interesting.

Gen nodded. and Arkady opened the door, letting them into the warmth and comfort of the mansion. Soft silence reigned in the halls. Despite the illusion of excess and leisure, Families were businesses. Everyone had to work, everyone had to earn.

"Get out of those clothes. Have a bath. I'm sure she'll summon you soon," Arkady said.

He left, disappearing into another part of the mansion. Gen paused in the foyer. The scope of the place nearly cowed him again. It was a shock to the senses each time he entered, like stepping from a cave into the light. The smell of cedar. Furniture gleaming with polish. Clean, tasteful fabrics hung on the walls and draped across chairs. Floors without a patina of ash. Cornices and molding gilded in silver and gold. More wealth here than he'd see in a generation of lifetimes.

Would have seen.

The Families were a necessary evil. Yes, people died because of their actions. It paled in comparison to the state's body count. More, they were not cowed by the brutal shadow of Khagan but burrowed under its skin and dared to strip clusters of gold from the bones. They offered wealth by the fistful to the loyal. All Gen had to do was what he'd always done—wet his blade and follow orders.

He climbed the stairs, savoring the clean scent on the air, smooth wood of the banister against his palm. Once in his room, he carefully removed each piece of clothing, setting them in a pile in the washroom. A dull throb beat in his cheek, and he raised a hand, touching the bloody cut there. The skin felt swollen, but not hot. No infection, then. He'd have to wash it well.

Steaming water poured from brass pipes into the porcelain tub, splashing against its sides in a torrent of crystal waves.

Three months ago, I would never have imagined water this clear. Hell, three days ago. What would Irina think of this?

He imagined her naked in the tub, breasts floating, hair like a halo. Legs slightly spread, her sex peeking from between creamy thighs.

That's a dead-end. Save it for now.

He took a breath, pushed it away, and climbed in. The heat felt good against muscles beat sore by exertion. He lay back and let it work out the knots of the past couple days. His mind drifted.

The taiga. Trees older than the city, older than the men huddling behind its walls. He smells them, weakflesh. They stink of rot and corruption. Stomping through the trees, loud. Insensate. They might as well be blind. Blind and stupid.

The first goes down in a spatter of gore. It never heard him. Intestines slip in thick ropes from its white belly. It keens in agony, so he rips its throat out.

More coming. They stamp and trample, and he is shadow.

He smells more corruption. Unnatural. It comes from the rods they carry, and inside, under the stink of chemical, is fire. He knows enough to skirt these men.

Another, alone. He drops from a tree, lands on its back. His weight bears it down, hind legs ripping it open to the spine. Jaws clamp on its neck, shake. A cry before death:

"Father!"

A thick snap, and the man goes limp.

On to the next. Pissing in a clearing. He rips its legs out. Lets it crawl across the leaves, weeping, smearing them with blood. The scent is rich and clean in his nose.

This one dies, and screams his name:

"Genndy!"

He shakes his head, disorientation throwing his balance for a moment. Something hits him in the side, and the world tilts. He wants to get up. Wants to push free from the grip of the forest floor. It refuses. The stink comes again, stronger. Men. Many of them. He hears the bark of their rods, catches the scent of fire.

The forest smells ablaze, but he sees no flames.

A man kicks him in the ribs. He tries to snarl, but his lungs are pressed tight, a mountain atop his chest.

"This one! Quickly! Get it on him!"

Claws out, or he tries, but nothing comes. His flesh refuses to respond. The world fades to a pinpoint, shrinking, shriveling. Like the first time he scented prey and the world opened up, only in reverse.

"Now! Get the stone on him now!"

He smells blood. It is not the men's.

Water, pressing against him. He'd sunk into the bath at some point. Gen came up, thrashing, red spirals trailing behind him. His cheek had opened again, bled into the water. Surfacing, he sucked in lungsful of air. Black spots danced in his vision.

How... I could've drowned.

Arkady sat across from him, on the lip of the vanity. He threw Gen a towel.

Ah, not drowned. Did he push me under? Another test?

Gen climbed from the tub and dried, forcing his self-consciousness down.

Let him look.

The weight of a new stone pressed into his chest, and he paused long enough to look. Black, with blue veins.

"A gift," Arkady said. He gestured to a fresh suit beside him. "Get dressed. We're late."

"Late?"

"Lia would have us for dinner."

Unfortunate phrasing.

Arkady turned to go, then stopped, glancing back one last time. "Ah, a waste. No matter. My congratulations to Mrs. Gen, regardless."

A blush worked its way across Gen's cheeks, and Arkady laughed, strolling from the room. Gen dressed in a hurry, grabbed the fresh greatcoat laid on his bed, and took the stairs two at a time. If anything, late was bad enough. He didn't want the food—or Lia—to grow cold.

The dining hall could easily fit at least three Dripping Buckets side to side. The similarities ended there, however. Great hearths took up a wall each, crystal chandeliers hanging overhead. As with everything else, hardwood encased the room. A massive table stood in the center, surrounded by high-backed chairs. Large enough to accommodate the entire Shkut Family. Tonight, however, the inner circle had the room to themselves.

Lia occupied the seat at the head of the table. As always, she was radiant, the sun before the stars. To her right, Boris, his ursine features furrowed at Gen and Arkady's entrance. Beside him, Dmitry graced them with a smile, raising his glass in greeting.

"Ura, comrades!" he said.

Arkady favored him with a smile in return and took the seat to Lia's left, Gen sitting opposite the veneficum.

Manners make the man. Irina, whispering in his ear.

When had that been? The winter formal at the veteran's hall? She'd spent weeks trying to train him, teaching him which fork went where and what to use it on. For a country which believed in the simple efficacy of the bullet, there were a dizzying number of rules about putting beets in your mouth.

After the third time Gen used the salad fork to scoop up a mouthful of auroch, she'd thrown her hands in the air.

"*Blyad!* Like teaching a bear to write." She picked up the fork, mock fierceness drawn on her face. "*This* is for salad." Set it down, picked up another. "*This* is for beets." And another. "*This* is for meat. The fork is the axle upon which polite society spins, you rutabaga."

Gen set the fork down and stared into her eyes. "*Polite society* is code for people who shit outside, thinking the neighbors won't hear."

She held his gaze for a moment, then burst into laughter.

"Is everything all right, Comrade Antonov?"

Gen blinked and looked up. He'd been staring at the silverware laid out beside the fine porcelain plate, a cloth napkin tastefully folded over the dish. Lia addressed him, concern on her face. Her eyes flicked sideways to Arkady, nearly imperceptible, then back to Gen. He forced a smile.

"Yes, fine, thank you."

Boris growled in his throat; a sound reminiscent of dogs protecting their territory. Gen looked across, felt that cold presence rasp across his mind again. He rested his hand casually on the knife to his right. Wondered if he might put it in the man's eye before Boris had a chance to blink.

A commotion from the hall broke the tension, and a Shkut soldier stumbled in, frost-rimed and harried. He paused long enough to scan the room, then made a beeline for Arkady. The messenger hunched over, whispers crackling. He stank of sweat and rotten vegetables.

Arkady's eyes widened, and he hammered his palm against the table. Silverware and dishes jumped, a discordant clatter following their movement.

"What?!" he roared.

The soldier backed away hurriedly. Arkady snapped his head to the side, a spiderweb of veins in the whites of his eyes. His lips pulled back from his teeth.

"Get your shit together, Antonov."

He stood, scooping his coat from the back of the chair, throwing it on with a flourish. Gen pushed his chair back, looked to Lia.

She smiled, gently. His heart ached for her attention. For a moment, he wondered what it might be like to rest in her bosom, to have her stroke his hair.

"Go," she said. "Business is business. I'm sure Arkady will follow up with us afterward."

Arkady glanced at her, opening his mouth to snap a reply. Instead, he swallowed it, got himself under control, and gave her a half bow, dazzling smile back in place.

"Of course. You'll forgive my outburst? Distressing news makes fools of us all, I'm afraid."

One perfect eyebrow arched; she inclined her head slightly. "Naturally."

Boris' flesh glowed like a steamed beet, his eyes never leaving Gen. Dmitry remained oblivious, emptying the dregs of the wine bottle into his glass.

Grabbing his coat, Gen gave Lia one last apologetic glance, then hurried after the taller man. Arkady stalked from the hall, heels clicking against the wood.

The dining room door closed with a soft rasp of metal, and they found themselves alone for a moment.

"What is Boris' problem?" Gen asked.

Arkady shrugged. He led them down a long hall lined with pictures of stern men and fierce women on the walls.

"He wishes he was you, I think."

"Why is that? I'm no one."

Arkady paused long enough to turn on Gen. He grabbed the other man's chin with long fingers, turning his face up.

"You are more than you think. And to me, you are *tovarich*. Think nothing less of yourself at worst. And at best, remember: Arkady the Shkut is my friend." He smiled. "Your enemies will surely tremble."

He released Gen and turned on his heel again, pushing through a plain door. The room beyond held little in the way of adornment. Simple and austere, trestle tables lined the walls, men dining at the benches. The air smelled of stew and fresh bread.

"I need three of the biggest, meanest bastards in here!" Arkady bellowed.

A murmur followed the pronouncement, and a scuffle of feet as men jostled for attention. In moments, a rough line formed in the middle of the room. Most of the applicants were large, tending toward soft. Arkady pursed his lips and pointed out three in quick succession.

An eye for talent, this one.

To a man, they looked cut for murder. Wide shoulders, hands capable of choking the life from a feral wolf. Most bore scars, and while it wasn't an indicator of quality, it was an indicator of experience and survival.

"Which of you can read?" Arkady asked.

One of the men, large enough to have to stoop through doorways, raised his hand. His bald pate shone in the candlelight.

"Your name?" Arkady asked, producing a pen and paper from the interior of his suit.

"Dyrkovich, sir."

Scribbling on the sheet, Arkady handed it to him. "You three. Be there. Now."

Drykovich turned to go.

"Oh, and Dyrkles," Arkady said. "Do not be late. Do not get lost. Unless you are fond of wolves."

The big man swallowed hard, then disappeared into the mansion, men in tow. Arkady led Gen through another door, cold air like a slap as they passed outside. He led them around the side of the manse, crushed stone of the walk grinding under their heels. They fetched up at a small stable.

"Pavel!" Arkady shouted into the night.

A slight man appeared from the dark. Skin the same tone as Arkady's, he wiped strong hands on an apron.

"Comrade?" he asked.

"Two, and fast," Arkady said.

Pavel nodded smartly and disappeared inside. He returned a moment later leading two solid chernomor: one black, one brown, already saddled. Arkady took the black. Though he hadn't rode since the war, Gen found his way into the saddle with ease. The horse danced a little, then calmed as it acclimated to his weight. He patted its neck.

He preferred riding to eating them.

Wasting no time, Arkady clicked his tongue once, and the horses broke into a trot, exiting the grounds and into the street.

"What's going on?" Gen asked.

"We've a rat problem. You're the exterminator."

A cold slither. The scent of blood on the wind.

Gen nodded, and they broke into a gallop.

Freezing rain fell. They rode the horses hard, lather rising on their flanks. The rhythm, scent of horseflesh, pound of hooves—the world slipped away for a moment.

Irkysk.

They'd come around the enemy's flank. Ten thousand screaming Altin Ordu caught flat-footed. His blood was up, and he leaned over his horse's neck, laid his rifle over a bent elbow. He sighted, brought down two pikemen, cordite and smoke like twin snakes in the air. Missed the next. And the next. The last round took an officer high in the skull, ripping his scalp off. The man flipped backward, falling into the ranks of soldiers.

Then they were among the foreign devils, and he cast the rifle away, saber out. It snapped left and right and left again, bloodying anyone daring to draw breath within a foot of him. Gore coated the lower half of his body, painted his horse red.

Screams filled the air, a symphony of pain and terror.

They slowed. Arkady dismounted first, Gen following. They'd come from Middle Street to the furthest northwest point of the city, the buildings slumped like weekday drunks, some leaning on one another, others threatening to spill their guts into the street. The smells of rancid meat and spoiled produce hung in the air, clinging to the stink of ash and soot and chemical taint like dogs stuck mid-fuck. The Scab, then.

Gen had only occasion to venture into this part of town once, to visit an old comrade. He'd found the man dying of cancer and kroc, mind a shambles. Some things there were no cure for, and he hadn't returned since.

If the Filth was the bad part of town, the Scab was its gangrenous limb.

Arkady's face formed a grim mask as they stalked through alleys filled with refuse, human and otherwise. Gen sucked in air, regretted the foul lungful he got in return. He pulled the stiletto and Bastard from their sheaths.

Ahead, light spilled from a squat clapboard building.

There. The killing begins there.

Arkady stepped over a wet heap that may or may not have drawn a breath. Gen followed suit. A group of three men detached themselves from the shadows.

Cut them!

Gen tensed, bent forward to rush the newcomers. Dyrkovich's features resolved in the dim light. He felt the potential trickle from him as quickly as it'd come.

Fuck, that was close. Nearly ended up ramming this knife down your throat.

Arkady motioned silently, the group taking up positions around the flimsy door facing the alley. It looked as if only rust and hope held the hinges together.

"Knock knock," Arkady said.

Gen kicked the door in.

KATYUSHKA LEONOVA – CHAPTER TWELVE

Even in these civilized times, myths of ancient stones persist. Stones dating back to the Plemya tribes, when the gods were said to walk the earth, shards of divinity, traits and memories carved from Mokosh or Zorya or some hellish demon.

— Iskusstvo Veneficum

Maks led Kat through the precinct to a back room.

Two men in crumpled uniforms sprawled on worn leather sofas, while three more lobbed darts at a dented, beaten dartboard. Cigareta, smoked to the butt, filled every ashtray to overflowing. Faded green botanical wallpaper, splotchy with smeared roses, peeled at the corners. She remembered something similar in her grandfather's house, though the colours had been crisp, unpolluted by smoke. Daily newspapers, cheap ink smudged to a grey slur, sat piled on corner tables. Their militsioner-issue greatcoats hung on a bent oak coatrack in one corner.

These men can read?

She doubted it.

"They went with the dead man's armpit option," she muttered to Maks. "With a subtle bouquet of fried onions."

He snorted a laugh.

Though the names escaped her, she realized she knew these men.

"Katyushka Leonova," Maks announced grandly, "welcome to the Officer's Lounge!" He waved his hands at the cramped room and added, "No officers allowed," in a stage-whisper.

Kat froze. All eyes turned to her.

When their attention slid to Maks, she sagged with relief.

"This is where off-duty militsioners come to relax," said Maks. "Well, those who either can't or don't want to go home. It's also where those looking to pick up extra shifts to pay off gambling debts or buy their side-silkies—"

"Side-silky?" asked Kat, interrupting.

"Ah, yes. Right. A silky is a Filth whore. A side-silky, however, is a cut above. That's a whore who tells you she's given up the trade and is now your girlfriend and so you have to support her or else."

"Or else?"

"Or else she'll tell your wife. Right, Maminov?"

The heavy-set balding man on one of the sofas groaned and looked away, shading his eyes with a hand like he meant to hide.

"Anyway," continued Maks. "It's really quite funny. You're sneaking around on your wife with a side-silky, and your side-silky is sneaking around on you. Though at least she's getting paid. Twice, I suppose!"

Katyushka considered the cold welcome likely awaiting her at home.

She'd filled the woodrack and made Fyodor breakfast and dinner in advance, but he'd still be an ungrateful little shit.

She blinked in surprise at the terrible thought.

That's the stupid stones, not me.

"I could come here after my shift?" she asked.

Maks wrinkled his nose in what might have been embarrassment if he cared what people thought. "Ah, well, you see," he said. "The Officer's Lounge is traditionally where the *men* come to relax, to escape the harping women in their lives."

"Sorry," said Kat, not entirely sure what she apologized for.

Was there a room like this—though no doubt much better appointed—at Kuznetsov and Alyokhin, where Fyodor worked?

Of course there is.

She imagined Fyodor drinking there, smoking cigars, lounging in plush chairs as she chopped wood, cleaned the house, cleared the lane of snow, and made dinner. Was that the real reason he was home late so often? Was he avoiding the 'harping woman in his life'?

"Gentlemen," said Maks. "I have a little job I require assistance with."

All five men perked up, the two on the sofas pushing into sitting positions.

"On or off the books?" asked one.

Maks made a sharp cutting gesture with a hand, shook his head in annoyance. Glancing at Kat he said, "No, no. Pribylov jests. All jobs are on the books and entirely sanctioned by Colonel Grinin."

One of the militsioners coughed, pretended to study the dartboard.

"There's a back-alley veneficum working in Shkut territory," said Maks.

"Without permission?" asked Pribylov.

Maks ignored the question. "My CI says he's mostly dealing in fakes, but he has a contact with someone offering surplus military stones. No one seems to know where they're coming from, which means we have to pretend to be real militsioners. The lovely Katyushka and I are going to go shut down his little shop and find out just who his contact is. Word is, this is a small-time one-man operation. No muscle to worry about. Just one old man. I need three brave men looking for a little overtime."

"Why three?" asked Pribylov. "You said one old man."

"Entirely on account of the pretty girl," said Maks, nodding at Kat. "She's Grinin's pet project and he's seen fit to dump her in my lap." He waggled eyebrows at the men and they dutifully smirked, attention again sliding to Kat. "If anything happened to her, Grinin would feed me my ass."

"What's worse," mused Pribylov, "being fed your own ass, or someone else's?"

"Depends on who the other person is," said the largest of the five militsioners.

Kat's grandmother would have said he had cave-bear blood, the underlying assumption that commoners routinely mated with animals.

Once again, all eyes focussed on Kat, though this time Maminov flushed bright pink with embarrassment.

"And there's Tsukanov dragging every conversation into the gutter," grumbled Maks.

Tsukanov grinned and winked at Kat. Somehow, it conveyed humour rather than invitation or innuendo.

Lips pursed, Maks pretended to study the five militsioners.

"Blood and bones!" snapped Kat, surprising herself with the vulgarity. "You already know who we're taking." She pointed at the heavy balding man. "Maminov because he's got ice for blood in a fight and is a fucking dance-master with a submission stick. Pribylov because, though he doesn't know when to keep his fucking mouth shut, he asks the right questions and notices shit the rest of you silkies miss. And Tsukanov because..." She gestured at the man. "Just fucking look at him."

Silence.

Maks and the five militsioners stared at Kat.

"What?" she demanded. "Let's fucking go, ladies!"

Spinning, she marched from the room.

"You heard the boss," said Maks, turning to follow. "Let's fucking go!"

After grabbing their greatcoats, Maminov, Pribylov, and Tsukanov hurried to catch up.

"I like her," said Tsukanov.

"She called you silkies," whispered Pribylov in mock shock.

Maminov trailed behind the others. "She scares me."

Out into the street.

North, into the Filth.

Long strides. Keep moving.

Walking at her side, Maks clapped Kat on the shoulder. The gesture was achingly familiar, reminded her she could never have this man she loved. Maks would never understand that some men just liked men. He'd be appalled, as if she'd lied to him all these years.

I'm not a man! It's okay if I love him!

Distracted, she stumbled over an ankle-deep drift of coal-stained snow.

I don't love him! That's not me!

For a heartbeat she considered telling him she wore his dead partner's memory stone, that she was Kostas Malakhov. She could tell him how Kostas was murdered, how the Shkuts ambushed him. Maks was a real militsioner. He'd know what to do.

No! Three! Only three people knew I was—damnit!—Kostas was going to be there. Maks and... and... Colonel Grinin?

That felt right.

Who was the third?

"That was great," said Maks, walking at Kat's side. "You play quiet and mousey so well I had no idea there was a tiger inside. And now this purposeful striding through the snow, brilliant."

"But?" she asked.

"You don't know where we're going."

He was right. Needing to flee her embarrassment at having spoken so, she'd stormed out of the Chernyshevsky Street Militsiya Bureau. Somehow, everyone followed. Probably a lesson there. Men were happy to follow anyone who seemed like they knew what was going on. Even a woman from secretarial.

"Left up here," said Maks. "We're going into the old smelting district."

"I thought that was north-east," said Kat.

"The new one is. The old one got so poisoned people started dying on their feet while they worked. The forges moved east and left everything behind. All the dirtiest most desperate and dangerous people promptly moved there on account of the low rent."

"Lovely," said Kat.

"Most of them really aren't. Don't know if it's the air or the water, but it makes for some ugly people."

The other three men caught up and walked abreast of Kat, forming a wide line across the street. Seeing the militsioner uniforms, pedestrians crossed to avoid them, or ducked into narrow alleys.

"Tell me you remembered your submission stick this time," said Maks, glancing at Maminov.

The balding man opened his coat to show what looked like a regulation-issue nightstick with a nugget of stone set in one end hanging from a loop.

"What's a submission stick?" asked Kat.

"Got it off a street-veneficum we busted," Maminov said with pride. "The stone on the end is a memory stone reject, can't hold memories. They get sucked in but aren't accessible after. But because of the kind of stone used, it snaps up memories in an instant."

Kat remembered. "Touch someone and it steals the last few moments of their life."

"Right!" said Maminov. "Touch them on the arm, and it'll get a few seconds. A head touch will steal several minutes. Leaves them confused. Often, they have no idea they're in a fight. Makes it nice and easy to whack 'em." He punched his open hand.

"Miss Leonova," said the hulking Tsukanov, "if you don't mind me asking, how did you get to be a militsioner?"

"Call me Kat."

Tsukanov flashed a boyish grin of gratitude.

"I guess," she said, "I volunteered."

"More like Grinin volunteered her," said Maks.

Everyone nodded commiseration. As if they'd all been volunteered for things they didn't want to do.

"I *told* you this was going to happen!" crowed Pribylov. "The war killed most of our young men. There's barely enough left to keep the forges running. At some point even the idiots in Khagan—"

"Keep your voice down or you'll be working the mines," hissed Tsukanov.

"— had to see women entering the workforce was the only solution."

"You read too many of those pamphlets the radical dissenter scum are always littering around," muttered Maminov, checking no pedestrians were in earshot.

"But the dissenters were right," said Pribylov. "I heard some of the factories hire women to work the floor. If this kind of change has reached Norylska, you know it's real. Kat, here, is proof."

Maminov's eyes widened. "Can you imagine how well-off Nora and I would be if she took a job? I wouldn't have to pick up so many of these overtime gigs."

"They'd raise the price of everything," grumbled Maminov. "You'd end up right back where you were, but now you're both working."

"In the next year or two," said Tsukanov, ignoring Maminov, "there's going to be another war. Everyone is playing at piece and diplomacy, but the Altin Ordu are gearing for war."

"Pfft!" said Maminov. "We'll crush them like we did last time."

"Not sure we crushed them," said Tsukanov. "Not even sure we won. If that winter hadn't been so hard, and if we hadn't got lucky severing their supply-lines, they might have made it to the capital."

"You're crazy!" said Maminov. "We have ten times the population."

"Had," said Pribylov.

Tsukanov nodded. "You remember the accuracy of their rifles? And the Altin Ordu army hands them out the way the militsiya hand out potatoes."

"I remember going weeks without seeing a potato," grumbled Pribylov. He patted his extensive belly. "Living off twigs and bugs and mud. So hungry you could feel your guts devouring themselves."

"Maybe we still outnumber them," said Tsukanov, "and I do mean maybe, but they're better equipped and better supplied."

"I once saw an Altin Ordu officer fight," said Maks, voice low as he mimed fencing.

The others fell quiet.

"Skinny little wafter in flowery pants with a huge poufy silk shirt. He'd been captured by a squad of infantry. Eight men. They had him cornered in a collapsed church."

Wafter. Kat swallowed the pain. The derogatory slang hurt more when Maks used it. As if one man loving another was a sin against the gods and nature. As if a man couldn't love a man and still be a *real* man.

"The squad was out of bullets," continued Maks, "because everyone was always out of fucking bullets."

The three militsioners nodded, lost in memory.

"So, these eight men with fixed bayonets have this Altin Ordu officer cornered. His gun is empty, so he tosses it aside. Contemptuous. And he draws this long toothpick of a sword. Eight men with solid iron gut-stickers and one wafter. The officer sketches something fast in the air, fucking *grins* at them, and bows.

"Oh, that's bad," said Tsukanov. "It's bad when they smile, but way worse when they bow."

"Fucking right it is," said Maminov. "I once shot a prisoner by mistake because he bowed. Turned out he was bending to pick up a crust of bread he dropped." He laughed. "I peeled potatoes for a month after that and was so fucking happy to be alive I didn't even mind."

"Right," said Maks, "you get it. He grins and bows, and stands there waiting, all relaxed and loose, like he's not facing eight men who are gonna spit-roast him. Finally, one of the infantrymen—scrawny little goat-fuck from Khagan—steps in to stab him. The wafter stabs him in the throat before his foot touches ground. I swear eight feet separated them and bang, this little Khagan tit is flopping about on the ground gagging on his own blood and everyone stands there watching until he finally stops." Maks looked to each of the militsioners. "You know what the wafter did next?"

"No," said Tsukanov. "No he fucking didn't!"

"Yep. He bows again with a smug little smile and says, 'next'."

"They should have rushed him," said Maminov.

"They shoulda fucking run away," said Pribylov.

"They rushed him," said Maks. "He killed four more before they gutted him, and one more after." He grunted a distracted laugh. "You know what they say, right?"

"If an Altin Ordu challenges you to a sword fight," said Tsukanov, "shoot him from a hundred yards off."

"Left at the next street," said Maks.

The other three men slowed.

"The Scab?" demanded Pribylov. "We're going into the Scab?"

"Weird how he didn't mention that one small detail, eh?" grumbled Tsukanov.

"What's the Scab?" asked Kat.

"Exactly what it sounds like," said Maks. "It's the crust of rot and dried blood that forms over a wound in Norylska. It never heals because we keep picking at it."

"Thinks he's a fucking poet," Maminov whispered to Kat.

"Gentleman," said Maks, "and Lady," he added, cocking an eyebrow. "If you are indeed a lady, though since you're here with the likes of us I'd have to guess probably not—"

"Fuck's sake," said Tsukanov. "Get to the point."

Maks fished four grey bandanas from within his greatcoat, holding them out in offering. Seeing Kat's expression, he said, "Tie it around that pretty face. It'll keep the stink out—"

"About three percent of the stink," said Pribylov.

"—and if it turns out we're not supposed to be here," continued Maks, ignoring the man, "it'll hide your face. Though since you're the only militsiya with beautiful eyes and great tits, people might figure it out anyway."

"Don't be crude," said Tsukanov, flashing Kat an apologetic wince. "Sorry. He's just..." He shrugged.

"I have nice eyes too," said Maminov.

Pribylov cast him an appraising glance. "Your tits are too hairy to be 'great'."

After deftly tying his own bandana in place, Maks handed out the others, helping each man tie it at the back. When he reached Kat, she turned, and he tied hers too. Crisp and clean, it smelled of harsh soap. She couldn't imagine the man doing laundry. Was he married? Did he go home to a wife each night after work?

Turning back to face him, their eyes met over the fabric. The bandana moved as he opened his mouth to say something, yet said nothing.

"Shit," said Pribylov, "we just lost Maks."

"Fuck that," said Maks, breaking eye-contact. "Let's go."

They followed him into the Scab.

The Filth stunk. Each neighbourhood came with its own bouquet of rot. Kat remembered joking with Maks years ago that you could drop her into any part of the Filth blindfolded and she'd know where she was by the stench.

Not me. Not my memory.

It seemed too real. There was nothing to differentiate it from any other memory. It was something from her past. Living with her grandparents while her father was in court. Eating Syrniki at that little bakery a block from their home back in Khagan. Joking with Maks about women even though what she really wanted to do was kiss his beautiful lips, take him into her mouth and—

Kat crushed the thought.

Pribylov was right. The bandana did little to filter the stink.

The stench of rotting meat and burnt auroch hair clogged her throat. A harsh acidi creek lurked beneath the less subtle flavours of the Scab. And they were flavours. Mouth closed, she still tasted them. Her eyes watered.

They passed men defecating in alleys. Misshapen forms lay curled in damp newspapers, sleeping or dead. Though the main street had been sloppily cleared of snow, leaving an ankle-deep cinereal slurry, the alleys were knee-deep, staggering paths cut through where some drunk wandered home.

"Here we are," said Maks, approaching a cramped clapboard building.

The walls bowed out, boarded windows glared at Kat like bruised eyes.

Swinging the front door open, Maks entered without first declaring himself as an officer of the law—*he never does*—and Kat and the other three militsioners followed him in.

Auroch fat candles lit the room a sickly yellow, stained the air with smoke and the gut-deep scent of burning hair.

A skinny man, bent over a makeshift table, sat at the far end of the room. Knowing Maks would be focussed on the street scum, Kat checked the corners. Nothing. The veneficum was alone.

The old man looked up from the stones arrayed before him, squinting at the intruders. "Customers!" he wheezed, voice thin and papery. "Welcome, welcome! Enter! I have the finest wares: bravery, happiness, self-confidence, guaranteed efficacy. Stones for fighting. Stones for loving. Stones for—" He cut himself off when Pribylov, Tsukanov, and Maminov arrived behind Kat. "Oh," he said. "There's rather a lot of you."

Entering the room, Pribylov went right, eyes scanning for lurking dangers. Maminov went left, submission stick clutched in his fist, ready to crack skulls. Massive Tsukanov controlled the centre of the room, a hulking tower of threat and muscle.

Kat followed Maks, three steps back, two steps to his right, the way she always did. Her hand slid into the inner pocket of her greatcoat, searching for the knuckleduster she didn't have.

"Fuck," she whispered, realizing she was unarmed. *What the hell was I thinking?*

"Not customers," said Maks, approaching the table. "Militsioners."

"Ah! The... uh... commission! You've come to collect your commission! Sales have been slow, but I have a few koyln set aside such fine gentlemen as you."

"We're not here for bribes," said Maks.

The old man sagged. "The Shkut Family sent you."

Maks grunted a laugh. "Strange as it may sound, we're actually here as militsioners. We'll take you, collect your fake stones, bring you back to the precinct."

"Strange," said the old man. He laughed, a choked cough. "Strange."

Maks shrugged. "What has the world come to, eh?"

"Knock, knock," said someone outside.

A heartbeat later, the door flew off its hinges, landing in a puff of ash and dust.

Two men strode into the back alley veneficum's shed like they owned the world. The big one, out front, looked oddly familiar, but she couldn't place the face. He wasn't on Kostas' mental list of scary baddies, henchmen, and low-life thugs.

The second man, stepping out from behind the first, froze Kat's blood. Swarthy and handsome, complexion hinting at Altin Ordu ancestry deep in his past, he was impeccably dressed. Kat remembered being stripped naked, kneeling on hard stone, seeing him through a sheen of blood. They'd cut her over and over, peeled strips of flesh from her chest and arms. Questions, over and over. Praying Maks would show up, save her. Praying he'd storm the gates before she broke. *C'mon, old buddy. Stride in here all cocky and be the hero you think you can never be.* She focused on the gun. Finally. Peace. An absence of pain, at the least.

Maks, where are—

Muzzle flash.

Kat staggered back a step.

Run. Run and hide. These are bad men. Dangerous. Run!

"Ark—" Kat's voice cracked. "Arkady."

GENNDY ANTONOV – CHAPTER THIRTEEN

Ever cut off an Altin Ordu's head? They don't bleed. Not like we do. Or maybe it was just the cold. You could always tell when they were coming. Those songs. They'd charge through the snow. Their guns froze. And that was okay, because we were better. Colder. At Irkysk, we were colder than anyone.

—Captain Boris 'Stinkteeth' Chernyshevsky, Khagan XIII

The door collapsed with the sigh of a corpse giving up its last breath. A glint of silver, and Gen risked a glance. Arkady holding a hand cannon. Then they were in motion.

Fast now.

The Shkut men filed in quickly.

A hush fell over the room. Gen swallowed, uncertainty making him pause. A skinny man stood in the center, lit by guttering candles dripping auroch tallow. Everything he wore fit poorly. Overlarge glasses perched on his nose, giving him the appearance of a mouse. His clothing hung from a spare frame. Ill-kempt hair trailed down his back in a snarled tail.

He does look like a rat.

Five militsioners stood in a semicircle around him, like a jury of hanging judges. Surprise painted their faces. That cold ripple in his head. Gen scanned them, mentally noting details.

Three hacks. Probably second-rate cops. Bald and fat. Seems like a Pig. Submission stick. Don't get hit with that fucker. Skinny with bad hair: Ferret. That one—the slab of meat—looks like he might skullfuck you if he gets too close: Auroch. Two officers. A pretty boy. And her. The mouse. She looks different. Like someone you might fuck now.

The brunette caught sight of Arkady as he slid into the room, eyes locking on him, gaze intense.

Something there. But what?

A twinge of jealousy shot through Gen.

For who?

He shoved the thought away in irritation.

No time for that bullshit.

Tension, thicker than blood. Thicker than fat and bone.

The gun roared. Someone screamed. Madness descended.

Pig hits the nearest man. Mikhail? Either way, Mikhail's forgotten his name for a minute. He stands there slack-jawed, the stick leaving him a gawping moron. Pig hammers a lead-lined glove into his skull, and Mikhail collapses like shed skin, blood trickling from the corner of one eye. Probably a crushed socket, likely permanent brain damage.

Ferret takes out Ivan like he's a stalk of errant wheat, wide blade whickering from its loop on his belt. It slams into Ivan's guts, splits him like overripe fruit. He coughs blood. Hard to scream when your diaphragm's been punctured. Clutches his stomach, thick ropes of his guts spilling from between his fingers. They're swollen like sausage links, his last meal still sloshing inside.

I know these moves. Taught them to green boys in the platoon. Dirty. Killers, to a man. What kind of fucking slime signs up to murder his countrymen?

The room stinks.

There's your answer. Shit.

The last remnants of humanity, dropped from the bowels of civilization. The world wavers, if only briefly.

Black-clad men slipping behind lines, slitting throats, shitting in dug wells. Altin Ordu? Turncoats? Men driven mad by bloodshed? It doesn't matter.

They're coming, a trail of dead in their wake. They're coming, and you're awake. Awake because the artillery won't let you sleep. The smell of rot won't leave your sinuses. And now you're awake because there's killing to do.

Auroch goes for Dyrkovich. The tall Shkut panics, runs the way he'd come, clearing the threshold in two impressive bounds. Slips once in the blood outside, slams into a wall. Recovers. The sound of his feet scrabbling for purchase, curses trail him as he flees into the night.

Five on two now. Technically, four. The woman is still hunkered down, body held prisoner by a frozen mind. Arkady's bullet rips the top of the shop owner's skull off. The former chandler's brains leak onto the floor in a red-green-gray soup. Arkady turns the gun on the brunette. She says something—his name?—and he pulls the trigger. The gun jams, the cylinder refusing to turn.

A moment of relief.

I don't know if I want her dead yet. Like ruining a work of art.

The brunette's partner—where is he?

Auroch comes at him then, a distraction. The other two angle for Arkady, the southerner backing toward the door, useless pistol dangling from his hand.

The wind gusts, and half the candles snuff it, just like that. The smell of their smoldering wicks reminds Gen of... something. Then it mixes with the stink of the Scab, and it comes back. Bodies. Burning bodies in the snow. Like pork, that stink. Death ablaze.

The world narrows.

Auroch comes. Hunched, arms out like he wants to embrace. Not bright. Probably doesn't have to be.

Too tall for his own good. Duck under his arms. He swipes like a buffoon in a play. It's a feint. Gen pushes upward, tries to gut him with Bastard. The muscled beast backpedals and his hands snap shut on Gen. A fist hammers twice into his ribs, knocks the breath out of him. Hurts like a motherfucker.

Stupid. Should've seen that coming.

Gen struggles, but Auroch has him pinned tight. The hand holding Bastard is trapped against his ribs. Auroch has a grip on his head and is pulling it to the side, straining Gen's neck. The big man leans in, wearing a feral grin.

Fuck. He's going to rip your throat out with his teeth.

Snap the free arm out. Stiff fingers into Auroch's windpipe. Like punching a wall. But it slows him. He stops lunging for Gen's throat, but the force of his massive hand is sending waves of ache into Gen's skull.

An impact against the ribs Gen's just left exposed. Pig's using the submission stick as a baton.

Downside to getting sloppy. Tactics go right out the window.

Upside: no memory loss, and I'm still in the fight.

Bonus downside: if the fat bastard breaks ribs, I'm definitely *going to remember that.*

Auroch tightens his grip on Gen, grabs the smaller man's head with one massive palm and *pulls.* Feels like Gen's skull is going to disconnect. To drive the point home, Pig hits him again.

Now.

Gen traps the stick with his free arm. Twists hard, ramming it into Auroch. The motion wrenches Gen's neck, but the pain fades as adrenaline burns it to the background. Auroch forgets what he's doing, drops his prey.

Gen staggers forward at the sudden freedom, turns the momentum into a killing stroke.

The stiletto slips under Auroch's chin as easily as a lover into a woman. It pierces the flesh under his jaw, punches through soft palate and into his brain. A scent, brief and intense, fills Gen's senses. Meat and fresh blood, a bouquet of slaughter.

Auroch doesn't know he's dead. Blinks. Tries to speak.

"Guh, guh, guh."

The scent again, carried on the stink of the dying man's breath.

A streamer of drool runs down Gen's chin. He's rock-hard below the waist.

What the fuck?

He pushes the feeling away, uses Auroch's bulk to kick off, gain distance.

He falls, but Gen's moving. Just the vague impression of an impact against the warped floorboards behind him. Pig is nowhere to be seen.

Probably circling around. Deal with him in a minute.

Arkady's backed into a corner by Ferret, the militsioner focused on the task at hand. He's easy. Bastard parts the base of his spine from his brain. In. Out. A slight crunch as the spinal column ruptures. No speech. Just a quick death.

An impact on Gen's ribs. Pig with his stick again. Sneaky. It hurts, but Gen escapes the intended effect. Pig lunges a second time, but he's too slow. Gen takes the hit on his coat, uses the opportunity to study his opponent.

Left-handed. Harder to fight, but not an Altin Ordu. None of these are Altin Ordu, which just makes them meat.

They circle one another. He might be slow, but he's still brutal. Pig lunges, two strikes in quick succession.

Nope, not slow. That's fuckup number two, fuckup.

Gen's on the defensive. Strike, block. Strike, block. No room to maneuver. He's backed toward a corner. Trips over something—Ivan? Hits the ground. The stick comes down.

Fu—

What was I doing?

Fog in the brain. Another impact. Pain. Why do I hurt? Who is thi—

FUCK

Something in his head seizes control. Gen might have forgotten, but it hasn't. It remembers the stink of men. The taste. The pain. Their fear.

The fat man brings the stick down in a sweeping motion.

Roll. Like falling from a tree. Twist, land on your feet.

Gen's back up, teeth bared in a snarl. A low rumble in his chest. Pig snaps the stick out, but Gen's ready. The state thug overextends.

Sidestep, turn.

Bastard chops down, takes three fingers holding the stick. Pig drops it, howling in pain. Clutches his hand to his chest. The stumps of his fingers pour thick blood over rumpled uniform.

Pick up the stick. Hit him once. The militsioner forgets he's bleeding out.

"Hi," Gen says.

He smiles. Gen nods at the wounded hand. The man looks down in horror. Gen hits him with the stick again. Again, the blank.

I could do this all night.

The terror of the militsiya. The things the people in the Filth have to do to avoid their gaze—to just survive the meeting some days. This feels justified.

He hits him. Again. Again. Again.

How many lives has this piece of shit stolen? We break our backs, and they grind our bodies into the dirt.

Again.

He's crying.

Again.

Never seen someone hit this many times with one of these.

"Hello?" Gen says.

Nothing. A blank stare. Whatever the stick's done, he seems to be trapped in there.

Again. And again. And again.

A clicking in Pig's throat, like a stuck cylinder. Like a beast unable to vocalize.

Gen rams the stick into his eye. The wood splinters with the force, stone dislodging into Pig's skull. Vitreous fluid, tears, and blood pour down his cheek.

Wherever he was, he's gone now.

More?

Check the room. There's always more meat.

The brunette. She's still squatting, hands over her head. Shelter of the flesh. But closing your eyes doesn't make it not happen. Irkysk proved that.

She's paralyzed.

Prey.

"Get the bitch! Get the stones!"

Arkady's voice snapped the blood fugue's hold on him. Gen paused, disoriented for a moment. The room an abattoir. Bodies littered like cast-off insect shells. Blood painting the walls, the stink of copper and shit thick in the air beside the candles.

The brunette bolted, rising and spinning in one fluid move. She disappeared out the door.

"Go!" Arkady roared.

Instinct pushed him, and Gen pursued.

He tore through the open door, into the street. Ahead, the woman turned a corner, disappearing into the warrens of the Scab. Gen followed.

Left. Right. Left. Left. Glimpses of her heels, smell of her perfume on the wind. Right again, over a rickety fence. Something small and dark barreled at him, and he swatted it away. Yelp of pain from the shadows, and a flash of guilt.

Not a dog, Gen!

Irina would *not* be impressed.

The brunette led him down an alley narrowing further and further as it went. Turning sideways, he caught sight of her scrambling up a short flight of stairs and sprinting away.

Fuck!

Gen rammed himself through the narrow divide, scraping back and stomach. The second he freed himself, he took a guess at where she might be.

There.

Hard left, up over another short wall. Leap onto a roof, clatter across. Below, the brunette bolted into the alley, glanced behind her. Nearly ran into the brick wall at the end. She turned, panic lighting her eyes.

Gen leapt down, landing gracefully. He'd left his knives back at the candlemaker's, but then, he shouldn't need them for this.

The woman backed up at his approach. She pressed her spine against the brick of the wall. Fear etched lines across her face, and guilt flashed again into his consciousness.

We doing this? Going to kill a woman? You've done some fucked up shit, Gen, but this... there's no redemption for this. Look at her.

The slither of an icy mind inside his own. Once again, it pushed something to the fore. An echo of Arkady's voice. *Kill the bitch.*

The guilt fled, leaving only the certainty of loyalty, the woman, and murder.

He took a breath, and a step forward.

KATYUSHKA LEONOVA – CHAPTER FOURTEEN

Ideas are a thousand times more dangerous than guns. If we don't let our people have guns, why would we let them have ideas?

—Tsar Khromov

Violence.

Arkady drew a revolver—*Nagan seven-shot, single-action, gas-seal,* a small voice supplied—and blew the veneficum's brains all over the back wall.

Kat froze. Couldn't move. Couldn't *want* to move.

The bullet hissed past her skull by a handspan at most.

The veneficum wasn't the target. She was.

Arkady adjusted his aim, thumbed the hammer back, and Kat stared down the barrel. Growls of rage and screams of pain as bad men killed bad men. Sounds of struggle, meat on meat impacts. Someone screaming in agony.

Duck left and go right when he tracks you.

She didn't move.

Click. The revolver jammed, Arkady blinking in annoyance.

Bullet creep caused by an improperly crimped round, supplied that too-calm voice.

Kat folded. Still on her feet, she crouched, hiding behind her knees, seeing the horrible world through a cage of fingers. Smaller. Disappear.

Screaming and blood.

Tsukanov, that beautiful monstrous slab of militsioner muscle who backed her on more busts than she could count, went after the mouth-breather from the Dripping Bucket.

Kill him! Kill him!

Kat wanted him on his knees, begging for mercy. She wanted to cut him, to carve him apart.

She wanted him dead.

Instead, she cowered.

Too fast. She watched everything. Arkady retreating, fussing with the revolver. Others fighting and circling. Maminov's submission stick lashing out, stealing seconds, stealing minutes. Pribylov going after Arkady. Maminov dispatching his opponent with ruthless professionalism and circling to attack the mouth-breather from behind.

Where's Maks?

She couldn't see him through her fingers, couldn't turn to look.

Mouth-breather murdered Tsukanov, drove a knife into his brain and shoved him aside like he was nothing, already forgotten. He grunted as Maminov hit him from behind.

Not on the coat!

Submission sticks only worked well when striking flesh.

Fat as he was, Maminov was a dancer. Ducking under fists of bone and muscle, he touched skin with the submission stick. Mouth-breather blinked, lost and confused, and then killed him anyway.

Kostas, the ghost in Kat's head, knew the type: Damaged from the war, they walked a razor-wire of fear and rage, violence the first answer to any dilemma. Mouth-breather didn't need to know who he fought or why. The fight—the killing—was all that mattered.

The mouth-breather beat Maminov to death with his own submission stick and then left it quivering in an eye-socket. He turned predator eyes on Kat.

Arkady yelled, "Get the bitch! Get the stone!"

And like that, as if the words broke him from the fugue of murder, the mouth-breather blinked and was a man. Wounded. Scared. Vulnerable. Doubting and fearing.

There's only one bitch in here, she realized, *and that's me.*

Kat ran.

Out the door someone handily kicked off its hinges. Nothing to slow her. Into the Filth.

Arkady screamed orders and she heard the heavy tread of feet behind her.

He'll never catch me. I'm the fastest man on the force.

No, she wasn't. She was the shortest woman on the force. The *only* woman.

Get the bitch. Get the stone.

Kat ran, knowing every street and every turn only *after* she'd made it.

She squeezed through a narrow gap, scrambled over a low wall, and ran.

Her side ached, a deep pain under her ribs like she'd been stabbed. Already wheezing, sucking breath. Gods above, she hadn't run since she was a child.

The hard wooden slap of cheap peasant shoes followed, grew in volume. The sour stench of man-sweat and blood.

Kat's old but expensive boots sliding in the ashen slush of the Filth, she skittered around a corner and into a dead-end.

She turned, back against the wall.

A cornered snake. Rabid rat terror.

He stood, arms wide, ready in case she tried to duck past. Empty-handed, his knives were gone. That was something, some small glimmer of hope.

He's going to kill you. He's going to take the stones.

Hard and round, they suddenly felt cold under her shirt. And that scared her more than anything. The thought this brute would tear her shirt off to get the stones, strip her naked, was somehow unacceptable.

She wanted to laugh for the insane irony.

Kat twitched as something seethed deep in her brain. Twisting vipers. Cave-lion rage.

Kill.

That wasn't Kostas.

She shrank back against the stone, one foot bracing against the wall for leverage.

Small.

Helpless.

Nothing.

A trap.

The big mouth-breather came, confident in his size and strength and speed.

Fear drained from her, left nothing.

Feinting left, she spun right, kicked him in the back of the knee. He grunted in surprise, leg folding beneath him. That put his flat bullet head at her height. Grabbing his hair in her right fist, she yanked his head back, driving two sharp left-handed punches into the bulge of his Adam's apple.

Kat shed her humanity, became intent and emptiness.

Spinning around behind him, she used the grip on his hair to smash his face into the wall. His nose broke, a wet explosion of blood.

Two hands in the hair, teeth bared in a rictus snarl, she slammed his head into the wall again.

Stepping back, she kicked him in the balls from behind.

Finally, a groan of pain.

That got his fucking attention.

Kill him. Finish him now.

But she wasn't who or whatever she thought she was. She was Kat. She could beat this slab of peasant muscle all fucking day and he'd still get back to his feet.

If he puts a hand on you, you're dead.

Spinning, Kat ran.

Blink.

Kat stood in Veneficum Lazarev's office.

The old man took the stones, laying them on the shelf with her name written on the rim in his careful, precise script. He looked exhausted, sunken and haggard, and for the first time she appreciated his advanced age. For a moment she wanted to ask after his health, but to do so would be beyond impolite.

Does he live alone?

She couldn't imagine this bent old man shovelling snow or chopping wood.

"Are you alright?" he asked. He looked like her grandmother used to when Kat came home with a skinned knee.

Am I?

Once again, her day was gone. She remembered arriving at the precinct, going into the veneficum's office to collect her stones, and then nothing.

Looking down, she saw her dress stained with blood and mud, her boots soaked through and scuffed. Somehow, she'd skinned the knuckles of both hands. Still damp, scabs hadn't yet formed. She felt like she'd punched a wall, fists aching.

"Everything hurts," she said.

Her lungs. Feet and knees. Hands. Bone-deep exhaustion like she'd sprinted a mile back in Lomonosov Prep School.

"Are you hurt?" Lazarev asked.

She checked herself, poking and prodding. Though she found many painful bruises, she was strangely surprised to discover she hadn't been stabbed.

"No," she said. "Yes?"

"Seriously hurt?"

"No."

Lazarev waited like he had all the time in the world and nothing and no one else mattered.

"What happened?" she asked.

He shrugged with a wince of apology.

Inspiration. "Give me the stones back," she said. "I'll tell you, and then you can tell me. I need to know."

"I can't," he apologized. "It's against the rules. The state owns your day." He touched her shoulder, the briefest contact. "Back in the war, there were more men than we could ever hope to provide memory stones for. After, the things they did, the things they *remembered*, broke them. You're a militsioner now. Maybe not frontline infantry, but I don't doubt you will see and do things in the line of duty you'd be happier not remembering."

Kat saw no sign of Maks on her way out of the precinct. Had they spent the day together? Did he know what happened to her?

No. He wears stones too.

What did they do all day? How could a couple of stones change her so much she came out looking and feeling like she'd been in a fight?

The state owns your day.

Staggering through an ankle-deep slurry of slush, the setting sun turning the horizon a bloody smear of coal slag and smoke, she walked home. Claustrophobic streets stank of iron and slaughterhouses. The haunting screams of butchered pigs echoed narrow alleys.

Home was a shithole. A two-room shed with mud and rags stuffed into the cracks. The woodpile around the side had collapsed because Fyodor had been careless in selecting which wood to take. She'd fix that later.

Hungry. So hungry.

I could eat an entire fucking auroch and still have room for ponchiki.

She twitched at the crude vulgarity. Where'd that come from? Auroch was peasant meat, tough and gamey.

Inside, Kat found Fyodor sitting at the table. She read anger in the hunch of his shoulders.

Did I forget to make dinner?

"I took the afternoon off," he said. "I took the afternoon off to come see you at work."

The memory stone. Had she seen him at work? Had she said something? Had they argued?

"I… I…"

"You weren't there," he said. "There were no secretaries there at all. No women."

"Colonel Grinin assigned me to—"

"You. Weren't. There. You lied. You lied to *me*."

"I didn't lie! It's just—The job changed. I didn't know that would happen, no one warned me."

"It changed today, all of a sudden?" he asked. He had that look, courtroom eyes, looking for loopholes, hunting for the weakness in her words.

"Yesterday," she admitted.

"Ah," he said. "Yesterday. Yet you failed to mention it last night. After I made you dinner."

Because the fact he put an ounce of effort into their life somehow made her wretched betrayal all the worse.

"I didn't lie," she repeated, desperate.

He nodded, understanding. "You conveniently forgot to tell me. You know what they call that in court? A lie of omission."

"I was so tired—"

"A *lie* of omission," he repeated. "Where were you? If you're not a secretary for the militionsers, what are you doing all day? Do you even have a job? Are you working the street? Are you a fucking side-silkie?"

Kat stared at him, stunned. She'd never heard him talk like this before.

Did he just call me a whore?

Shocked hurt.

"Did you talk to anyone there?" she asked. "Did you—"

"Why would I talk to anyone?" he demanded.

"If you'd just asked—"

"Oh? This is *my* fault now? Why would I need to ask? I *trust* you." His fists clenched on the table. "I trusted you. Why do I have to go asking what my girlfriend is up to? Can you imagine how embarrassing that would be?" He shook his head, appalled. "You weren't there! So, I'm supposed to ask where my girl is? No," he said, shaking his head, "you're supposed to tell me."

"I'm sorry," she said. "I…"

Why hadn't she told him about Maks and the fact she wasn't a secretary?

I was scared he'd be jealous.

Was that true?

Maybe? A little?

Fyodor pushed back from the table and stood. "I'm going to the office. Got to get caught up on all the work I missed this afternoon."

He wouldn't look at her.

I hurt him.

She'd betrayed his trust. She'd been thoughtless and selfish.

"I'm sorry."

Grabbing his coat, Fyodor stomped out of the house, slamming the door behind him. The walls shook, dust raining from the ceiling.

Kat stared numbly at the unlit woodstove, the empty woodrack.

"Fucking asshole," she said.

GENNDY ANTONOV – CHAPTER FIFTEEN

There are few excuses for a dedicated Kievan to have a hangover: Drank his weight in vodka. Fell off the roof while drinking vodka. Kicked by an auroch while drinking vodka. And, of course, having one's ass handed to him by his wife after a night of drinking vodka.

—D Puskyn, Exile

A red dream. Cut from flesh and bone, bathed in blood from the grinder until its skin is raw and pink. Shadows, a coven. A sisterhood. The Night Witches. They moved through the battlefield like smoke, and where they passed, men fell like chaff blown from a field.

Small. Shockingly so. Wisps made flesh. They were something else, something dug from the stone mines. Rumor and lie. But it reached Altin Ordu ears, and when men died behind their lines, the ripple of terror was a cold wave you felt from the Kievan front.

That's what she was, then. A Witch. A wraith. The embodiment of darkness beneath the earth, with the strength of stone. Her fists, like a jeweler's hammer.

Tap. Tap. Tap.

Insistent.

Tap. Tap. Tap.

In his skull.

Blink. Arkady's face hove into view, a grin across his dark face.

"She rung your bell good, eh, comrade?"

Gen groaned and sat up. His face ached like someone had used it as a blacksmith's hammer. The inside of his skull throbbed, the echoing ring of the anvil in response. He moaned again, held his head in his hands.

"Fuck," he muttered.

"Come, get up," Arkady coaxed him.

He offered Gen a hand. Gen took it, letting himself be helped to his feet. The world spun for a moment, Arkady putting a steadying hand on his back.

How the fuck did she manage that?

Memory stone, dipshit.

Gen shook the voice off. Arkady regarded him with a wry smile.

"Come, we have business," Arkady said.

Gen hesitated. He'd expected the man to be furious. He'd lost the woman. Failed.

Arkady made it to the end of the alley, turned. "Come, already." He saw the look on Gen's face, shrugged good-naturedly. "I'm not angry. The Shkut reach is nearly as long as our pockets are deep. Besides, you killed three militsioners! Amazing!"

Relief flooded Gen's core, the cool wash of emotion soothing prickles of shame. He hurried to catch up. Fat flakes of snow had begun to fall by the time he reached Arkady. The other man looped an arm around Gen's shoulders.

"Three on one! Fuck, what a story! And the big one!" he crowed.

He mimicked the fight, ducking and weaving as they moved through the streets. Gen allowed himself a small smile.

Victory from defeat. The Kievan way.

The temperature dropped as they walked, the snowfall becoming a white wall threatening to coalesce into a blizzard with each gust of wind. By the time they reached the Shkut mansion, Gen's bones ached, and snot ran in a continual runnel that froze on his upper lip in a stubborn crust, no matter how many times he wiped it away.

Square of the Fathers. Gen had begun to think of it as home.

Irina is home.

A second home, then.

Arkady led them up the stairs, valet nowhere in sight. Once again, Gen paused in the foyer. Each time he returned, the beauty of it nearly sucked the air from his lungs. Someday, Irina would have this.

"Come," Arkady said, breaking the hold the mansion had on him. He did not wait, but took off at a purposeful stride, Gen jogging to catch up.

Arkady led him through a series of corridors, the way leading to stairs down, and more corridors. Arkady remained silent during the procession, suddenly somber after their gregarious walk home. Truth was, Gen was thankful. He ached all over. Between the beating from the girl and the fight with the militsioner thugs, he needed a little quiet.

The end of their journey was an alcove cut into a wall of stone. Gen wasn't sure how far down they'd traveled, but the air was cooler here than in the mansion, carrying a musty, wet smell.

The statue of a woman was carved from the wall. Hair surrounded her head in a halo. Two babes suckled at each bared breast, the rest of her clothed in layers of fabric lifted in pleats by invisible hands. Her flesh, where it showed, was wrinkled and swollen all at once. In all, it gave the impression of someone drowning.

"Marzanna," Gen breathed.

Arkady knelt before the statue, then stood, turning to Gen with a small tumbler in his hand. He produced a knife.

"On this day, Genndy Antonov, you become a brother of the Shkut. Do you accept?"

This is it. What all the spilled blood is for. Don't you dare back out.

Gen wet suddenly dry lips. "Yes," he said with more conviction than he felt.

He should worry what Irina might think. He should worry about his child.

That's why you're doing this! Would you spit in the face of the man who made you? Who will help you provide?

Throw this away? No.

"Defend the Family, keep our secrets, and keep your promises?"

"Yes," Gen said.

"And will you forsake all others before the Family?"

Which family?

"Yes," Gen said.

"Your hand," Arkady said.

Gen stretched out his palm, and Arkady made one quick pass with the blade. A line of crimson welled from the cut. Arkady turned the wound over the tumbler, letting ruby drops fall into the vodka inside. It formed a bloody cloud. Arkady closed Gen's fingers, then embraced him.

"Welcome to the Family, brother."

They separated, and he raised the glass, took a sip, passed it to Gen. Gen repeated the process, then poured the rest out at Marzanna's feet.

Arkady's grim demeanor passed, and a smile lit his face.

"Come, I have gifts!"

"For me?"

"No, your silky girl. Yes, for you. And Irina. And your child. You're family now. Family does for family."

A carriage! They'd hired him a carriage. Dangerous to be seen with that kind of wealth in the Filth, but he was Shkut now. He *was* the danger. It pulled up a block away from his home—no need to startle Irina. He trudged through snow grown shin-deep during his time with Arkady, the going slower with the packages he carried. Ahead, Irina.

Shame warred with a host of other emotions, creating a slurry in his chest. Three days was a long time to be gone with no word. Briefly, he tried to compose an excuse as to why he'd been gone on a walk for three days. Then he hefted the gifts he carried as they tried to slide from his grasp and realized he wouldn't need to.

He climbed the steps and pounded on the door.

Footsteps inside.

The door, opening, spilling warm light onto the blanket of white.

Irina.

Her face, a war. Sorrow, joy, rage.

She pulled him in. Pushed him away. Slapped him. Screamed. Her fists against his chest a thousand times. He dropped the packages and folded her into his arms, her voice muffled, the words clear regardless.

"Bastard bastard bastard bastard...."

And then some.

Finally, the words trailed off to sobs, and sobs to silence. She pulled away, sniffed. Wiped her eyes. His own were as dry as the steppes.

"You must be cold," she said, pulling her shawl around her.

"Freezing."

"There's a fire."

"Yeah. Smells nice."

Liar. Smells like the Filth.

"Come in, then," she said.

She stepped in the door. Gen followed.

Opened packages littered the room, glitter and gold shining in the firelight. Irina pulled a mink stole from its box. Beside him, another box Arkady had given him. The stone inside a swirl of green and red.

"Loyalty. Lust," he'd said.

"For?"

"For you. For Irina."

Gen frowned, and Arkady laughed.

"It's not so bad as that, tovarich! Shkut men must be happy and undistracted to do their work. This will simply ensure both."

Gen took it, tucking it away in his coat. Despite his misgivings, he didn't want to appear ungrateful.

Irina twirled. Gen didn't know where Arkady had found the mink, but the man had impeccable taste. Her eyes shone. She held it out, wrapped it around her neck.

"It looks good on you," Gen said.

He picked the stone up and stood, walked to her, grabbed the ends of the fur. Pulled her in close. She tilted her head up. He felt the baby squirm in her belly as they pressed close.

"There's more where this came from, you know," he said.

"More?" The light in her eyes faltered.

She stepped back and he let the ends of the stole fall. Irina unwrapped it, threw it in the box. She opened her mouth, closed it. Her eyes blazed in the firelight, fists clenching and unclenching. The vein in her forehead, the one he'd named Irishka—*Little Irina*—throbbed in her temple.

"I thought—hoped—when you returned, you were done. This was a one-time thing. But *more?* Gen, no."

He stepped in close, his own anger rising. "Ungrateful," he spat.

"Un*grateful?*" she said, incredulous. "Every night, I built you a fire. Made you dinner. Hoped you might come home. When Mrs. Varvara came to ask about you, I told her you were consulting for the militsiya. When you still didn't return, I went to the Bucket, and *pleaded* for anyone there to tell me where you'd gone. Ungrateful, you sonovabitch? I kept the fire burning for you!"

She raised her arm as if to strike him.

Slither of ice-cold purpose, driving instinct.

His arm came up, slapped the hand away. He grabbed her by her hair, yanked her head back.

"Never..." he said.

Tears stood in her eyes. He faltered, let her go. Irina retreated, pulled her shawl tight. But she did not cry.

"Out."

"Irina—"

"Out! Get out of my house, Genndy Antonov! Go to the wolves!"

Her tone was iron. Her tone was steel. He turned and gathered his coat, slipped it on. Set the box with the stone in it on the table. Opened the door. Outside, the wind had picked up. Snow pricked at his skin as he hesitated on the threshold.

"Out," she whispered.

He stepped out. For a moment, light shone in a wedge on pristine drifts. Then the door closed, and the night swallowed it.

Gen's head throbbed.

Failure.

Alone.

Failure.

Alone.

Fuckup.

Idiot.

Failure.

He walked blind, barely aware of the plummeting temperature. Lost in his misery, it wasn't until the chandler's loomed from the wall of snow that he looked up. The place smelled of death. He pushed past the door still hanging from its hinges. The bodies had been removed, but blood decorated the floor and walls, dried to a brown crust. The stink of copper, tallow, and smoke hung in the air. He didn't care. It was out of the cold.

Hateyouhateyouhateyou

A few minutes spent casting about the room. Arkady had taken his gun with him, then. Nothing to be done for it. He'd have to survive.

Ha, is that what you do?

More searching. A half-empty bottle of vodka. He spun the cap off, swallowed until he choked, sputtering and coughing. The stones around his neck rattled, beating a tattoo against his chest.

Useless useless useless

He pulled them off in a fit of rage, let their chains pool on the floor. Disorientation. Alone. Alone as he'd ever been. A sort of calm settled over him. In his head, fractured parts of the whole began to take shape.

Arkady at the Bucket.

Arkady when I slept.

Arkady with his fucking Family.

He looked at the stones again. Pieces began to fit. Loyalty. Cold purpose. Murderous intent. Did the order matter?

He reached out. Paused, fingers twitching. A breath. Another.

Irina.

The thought a barb. A goad. A promise.

Cold purpose. It settled over him like a mantle.

Intent next, and his mouth watered at the scent of blood.

Loyalty.

Rage bubbled up in him. He'd been used. Lied to. He was just another of Arkady's *golubois*. He reached into his jacket, pulled Bastard free, and hammered the hilt into the stone.

It detonated.

Pieces of the rock scraped his chin, drawing blood, the rest littering the floor, blood-red garbage.

Like my heart.

He slipped the chain under his shirt, finished the vodka. Tossed the bottle at the wall, and it exploded into shards.

In place of calm, rage welled in him. Outside, the wind howled, snow shattering against the walls of the chandlery and piling in the broken doorway. Inside, in the empty places he saved for Irina and the baby, a black tide rose, filling the hollows. He nurtured it, savored it. Honed it like a razor, sharp enough cut slivers of his heart, and that too he pared down until it was the shape of a blade.

If the world wanted blood, he would give it blood.

KATYUSHKA LEONOVA – CHAPTER SIXTEEN

Fascism is nothing but capitalist reaction; from the point of view of the working man the difference between the types of reaction is meaningless.

—Lev Davidovich Bronstein

Coat slung over her shoulder, Kat stood in line to get into Veneficum Lazarev's office. An unexpected storm during the night caught the sootmen off-guard, and everyone was late to work after having shuffled through knee-deep snow. There'd been a moment when she first stepped outside when she gloried in the beauty. The world was clean and pristine, perfect glistening white. By the time she finished chopping wood, making that night's dinner for Fyodor, hand-washing their laundry and hanging it to dry in the bedroom, the forges and smelting furnaces had returned Norylska to her usual cheerless grey.

Next in line to enter, she waited as a militsioner exited Lazarev's office. Looking her up and down with a blink of pleased surprise, he passed by, disappearing into the precinct main hall.

Do I know him?

She imagined Fyodor's anger: Did you smile at that militsioner? Were you *flirting?*

No! I would never!

He hadn't come home last night. For hours she lay awake, listening, waiting for the rattle of the doorlatch, praying to hear him stomp about fetching blankets so he might sleep on the sofa.

Previously, he'd always returned, no matter how angry.

But this time she lied, betrayed his trust.

She berated herself for not doing better, for hiding the fact she wasn't in the secretarial pool. She should have said something! She should have been honest. She had nothing to hide!

Or did she?

There was, she decided, simply no acclimatizing to the idea of memory stones. Having a second life she couldn't remember was an impossible burden. Guilt ate at her because she didn't know what she'd done. She would *never* know. That knowing she couldn't know, had she taken that as permission to do awful things? If she didn't know what she'd been up to, whether she'd been faithful to Fyodor, how could she blame him for doubting?

Kat glanced at her scraped knuckles, gently prodded the many bruises peppering her ribs.

She felt more like she'd been in a fight than unfaithful.

Impossible!

How could she fix this?

How could she make it up to Fyodor, show him their life together was more important than this damned job?

I have to quit.

She tried to imagine walking into Colonel Grinin's office, telling the militsiya officer she was finished. The thought terrified her more than facing Fyodor's wrath.

Fine, then. Not that.

Maybe she didn't have to face Grinin at all. What if she told Lazarev she quit? He could tell Grinin. The old man seemed nice. He'd understand—

"That's fine," said Penkin, Lazarev's assistant. He stood holding the door for her, waiting with his ever-present expression of barely contained annoyance. "I'm sure the criminal svoloch of the Filth will hold off until these militioners are on the job."

Startled, Kat glanced over her shoulder at the line of men. Caught staring at her ass, the militsioner directly behind pretended to study his shoes. Everyone was waiting for her to enter the veneficum's office.

"Sorry!"

Embarrassed, she ducked past the slim man.

Someone in line muttered, "Penkie, you goluboi, you just ruined the best part of my day."

"Ah," said Lazarev, waving Kat into his office, "my favourite militsioner."

She waited until he closed the door behind her. "I don't... I can't do this. I shouldn't be a militsioner. I shouldn't even be a secretary." Tension built behind her eyes, the need to cry, to let the pent emotions free. "I shouldn't be here at all!"

"Okay," he said. "It's alright. Tell me what the problem is. Things went badly at home with your quietly angry boyfriend? Let me guess, he feels threatened because it turns out you're much stronger than you thought."

"What? No!"

Her denial rang false. Was there something to Lazarev's words? After all, she'd taken the job in spite of Fyodor's many arguments against doing so. Was this the first time she'd ignored his desires?

"Not at all," she added. "It's..." Ashamed, she hesitated to tell him she'd lied about her job. "I'm not cut out for this kind of work." She showed him the scrapes and bruises on her knuckles. "*This* isn't me."

He didn't look surprised. Instead, he said, "I think perhaps you're stronger than either of us suspected."

He did? What did that mean? Did he know something?

"I have to quit," she finished.

"Follow," said Lazarev, heading into the vault at the rear of the room. "Toss your coat on one of the tables."

She wanted to argue, wanted to turn and march out of the Chernyshevsky Street Militsiya Bureau. Instead, she did as instructed. Really, what choice did she have?

Pulling on his leather gloves, Lazarev collected her stones from the shelf. Was there another small stone on the traits necklace? Not having previously counted them, she was unsure.

"No," she said, "I don't want those."

"You misunderstand," he said, holding them out in offering. "You can't quit." Seeing her expression, he added, "*This* you can't quit. You need to be Militsioner Katyushka Leonova to leave the force. You're only her when wearing the stones."

"Can't *you* tell Colonel Grinin this was a mistake?"

He snorted in wry amusement. "This directive isn't Grinin's idea, it came from Khagan. It's nationwide. All across the country women are being tested much as you are." He held up a silencing hand when she tried to speak. "I know Grinin from the war. He seems nice, for a militsiya officer, and to be sure the years since have softened him. Somewhat. But if I march into his office and tell him Khagan made a mistake by putting women in roles previously held by men, I'll likely be sent to the mines as a traitor to the state. If I tell him he personally made a mistake by choosing you, he'll shoot me right there in his office to save himself the paperwork."

"You exaggerate," she accused.

"Do I?" Again he lifted the two necklaces toward her. "If *you* do it," he said, "it's different. The failing becomes yours rather than his. But either way, you have to be wearing the stones. You aren't officially a militsioner without them."

Accepting the stones, Kat sagged in defeat. If this was the only way, she had no choice.

Sliding the necklaces over her head, she tucked them under her shirt.

Memories.

The abandoned candlemaker's. The back alley veneficum, head exploding as Arkady shot him. Maminov, Pribylov, Tsukanov. All dead, slaughtered by that dead-eyed bastard who chased her through the Filth.

The shot that killed the veneficum was meant for me.

With perfect clarity she recalled the vicious sound of the bullet hissing past less than a handspan from her face.

Arkady wasn't surprised to see me there.

Get the bitch. Get the stone.

He knew *I was going to be there.*

Just like last time.

No, not quite. This time they weren't waiting, though they did arrive moments later.

Who knew they were going to visit the veneficum?

Maks. Maks knew.

Anyone else? Had the order to bust the man come from above?

She didn't know, but it seemed likely.

Colonel Grinin. I told Grinin—No! Kostas told Grinin he wanted to follow a lead and—

And they were there waiting for him.

Stripped naked, hands chained over her head. Knees on cold stone. The man with the darting tongue and snake-twitch carving flesh from her. Cold and inhuman.

Ushakov! That was Ushakov, the Shkut torturer.

Arkady was an avtorityet, a brigadier in the same Family.

Kat swallowed a leaden lump of terror. *The Shkut Family wants me dead.*

One of Norylska's largest crime families, the Shkuts, practically owned the Filth.

Why me?

She was no one!

"If you want to see the Colonel now, you may," said Lazarev, gesturing toward the door. "I do apologize, but I have a lot of militsioners I must process this morning."

She stared at him, unmoving, her mind a chaotic maelstrom. If she quit, she'd lose access to these stones; she'd be timid Katyushka once again. If the Shkuts wanted her dead, she'd be helpless. Without the memory stones, she wouldn't know she was in danger!

I need these stones.

What she really needed was a fucking cigareta and vodka to calm her nerves.

Maks and I will—

Good old Maks. Maks, whom she loved and could never have.

Maks who may have betrayed her to her death.

No. Grinin. It must have been Grinin.

"Miss Leonova?" asked Lazarev.

"I can't quit," she said. "That's not the kind of man I am." She winced at the slip, but Lazarev ignored it.

The veneficum beamed fatherly pride. "I will admit I hoped you'd change your mind. I knew there was a hidden strength in you."

He believes in me. No one had done that before. Certainly, no one ever suggested there was a strength to her, hidden or otherwise. Kat's chest tightened with emotion and she wanted to cry for this small kindness.

"Please remember," continued Lazarev, "if you need more help getting through the day, dealing with the many difficulties a militsioner must face, you can always come see me." He gestured at the shelves of ordered stones. "Most men are too prideful to admit they need help." He winked. "And yes, prideful does mean stupid."

For a heartbeat she wanted to hug the old man with gratitude but remembered such displays between men were frowned upon. The last thing you wanted was someone questioning your sexual preferences; particularly someone as dangerously intelligent as Lazarev.

She didn't remember she wasn't a man until she had her greatcoat from the locker and was out in the precinct hall, following good old Maks who may have betrayed her out the front door.

Maks paused in the street, watching a team of sootmen shovelling ashen snow into waiting wagons. Two blocks to the west a train of huge wagons rumbled north into the reducing district, groaning under their burden of paraceratherium corpses. With a look of distracted concentration, he began patting down the pockets of his greatcoat.

"Left breast pocket," said Kat.

Fishing out the dented cigareta tin, he propped one between those beautiful, perfect lips. Seeing her expression, he frowned and offered her one too. Accepting it, she snatched a lit smoke from the mouth of a militioner returning at the end of his shift, using it to light hers.

"There's fucking two of them again," muttered the militsioner when she returned his cigareta.

After Maks used hers to light his own, she said, "I need a drink."

"Blood and bones," he muttered "Finally!" He set off; shoulders hunched.

Kat jogged to catch up.

"You listened," said Maks.

I did?

Having no idea what he was talking about, she said, "Don't let it go to your head."

"This is the first day you're not wearing the nun-bun. The makeup, snug sweater, and fitted shirt are maybe a bit much for the Filth but are still appreciated. Ilyushin damned near swallowed his own tongue when you came strutting out of Lazarev's office."

"I don't strut."

She wanted to say she hadn't dressed for him; her choice of clothes was entirely professional and none of his business anyway.

Except the sweater she wore was a little thinner than the weather demanded, and perhaps the bra beneath did lift things a little more than decorum required. The long skirt, which clung to her hips, narrowing enough toward her knees to show off her curves, had looked great in the morning.

I can't run in this fucking thing! What if get in a fight?

Fleeing through the Filth. Cornered by the vicious brute who killed her friends.

I barely knew them!

That wasn't true. She'd been on scores of arrests with those men. She knew Tsukanov from the war, served in the same unit. Pribylov knew she was goluboi and didn't care!

I don't like men!

She stumbled, confused.

Yes, Maks was a good-looking man. But her feelings for him were all Kostas'. She didn't love him. She didn't want to lick every part of him, bite that pert apple of an ass, feel him inside her—

Kat crushed the growing mental image.

Yeah? Why are you dressed like this, if not for Maks?

No. It wasn't about him, it was about Fyodor.

About, or for?

Strange that she saw it now but not when she dressed in the morning. Earlier, she'd simply picked out clothes for the day.

Fyodor isn't the only one who can be quietly angry.

This morning, doing all the chores, doing everything she could to apologize to Fyodor, she'd felt guilty. Now, she found only anger.

Of course she didn't tell him she wasn't a fucking secretary. He would have been angry and put his foot down and bullied her into quitting. There wouldn't have been a discussion, and she'd have caved like the weak pustyak she was.

I get it, she thought, remembering what Maks said on her first day.

She wanted to wear the stones home because once they came off, she'd be her weak, pathetic self.

I want to wear these and have real argument with Fyodor. This time, she wouldn't let him run away; she'd force a confrontation.

Except she wouldn't. At the end of the day, the stones would end up on a shelf in Lazarev's vault.

What must it be like to be a veneficum? She imagined living, surrounded by lost memories, lives waiting to be once again picked up.

Does he ever get curious?

Did he touch the stones, just for a moment, to peer into the lives and thoughts of the militsioners?

Already wrestling with the additional memories of Kostas, she couldn't imagine the nightmare of sorting through dozens. It would break her, drive her crazy. She'd never know who she was.

I don't love Maks, that was Kostas. I don't even like him.

And yet here she was in a tight sweater and skirt.

Double-think. That's what her grandmother used to call it. Doing something for a superficial surface reason while pretending you didn't know the true, underlying impetus.

Was her anger at Fyodor the superficial reason?

Fuck, I don't know!

Kat scowled. Grandmother would not have been impressed by her crude language.

Recognizing where they were going, Kat said, "The Dripping Bucket?"

She hesitated. She'd first seen that huge mouth-breathing bastard who murdered Maminov, Pribylov, and Tsukanov here.

"Where else?" he asked over his shoulder.

Fair enough. They did come here a lot. Usually during their shift, but sometimes she and Maks met up after work for a couple of drinks. He was a different man then, his cocky veneer gone. Quiet. Introspective. Lonely. Sometimes he drank too much and slurred his words, stared blearily into his cup. Those were always the most exciting times as she half prayed, he'd get drunk enough she might take advantage of him. Of course, she never did. She'd help him stagger home, enjoying the solid weight of him against her. She'd see him into the door, resist the urge to hug or kiss him, and walk the rest of the way alone. She always told herself it was because she wanted to make sure he didn't fall over and freeze to death, but that was double-think. What she really hoped was someday Maks would invite her in. Maybe, at first, just for one last drink. But things would move on from there and—

"Here we are," said Maks, pushing open the door and entering.

Kat followed him in, trailed behind admiring the broad shoulders and slim hips as he weaved between tables toward an empty one in the corner.

She checked the bar. No Arkady. No big mouth-breather. Scanning the room, she saw no Shkut men she recognized, though there were always new shestyorka—errand boys, lookouts, and informers—hoping to earn their way into the Family.

Claiming the seat in the corner so she could watch the room, Kat shed her greatcoat, slinging it over the back of another chair. Aware of the many watching eyes, she waited for Maks to fetch drinks.

He returned in moments, placing a dented mug of vodka before her. He removed his own coat, sitting across the table.

"We need to talk," he said, jaw set.

A rush of heart-crushing fear ran through her, mind going blank at the thought of confrontation. When Fyodor said that, it was trouble. She always knew she'd done something wrong. Worn the wrong dress or said the wrong thing to the wrong person.

The fear passed, snuffed. This wasn't Fyodor, and she didn't give a flying goat-fuck what the pathetic pustyak thought.

"We do," she agreed.

Maks studied her over the rim of his tin mug. "That back alley veneficum. You left. You just..."

Get the bitch. Get the stone.

"I was chased." She hesitated to say more, to give away what she knew.

"I thought you'd been fucking murdered!" he snapped, suddenly angry.

The need to apologize rose and died a cold death.

"When I left," she said, watching him for a reaction with the training and experience of a veteran militsioner, "the big guy followed me out. Which I guess you somehow missed?"

Eyes narrowed, Maks said nothing.

"Everyone else was dead. That left just you and Arkady in the veneficum's. And his gun was jammed."

"He ran," said Maks, voice tight. "I had to let him go because I had to fucking chase after you. Which raises an interesting question."

"Does it?"

"Indeed." He sipped vodka. "A Shkut kryshas—a skilled killer for the Family—chased you. A big man. A man who just killed three militsioners—veterans from the war no less—like they were fucking nothing." He drank again, swallowing with a show of teeth. "And he couldn't catch you?"

Oh, he caught me.

Kat froze, unsure what to say. Should she tell him she wore Kostas' memory stone, that Lazarev had given her the traits to survive on the job? Blood and bones, she didn't even know what traits she had! She remembered the cold joy of violence, annoyance she wasn't strong enough to kill the big man without undue risk. Yet she hesitated. Maks knew Kostas was going to be in that alley, and he knew they were going to visit the veneficum. Though he brought the other militsioners along for support, she couldn't rule him out.

The thought he may have betrayed her, sold her to the Shkuts, broke her heart.

Maybe he doesn't love me the way I love him, but he's a good man.

At least when the stones came off. Those evenings when they went for drinks after work, he was a different man. Confidence gone, replaced by a quiet thoughtfulness, he became tentative, shy. She loved him even more those times.

"He caught me," she said, voice quiet.

Maks blinked in surprise. "He let you go?" he demanded, incredulous.

She shook her head, showed him the bruised and scraped knuckles.

He burst out laughing. "You feisty little minx! You surprised him! He underestimated you, and, let me guess, you kicked his balls in."

Remembering how good it felt to smash the big man's face into the wall, Kat nodded. "When he fell, I ran away."

Not a complete lie.

Fishing the dented cigareta tin from his greatcoat, he popped two into those beautiful lips. Amused, she watched him search his coat for matches. Not finding any, he cursed, and went to the bar.

He returned with two lit cigareta in his mouth, and two more vodkas. Sitting, he placed one drink in front of her and withdrew a smoke, turning it to offer the unlit end.

Leaning forward, Kat accepted it with her lips.

Their eyes met.

Why? Why did you fucking do that?

Maks laughed, an awkward stumbling thing, as she sat back. "You know, there was a time when I thought you maybe had the memory stone from someone I knew." He inhaled hard on the cigareta, let the smoke curl from his nose. "But he would never do that."

Are you kidding? Kostas dreamed about sucking your fingers.

And other parts.

Kat's breath caught, a warmth spreading from deep inside. *Just the vodka. Just the vodka.* She didn't want to climb across this rickety table and fuck him right here in the Dripping Bucket like a cat in heat.

Gods above and demons below! What got into her?

It's Kostas.

Kostas and maybe the vodka. She never drank. Hell, she never smoked either, but here she was smoking and loving the delicious naughtiness of it. The world swam liquid and soft with warmth.

Kat slammed back the rest of her vodka and immediately wanted more.

I don't want to be me.

Her skull was a prison, and she was trapped inside. She wanted out, a moment's respite from the fear and doubt and worrying over what others thought. It was fucking exhausting.

What would Fyodor think, if he saw me now?

She tried to imagine his horrified shock to discover her smoking and drinking with a handsome man in a shit-hole tavern in the Filth. He'd leave and never come back.

Good! Fuck that insecure pustyak!

Gods, she wanted to punch him so bad, smash his face into a wall like she had that big Shkut brute. Teeth scattered about the street, Fyodor sobbing in broken misery as she drove his smug face over and over against unforgiving stone.

She drew a calming breath. Much to her shock, the thought of violence had further warmed things down south. She wanted to rut like a filthy beast, clawing and biting, grinding so hard it hurt—

She supposed she could understand, at least in theory, Kostas' love for Maks, but why did he hate Fyodor so much?

Does he?

Kostas was memory stored on stone. The man was gone, dead.

"I'm sorry I got angry," said Maks.

It hit her like a punch in the face: Not once in the years she and Fyodor had been together had he ever apologized. It wasn't that he was perfect, or never made mistakes. But somehow, when he did, they were nothing, forgivable. Not his fault.

Nothing ever is.

"Can I tell you a secret?" asked Maks, using the ember of his cigareta to light two more, and passing her one.

Kat's heart screamed with joy. "I guess," she said, accepting it between two fingers.

"You're not at all what I expected."

"Oh?"

"Colonel Grinin briefed me, told me all about your family. About your father. You went to the best schools in Khagan. You come from money."

"You didn't think we could have drinks and share a few smokes because I know how to read?"

"I know how to read," he said, defensive. "It's just… I feel weirdly comfortable with you."

I feel it too.

"I feel like I know you," he added. He studied her through a haze of smoke, perfect lips pursed as if begging to be kissed. "Any luck yet? Figure out whose stone you're wearing?"

Shit.

Kat shook her head. "I think maybe a whole bunch of militsioners have worn the stone over the years. Too confusing."

"Yeah, it couldn't be him anyway."

"Him?" she asked, knowing the answer.

"My old partner."

Why can't it be him?

"I miss him," Maks continued. "Kostas was a good man. A friend. Best I ever had. Didn't matter he was goluboi."

Kat sat stunned. Maks knew Kostas liked men. Kostas, afraid of losing his friend, had lived in fear of being found out.

Men. Fucking typical.

GENNDY ANTONOV – CHAPTER SEVENTEEN

There are few things more fucking annoying than a man who won't fucking die the first fucking time you fucking kill him.

-Ratman, The Scab

Blank. White like snow. Pain, coming in a throbbing wave. Sound following. A low thrum.

Blood?

Mine?

Someone throws a fist. Gen ducks to the side, snaps one, two quick jabs into their ribs. Something burns in his ribs. Wet heat against one hip, slipping down the outside of his thigh. Someone hits him from behind, the impact rocking his skull.

His nose is bleeding. Thick and coppery, clogging up his throat. Need to spit, clear it out before he pukes. Swallow instead. Blink the sting from the eyes. Gods below, it fucking stings.

When did that happen?

Men come at him, shapeless shadows in the stinking dark of a vast echoing space. A warehouse? Abandoned factory? No matter. They're nearly on him. Gen slips to the side of the nearest, grabs the man by the back of his head. Helps him along, Gen straightening his arm, snapping it out rigid as an iron bar, smashing the assailant's skull into the nearby brick. His nose disintegrates with a wet crunch.

Momentum's a bitch.

The thug collapses into a gurgling heap, and Gen stomps on his neck, crushing off the agonized sounds. Another, coming up with a knife. Blade sharp enough to glint in the dark. He lunges, Gen steps back. Lunge, back. Lunge, back. He's driving Gen somewhere.

Another impact, and Gen tastes blood. The warehouse blinks out.

Where? What the fuck is happening?

Movement in the shadows. No time to contemplate. No time to stop. New pain, joining the others. Inside his bicep. Feels like someone tried to peel him.

Glint of blade in the half-light.

Gen takes the opening. Moves in instead of out, and the blade cuts a bright line across his ribs, opening the wound already there deeper. He roars in pain and traps his attacker's arm. Lock the joint. Hammer down with elbow, weight behind the blow. The arm snaps. Knife man screams, blade clattering to the floor.

Knee into the man's ribs, snap of another bone. Ragged breathing. Probably punctured a lung. Gen stoops, scoops up the knife. Lunges forward and—someone hits him between the shoulder blades.

Flicker.

An inferno burned through him, weight pressing him down.

What the fuck is happening?

Fuck.

Some big bastard has him pinned. Gen casts around for a lifeline. The man with the knife lays slumped against a wall, hilt of his blade protruding from the top of his skull. Smashed head forms a crumpled heap on the floor. Another shape sprawled in a corner in a deep pool of shadow. A limb, seemingly placed at random, hangs from a rafter.

No weapons nearby.

The big man raises a stick. Gen tries to raise his hands to defend, but the man on his chest has Gen's arms pinned with his thighs. He brings the submission stick down. Gen turns his head, the blow grazing his skull.

Big man bringing the stick down again. Gen flexes his hips, thrusts upward, throwing his attacker off. To his credit, the man keeps a grip on the submission stick. Gen continues the movement, rolls to his side. Snags the stick and wrenches it out of the man's hand.

Turns the roll into a somersault, comes up behind his attacker. Uses the stick like a garotte, hands at each end, careful to stay clear of the stone. Gen shoves his knee into the brute's spine and heaves back. Rewarded with the crunch of a smashed windpipe. The man still struggles, and Gen pulls back harder, harder, until the big man's neck snaps.

He drops the limp bundle, throws the stick away. It clatters into a corner in the dark. Wrenches the knife from the skull of the corpse against the wall.

A small office occupies space on the far wall, and Gen limps over. Kicks in the door and drops into a chair too ratty for the former owners to take with them. Dyrkovich is still there, propped up on a couch, unconscious.

Gen waits. The battle rage wears off.

He remembered the day before.

*

Arkady lit a cigareta while Gen recounted his encounter with Irina, nodding in all the right places, making all the right sympathetic sounds. Gen suppressed the urge to feed the man his teeth. When he finished, Arkady patted his shoulder.

"It happens. Not everyone understands what it is to be a Family man. She'll come around. You'll see."

Gen nodded; considered that had he not been pulled into the life in the first place, he'd never have to worry about her coming around. His rage surged anew and he took a deep draught of the vodka he'd poured. It burned, a numb wave following in the wake of the fire. His anger cooled a fraction.

Arkady rounded his desk, pulled a sheet of paper from the blotter there. "I have a present for you."

He held it out. Gen took it, scanned the name scrawled there.

Dyrkovich.

The goon Arkady recruited for the job at the chandler's. The bastard ended up fleeing faster than a man convinced his cock is on fire and the only thing capable of putting it out is distance and speed.

He spends men like money.

Another thing to add to Arkady's tally. Despite the ugly realization he'd been used—likely anyone not in the inner circle was a pawn—Dyrkovich had abandoned his men.

A flash of memory, like a spark to tinder.

Fog clinging to the earth like a jealous lover. Through it, shadows. Altin Ordu , advancing. The first shots rang out when they were hundreds of yards out. Kievan men fell like threshed wheat, heads popping like pinched ticks, holes opening in chests and throats, legs dissolving in a mist of blood and bone. As deadly as they were with a blade, the bastards must've had eyes like a hawk to hit men at that distance in poor visibility.

Then the chant came. Gen spoke enough Altin Ordu to understand, and he felt a chill shake the line as others translated for themselves.

Demiri vur!

Eti kes!

Ruhu kurtar!

Kemikleri yak kömür et!

Sal onları!

Sal onları!

Men broke from the lines, rifles forgotten. They scrambled up the sides of trenches, slipping on ice and hardened mud. Those that slid back down, the commissars filled with bullets.

No man leaves.

Every man fights.

Gen sucked in a breath, turned that rage into an arrow. Arkady laid a hand on his shoulder, voice in his ear.

"For you, my *Volk*."

The man's breath stank of cinnamon and tobacco. It lingered, grew in strength. Became overwhelming, turned sour and putrid.

The memory shattered.

*

Exhausted. He hadn't been expecting the ambush. Should've known it was too easy, creeping in, knocking Dyrkovich over the skull. The man still had a goose egg decorating his bald pate, so that was something, at least. Gen hated it when it felt like he'd done too much work for too little reward.

He wondered if Arkady set him up. Did the man know what was waiting here? Or had Dyrkovich hired goons of his own? Regardless, it spoke of paranoia that it had come to this. Though whose, he couldn't be sure.

Gen should've been used to it. The default state of the Kievan citizen is paranoia. The state watches you. The militsiya watches you. Your parents watch you when you're a child and threaten to turn you in, and when you're grown, your wife watches you, you watch your wife, and your neighbours watch the both of you.

Ironic that a state so repressed would make voyeurism its national pastime.

He laughed a little, causing his muscles to spasm, and it turned into a groan. He seriously considered asking Dmitry for a stone that suppressed pain.

Barring that, a vat of vodka.

Dyrkovich echoed his groan a moment later, the tall man coming round. He blinked red-rimmed eyes and squinted against the dark.

"Tomas?" he asked. "Bendzhamin? Nikolay?"

When no answer came, he pushed against the couch. Gen leaned in and slammed the blade through his shoulder, hard enough to pin him to the back of the furniture. He screamed, a high-pitched sound like a cat in a grinder.

"Fuck!" he sputtered when he regained his speech.

"Shut up," Gen said.

Dyrkovich's eyes widened, flicking from side to side, searching the dark.

His gaze landed on Gen, and he blanched, already pale skin nearing the colour of milk. "You! Ah fuck! I'm sorry, comrade! I didn't want to die! I have a family to feed, a baby on the wa—"

"Shut. Up," Gen repeated. "Let's talk about personal responsibility. Yours and mine."

Dyrkovich opened his mouth as if to reply, and Gen shook his head. The other man shut it with a snap. Gen reached into the pocket of his greatcoat and pulled out three long needles. Seeing them, Dyrkovich blanched again.

"You know what these are?" Gen asked, laying them out beside him.

Dyrkovich nodded.

"I want to hear you say it."

"Broadheads." A loud swallow followed the word.

They'd used broadheads in the war. Thin flexible tubes of steel, they fit just about anywhere. But when you pressed a knob on the end, they opened to form a four-bladed arrowhead, narrow at one side and wide at the other, razor-sharp, barbed on the end. Impossible to remove without surgery or brutally fucking someone from the inside out. Some motherfucker in the OSD came up with the idea. But then, that's what the OSD did. Came up with ideas and generally acted as motherfuckers.

Gen threaded them one by one onto a thin fishing line, securing them with a knot on each knob. When he yanked the string just so, they'd all snap outward at once. Dyrkovich watched, sweat beading on his forehead.

When he finished, Gen held up the string, broadheads dangling from it, inspecting his work. Dyrkovich broke the silence with a thunderous fart.

"Ah, sorry, my stomach acts up when I'm anxious."

"Are you anxious?" Gen asked. "I hadn't noticed."

He pushed himself up and stood over Dyrkovich. "Open."

Dyrkovich stared, eyes watering with tears. "I'll tell you whatever you want, just... just don't. Please."

Gen squatted until he was a height with Dyrkovich. "I know you would. But I have no time nor tolerance for lies today, friend. This will just ensure you tell the truth quickly and efficiently."

Dyrkovich shook his head. Tears *did* stream down his face, then. "I can't. I can't. Please don't make me. You can't make me."

Another fart.

Gen reached out and hammered on the hilt of the dagger, sending it quivering in Dyrkovich's shoulder. The man screamed again.

"Consider the alternative," Gen said, and thumped the hilt once more for good measure.

Coughing, crying, snot running down his face, Dyrkovich shook his head, snapping it from side to side.

This motherfucker.

Gen lashed out, his fist connecting with the man's chin. Dyrkovich's skull rocked hard, once to the side, and he went limp. Squeezing the soldier's jaw until his mouth opened with a *pop*, Gen threaded the broadheads down the man's throat, then played out the string until he could sit again.

Fart.

Starting to smell like a spoiled cabbage factory in here.

Irina never did like that stink.

Do you blame her? Boiled cabbage is the snot of the vegetable world.

He patted Dyrkovich on the cheek. When the man didn't stir, Gen horked up a wad of phlegm and spat it in the man's face. Dyrkovich woke sputtering, eyes gummy and squinted.

"Morning, sweetheart," Gen said. He leaned back, put one leg over the other. "Now. How did you know I was coming?"

Dyrkovich shook his head, sending the string swaying. The sensation caused a flicker of realization to flash across his face. Terror peaking, he stopped, frozen, eyes wide. Gen gave the string a little flick, and Dyrkovich blurted his answer.

"I didn't! These Gruzdev men—they owed me. I'd done a job for them a while back. Please don't kill me, please don't kill me!" he winced, as if the admission might cause his insides to detonate.

"No one set me up?"

"No, I swear it on my mother's life!"

"You're just a coward?"

"Yes! Now will you let me go?"

Gen paused a moment, searched the other man's face.

Dyrkovich farted again, and as if that was a lock breaking free, blurted "I know where Arkady keeps his codebook!"

Interest prickled Gen's ears. "Codebook?" he asked.

"It's this... thing. All kinds of info about cops and stones and such. When he's drunk, he brags about it. But only in private."

"How do you know about it, then? Seems like something someone who doesn't want to die would say." Gen twitched the line again.

Fart.

"He made me take care of a date of his once. Told the boy everything. The boy told me, like I'm telling you. It's in his room, under the floor. Let me go now?"

"You killed him?"

"The goluboi?"

The word dropped from Dyrkovich's lips with disdain. Gen's face hardened, and Dyrkovich's eyes widened as Gen's fingers tightened on the string.

Fart.

"No, please. You don't understand. You don't get it! What they're turning you into! An *animal!*"

Gen thought of Irina. Of the things he'd already done in the name of the Family.

"Too late," he said.

He pulled the string.

The broadheads opened all at once. Dyrkovich froze, and the dual stench of shit and urine filled the air as the man soiled himself. He opened his mouth, and a rattling moan of agony echoed in the room, blood trickling from the corner of his lips. His chest heaved, face flushing with pain.

"Ah-ah," Gen admonished. "Fear makes it worse. Hyperventilating, shaking, trying to speak. You'll drive the barbs deeper."

Tears rolled down Dyrkovich's cheeks. The moan was a constant low sound in the air, as if he was deflating. Gen tugged the string, yanking the barbs up by a tiny increment. The trickle of blood increased from Dyrkovich's lips. He gurgled when he breathed, wheezed. The moan had stopped.

Severed his vocal cords.

"Now. That conversation. When you're asked to support a comrade, you support. The. Comrade."

Gen tugged on the string for each of the last three words. Dyrkovich grunted in pain, breath coming like a teakettle. Blood bubbled in his nostrils, the whites of his eyes turning a sickly yellow.

"Ah, your liver. That's got to hurt. Yeah, the harder I pull, the more the barbs sway. Probably all tangled in your lungs. Your throat likely feels like shattered glass.

"You know, I once saw an Altin Ordu take five of these into his guts. But the OSD officer doing the questioning wasn't so kind. He went in through the ass."

Dyrkovich's throat bobbed, and with each tremulous motion, more blood slipped from his lips. He slumped, dagger in his shoulder pulling at the wound there, cutting deeper. The pain prompted him to slam himself upright, kick his feet in agony. His lips worked soundlessly as the barbs turned his insides to a slop of meat.

The tall man's eyes rolled, and he opened his mouth as if to scream, unleashing a tide of red and yellow-streaked vomit. It poured down his chest in a sheet, pooled in his lap. Thick black clots clung to mucous-like streamers of bile. Dyrkovich coughed, again and again.

More blood, a red tide. Gen helped it along, yanking the string until something gave way. The closest broadhead ripped free, bringing chunks of tracheal lining with it. Other pinkish lumps of flesh came on their heels, soft wads of the man's tongue. Behind that, a mass of teeth, and strips of soft pallet.

Dyrkovich leaned forward and screamed silently, the sound a rasp of air in the dead of the warehouse. The movement and his weight forced the dagger in his shoulder upward, and the man's arm separated with a pop.

Blood rushed from the stump of the severed limb, Dyrkovich rolling on the floor to escape the pain. Gen watched, then knelt beside the man. With skill borne from battlefield practice, he set a crude tourniquet on the stump, cinching it until the bleeding slowed to a trickle. Then, with methodical care, he set Dyrkovich back on the couch.

That done, he sat back in the chair, string in hand again. Dyrkovich's eyelids fluttered. He came to, fixing on Gen, lucid for a moment. Shock was setting in, then.

"You'd wonder how much pain a man can endure before he passes out. How much damage inside. I've seen men take days to die, their guts in their hands. I've seen men with ruptured insides suffer in incredible pain as their body poisons itself from ripped intestines and broken organs. Short answer? It's a lot, comrade.

"You warn me of the Family turning me animal. A monster. I say the state already made me one. At least I'm not a traitor."

He slammed the dagger into Dyrkovich's other shoulder, and tugged the string just a little.

Another silent scream.

This would take all night.

KATYUSHKA LEONOVA – CHAPTER EIGHTEEN

Altin Ordu preach the freedom of their people, proclaim the strengths and victories of their democracy. They are blind. Social-Democracy is objectively the moderate wing of fascism.

—Tsar Besarionis dze Jughashvili

Blink.

Kat stood in Veneficum Lazarev's office. The old man, leather gloves in place, had already turned away, placing her necklaces of memory and personality stones on the shelf with her name. Strangely numb, off balance, she stared at the neat handwriting.

Not in a million years could I write that neatly.

She barely felt capable of standing, her lungs ached like she'd spent the day strolling the smelting district. Coughing, she tasted stale cigareta and a back of the throat burning reminiscent of paint solvent. It reminded her of the first time she met Maks, and their visit to the Dripping Bucket.

"You alright, Miss Leonova?" Lazarev asked, turning back to her.

An instant ago she stood here telling him she wanted to quit the militsioners. Now, she was empty, exhausted. Not like the day she came back bruised and beaten, but emotionally wrung out.

Was I smoking?

Licking her lips, she knew the answer.

Proper women don't smoke!

All through school they hammered into the girls what *Proper Women* did and did not do. Proper Women were polite. Proper Women were kind. Proper Women were quiet. Proper Women listened to their fathers and husbands.

She almost laughed at the thought.

Proper Women don't work for the fucking militsioners.

She wobbled unsteadily and leaned against the nearest chair for support.

Am I drunk?

Proper Women definitely didn't get drunk. Though, come to think of it, sometimes her grandmother got giggly late in the afternoons.

"What?" she said, having forgotten the question.

"Are you alright?" Lazarev repeated. Eyes rimmed in red, he looked like a man who hadn't slept in years.

"I don't know," she admitted.

"You aren't hurt, are you?"

"I… I don't think so." Checking herself for new wounds, she discovered ashen mud staining the front of her long skirt. Had she fallen in the snow?

Or was I kneeling in front of—

Flushing with heat, Kat crushed the thought.

Proper Women definitely didn't do that.

"Though militsioners rarely take advantage of it," said Lazarev, "part of my job here is to help the men—and women—" he added, with an apologetic shrug, "deal with the traumas of the job. Just because you can't remember your day doesn't mean there aren't stresses that come with such a lifestyle."

Lifestyle. Like she'd picked an unconventional hat.

Like this was a choice.

What could she possibly talk about? Should she tell him of her difficulty at home, how the job put a strain on her relationship with Fyodor? She needed this to end!

I want my old life back!

"I was going to quit," she said, instead.

"Yes, I remember." Scowling at a desk, he straightened a pile of loose-leaf paper. "The moment you put the memory stones on, you said, and I quote, 'I can't quit.' You sounded very sure, very purposeful. I was impressed with your strength of character."

"You were?"

Had any man ever been impressed by anything about her unrelated to a body part?

"Very much so. A moment later you strolled out of my office. I didn't see you again until just now." He glanced over his shoulder at the shelf with her stones, hesitating. "I'm not supposed to talk about anything that happens before the stones come off."

Yesterday she returned looking like she'd been in a brawl. Today she came back drunk and stinking of cigareta, impossible as that was. She desperately wanted to hear something—anything—of her other life.

"Obviously I can't share details," he said.

"Please. I just…" She just what? She didn't know what she was asking. That other life was hers and yet it belonged to the state. What good could come from bringing that home? "Is this a mistake?" she asked. "Is me being here a mistake?"

Lazarev studied her with a look of fatherly concern. "A moment ago, you seemed happier. Relaxed. You seemed…" he shrugged, "comfortable in your skin."

Whatever she'd done to get these stained knees made her happy? "Comfortable in my skin?"

"Even more than when we first met." Lips pursed, he hesitated. "I don't know you outside of this place." He waved a hand at the vault and stones. "But if I didn't know better, I'd say you are gaining something incredibly valuable from this experience. I think you're learning who you really are."

Who I really am?

What did that mean?

She knew who she was. She was Katyushka Leonova, daughter of the disgraced Nikhil Leonov, former Secretary of Finance for Yuryev Industrial, one of Kievan's greatest arms manufacturers. She was the soon-to-be-fiancé—and then wife—of Fyodor Ozerov.

She was defining herself by the men in her life.

Kat swallowed the thought, choked it down.

"I have to go," she said, backing toward the exit. "Fyodor will be waiting for me."

Lazarev dipped a shallow bow. "You have a good evening, Miss Leonova. I know this isn't easy. I truly am sorry for that."

Evening? In the windowless vault, she hadn't a clue what time it was.

"It's not your fault," she said, letting herself out.

Turning, she found herself face to face with Penkin's disapproval.

"Sorry," she said, pushing the door closed behind her.

Penkin's nose twitched like an annoyed rabbit. *Or an angry rat.* He didn't move to let her past.

"I realize," he said, "that the sample pool for early research is small. An N equals one experiment, if you will." His breath stank of onions.

She'd studied science but suddenly couldn't remember any of it. She wanted to lie down or eat buttered toast or both. *Toast. Yeah, toast would be great right now.* "What?"

"Women in the workforce," he said. "You're the only one here."

"Ah. Yes. N equals me." Finding that funny for reasons she couldn't imagine, she giggled.

"Quite," he said. "I've done the math."

"Math?"

"Indeed."

"You really hit those consonants," she pointed out. "The T in quite. The last D in indeed. Percussive. Wet." She hid her surprise at herself behind a raised eyebrow.

For a fraction of a heartbeat his smug certainty faltered.

"The math," he repeated. "You spend more time in Veneficum Lazarev's office each morning than any of the men. You do the same again at the end of the day."

Is he jealous of my time with Lazarev?

"If," he continued, "the department was to replace half the male staff with women," his tone left no doubt as to his feelings on the wisdom of such a decision, "I calculate it would take Lazarev three days just to assign stones to each militsioner each morning."

Something inside Katyushka turned hard like stone.

She leaned into the pompous little fuck, her nose a finger's width from his. "How about you get out of my way before I use the corner of that desk to smash your teeth down your fucking throat?"

Total calm. No fear. No thrum of nerves. Cold empty.

She made a show of examining the bruised and scraped knuckles of her right hand.

Penkin retreated to his desk with an appalled huff containing more than a little fear.

Kat let herself out of his office.

Locker room. Coat. Out into Chernyshevsky Street.

Deep drifts of ashen snow sat where the sootmen, unable to keep up, piled it for later retrieval. Fat flakes, damp and heavy, fell straight down. No swirling dance. Oil lanterns lining the main streets turned the scene a warm yellow at odds with the freezing cold.

This is the most beautiful snowfall I've ever seen.

She wanted to lie down in street with her mouth open, catch the pure flakes before Norylska tainted it the way it corrupted everything. Stained streets. Stone buildings blackened by centuries of soot. The sky an endless pall of smoke and ash and winter storm clouds.

Hadn't there been a time when mud and snow were two different things?

The city moaned, the creak of shrinking wood. Off to the north the furnaces rumbled like sleeping dragons. Never silent.

Norylska groans.

Kat set off for home. Fyodor would be there.

He'd be angry.

Again.

Still.

She'd explain she tried to quit, wanted to quit.

Somehow, she'd make him understand. They'd get through this. They'd get back whatever it was they lost. This was all her fault; somehow, she'd make it right.

They could be happy again.

Again?

Were you ever happy?

"Of course I was," she said, breath pluming hot like a forge bellows. "I had everything. A good man who was going to be someone. I was going to be a great wife, a fantastic mother."

Weren't those the things defining a woman's happiness?

Passing a tavern, yellowing lanternlight sneaking through stained windows, she slowed to listen to the voices within. They sang songs from the war, great rousing choruses of '*And we watched the fuckers burn, burn like bails of grass, and when the fuckers ran, we shot them in the ass!*'

Looking back the way she came she saw her footprints weaving erratically through the snow.

Gods above she wanted a pivo to wash the taste of stale smoke from her mouth.

There'd be men in the tavern. Men from the war. Hard men. But even among the hardest of men there were men like her, men who liked—

"I'm not a fucking man!" she shouted.

"Would you like to be fucking a man?" someone shouted back.

Spinning a circle, she saw no one. Suddenly scared, Kat hurried home.

Seeing the woodpile covered in a heavy blanket of snow, Kat stopped to shovel it free. The work cleared her head and she found herself hesitating at the door, dreading what might await within. Would he still be angry? Would he be there at all? What if he left?

"What if he *did* leave?" she whispered.

What then?

She already did all the work around the house. She cooked and cleaned. She chopped the wood and shovelled their walkway.

He pays for everything.

The rent on this cramped shack. The groceries she walked into the Filth to buy.

I have a job now.

Having been there less than a week, she hadn't been paid yet, but Colonel Grinin said her new position paid twice what a secretary earned. Surviving on a secretary's salary would have been tight, but now she could afford both the rent on this shit-hole, and groceries.

Yet, the thought of Fyodor leaving terrified her. Proper Women didn't live alone. Father would want her to move back home. She'd lose what little freedom she had.

Deal with whatever happens, she told herself. *You'll get through this.*

This was just a rough patch brought on by the sudden changes.

We'll get through this.

Taking a deep breath, Kat pushed the door open. Inside, she found Fyodor scrambling eggs on the woodstove. Warmth flushed her face, the smell of eggs and cheese awakening a deep hunger she hadn't noticed.

Seeing her, he flashed a grin. "I thought you might be hungry. Got fresh eggs from one of the markets in the south. They had that aged cheddar you like too."

He hefted the cast-iron skillet, showing off the food, and she never loved him so much.

"You did this for me?"

"Of course." He scraped a heaping pile of cheese and eggs onto a waiting plate. "I know you're working hard, and this wasn't the job you wanted. But it's the militsiya, and you can't exactly refuse them." He shrugged. "And you're right. The extra money will help. We could be into a real house in the south early next year. Fresh vegetables every day. No more shopping in the Filth. Maybe the occasional—"

Fyodor stopped, seeing the state of her dress.

Looking down, Kat realized she hadn't appreciated how bad it was. Snow and ash stained the front. She really did look like she'd been kneeling in the street.

"I fell," she blurted.

Placing the plate on the table, he took her in his arms. "Are you alright? Are you hurt? What happened?"

"I..." She couldn't tell him she didn't know.

Fyodor's nose wrinkled in distaste and he leaned close to sniff at her. "Have you been *smoking*?"

She wanted to deny it, but she knew she had. The bitter taste of cigareta filled her mouth.

"You have," he said, not waiting for an answer. "And you've been drinking! Gods above, I smell cheap Filth vodka all over you!" He retreated a step, creating a distance further than the single stride. "Who were you with? Were you drinking with militsioners? Is that why you've been home late each night?"

"No! I—"

His eyes changed, became cold, distant. "Do not lie to me."

"It's work," she said. "I have to wear a memory stone. All militsioners do."

"I'm a lawyer," he said, voice low with anger. "Don't tell me things I already know."

"When the stones come off at the end of the day, I come straight home to you, I swear."

He gestured at her stained knees. "And what happens before the stones come off?"

"I don't know!" she snapped. "I'm not wearing a fucking memory stone right now, remember?"

"You might not know," he said, "but *I* know." Jaw tight, fists clenched, he loomed over her. "You've been drinking. You've been smoking. You practically reek of men."

Kat shrank before his anger.

Was it true? She couldn't think. Couldn't speak to defend herself. It felt like she was caving in, fleeing the confrontation.

"You're fucking someone at work," Fyodor said.

The horrible bluntness of the accusation.

The fact she'd wondered the same while standing in Lazarev's office.

"Staying late," he said, nodding to himself. "Smoking and drinking." Building his case, as if she were on trial. "The lies about your job." Judge and jury. "It's the only explanation."

"You come home drunk and stinking of cigars all the time!" she lashed out, surprising both of them.

He flinched, and she saw something there. A flash of guilt smothered in an instant.

Demons below! All those nights he came home smelling of perfume, and she'd taken his word it was the waitstaff.

I'm an idiot.

The door swung open, bang of wood against the wall a death knell for the conversation. Four men strode into the little shack like they owned it. Hulking shoulders in stained and much-patched militsiya greatcoats from the war. Big men. Scars and tattoos, ears and knuckles forever swollen from fighting. Bad men.

As they spread out a fifth in an expensive suit entered. Narrow shoulders, slim hips, he had the build of a Khagan ballerino. Heavy lidded eyes, dark, like a Altin Ordu prince. Only the black under the eyes was missing. One of the slope-headed men came damn close to bowing to him and they all scattered from his path.

Among these bad men, he was the baddest.

"Who the hell are you?" demanded Fyodor. "Get out! I'll have you know that I'm a lawyer at—"

One of the men grabbed him by the throat, pinned him to the nearest wall.

"At Kuznetsov and Alyokhin," said the bad man holding him. "We know." He squeezed and Fyodor's face purpled. "A fuckin' peep from you, and the sootmen'll find you in a fuckin' drift, yeah?"

Fyodor nodded.

"Good."

Gaze languorous, the slim man studied Kat. "Different." he mused. "Sometimes it's like that, you know? Some people are what they are. One layer. Like Antipov here."

The thug did bow this time.

"Antipov is always Antipov." He shrugged, the slightest lift of one shoulder. "No matter what you're wearing."

What I'm wearing?

Confused, Kat suddenly felt ashamed by her humble shack, the snow and ash staining the knees of her dress. Of Fyodor for making no attempt to protect her.

"But you, my dear." He offered a sad smile. "You are someone entirely new." He glanced about the room, studying the blunt simplicity as if disappointed. "You're not what I expected." The hint of a shrug. "The old man has no taste for art. He can't appreciate..." He waved a hand at her with a sigh. "Still. Business must."

He's insane. He made no sense, a rambling madman.

"You're in the wrong house," she said.

He gave her a look expressing exactly how pathetic the attempt was.

"I don't want you," he said. "I have no desire to hurt you. Though your quietly angry boyfriend over there..." Onyx eyes turned on Fyodor. "Him, I'd like to break."

"Please don't," she pleaded.

He shrugged, unmoved. "I want the stone, and you're going to give it to me. If you don't... Antipov?"

Antipov landed a crushing punch to Fyodor's belly and stood over him as he crumpled to the floor in a foetal ball. "More?" he asked.

"Not yet."

"I don't have any stones," said Kat. "No jewellery."

The slim man blinked in surprise, brushing at the collar of his impeccable suit. "Not even an engagement ring?"

"No."

He scowled at Fyodor. "Anitpov," he said. "Again."

Antipov kicked Fyodor, hard. Raising a foot, he asked, "Should I stomp his head in?"

"Not yet."

Antipov returned his foot to the ground and stood waiting. Punch a man. Break his skull under your boot. Or do nothing. All the same.

"No," said the slim man, attention again on Kat. "I'm not interested in anything you own. I want the memory stone you wear at work. You'll find a way to separate yourself from that chisel-chinned idiot of a partner and bring it to me. Tomorrow."

He gave her an address deep in the Filth and had her repeat it back.

"If you don't," he said, "I'll come for you. I'll find you, no matter where you hide. I'll have Ushakov skin you alive. I'll peel your boyfriend like a fucking grape."

Frozen, Kat couldn't move. Her thoughts spiralled to nowhere, a whirling storm of fear. "I can't! If I return to the precinct without the stones, they'll assume I stole them. I'll be shot as a traitor."

For a moment he stared at her in disbelief. Bursting out in surprised laughter, he slapped the thigh of his immaculate suit. "Oh, dear. We often bite our own ass. It's the curse."

"W-What?"

"Would you rather be shot, a bullet in the brain," he touched a slim finger to the centre of her forehead, "or skinned alive over the course of several days?"

"Just give him the stones," Fyodor moaned from the floor.

"Fucking grow a pair of stones!" she snapped back.

Antipov blinked in surprise, hid a smirk behind a meaty hand.

"Indeed," said the slim man. "Bring me Kostas."

Kostas? The name meant nothing.

"That address," he added. "Tomorrow. Please."

It almost sounded as if she had a choice.

Well, you wanted to quit.

Kat laughed at the absurdity of the thought as four frightening men and one utterly terrifying man exited the shit-hole that was her home.

GENNDY ANTONOV – CHAPTER NINETEEN

There are few truly terrifying things in life, fortunately rare as gold coins: A wise man's fear; loss of one's self, when a good man goes to war. Of the those, I fear the third the most. When a good man is pushed to violence, he is unleashed. There is no atrocity, no act of horror beyond his reach. The walls he erects around his heart don't keep you out. They keep him in.

—D. Puskyn, Exile

Gen stumbled into the Dripping Bucket feeling like six miles of bad road on a five-mile stretch. The bleeding had stopped for the most part, though clotted scabs stuck to his clothing, pulling and cracking as he moved. In all, he'd prefer not to repeat the experience. But that was the way with life. The philosophers were fond of saying that you got what you needed, not what you wanted. Though, Gen wasn't sure he *needed* an ass-kicking every couple of days.

The Bucket was mostly empty this time of day, the combined stench of cold wax from snuffed candles, stale kvass, piss, and congealed grease hanging in the air like a teen's crusty blanket lurks beneath their bed. The career drunks needed pay in order to drink, after all. A vicious cycle, that. Work paid you and you paid the bar and then back to work so you could do it all over again. A snake eating its own tail. Or, more accurately, a snake trying for its tail and repeatedly ending up with a mouthful of ass.

On his way in, he passed a small dark-haired man nursing a mug of something black and foul. Gen spared him a glance and nearly lost a step. Pyotr. The debt-collector. The man didn't look up, however, too absorbed in the depths of his drink and whatever misery lay drowned within. One hand played with a gold band, turning it over and over. It made a simple clicking sound as it tapped against the rough wood of the booth's table.

An echo of something—sorrow, perhaps—triggered a cascade of memory.

The ring was cheap. That is to say, cheap by anyone else's standards, perhaps. But he'd not marry her without it. Not so much for tradition, but because he wanted her to see he could provide. He could afford the things she wanted, needed. He could keep his promises.

When the jeweler told him the price, Gen's heart nearly withered. He stood, staring in disbelief, mouth open. 40 koyln! He could feed himself and Irina for a year for that price! And yet... the way her eyes glittered when she'd seen it.

He'd trudged from the shop, hands in pockets. Another man, passing, clipped his shoulder, and he looked up. Small and dark, hair swept back, he flashed Gen a grin.

"You look as if someone's trod on your cat, tovarich! Did this man take you for a ride?"

Gen shook his head, half-paying attention as he tried to think of ways to raise the money. He moved to get around him. The little man stepped in front of Gen again.

"I can help," he said. A purse flashed before Gen's face, its weight evident.

Pyotr was indeed helpful. Magnanimous, even. In the end, he'd bought the ring. And found himself married to two people, the loan shark never far from his thoughts.

The tapping of the ring pulled him from memory. Surely this man had a family to feed as well? For the briefest of moments, Gen nearly felt sorry for him.

Cold logic dropped into place, followed by predator instinct.

He remembered animals like Pyotr wouldn't exist if such a thing as fair pay did.

He considered smashing the man's skull into his mug and slitting his throat with the ceramic pieces. He considered confronting him and laying down the law as only a Shkut man could. In the end, he decided to take the middle road. He kept walking, pretending as if he'd never seen the little weasel.

He pulled up a stool before the bar and laid a koyln down. The slab of meat calling itself a bartender, Shchukin, raised an eyebrow and continued cleaning the glass he held. Not big on words, Shchukin. Gen liked that in a man. Too much talking with these kids. Too much... everything these days.

Shchukin set the glass down, extracted the towel from inside, and filled it with something masquerading as vodka but smelling like the inside of a factory furnace.

Gen raised it. "Ura," he said and took a long swallow.

It tasted worse than it smelled but did the trick. A warm wave of pleasant numbing spread through Gen's limbs, easing the worst of his aches. Shchukin lifted his eyebrow again and brandished the bottle. Gen wasn't sure if it was a threat or an offer. He shrugged, and the bartender filled the glass.

Again, Gen took a drink, though smaller this time. Whatever the shit was, it had the distinct aftertaste of burnt flesh. He opened his mouth to ask and decided he didn't want to know.

"Old lady's been in here a couple times," Shchukin said.

Irina?

Gen swallowed the swell of anxiety and hope threatening to rise in his chest. "When was this?" he asked.

Shchukin squinted, brow furrowing like a landslide.

Like watching a mountain try to remember where it put the butter.

"Few days back," the bartender said.

Hope died like a bird on the wing, spiraling into the depths of his guts. She hadn't been back since their fight the night before, then.

Two nights?

That submission stick had done a number on him.

Gotta stop getting hit in the head, genius.

He took another shot of vodka. Shchukin spoke up again.

"That fight the other day. You did good. These boys need their skulls cracked once in a while."

Never said more than three words in all the years I've known him, and now he's a cult of personality.

Gen stared at him, puzzled. "What's this all about, Shchukin? Your lips are usually tighter than a babushka's asshole."

Shchukin winced.

Probably thought he was being subtle.

"We all saw who you left with. A Shkut man! You done good, Gen. Boy from the neighborhood, getting in with the Family. Makes people feel safer around here. Makes 'em feel like they've got a stake in the Filth now, like things might get better. Shit, the Bucket's hasn't had a blowup in days."

It was Gen's turn to wince. "Yeah, well. It's a job, and I'm only one man."

"Ah, but one man—give me a lever and a fulcrum large enough, and I can move the world, right?"

"Yeah, sure," Gen said. "You just have to be careful it doesn't roll over your foot."

Shchukin looked about to say something else, but fate or providence interrupted in the form of a man taking a seat to Gen's left.

Scents of wool and booze. Gunpowder. Sweat.

No blood, though, and he was thankful for that. He relaxed a fraction. The man to his left struck a match, the acrid stink of Sulphur flaring to life for a moment. He lit his cigareta and shook out the match, tossing it on the bar top.

Shchukin pushed a glass of something dark and amber over to him, and Gen turned to look at the man beside him.

Osip?

Ten thousand screaming men, standing at the lip of hell, and Osip looked no more perturbed than he did any other day. He ran a hand through his hair, lifted his rifle, and grinned at Gen.

"Good day for killing, yeah?" he said.

His accent lilted, hair straight and dark, eyes the color of muddy shadow.

The Altin Ordu, creeping through the snow like Solostian leopards, sprung forward, slick and silent. Or as silent as an Altin Ordu was able, wearing colors loud enough to set off an avalanche. The Kievan line rippled with the impact, slipping back and firing.

Altin Ordu went down like stalks of harvest corn.

Another wave, another salvo.

Then the rifles were empty or jammed, and the Kievans moved to knife and saber, maul and axe. Even taking five to their one, the Altin Ordu were outnumbered here, and eventually their line weakened, then snapped, survivors fleeing. Or attempting to.

An order from the back, the commissars repeating it for clarity.

Cut them down.

Osip, screaming something high-pitched and unintelligible, a knife in each hand, laying into the fleeing Altin Ordu line like a starving bear. Gen followed suit, teeth bared in a rictus grin. Slaughter. Hot, unending slaughter. The snow turned red. The earth unfroze just enough from the warmth. Mud sucked at their boots.

The Altin Ordu poured on speed, but it wouldn't be that easy.

Osip snatched at the bandolier on his chest, pulled away a sphere the size of an apple. Yanked the cap at the top. Hot fizzing filled the air. He threw it and—

An explosion. Parts of men raining everywhere. A cheer from the Kievans. More grenades made their way down the line. Altin Ordu detonated until the Kievan line could no longer reach them, and even then, the bloody earth at their heels erupted in celebration.

"How's the weather, sergeant?" Gen asked conversationally, over the rim of his glass.

Osip glanced around, realized Gen spoke to him. He blinked, as if trying to focus. A grin spread across his face like a cloud in water.

"Genndy Antonov! I'll be fucked sideways!"

Gen smiled and took the man's offered hand. His grip was strong but shook just a little all the same. Sadness dropped across Gen's heart like a passing shadow. He'd seen it before. Battle sickness. Men went to war. Sometimes they came back the same on the outside; sometimes with new scars rearranging their features like an earthquake reshapes a mountain. Inside, however, they all shared the same trait: a thick twisted wound across their soul. If a man is a book, as Lavrenti wrote, then war rewrote it from page one.

Gen let the handshake drop, and the smile slipped from Osip's face.

"What've you been up to lately, sergeant?" Gen asked.

Osip took a drag from the cigareta, exhaled smoke in a lazy blue-white plume. "This, that, the other. You know how it is. A man gives his all to his country, and his country asks him to bend over because the mouth has gone dry and a good soldier doesn't chafe his superiors."

Gen laughed.

"But you!" Osip gestured, then made a face. "I would say you look well, but it seems you've taken my metaphor perhaps a bit too literally. You haven't taken to fucking bears, have you?" Humor slipped away and concern writ itself across his features. He leaned in. "Are you well, brother?"

Gen took a slug of vodka and nodded. "Well enough."

Osip leaned back, sucked on the cigareta until the cherry glowed red. "Aren't we all. What are you up to these days?"

"Working for... invested people."

"Ah," Osip winked. "Family man."

Gen stared, blinking in disbelief at the quick deduction.

Osip laughed. "Obvious, brother. You've had your ass kicked, but in nice clothing." He took a drink, then squinted at Gen. "Do they treat you well?"

Tell him the truth. If an old soldier understands or appreciates anything, it will be that.

Gen hesitated, caught between an easy lie and the truth.

Osip nodded in the space of the silence, cigareta a stump between his lips. "Then why do you do the work? Ah—" he held up a hand. "Duty, no? You have a wife, a child, perhaps. A reason to break yourself? The money is good. I understand. Old soldiers—of which, there are few—you can teach new tricks. Vasily is an accountant. Penkin an administrative assistant, whatever the fuck that means. But you can never beat who we are out of us. What we will always understand, below the layers of clothing and skin and pretense, is blood and money make the world turn. And that is where we shine. We are survivors, my friend."

He finished his drink and slammed the glass on the countertop, then swept his hair back. "Now, if it were me, I'd find a way to take my share. But I understand, not everyone is about rocking the boat. Sometimes the easiest path is that of least resistance."

Easy path? Motherfucker—

Osip stood, interrupting the thought. He pulled his scarf tight, stopping to lay a hand on Gen's shoulder. "I suspect you'll have to make a choice, soon, tovarich. Family, or family. You know which I mean. I wish you luck."

He walked away. Gen counted to five, then called out to him.

"Osip."

The footsteps stopped, and Gen turned to find his old comrade waiting with a grin.

"Can you still find things? Like the old days?"

"What kind of things?"

Gen beckoned him over, then snagged a stub of pencil from Shchukin, scribbling a list on a napkin. He handed it over. "Hard to find."

Osip read, then nodded. "Meet me at the old watchmaker's tonight."

He tucked the paper away and scurried off. When he had gone, Shchukin raised an eyebrow. Gen waved it away.

"No, this is the first *good* idea I've had."

Shchukin shrugged.

"Trust me."

The bartender rolled his eyes.

"Smartass," Gen said. He finished his drink, dropped another koyln on the counter, and strolled from the bar and into the day.

The 'old watchmaker's' was once a respectable store at the end of the Scab, before the urban blight spread. Chenikov and Sons provided everything from pocket watches to grandfather clocks, with a light trade in illegal weaponry behind the counter. Now, it was just another burned-out shell, the militsiya long having raided it and put it to the torch, and the owners to the rope.

Night fell, and with it, the temperature. Gen stood just inside the doorway, watching the street.

Probably ratting you out. You haven't seen Osip in years. What makes you think he wouldn't use you for a dime and a kroc fix?

Gen ignored the voice. While likely true of most people he'd met, Osip was a different breed. No stranger to avarice or self-interest, true, but the man was certainly in it for more than pocket change. If he'd offered to help Gen, it was because he thought either the payday was good, there was mayhem to be had, or both.

Another hour passed in the dark, and Gen stomped his toes to put circulation back in them. Norylska groaned as cold set in, factories belching smoke into the sky. This city was like an old whore—stinking, cold, and diseased.

There. Behind us. The scent of tobacco. Tread of boot.

Gen spun, Bastard in his hand. He'd had the foresight to retrieve the blade from the chandler during his last visit. And despite the pain the movement brought, he felt more secure with a few inches of good steel in his hand.

Osip emerged from the shadows of the interior doorway, just past where the ceiling sagged like a pregnant sow. He raised his hands.

"I'm wound-free, thanks. I'd like to keep it that way." Gen sheathed Bastard, and Osip turned and disappeared back into the guts of the building. It didn't take long for Gen to catch up, though it was a surprise when he did. The former fixer had converted the back end of the watchmaker's, tearing out the floor and digging into the earth. It sloped down until they were below ground level, then the tunnel ran another twenty feet before opening into a spacious area that must've taken Osip months, if not the better part of a year, to dig out.

A table and chairs sat in the center, with workbenches against one wall. Against another, crates of weaponry and explosives of all shapes and sizes. Two men sat at the table, poring over a map. A third joined them shortly after a wooden bang echoed down the hall. Gen ducked back out for a moment and saw the light from above had been cut off. Osip had installed a false ceiling, to make it appear as if the watchmaker's had never been re-occupied.

The men took a seat at the table, with Osip at the head. He leaned back in his chair and lit a cigareta.

"It's a fine day for killing after all, isn't it, comrade?" he asked.

Gen grinned, then leaned over the table, looking at the maps Osip had secured. Floorplans of the Shkut estate, and relevant routes. Incredible work on such short notice.

Maybe. Maybe he was already up to something.

Not my problem.

"Let's begin," Gen said.

KATYUSHKA LEONOVA – CHAPTER TWENTY

Memories and traits can be stored on virtually any type of stone. The use of lesser stones, those softer and more prone to breakage and crumbling, is ill-advised. The harder and more structured the stone, the more accurately it can retain the complexities of personality and memory, and the longer the information will last. Inferior, less structured stones suffer degradation over time.

The wealthy of Kievan prefer to use the highest quality diamond for its quality of storage and longevity. Traits stored in diamond have been known to be perfectly retrievable hundreds, even thousands of years later.

'Street' stones are made from less expensive crystals or even everyday pebbles in truly desperate situations. Agate, kyanite, quartz, and obsidian are commonly chosen for their structure and relative inexpensiveness.

—Iskusstvo Veneficum

Fyodor wouldn't look at Kat as he rose from the floor, brushing himself off. Face set in a terrifying scowl she feared might erupt into violence, he glared undirected rage at everything but her. His clenched fists shook like he wanted to lash out, smash something. She'd never seen him so angry. Not a big man, she suddenly realized he was still more than capable of killing her.

Kat shrank back, moved to put the table between them.

Focussed on the floor, he didn't notice.

"There were five of them," he said. "You can't—" Lip curling he continued. "You can't fight five. If there was just one, that slimy little fucker, I would have killed him."

Liar.

He would have done nothing. The well-dressed man with the heavy eyes didn't need the rest of them. They were for show. He would have killed Fyodor in a heartbeat, shot him through the head with the revolver hidden in its underarm shoulder holster.

"He had a gun," she said. She hadn't noticed noticing, but now she spoke it aloud, she knew it to be true. She could almost tell him what kind it was, the name on the tip of her tongue.

"You were in danger," Fyodor said to the floor. "Vulnerable. If you weren't here, I would have taken the gun and killed them all."

Bullshit. You were too busy curling up on the floor to notice the gun.

She wanted to kick him like Antipov had.

"I know," she said instead. "I'm sorry."

Because once again it was her fault. It was her fault they came. It was her fault Fyodor hadn't been a hero.

"We have to go to the militsioners," he said. "We have to report this."

I am a militsioner. Kat crushed the urge to laugh.

Fyodor waved a hand at the mud and slush the men tracked through their home. "A fucking mess. We have to report this, and you have to quit. No more drinking and smoking. No more job. No more stones. No more pretending to be a man."

How about you pretend to be a man.

"I told you not to take this job and you ignored me." He managed to focus on her feet. "You did this to me. To us. This is your fault."

He was right. He was always right.

"You'll quit in the morning," he said, attention moving up, focussing on her stained knees. "I've been eating cold dinners and doing women's work and you're coming home drunk and smelling like men. Unacceptable. Your father would be so disappointed."

A maelstrom of emotion waged war in her chest, crushed her heart, made breathing difficult.

You don't own me! They weren't married. Demons below, they weren't even engaged!

"I can't," she said.

Finally meeting her eyes, he said, "You quit, or we're done."

She wanted to tell him to get the fuck out. She wanted to scream and rage, to smash his smug face. But she'd sunk so much time and energy into this relationship. Years. They were going to be married. They'd get out of the north, buy a real house and have children. She'd be a mother, the centre of the family the way her grandmother was. A few days ago, their future had been all potential and promise.

All the shit I tolerated would be wasted.

His late nights. Him coming home stinking of cigars and perfume. Why was it okay when he did it?

She wanted him to leave and yet was terrified of being alone. From a good family—at least by Norylskan standards—he'd soon be a partner in the law firm. They'd even talked about moving to Khagan in a few years. Kuznetsov and Alyokhin had branches in every city; they could live anywhere. Marrying Fyodor would be a step in bringing her own family name back into good standing. Her father would be proud.

If he leaves, I'll be stuck in this armpit forever.

Arms crossed, Fyodor waited.

Kat sagged with defeat. "I'll quit."

Wanting more, knowing she'd give it to him, he said nothing.

"Things will go back to normal," she said.

How? How could anything be normal now?

"But I have to give that man the stone. If I don't, they'll kill us. Both of us."

Whatever we're in, we're in this together.

"I'm going to stay with my parents until you've sorted out this insanity," he said. "As long as you're wearing those stones, and are doing gods know what with whom, I can't trust you. I can't be with you."

Liar. Coward. You're running away like you always do.

"When it's done," he said, grabbing his coat off the rack, "and you're once again my Katyushka, come and find me."

He left without another word.

"Your concern for my safety," she said to the closed door, "is truly touching."

She wanted to cry. That criminal treated her with more respect than Fyodor ever had.

Kat fetched Fyodor's cognac from the cupboard. Never having given it much thought, she laughed when she examined the bottle. It was expensive, costing nearly a week's groceries. Spinning the top off, she lobbed the cap in the general direction of the garbage.

Not gonna need that again.

Drinking from the bottle, she collected the lantern from the table and headed into the bedroom to hunt for cigareta. She found a pair of cigars in a sealskin pouch.

They look like fat dark cocks.

She bit one end off the cigar, spitting it into the corner, and lit the other from the lantern.

Kat retired to the bed to smoke and drink, ashing onto the floor when needed.

Shouldn't I be crying?

It seemed appropriate. Her life was falling apart. The man she loved was either going to leave her or already had.

'When it's done and you're once again my Katyushka, come and find me.'

Imperious motherfucker.

She drank.

What do you actually love about Fyodor?

He was handsome, had a good job. He'd be a good provider. With him, she'd have a stable, secure future. Children—though come to think of it, she couldn't imagine him as a father. Not that her own father had been much of one.

Maybe that makes Fyodor perfect. She laughed at the thought, spilling ash onto the bed.

"Fuck." Brushing it away with a careless sweep of her hand, she left a grey smear on his side.

I'll wash the sheets in the morning.

Why? Was he coming back? Did she want him to?

Kat smoked the cigar to a blunt, damp stump, crushing it out on the side table. At some point, the fire in the stove went out and the temperature fell. Cuddling the bottle, she crawled under the heavy blankets.

It was nice, quiet.

All her life she'd been surrounded by people. Each one had expectations she'd molded herself to conform to. Her teachers and classmates. Grandmother. Father. Fyodor.

"How do you know who you are," she asked the bottle, "if you've never been alone?"

The bottle had the answers; she drank them all.

Kat dreamed.

Stripped naked, arms chained above her, Kat knelt on the hard stone floor of an abandoned warehouse in the Scab. Lines of cold fire cut her sides where someone carved away strips of flesh.

Angular and bony, this wasn't her body.

Sheened in blood, she looked up at the man asking questions.

Delicious eyes, heavy and dark. He'd been handsome in her kitchen, but he looked different now. Maybe younger. But the changes weren't in him, they were in how she saw him.

Some people are what they are. No matter what you're wearing. But you, my dear, are someone entirely new.

"How did you figure who our man was in the department?" he demanded. "Were we sloppy?"

Something about the question bothered her.

Shouldn't he be asking who *the leak was?*

No, because he already knew. He only cared how she knew.

The other man, reptilian cold and twitching, darting snake-tongue, cut her again.

She wanted to scream that she didn't know but this wasn't her dream. She was caught in another man's nightmare.

Heavy eyes, lids dark, handsome face a handspan from hers like he was going to kiss her. "Tell me," he said. "Tell me and this can end."

But she knew if she told him, he'd kill her and destroy the stone.

Maks, where are you?

He was supposed to be here. He'd come. He'd save her.

Have to hold out a little longer.

They cut her again, peeled a sheet of skin back, left it hanging at her slim hips.

Maks. Please.

GENNDY ANTONOV – CHAPTER TWENTY-ONE

In orthodox Kievan religion, there are six hells—one for each vice: Avarice, Lust, Sloth, Vanity, Pride, and Gluttony. Notably missing is Wrath. Even more notably missing from the grouping under those sins is pure murder. Murder due to greed, lust, or any of the aforementioned is a damnable sin. Which is to say that in Kievan culture, murder via wrath is always justified. And state-sanctioned murder is always forgiven.

—D Puskyn, Exile

It cost Gen every last koyln of Arkady's gift to hire Osip and his men. While Osip may have been a friend and former brother in arms, the man was mercenary to his core. In the end, however, it left Gen with three solid—*Expendable*—soldiers, explosives, and a handful of cheap military stones for the men.

As a final precaution, Gen handed Osip a gold band, and in return received a stone of his own. Brutality and cold purpose were useful, but Gen needed an edge. Going outside the Family made him nervous in a way even the confrontation at the chandler's hadn't. If Arkady discovered he'd sourced a stone outside the Shkuts, there was no telling what the man might do. He might be able to pass off the destruction of one stone as a casualty of a fight, but the appearance of a new one? Harder, he thought.

The Families weren't big on motivation. All yours should come from the ones running it. 'Finding' a new stone meant you'd taken initiative. Taking initiative meant you were ambitious. And ambition meant you wanted someone's job, so better you disappeared in the snow than someone else find themselves demoted. Promotions came from above, after all. Not below.

Gen inspected the rock Osip had procured, holding it up to the light of a lantern hung against a wall. He'd told the man he needed something *exceptional*, but this looked like nothing more than colored glass. Osip assured him the stone was obsidian. In that, it seemed he'd been accurate. Glassy black with an occlusion where the facet turned nearly transparent, it looked like smoke frozen in rock inside. Its chain, silver, glinted in the light of the basement.

"Who's in here?" he asked.

Osip shrugged, plucked the cigareta stub from his lips. "An inmate. Some poor soul locked in the gulag." He gestured with the stump of his smoke, tendrils punctuating his words. "Why do you want something like that, anyway?"

Gen turned the stone to one side, then the other, watching light catch the black facets. Finally, he lowered it.

"Muddy the water. If they suspect anything, if anyone comes after me, tries to make me talk, I'll have this in my head."

Osip snorted. "Good plan. Insane, but good."

"Like your cooking."

Osip hiccupped a laugh. His borscht had been legendary for putting men in the infirmary due to intestinal trauma the next day.

The thought brought Irina's own cooking to mind. The heavy rye, dark as a moonless night on the tongue, her stew—savory, thick. A man could eat a bowl and easily skip the next couple meals. The thought brought a brief smile to his lips as a memory surfaced.

"Genndy Antonov!" she'd admonished him.

Gen looked up from the bowl of stew he'd demolished, puzzlement writ on his features. What could I have done?

"Did you even taste it?"

He gestured feebly with his spoon. "It hit my tongue on the way down."

She tsked and took a sip of her own, the bowl still three-quarters full. He tapped his fingers on the table, looking longingly at the pot on the stove, still steaming, still filling the kitchen with the scent of heaven.

She sighed in exasperation. "Go, get more."

Gen practically leapt from his chair, hastily scooping the thick gravy and meat into his bowl. It was a rare treat to have seconds when you had to make a budget stretch, and he wasn't going to waste the opportunity.

Bowl full, he charged back to his seat, tearing off a hunk of bread and sopping it in the gravy. He tore into it with gusto. Irina snorted, then burst into laughter.

"Use a spoon, you godsdamned auroch!" she teased.

"You hear me?" Osip asked, breaking into the memory.

Gen blinked, shook it off. "No, sorry. Thinking."

"Mmhm."

Osip turned out to be a font of information in regard to stones. There was little the man didn't traffic, and he had a near-encyclopedic knowledge of illicit goods. He paused from packing a wad of explosives into a satchel.

"You know what you're getting into with that?" he asked, pointing to the stone still dangling from Gen's hand.

"Some idea."

Osip snorted. "The basics, then. That is a stone crafted by a master veneficum. I don't deal in half-measures. The man on that stone is a nightmare. Let me give you a rundown.

"At Mirmysk, he'd disposed of an entire village after the state learned of Altin Ordu infiltrators. You know Kievan philosophy: Better a thousand dead innocent Kievans than a single living insurrectionist.

"At Cherblynka, he'd overseen camps where Altin Ordu prisoners were stripped of their selves, then the hollow flesh burned down for tallow. The pile of stones was said to have filled an entire paracera cart.

"At Red Pass, he'd investigated rumors of an entire battalion going cannibal. Then recruited them into the Office of Strategic Defense. People missing in the neighborhood? Probably a hungry militionser.

"After, he crafted the stories the state used to ply the minds of the public. Mirmysk: bad well water. Cherblynka: a plague—the bodies had to be burned. Red Pass: rumors put forth by the Altin Ordu menace—the morality of the Kievan man remains unassailable.

"Each incident, an atrocity. Each atrocity, a patriotic gesture. He was the right hand of the Tsar, the knife in the dark.

"The man was a war criminal, Gen. A sadist. That's who you'll be sharing space with. It's not just memory. You wanted to confuse anyone tracking you—this is the stone."

Gen looked down at the obsidian dangling from his hand. The war made everyone criminals. Why would this be any different?

"How's it work?" he asked.

"When you put it on, he's going to slam into you. Two minds in the same space. It'll be unpleasant. You might experience drift—the moment when one personality fights for dominance over the other. You'll definitely experience bleed—it can't be helped. Your man in there is whole. He's going to want to ride along. Hell, he might not even let you take the stone off in the end.

"You still want it?"

Gen thought on it. If he wanted to win this fight, he needed every weapon he could pull. Especially the unexpected ones. He needed the little brunette milistioner from the Bucket to trust him so he could pull this plan off. And that meant thinking like someone else.

Coming to a decision, he nodded.

"I'm ready."

Osip sighed, made a dismissive gesture. "Your funeral."

He went back to packing the explosives.

Gen sat cross-legged on a rough mattress one of Osip's men dragged in from only gods knew where. With deliberate slowness, Gen lowered the chain over his head. The stone came to rest against his chest, alongside the others.

It was cold.

Cold like iron in winter.

Cold like the grave.

It spread from the stone, crackled in his veins, rimed his bones, speared his heart.

A tremor built in his guts, rising to a crescendo like a wave reaching its crest. He shook and fell to his side, teeth chattering, blood-flecked foam pooling at the corner of his mouth as some small vein in his guts ruptured with the churn of muscle. It tasted of seawater and iron. Vision winked out like a hood pulled over a lantern.

A barrage of half-formed images and sensations—skinned men and women, children little more than burned husks on the tundra, the taste of flesh, the stink of Khagan alleys—assaulted him. Something cold and clinical pressed against his mind, looking for cracks like water seeks to seep into a dam.

Gen fought back, imagining his thoughts a seamless wall, his person unassailable, barbed and aflame.

Finally, the attack ceased, the intruder conceding a stalemate. The room came into focus, Osip kneeling beside him. He offered Gen a tumbler of water. Despite it being warm, Gen drank the glass down. It cooled the fever in his throat, the raw sensation indicating someone had used his alimentary canal as a tunnel, crawling along it with sharpened knives. He leaned back and closed his eyes.

A presence pushed into his head, unsubtle, determined. It rifled through his memories, shuffled his thoughts.

You're a bit of a disappointment.

Gen winced at the voice.

"Are you well, comrade?" Osip asked.

Gen opened his mouth to reply that he was the opposite. Whatever Osip had brought him seemed to be poisoned.

Tell this man nothing. I am poison only to those who reject me.

He bit off his reply, cleared his throat. "Fine, thanks. Drift was bad."

Osip nodded, took his seat at the table again.

"How long was I out for?" Gen asked.

His voice rasped against his tongue.

"Several hours. It is night now. Should we wait?" Osip asked.

Gen frowned. "For what?"

"You to recover."

"I'm fine." To prove it, he pushed to his feet.

The room doubled for a split-second, brown clay of earthen walls becoming rigid granite all around. Steel bars blocked the exit. Blood trickled in rivulets down the hall outside. Then it vanished, and Osip and his plain, unbloodied hideout lay before Gen again.

Osip watched him, then nodded. "You should get back if we want to do this before dawn, then. We'll follow behind."

"An hour after I arrive. No sooner, or they'll think I'm up to something."

"Yes, yes, I know. Now go, tovarich."

Gen nodded and found his way from the hideout, one of Osip's underlings opening the way into the watchmaker's. Above, it was as it always had been—a broken shell. Outside, night came clear and cold. His breath made frosted plumes in the air and the stars threatened to cut swathes from the black, so sharp were their points.

Do you know this song?

A melody began in Gen's head, and he whistled as he walked. Snow crunched underfoot, a percussive counterpoint. He was never so happy as when he was about to pull off a plan.

Is that my joy? My song?

Yes? No? Maybe he was being paranoid. Bleed didn't work that quickly, did it? Yeah, paranoia.

Yeah, that's all.

The tune died on his lips, and Gen made his way back to the Shkut mansion in silence.

Irina played through his head like a zoetrope in the rickety cinema on Puskyn Way. Irina, dancing in the snow. Irina, her face taking up his sight, cool hands to each side of his head, a slight curl to her lips. Irina, fierce, hands on her hips, eyes like black coals, an ember in each tiny fist.

Irina, Irina, Irina.

A litany.

An accusation.

The slight swell of her belly filled with child, the curve of her calves, the arch of her back. The smell of her neck in summer—soap and sweat and some indefinable scent, of a day's work cutting and cooking and laboring. Vegetable, bread, and broth. Sex and hunger.

Sustenance in the dark.

You mourn as if she has passed.

Might as well have.

A shame. Attachment brings sorrow. Sorrow is a crack in the heart. And in Kievan, ice forms in the cracks, forces the foundation apart. Breaks a man as surely as wedge and hammer splits rock.

Shut up.

The voice quieted. Gen stalked past dark homes, quiet alleys. The cold kept all but the most enterprising criminal out. He supposed, in that, he might be found admirable.

When did this happen?

What? When did what happen? This slide into what he'd become? The war, perhaps. Maybe sometime after. He'd been happy for a time. Or thought he was. Determined to make an honest living. Raise a family, be a father unlike the one he'd known. Open hand over clenched fist. He'd nearly succeeded. Maybe would have, had he not met Arkady.

The rasp of scale on stone. The low rumble of growl.

Melancholy dulled, lost its edge. In its place, anger.

This, I know.

You know loss? You are just a monster.

Monsters are people too. You need me. Here, a gesture of goodwill.

A flood of imagery. *A shack in the Filth, laundry flapping from frayed lines in the meagre yard. A man approaching. A woman, running out to greet him, hair gold, frame slight, lips stretched in joy. The man, pulling up short, the smile of recognition falling like a dropped stone.*

The scene flickered.

The interior of the shack. The woman hung from a ceiling beam by a hook through her ankles. A crying child on the floor. The man, sharpening a blade.

Another flicker.

Blood, a pool. Child's fingers dipped in it. Bone and fat glistening in a fly-blown heap. The child, fingers in its mouth, red around the lips.

The image faded. Gen found himself leaning against a wall, breath coming in ragged gasps. Tears stung his eyes.

Who?

My mother. Not all monsters are born. Some are made.

Gods below.

This is what they do.

Not my Irina.

No, not your Irina. Not with my help.

Gen sucked in a cleansing breath, pushed off the wall. His step quickened. In his chest, purpose. In his head, ice sharp as razors.

KATYUSHKA LEONOVA – CHAPTER TWENTY-TWO

Nothing drives progress like war. Even an art as venerable and well-studied as that of the veneficum has room to evolve. Early in the last war it was discovered the entirety of a man could be stored on stones constructed of what amounted to compacted mud. While there was considerable loss, and the decay rate of the stored memories was devastating, it was found such stones could be dissolved in water and then imbibed by a subject (host). In many cases the personality stored on the stone (parasite) was able to subsume that of the host. Typically, the parasitical personality slowly lost control as it was filtered, urinated, and defecated by the host.

The practice was the basis of an incredibly successful campaign of assassinations and political manoeuvres leaving the intact host to suffer the consequences.

—Aleksandr Shelepin, Chairman of the SSU (Sekretnaya Sluzhba Ubiystv) 1537-1539

"Fuck me," said a splintered voice.

Kat opened one eye. The other, crusted closed, didn't budge. She peered blearily about the bedroom.

Who said that?

No one. She was alone.

"Fuck me," she repeated to make sure the voice was hers.

It was.

Tangled in the blankets, she held the cognac bottle clutched to her chest like a baby. The lantern sat dead and accusing on the side table. She'd left it lit and it burned through near two days' worth of oil as she slept.

"Fff…"

Fuck it. Too much effort.

Still holding the bottle, she levered herself into a sitting position. The room tilted, turned with a gut-wrenching twist, and she vomited all over Fyodor's side of the bed.

Justice.

Justice stank and left an awful aftertaste.

Pushing the sheets away, she stared at the crust of ash and mud staining the front of her long skirt. Had she taken off the wool leggings she wore beneath at some point during the night? They were nowhere to be seen.

Gods above it's cold in here.

The stove had gone out hours ago. Only the residual warmth of the iron saved the room from freezing.

Kicking her way out of the skirt, a titanic battle she almost lost, Kat found her knees bruised and scraped. Her right shoulder hurt, a bone-deep ache at the base of her neck. Climbing from the bed, she huddled the blanket about her shoulders and staggered to the mirror. Stared, blinking, at the huge bruise.

"Are those teeth marks?"

Kat leaned closer, trying to make her eyes and brain cooperate.

"Those are fucking teeth marks."

Rather than think about what that might mean, she headed for the kitchen.

Load wood into stove. Kindling. Twigs. One log. All one-handed as the other kept the blanket in place. Hunt for matches, one eye still gummed closed. Spot the eggs Fyodor made last night. Cold, cheese congealed.

"Food," she said, grabbing a handful of egg and jamming it into her mouth.

Nothing ever tasted so good.

What was she… matches. Right.

Find matches. Light fire one-handed.

Stare at flickering wisps of flame, watch them wink out.

"Fuck."

The wastefulness of requiring more than a single match to light a fire angered Fyodor. He'd spend half an hour carefully constructing the layers, making sure everything was perfect. Then, when everything met approval, he'd light a half dozen different spots around the kindling with that single match. *One match,* he'd say with such pride. Like he'd managed the fucking impossible. Like he deserved an award or something.

More matches. More cursing.

"Fire!" she croaked when it finally lit.

Kat returned to the table, sat before the gelid eggs. Shovelling them into her mouth, she grinned in vodka-numbed contentedness. Simple. Empty.

"Numb dumb," she said, laughing. Fucking chair was freezing. "Numb dumb cold bum."

This was so much better than feeling.

After melting snow on the stove, she scrubbed her face until she could open the other eye. Dunking her head, she rinsed the crusted vomit from her hair.

It was funny, really. Her life was either falling apart, or already had. One of the biggest crime families in Norylska threatened to skin her alive. To make them go away, she'd have to steal a memory stone from the state, which would result in being shot in the head. Instead of fear or horror, or any of the sane emotions attached to being doomed, all she really felt was horny. And she wanted to shop. She wanted a good grinding fuck, and then wander the nicer markets in the Square of the Founders.

Eggs finished, Kat stared at the empty plate. Fyodor's family gave them that collection when they moved in together. She pushed it away. Kept pushing until it fell off the side of the table and shattered on the floor.

Putting another log in the stove, opening the flue so it burned hot and fast, she returned to the table.

"What am I going to do?"

What if she left Norylska? Pack a few essentials and hire a carriage to take her away. Kayerkan was the nearest town, but it was west. The men hunting the megafauna Kievan burned for oil used it as a stopover before returning to Norylska. She'd heard trappers say that if Norylska stank, Kayerkan was like having your head halfway up a three-week-dead paraceratherium's ass.

She wanted to go south, all the way to Khagan. Snezhnogorsk, the nearest town to the south, was two weeks away.

I have no money.

Fyodor, being the man, took care of everything, kept it all in the bank. Each week he gave her what she needed to buy groceries. He always talked about how near 'the ragged edge' they were, but then had money for cognac and cigars.

I can't afford to hire a carriage to take me to the southern gate, much less to Snezhnogorsk.

"I'm a prisoner of economy." A line from some play she saw at school.

Women might take factory and office jobs in Khagan, but it wasn't the case here. This was Norylska, the old world. This was the last place change reached. When her family left the capital, the Tsar had recently announced gas lines would run through the entire city to light the streets at night. That was several years ago. She imagined well-lit streets, no drunken sootmen climbing poles to refill the hanging lanterns.

All women are prisoners of economy.

Except for those women running the crime families. How strange that was. It had always been that way, but she had no idea why.

Gotta start my own crime Family.

Right. Katyushka Leonova, master criminal.

The old man working the fresh grocer once undercharged Kat. She brought it to his attention rather than risk the guilt of a free potato.

Anyway, she'd soon be too busy getting skinned alive and shot in the head to start a crime Family. Then there was the fact most of the crime families had ties to the Tsars. Most were either related to previously deposed Kievan rulers or were extended family of Tsar Khromov. Rebel poets and self-proclaimed intellectuals said the Khromov family were nothing more than the most successful criminals.

"Focus," Kat told herself. "You have two choices."

Take the memory stone to the Shkuts and get a bullet in the brain. Tell the militsioners what happened and be skinned alive.

She couldn't run.

Fyodor, no doubt cowering in some brothel, was no help at all.

Her father? She didn't have time to wait for him to sober up enough to understand what was happening.

"I need help."

Three men came to mind: Colonel Grinin, Maksim Tkatchenko, whom she'd been partnered with, and Veneficum Lazarev.

What if she went to Grinin?

"He'd think this was all my fault and make sure I couldn't take the memory stone."

In a few days the sootmen would find her skinned and frozen corpse in a snowdrift. Or maybe in the spring. That's when they found most of them. Gods, how many weren't unlucky drunks? How many of the stiff dead were left there by one of the crime families?

Probably most.

"What about Maksim?"

She remembered her first day. Instead of taking her directly to the veneficum, he'd dragged her to the Dripping Bucket. He drank and smoked before noon, joked about taking bribes, and showed no respect for the work of the militsioners. He was everything her grandmother warned her about in bad men, too handsome and sure of himself by far.

"Fine," she said. "Lazarev seems nice."

He listened, seemed to genuinely care about the militsioners wearing his stones. He'd want to help.

"Yeah, he'll *want* to help."

Sad as it was, that was still better than her other two options.

Decision made, Kat rose from the table and returned to the bedroom.

Tossing the blankets atop the vomit to hide both the sight and the smell, she dressed.

She never did find her wool leggings from the day before.

The eastern sky brightened as she walked, turning pale and sickly yellow with no promise of warmth. Another storm blew in as she slept, dregs of it still falling. Snow hid the woodpile from sight, piled thigh-deep in the narrow alley between their shack and the neighbor's. Shoving through, she stumbled into the street. Though the sootmen crews had already been through, grey drifts reached past her ankles.

Kat headed north, stepping in the boot prints of those who had gone before.

The more she thought about it, the more she realized she might be overreacting, worrying about nothing. All militsioners wore memory stones. It made sense criminals wanted to get their hands on the stones of those who witnessed a crime. Destroy the stone, destroy the evidence.

This must happen all the time.

No doubt the Shkuts assumed she was naive and gullible and would hand over the stone without a fight.

I'll talk to Lazarev. He'll know what to do.

They'd send a team of militioners to get the bad men and bring them in. She'd stay somewhere safe until they were all locked up. Once that was done, she could quit. No one would blame her.

By this time tomorrow, everything will be back to normal.

Fyodor could crawl out from whichever rock he was cowering under.

She'd have to clean up before he came home.

Shit. That fucking plate.

He probably wouldn't notice.

She arrived at the Chernyshevsky Street Militsiya Bureau before the morning-shift militsioners. Skipping the locker room, she headed straight to Lazarev's office.

Penkin answered, blocking the doorway with his damp dislike. "You're early."

So clean shaven his face looked raw, dressed in a crisply ironed suit, he looked all too awake and alert.

She hated him. "I need to see Lazarev."

"*Veneficum* Lazarev, is busy.

"Then I'll wait."

"Agreed," he said, beginning to close the door.

Kat jammed a foot in the way. They both stared at it in shock, her more surprised than he.

"I'll wait in your office."

"That's hardly—"

"No," she said, "I don't mind."

"I don't think—"

She shoved past him like he was nothing. Rather than risk contact with a woman, he retreated.

"Oh look," she said, spotting a tray with a steaming mug of coffee and a pile of pryaniki, those honey spice cookies her grandmother used to make. "Did you make those?"

Caught between denial, pride, and anger, Penkin hurried after her. "They're for Veneficum Lazarev."

"Not to worry," she said, "I'll bring it to him." Collecting the tray, she turned on the assistant. The mug sloshed dangerously. "Careful. Don't bump me or I'll spill."

Eyes wide with horror, Penkin raised his hands like she'd pulled a weapon.

"Get the door, would you?" Kat asked, adding, "Thanks," before he answered.

Penkin pushed the door open and she entered Lazarev's office.

The veneficum stood at one of his desks scowling at the heaped paper like he'd lost something. Glancing up, he blinked at her in surprise. "My coffee. I was beginning to wonder if he'd bring it before it got cold."

"I didn't want you to burn your lips again!" Penkin called over Kat's shoulder.

With one foot she kicked the door closed on the assistant.

Taking the mug, Lazarev nodded his thanks. "Penkin treats me like I'm a senile invalid," he grumbled, taking a sip. "Ow, that's hot!" Depositing the mug on one of the desks, he spilled coffee over a pile of yellowing paperwork. Turning his attention to the pryaniki, he examined each with a critical eye. "The best ones are soft on the inside," he explained, "but sometimes Penkin overbakes them. Lift the tray a bit, would you?"

Kat did as instructed.

"Now," he said, "see how the glaze is uneven? That's actually a good thing. The thicker parts will give you more of the honey flavour, but the thinner areas are more likely to caramelize. My mother used to make these every Novogodnyaya. Penkin makes them whenever he wants to ask for a day off. I hate to say it," he flashed her an embarrassed glance, "but Penkin's are better. A hint of ginger, a dash of vanilla and nutmeg. He's a fastidious and pompous little shit, but he makes the best pryaniki." Selecting one, he popped the whole thing into his mouth. "And I have no idea where he finds vanilla in Norylska," he said around the cookie.

Lazarev took the tray from Kat, lifted it in offering.

Selecting a pryaniki, she tried a small nibble. It was honeyed heaven.

"I bet he gets a lot of days off," she said.

"Far more than Grinin knows about." Turning away, he found a stack of papers to balance the tray on. "I must have lost track of time. Is there much of a line in the hall?"

"I'm early," she admitted. "Sorry."

"Nonsense." Lazarev waved her apology away. "I rarely get to share my cookies. Militsioners are..." He shrugged. "They get oddly uncomfortable when you offer them treats reminding them of home and better days. That handsome Maksim Tkatchenko cried like a little boy when I gave him one of Penkin's homemade churchkhela. Now he won't even look me in the eye. Like having emotions is a weakness. Or at least expressing them in front of another. Though perhaps he's different with you?"

Was he? After that one morning in the Dripping Bucket, he acted like they'd never met.

Technically, I guess we never have.

It felt like there were two Katyushkas: The one she knew—the quiet and well-behaved Kat she'd been her entire life, and the one who drank and smoked and came home late. Gods above, she wanted to be that Kat right now!

"I suppose," said Lazarev, "if you're here early it's because you want to talk about something? I can't tell you how refreshing it is to finally have a militsioner on staff willing to make use of my services."

Unsure, terrified of what the veneficum might say, who he might report this conversation to, Kat hesitated.

Tell him. Tell him everything.

There was no way criminals had never tried to get hold of a militsioner's memory stone. That was probably why Lazarev gave that speech about being shot as a traitor to the state.

The man with the heavy eyes found it particularly amusing when she mentioned her fear of being shot. He probably heard that all the time. His reaction had been strange, however: *We often bite our own ass.*

Was that some strange way of saying, 'We are our own worst enemy'?

"I need to tell you something," Kat said, straightening her shoulders.

Lazarev waited with calm patience.

But what to say? She had no idea why the bad men wanted the memory stone because she couldn't remember anything that happened while she wore it.

I'll be able to explain everything if I can tell him why they want the stone. Once she had it on, she'd understand the reason for last night's visit. *Stupid, really, to try and discuss this without knowing everything.*

"If I could have my memory stone for a moment?" She looked past the veneficum, at the closed vault door. There were two necklaces in there, on the shelf with her name. Gods, she wanted the second one. Confidence. Bravery. Whatever else was on there.

"For a moment?" asked Lazarev, rising and heading to the vault. "Aren't you about to start your shift? Have I come in on the weekend again?"

"And the personality stones, if you don't mind," said Kat, only half-listening to the veneficum's prattle.

Lazarev stopped, back turned to Kat, one hand on the door. "Are you sure? The trait stones are meant as support when on-shift, to help you though dangerous situations. They're ill-suited to open communication between patient and veneficum."

On one hand, she saw the logic. A trait to help you face down a danger-ous criminal might hinder other situations. But how could honesty and bravery be an issue when having a difficult conversation?

Lazarev opened the vault door and Kat spotted her stones. She wasn't sure why she'd assumed honesty and bravery were among them. Maybe there was no place for such in law-enforcement. What if militsioners needed to bend the law in order to effectively enforce it?

I might not be brave, but no one ever accused me of being dishonest.

At least not before Fyodor accused her of having an affair at work.

I would never!

She might not know what she did while wearing the memory stone, but she knew who she was.

You know who you were.

Once the trait stones were on, she had no idea what kind of person she became.

"Yeah," she said, following Lazarev into the vault. "I need the personality stones too. Actually, can I have them first?"

Pulling on his leather gloves, Lazarev collected her stones. He held out the traits necklace.

Accepting it, she slid it around her neck, half expecting a sudden rush of strange emotions.

Nothing.

"Are you alright?" asked Lazarev.

"I expected there to be more," she admitted.

"Personality separates us from animals, us from one another. It's no surprise we think of it as being this big thing. In truth, we're more similar than we are separate. Those people who are truly different can't fit in. They live in mud huts in Taymyr Forest. They're the ones the sootmen find drunk in alleys or dead in a snow drift. The rest of us..." he lifted one shoulder in a half-shrug.

Kat considered Fyodor's self-centred distance and her own need to please. Lazarev's kindness and Penkin's smug loathing. Helping herself to another pryaniki, she said nothing.

The veneficum offered the memory stone necklace. "Is everything ok?"

A moment ago, she'd been ready to spill everything. She only wanted the personality stones to give her the courage to say what needed to be said. Now, she wondered if she was making a terrible mistake. Maybe she'd be better off dealing with this herself. She could give the stones to that handsome and well-dressed criminal.

Fyodor has money. She was suddenly sure he'd been tucking funds away for years. Probably since before they met. She'd get it out of him and use it to get out of Norylska.

Lazarev asked you a question.

"I'm not sure," she admitted, confused by the conflicting emotions and desires.

Kat took the necklace, studying the rock at the end of the chain.

Who are you?

She wasn't sure who she was talking to—herself—or the memories trapped within.

Donning the necklace, sliding the cold stone under her shirt, she realized she was an unbelievably naïve idiot. Grabbing another pryaniki, she jammed the whole thing into her mouth to buy time to think.

The sweet cookie turned to sodden ash in her mouth.

That was Arkady. Arkady was at my fucking house.

The Shkut avtorityet knew where she lived.

They knew the firm Fyodor works for, she remembered.

They knew everything about her.

The dream that wasn't a dream. Arkady watching Ushakov, the Shkut Family torturer, peel the skin from her ribs. No, from Kostas' ribs.

Bleed. She'd heard about that. Sometimes memories and traits stored in stone stayed with the wearer for a while after the stone was removed.

'How did you figure who our man was in the department?' Arkady had asked Kostas.

To think she'd considered taking the stone straight to the Shkut without telling anyone!

He'll kill me the instant he has the stone.

She knew she was right. Or half-right.

He'll torture me first, to make sure I've brought the right stone.

He'd kill her after.

Perhaps a few years younger, the Arkady from her dreams—the Arkady Kostas remembered—was the same man she met in her kitchen. And yet he was so different. Where she saw an Altin Ordu Prince with heavy eyes, Kostas saw a cold-blooded killer of men. Sure, while he found the Shkut avtorityet attractive, slim and fit, he focussed on totally different aspects. She saw dark eyes and re-fined features. Kostas saw slim hips and a slight curve to his spine Kat hadn't even noticed.

The militsioner whose stone she wore had known Arkady for years. But when Kat met him, she saw someone entirely new.

Some people are what they are. No matter what you're wearing. But you, my dear, are someone entirely new.

"Are you sure you're alright?" asked Lazarev, interrupting her thoughts. "You seem distracted."

Grabbing Lazarev's coffee, she washed down the cookie.

Arkady came to her house and demanded the stone. That not only meant he knew where she lived, it meant he knew whose stone she wore.

"Sorry," she said, replacing the mug on the desk. "Thought I was going to choke."

Lazarev looked unconvinced but didn't push.

Only three men knew I was going to be in that alley: Maks, Colonel Grinin, and Lazarev.

She studied the veneficum. He waited with patience.

But how many know whose stone I wear?

Maks suspected, she was sure. And everyone reported to Colonel Grinin.

She had to trust someone, right?

The fuck you do.

"I better get to work," she said, grabbing another pryaniki and heading to the door.

Lazarev watched her leave with a look of bemused tolerance like her grandmother always wore when Kat explained whatever insane thing she wanted to try next.

Passing through the veneficum's office, she let herself out, closing the door behind her. Penkin, bent over a stack of papers he was rearranging, ignored her. His shirt hung open and she caught sight of the necklace within. He wore a half dozen stones.

Gods, if this was his personality after being improved by Lazarev, she shuddered to think what he'd be like without them.

Exiting Penkin's office, she ran into Maks. His hair, never neatly brushed, was a disaster.

He stood frozen, hand reaching for the doorknob, blinking at her. "Sorry. I didn't know—that is—I thought—"

She'd been so focussed on Arkady's visit and figuring out who she could trust, she'd given no thought to the previous day.

"Oh my fucking gods," Kat said, as it came rushing back.

"Sorry?" said Maks.

Kneeling in the snow before him, his hands tangled in her hair.

Against the wall, leggings at her knees, skirt bunched at her hips as he knelt behind her.

Savage grinding need crushing thought.

He took her from behind.

'Bite my neck,' she commanded. He obeyed. 'Harder. Bite harder you fucking pustyak.'

"We fucked in the alley behind the Dripping Bucket," said Kat.

"That didn't take long," muttered Penkin, somewhere behind her. "What, two days? Three?"

She ignored the assistant.

"Um," said Maks, backing away. "Do I know you?"

GENNOY ANTONOV — CHAPTER TWENTY-THREE

To the criminal elements of Norylskan society, planning further than a week in advance is as alien a concept as true loyalty, charity, or service. In the Families, one knows neither the hour nor day of their demise, but it said it is closer than the death they expect.

— D Puskyn, Exile

Lia and Dmitry greeted Gen at the door of the mansion. An odd enough occurrence in itself, made odder still by Arkady's absence.

"Where is—" Gen began.

Trepidation ran through him, alongside a thrill of fear. Did they know already? Had Osip turned coat so easily, or perhaps one of his men?

Lia smiled, cutting the train of thought off. The brilliance of it dazzled him, sucking him into the undertow of her personality. "The prodigal son returns!" she said.

Dmitry clapped him on the shoulder. "Arkady has retired to his quarters. But he told us of your deeds in regards to the militsiya! Boris himself could not have done better."

Gen glanced around, looking for the Shkut assassin. Relief must've shown on his face at the man's absence, because Lia laughed, a light, tinkling thing.

"No, he is not here."

"Who?" Gen asked, feigning innocence.

Lia tsked. "It is no secret the man dislikes you. He's inspecting the guards. One must give the wolf tasks, lest it devour the sheep." She put an arm around Gen's shoulders, skin warm and soft where it brushed against the back of Gen's neck. She leaned close, lips leaving a trail of raised flesh and hair in the proximity of their wake. Her breath hot against his ear, making his skin tight. "A boon for our favored son."

She smelled of vanilla and musk, and despite himself, Gen found he had an erection at the combination of her closeness and scent. She noticed its pressure against her thigh and released him, laughing again.

"You must learn to relax. You wouldn't be the first man in this Family I've fucked."

Gen blushed, and she walked away, heels clicking on the stone floor. Dmitry gave Gen a friendly wink and followed close behind.

"Come," she said, beckoning. Gen waited a moment, then trotted to catch up.

Lia led Gen to a yet another part of the mansion he hadn't visited. As they went, he wondered at the size and sprawl of the place. If the families kept homes like these, what must the Tsar and his ministers live like?

Sparse and utilitarian, the wing lay behind a solid door in the wall. The floors were simple poured stone, the walls brick. They passed what looked to Gen like several cells, coming to a stop at a door identical to all the others. Lia paused, and turned back to Gen, Dmitry posting up beside the door.

"I have a present for you, Genndy Antonov. Rather, Arkady has a present for you, but I insisted on presenting it to you."

What game is this?

A play. For power, perhaps. To reel you in deeper. To indebt you to the Family. Or a simple demonstration. The best motives are the ones you do not discover until it is too late.

As if they'd rehearsed it, when she finished her speech, Dmitry opened the door. The interior of the room was small by the standards of the mansion. Perhaps ten by ten. In the center, a simple chair, and bound to it, a naked man.

Holy fuck.

"Holy fuck," Gen said.

Pyotr, the debt collector.

They'd worked him over a little, as one tenderizes meat. His hair was disheveled, and a trickle of blood ran from the corner of his mouth. One eye swelled in a purple goose egg, and his nose whistled when he breathed. Upon seeing Gen, he opened his mouth to say something. Lia cleared her throat, and the man blanched, snapping his lips shut.

"He had the poor taste to approach Arkady, looking to settle your debt. Now, that's not unheard of, for a collector to contact a man's employer. But Arkady had already made it clear Pyotr here was not to trouble either of you. So, here we are."

Ah, a woman after my own heart. I wonder how this man will bleed? I wonder if it excites her as it does me?

Gen found he was still hard. He growled internally. The only response in return was laughter from the voice.

The sound of wood scraping against stone brought Gen out of his fascination with the man held captive. He looked round. Dmitry stood behind another chair he'd brought in.

"Please, sit," Lia said.

Gen blinked, backed up a step. She laughed again.

"Oh, my dear, sweet Gen. You are perfectly safe. Sit."

Fuck no. Trust? Insanity.

A brief flash of intense paranoia rushed through Gen. On its heels, recollection not his own, of being called into an office. There had been a chair there, as well. When he woke, it had been replaced with the cold stone floor of the gulag.

He pushed the feeling down and sat anyway, the newcomer in his head running a stream of invective at his blind trust. Lia shrugged from her coat, Dmitry pulling it from her and folding it over his arm. Her arms and back were toned and muscular. She rolled her head from side to side, then reached to her back pocket, pulling on a pair of white fingerless gloves. The knuckles bulged with padding.

Lead-lined.

"Despite what you may think of the Family," she began, "we check up on our people. We want to know what kind of men we hire. Now, Pyotr here," she circled his chair. His eyes widened, whites nearly obscuring his iris. "Thinks you're unreliable."

She shot a quick rabbit punch into the back of the man's skull. His head rocked forward, and a cry of pain erupted from his lips.

Sloppy. Risks unconsciousness.

"I think that's disrespectful."

She made another circuit of the chair, and her fist lashed out a second time, smashing into his face. The swelling around his eye burst, sending a torrent of blood down his cheek, slipping down his neck, staining his chest hair.

"Behind him again.

Yes! Better! Hare him. Let the fear and pain build! This is artistry.

"I think it's an insult to the entire Family," she punctuated this with a punch to the base of his neck. He screamed. "After all, we chose you."

Another punch, and his ear burst into a bloody cauliflower.

Ah, too much force again. She is erratic. Interesting, but risky. As in all things, the application of misery must be precise.

"We trust you."

She grabbed Pyotr's shoulder, put one hand on his other to steady her grip, and yanked. The arm dislocated with a sickening pop.

Oh Gods, she's mad.

"We love you," she said, and dislocated the other shoulder.

Bravo!

Pyotr trembled in the chair, snot running from his nose, mixing with blood from his eye. She leaned in until she was on a level with the man, punched him once in the stomach. He vomited, puke splattering the floor, and gasped for air.

She sat on his lap, unmindful of the slop gathered there.

"You are ours," she said.

She shoved her thumbs into Pyotr's eye sockets, pressing until the orbs burst with a squelch, vitreous fluid staining his cheeks. He screamed, its pitch rising and skirling into a chiaroscuro of agony, echoing off the walls. Satisfied, she nodded, stood, and took her coat from Dmitry.

"Let him learn," she said.

Dmitry approached the man and dropped a stone the color of mud over Pyotr's neck. A pause in his misery, then the keening began anew, higher-pitched than before.

Lia turned to go. "Ours," she said on the way out, patting Gen on the cheek. He did his best not to flinch in response.

She'd nearly reached the door when a messenger appeared. He stepped to Lia and whispered something in her ear. She nodded.

"Find Arkady and inform Boris. Dmitry and I will join you shortly."

The messenger turned and ran back the way he'd come. Lia paused on her way out.

"It seems we have visitors. Join us when you can. I'll not rob you of this gift."

She left, sweeping from the room, Dmitry following close behind.

Pyotr continued to scream. Gen came to stand over the man. He held no love for the little weasel, but this seemed cruel for its own sake. To Gen's mind, punishment should fit the crime. Pyotr had done nothing to warrant this sort of retribution aside from falling to avarice.

Lessons learned are lessons never forgotten.

Maybe.

Gen pulled the stiletto from inside his coat and rammed it into an eye socket. The screaming stopped, and Pyotr stilled. Somewhere distant, gunfire echoed in the street. Gen left the corpse to cool.

Gen left the private prison the way he'd come. Outside, the sounds of combat grew louder as Osip's men struck from the dark. Gen considered it a good sign they'd survived this long. He moved to a window, chancing a glance out. Men moved in the dark, mansion lights catching the glint of steel. Gunfire rebounded from the walls and muzzle flashes lit a nearby alley.

Gods, tell me they're at least moving about.

You paid for muscle, not brains.

I paid for both, fucko.

As if on cue, the stables detonated. Horseflesh and fire erupted into the sky, and the mansion shook. A Shkut soldier watched, open-mouthed, as debris launched upward. His neck craned, up, up. A falling hunk of horse ended his fascination abruptly, flaming torso smashing him to the ground. Gen snorted a laugh despite the situation.

Get moving, genius.

Gen turned and moved swiftly through the house. Up one flight of stairs, turn right where he would normally take a left. He knew a long hallway stretched from the next landing. Arkady usually had two men guarding his door.

Another explosion from outside, and the front fountain became a cloud of shrapnel. Screams, and more gunfire. Gen heard running from above and ducked into a nearby alcove. Arkady's guards pelted by soon after, down the stairs and out the front door without a glance to either side.

Gen took the stairs two at a time.

Hope you can count worth a shit.

He gained the landing, breathing a silent prayer of thanks for the empty corridor. Arkady's door stood on the right, clean white, gilded at the edges. Gen knelt, peered in through the keyhole, then listened. Empty.

The lock gave up the ghost on the first attempt.

Arrogance. A humbler man would've sprung for an expensive lock.

Gen stepped inside, letting the door close quietly behind him. He took in the room at a glance. The bed: carved hardwood, clean sheets. A bureau to one side, a mirror attached to the back. Several small boxes stood atop it amidst an array of jewelry. A wardrobe crowded one wall beside a comfortable-looking chair. On the other, a bookcase from which books overflowed onto the floor.

Step across the floor. Light. Tap here. Tap there.

Tap.

Tap.

Hollow.

He knelt, using Bastard to pry at the loose board. It popped easily. He pulled it away. Something sprung past him, green and slick. Gen rolled away on instinct, coming up on his knees. Across from him, a jewel viper lay coiled on the floorboards. It regarded him with glittering black eyes, tongue flickering between its lips. It opened its mouth, presumably to hiss, and a voice issued forth, like steam from a kettle.

"Traaaaaaaitoooooooooooor."

Fucking veneficum.

It sprung at him, fangs dripping venom.

Gen swiped at it, trying to knock the thing away. If it got those fangs into him, he was well and truly fucked. He struck it in the head, yanking his hand back after impact, instinct telling him to protect vulnerable flesh. The snake flew across the room, impacting the wall. Bright fire burned across his fingers and he hurriedly wiped the splashed venom on his trousers.

Close.

He'd seen a man bit by a jewel snake once. Once was enough. The venom ate the man from the inside out, and in the end, he'd died coughing up his own guts.

A hiss, and the snake struck again, flying across the room, directly for his throat. Gen was ready this time, and ducked to the side, snatching the little beast from the air. He gripped it behind the head and slammed its fangs into the wood of the floor.

It made an unnerving, muffled scream as he leveraged the thing's skull forward and snapped off the barbs.

Still holding the monster tight, Gen reached into the hollow where the book lay and pulled the journal out. Then he slammed the snake against the lip of the opening. It went limp in his grasp, and he tossed it into the hole. Once finished, he replaced the board and went to the window.

You'd better hope your friend isn't a corpse.

He ignored the voice and glanced around once more. Outside, fires lit the street, but from here, darkness still cloaked the alley. Hedging his bets that Osip was both alive and not already bought by someone more enterprising, Gen tossed a couple of Arkady's rings into the bag with the book, then opened the window. He dropped the bag without a word, listening for a moment. Satisfied there'd been no sound of impact, he closed the sash.

Take the fangs from the snake

Gen pried them out and slipped them into a pocket, cleaning up the rest the best he could, peering out the door before leaving. The hall remained empty.

Lucky fuck.

Gen stepped out and hurried down the stairs, out the front door. Shkut men lay in various states of disarray and defeat. Bullet holes leaked precious fluids into the earth. Burns bubbled and blistered, smelling of singed pork. Some men bore fresh gashes promising to heal into impressive scars should they survive infection. The thought triggered a flash of trauma.

Field chiurgeons tying off limbs with tourniquets to stop blood loss. The crude sound of a half-dull saw trying to rip through stubborn bone and doing a half-assed job of it. Men, screaming. An endless cacophony of agony. The stink of alcohol, stench of blood and infection.

Doctors worked overtime, swaying on their feet, masks tied tight against the assault of gangrenous gasses. There, the sickly-sweet odor of rot held sway, a miasma of near-death.

Outside the tents, limbs piled high in necrotic fly-blown heaps.

Inside the tents, horror to last a thousand lifetimes.

The world was an abattoir.

A nearby soldier asked for water. Water. Water. The memory shattered. Whatever military stones Osip found for his men, they were worth every koyln.

Someone hailed him, and Gen turned. Arkady stood near Boris, one of Osip's men a cooling corpse between them. Rage heated Gen's blood at the sight of the two of them. He looked away, as if distracted, then back.

Another of Osip's soldiers burst from the shadows behind Boris.

Yes!

Boris turned and swept the man's head from his shoulders with casual contempt, the wide blade he carried whickering through flesh and bone as if they were paper. He turned back and grinned at Gen.

Fuck!

"Come, tovarich! We've got them on the ropes!" Arkady called. "Show our brothers what you can do!"

Gen trotted over. Others joined him on the way, and soon the Shkuts stood in a knot. Boris' smile faded by the time Gen reached them, but by then, Arkady was in high spirits. He slapped Gen on the shoulder.

"*Now* you'll see something, brothers!"

Gen looked around. The fighting appeared to have died off. He looked a question at Arkady, who just pointed. Gen followed the gesture. Two of Osip's men—the ones from the tunnel—were hemmed in by Shkut soldiers and stood at an impasse.

"For you, my Volk," Arkady said.

Meat. They're meat. For the cause. For Irina.

Gen rolled his shoulders. The men watched as he approached, apprehension clear on their faces. They let him draw close, as though he were an ally. By the time he stopped, he stood nearly toe to toe with the first man. Gen looked into his eyes. The color of Irina's eyes.

Another one, then. When will you cease to break the trust of those you rely on you?

He disemboweled the man, Bastard making a neat incision into his stomach, coming up and around. The mercenary's eyes widened, thick wet weight of intestine slopping against Gen's shoes, followed by a flood of gore. The man collapsed into his own entrails.

Meat.

The other wept.

"At least fight back, putya!" someone yelled from behind them.

As if the words were an incantation breaking a spell, the remaining man snapped from his torpor. He raised his pistol, a battered Gruzyev five-round.

Duck.

Gen ducked.

The pistol bucked in the man's hand, and Gen came up, turning to the side as he did. Osip's man came at him then, pistol forgotten, heavy blade in his hand. Less elegant than a cavalry saber, just as effective.

He chopped down with it, and Gen let the blade ricochet off Bastard. It threw the man's swing wide, and Gen stepped in, planted the stiletto in his armpit. His opponent screamed, nerveless arm dropping the sword.

He raised the pistol again. Gen grabbed it, turned it inward. He rammed it against the man's ribs. They struggled, Osip's man trying his best to stop the hammer with his free hand, despite a coating of blood.

Gen grabbed the hand, broke the thumb. The man grunted in pain, He brought his knee up, smashing it into the inside of Gen's thigh. Gen flinched back, a rolling ache throbbing into his groin, grip weakening. Triumph shone in his opponent's eyes as he regained control of the pistol. He took aim and Gen dove to the side as another shot thundered in the yard.

Up a final time, hacking Bastard into the inside of the man's elbow. A thick runnel of blood poured from the incision, slicking weapon and flesh. The hired soldier's hand weakened as severed nerve lost the impulse to clutch. He sucked in breath in a hiss of agonized air. That alone would do for him, but Gen's blood was up. Gen seized the man's wrist, turned the pistol, pressing it against his opponent's jaw.

Terror, pure and undiluted, flowed from the man, smelling like the piss down his leg.

Gen pressed his opponent's finger against the trigger, using so much force the bone snapped. The gun roared, and the top of Osip's hireling's skull vaporized. Gen squeezed the trigger until the hammer fell on empty chambers and what remained of the man was a corpse with a ragged stump for a skull.

He dropped the body and turned. The Shkuts had gathered to watch. Silence filled the yard.

Do something.

Yes, kill them all.

Gen bowed, then looked at Boris, and smiled.

Arkady began to applaud, the sound like the tolling of a broken bell.

KATYUSHKA LEONOVA – CHAPTER TWENTY-FOUR

Those who are truly convinced they have made progress in science do not demand free-dom for the new views to continue alongside the old, but rather the substitution of the old views for the new.

—Vladimir Ilyich Ulyanov

Kat paced the sidewalk in front of the Chernyshevsky Street Militsiya Bureau, waiting for Maks. Black clouds ate the sky, dumped snow like they'd been eviscerated. Teams of sootmen scampered to keep up with the downfall, filling wagons with the ashen slurry and hustling it off to wherever they took it. One of the sootmen found a frozen body, stiff and contorted. Dragging it from the waist-deep drift, he wrestled it onto the wagon and returned to shovelling.

Her shoulder ached where Maks bit her, a constant reminder.

No, no, no. That wasn't me.

Except it was.

She remembered everything. Kissing. Licking. The way he spun her against the wall, hiked up her skirt, dropped to his knees, and buried his face in her from behind. The sudden cold of being exposed a delicious contrast with the heat of his tongue. He didn't stop until an orgasm shook through her, turned her knees to pudding.

'Fuck me,' she ordered. 'Fuck me from behind.'

Rough hands.

She needed this, wanted to howl like those cats who rutted in the alley every spring.

'Bite my neck,' she demanded. Maks obeyed, growling. 'Harder. Bite harder you fucking pustyak.'

"Not me," she said aloud.

She wanted to believe she lived two separate lives. There was Katyushka Leonova, the proper young lady who went to the best schools and was going to marry a lawyer and raise a family and live in a nice house in the south. And then there was Kat, the militsioner who came home with bloody knuckles from fighting, who fucked her partner behind some dank tavern, who smoked and drank and… and… and felt alive in ways Katyushka Leonova never had and never would.

Maybe as Katyushka she could pretend that was true. But here and now she remembered everything, and it all looked like one life.

I was angry at Fyodor. That's why I did it.

That was a bullshit excuse. She hadn't thought about him once the entire time.

I was drunk!

While true, that wasn't it either.

She fucked Maks because she wanted to.

The rest of the day came back to her as she paced.

Still pulling on his greatcoat, Maks exited the precinct looking confused and worried.

"Sorry," he said, joining her on the sidewalk. "I just… you know… memory stone. We've never met when not on shift."

"We meet every fucking day when you stare at my tits and pretend you don't know me."

"That first time we met, you didn't have a memory stone yet. I was already wearing my stones."

"So? You can't be polite?"

"Ah," he said. "I'm…" He grimaced, looking off down the street. "There's me at work, who likes crowds and people. He can say and do anything."

"Like fucking women he barely knows behind taverns?"

He winced. "And there's me. The real me. The me who stays home with his books. The me who can't imagine why anyone would like him. The me would never talk to you, couldn't even make eye contact. Fucking coward. I hate him."

"He sounds nice."

"Then why did you fuck me instead of him?"

"I've never met him."

This was going all wrong. She'd been ready to rage at Maks, to blame him for everything. He tricked her! He lured her to the Dripping Bucket and got her drunk and then took advantage of her in a fucking alley!

But it wasn't like that at all.

She remembered vodka after vodka, chasing each with a delicious cigareta, studying Maks through the smoke, deciding she wanted him. She wanted to feel good. Nothing else mattered. She was tired of every decision being about making someone else happy. The constant worry of what others thought was exhausting.

She gave him smoky eyes until even a dimwit would know what she was thinking.

She'd half-dragged him into the alley.

He'd resisted, saying this was wrong, pointing out she was engaged.

'I'm not,' she admitted. 'I lied about that.'

'But still,' he said.

'Anyway,' she added. 'He left me.' Which was maybe a half-truth at best.

'I'm not sure—'

Then her hand was in his pants and he finally shut up.

How did this happen?

"Look," said Maks. "This... We're not supposed to—"

"Militsioners aren't supposed to fuck their partners?"

She wanted to tell him about Kostas, how he loved Maks, how he died praying his partner and only friend would save him.

But he didn't.

Maks should have been there, but he wasn't. As much as Kostas loved him, Kat didn't trust Maks.

In spite of everything, she realized she regretted none of the previous evening.

What's to regret? When I take the stones off, I won't remember any of this.

At the end of the day she'd go home and hope she hadn't lost Fyodor forever and she'd work even harder to make him happy, to keep him.

'I hate him,' Maks had said of the man he was without his stones. She understood that the sentiment. She didn't like proper little Katyushka either.

"I need a drink," said Kat.

"Gods above, woman. Back to the Bucket for another round?"

Their eyes met.

Awkward silence.

"I mean..." Maks rubbed at his brow, busied himself fishing out a cigareta she knew he couldn't light.

Kat took it from him, threw it into the snow. "Let's go." She set off without waiting.

Maks stared at the crumpled cigareta for a moment before following. "You know why I never have matches?"

She knew immediately. "Because you don't smoke at home."

He nodded. "Long ago I figured out that I smoked while working. You can only go home with that taste in your mouth so many times before you figure it out. But Home Maks thinks it's a disgusting, stinking habit and is angry at me for smoking. My clothes reek of it. He hates washing them."

"So he never brings matches to work."

"Yep. Sometimes he punishes me by wearing uncomfortable underclothes or not bringing money for lunch. Asshole."

In the evenings, candle-lit and warmed with vodka and pivo and the scents of whatever they were making in the kitchen, the Dripping Bucket possessed a semblance of, if not class, at least hominess. First thing in the morning, hangover from the previous night still haunting your thoughts and bowels, the floor sticky with spilt drinks, the place stunk of stale cigareta and desperation. The morning sun pissed in through filthy windows.

Someone lay curled under a table. Dead or sleeping, Kat couldn't tell and didn't care.

Taking a seat at the bar, Maks grabbed the last lit candle and used it to light them each a smoke. The bartender brought vodka and a beer without being asked.

"Fuck off until we call you," Kat told him.

He took one look at her militsioner greatcoat and fucked off.

"We need to talk," she said.

Something in Maks seemed to crumple, and he focussed on the dented and stained bar. "Here we go."

"What?" she blurted, confused.

"Let's pretend you're you and I'm me."

"A stretch," she said, "but fine. Now what?"

"You're from the south. You have a good family. You either have a fiancé or at least someone who wants to be your fiancé."

She didn't bother correcting him.

"You're smart, and you're educated," he continued. "And let's be honest, you look like that," he waved a hand at her.

"Like something a cat puked up on your front step?"

"Sure, if cats vomit stunningly gorgeous women. You are, in every way imaginable, out of my league."

Was she? She didn't feel like it. To be honest, she felt more comfortable with Maks than she ever had with Fyodor. With Maks, she didn't have to pretend.

"So," said Maks, "There's only one way the words, 'We need to talk,' can end. You'll say you made a terrible mistake. You'll say it was the vodka. You'll say you want a new partner, or maybe you'll quit, and I'll never see you again." He inhaled hard on his cigareta, let the smoke curl from his nose. "And I'll have one more reason to dread putting the stones on each morning."

"Bone memory," she said, remembering that first conversation. Though last night put a whole new spin on the words.

"On the high side," said Maks, flashing a fractured grin, "the next man to wear that stone is going to have to live with the memory of me fucking him behind the Dripping Bucket."

That was Kostas you were fucking, not me.

But that wasn't true. Or not entirely true.

For all his bluster and jokes, Maks looked like a little boy hiding his hurt. She couldn't figure it out. Did he feel used, or was he worried he wouldn't get to have sex with her again?

Kat pushed the thoughts away. None of it mattered.

Obviously, Veneficum Lazarev knew whose stone she wore. As the commanding officer, Colonel Grinin would know as well. And Maks... she remembered the look he gave her the first time she took his cigareta, all the times he almost asked.

He knows.

Or at least suspected.

He joked about taking bribes, and clearly had dealings with criminal elements. He'd been left alone with Arkady, a Shkut Avtorityet, and blithely wandered away unharmed. Maybe he really did have to let the man go because he went after Kat, trying to save her from the goon who chased her. Or maybe he didn't.

Gods above! That was Arkady here in the Dripping Bucket with the huge mouthbreather the first time Maks brought me here!

What were the odds they drank at the same bar and didn't know each other? Maks and Arkady probably came here for a drink after she fled, assuming she was dead.

He was Kostas' partner and now he's yours.

Who decided which stones were assigned to which militsioner? Was it Grinin's decision, or Lazarev's? What if both Maks and Grinin were in the Shkut pocket? There were too many coincidences for them to be coincidences.

If Maks wanted you dead, he could have murdered you behind this shitty bar last night.

Her thoughts spun useless circles, a dog chasing its tail. She wanted to tell Maks everything but couldn't trust him.

So? What are you going to do?

She wanted to hunt Arkady down and beat him to death with her bare hands. She wanted to find somewhere safe to hide until all this was over.

"Wow," said Maks, retrieving his dented cigareta tin and fishing out two more smokes. "That is the longest a woman has ever spent trying to figure out how to tell a guy it's over."

She needed a moment of space, room to breathe. She needed to *think*.

Kat slammed back the last of her vodka and stood. "I have to go to the bathroom." On a sudden impulse, she leaned in and kissed him on the cheek. "Order another round. I'll be back in a moment."

"Your fiancé is an idiot," said Maks as she headed to the rear of the building.

GENNDY ANTONOV — CHAPTER TWENTY-FIVE

Punishments for infractions against Norylskan Families are varied and imaginative. From the Gruzdevs' propensity for roasting men over coals, or the Shkut favorite, drowning, to a panoply of other horrors, there is no lack of ways for men to die. But for traitors, there is only one punishment, proscribed by a centuries-old unspoken law, agreed upon by all Families: The Flaying. To see a Flaying in person is a spectacle never forgotten. To receive a strip of the dead man's flesh is to receive a blessing from the gods.

—D. Puskyn, Exile

Mirmysk. A child crying. Bodies laid out in neat rows, unmarked aside from the broken sclera of their eyes, snow stained beneath them. Just outside town, the militsiya dug a trench, wide enough to lay bodies head to toe, long enough for the tallest man. Digging was slow in the permafrost, but still the men made good time. The earth may have been frozen, but these men were colder.

Sobek walked down the line of bodies, pointing out a male here, a female there to the officer at his shoulder. Soldiers dutifully took them and dragged them to the cart where six or seven others were already piled.

Altin Ordu.

Not so different when they tried to blend in. But Sobek knew them, knew the stink.

The sound of wailing reached him, and he paused.

"Is that a child, major-general?" he asked the man at his shoulder.

"Y-Yes, sir."

"Why wasn't it dealt with?"

"They're children, sir."

"Interesting. So, you'd propose that children are incapable of becoming monsters?"

The man looked lost, turned his head toward the sound. Sobek drew his service revolver and shot the officer in the face when he turned back. Sobek gestured to a stunned soldier standing nearby.

"You, you're promoted. Have this one buried."

The man nodded smartly, shouting out orders over his shoulder, joining the OSD officer on his rounds.

Children could grow to be monsters, after all.

Gen woke from the dregs of the dream, shook off his passenger's clinging taint. The woman next to him stirred in her sleep. Guilt took the place of Sobek's memory.

So easy to smother her, free yourself.

A ripple of disgust passed through Gen.

Shut up.

In the absence of morality, there is only freedom. Right and wrong, constructs of weak minds. Every action a ripple. Every ripple, a future effect. Killing this woman may save another. Who knows what these whores carry? She may fuck the life out of a great mind someday. And you would be to blame.

Gen pushed the voice back.

We're all just trying to fucking survive.

He looked at the woman again. Lia offered her after their victory over Osip's men. Small and lithe, she was pretty in a simple way, brunette, straight hair. Nothing like Irina. Something like the militsioner from the Bucket. Then, he supposed that was another Shkut manipulation.

He stared at the curve of the silky girl's back, the swell of her ass, half-hidden by the sheets. His cock stirred at the memory of how tight and wet she'd been. How willing. How wild. It would be so easy to take her again.

He tore his eyes away as another wave of guilt crashed into him. He pushed off the bed in defiance of temptation.

It's well and truly dead then?

Irina?

Never. This is just a slip on the path. Besides, everyone knows Family men keep silkies. Even their wives. Especially their wives. Irina once joked, "You should have a girlfriend, to take the pressure off me." She would see this as a boon.

Even as he thought it, he knew it for the lie it was. Would Irina care? More, would she be able to forgive?

Would you?

He knew the answer to that. Wondered if all he'd ever seen in her was pride in landing this pretty little thing with a pert ass and strong legs. Wondered if Irina had been more than a wet hole and an ideal for him.

No—you loved—love her.

Maybe. He looked at the silky girl again. Considered how easy it had been to fall into bed with her.

If it wasn't before, their marriage was fractured so completely now, he could never repair it. Even should he somehow manage to hammer it into a semblance of the shape it once had, it would be weaker at the bent places. Easier to break again.

His head hurt. He shook the thoughts off, stalked to the window and flipped the curtains aside. Still dark. Sometime between deep night and dawn, then. His mind raced, chasing itself with rationalization and incrimination. Bending his will to the task, he forced his thoughts into a semblance of order.

Fortune smiled on him, it seemed. He'd stolen Arkady's book. No one noticed.

Eyes heavy with the remnants of sleep, he scrubbed his hands over his face, felt the callouses on his palms against his cheeks. Callouses built on a lifetime of work. Honest work.

Will you stop being such a putsyak?

He snorted. No man could rightfully call him that. Here, he was murder incarnate. Maybe he'd always been. Despite everything this Family had put him through, maybe they'd done him a small favor. He'd hidden inside himself for so long and so deep, he'd been living as only half a person. A man could be complex. A man could be many things.

A man can be a monster, too.

His throat was dry as the steppe in summer. He found the bedside pitcher in the dark and poured himself a glass of tepid water. The taste loosened vodka still hiding in the crevices of his gums, and last night's celebration returned.

"Paid a visit to the little bitch," Arkady said.

The announcement took Gen off-guard, the words circling in his brain before landing on their subject, sinking talons of understanding in. "The militsi—"

"Katyuskha. Kat, yes."

Gen gave him a puzzled look. "Why would you do that? Visit a militionser's home? Wouldn't she be trouble?"

Arkady shook his head. "Not off-duty. They only get those stones while they're working."

Unease wormed its way into Gen's guts. "Kill her, then?" he asked as nonchalantly as possible.

Arkady shook his head. "Just a warning. And an ultimatum. We—" he spread his arms to indicate the room, drink sloshing over the side of his glass "have worked too hard for a single cockroach to bring us down."

"Did it work?"

Arkady took a sip of his drink. "If it didn't, we won't have to worry, regardless. She turns it over; the state executes her. She doesn't; we do. Stupid to fall so deeply into such a trap."

Clever.

"How do you mean?"

Arkady pointed at Gen. "You know what you know, yeah? Hard work, killing. Your letters, numbers. No pretense. You came up in the streets. Your knowledge is practical, applicable. This woman," he spat the word with contempt, "strives to rise above her station. Small and weak, overeducated, but somehow never attended a single seminar on venificum theory, never an ounce of intellectual curiosity as to what might be hung around her neck from day to day. For all she knows, they could be toxic. Stupid, for one who spent a small fortune at university."

He has a point. What about your stones, Genndy Antonov?

I know what's in my head. I ditched the bad rock.

Did you?

Again, that knot of unease. The spark of a plan. Kat had gone to university. Gen had already had Osip transcribe a page from the book. It was in no language he knew, despite speaking Kievan, a smattering of Altin Ordu, and just enough Solostian to ask for a blowjob. But maybe, maybe this woman would be able to help. A mutually beneficial agreement.

The silky girl stirred in his bed, dragging Gen's attention back to the present. He gathered his clothes and dressed in the bathroom, then slipped out the door. The mansion was quiet and would remain that way until late morning. Kievans were fond of their vodka, but too much was too much.

Once outside, he took a moment to find his bearings. Snow fell in thick curtains, muffling sound. City lights played out as hazy yellow globes. Somewhere nearby, sootmen worked in shifts to clear ash and snow-choked streets.

He made his way down one alley, taking a dogleg to the left. A flowerpot leaned against a rickety fence, cracked from disuse. Gen gave it a kick, the package with the book tumbling out. He knelt, checked the contents, and satisfied, tucked it into his coat.

Osip was worth every penny.

The Bureau was somewhere to the south. Gen had never been but figured it shouldn't be too hard to find. Look for the building pedestrians avoided, the citizenry resented, and the miserable bastards who worked there hated.

He shoved his hands in his pockets and made his way there, snow erasing his passage.

Fuck, it was early. Miserably cold, snot running in a constant stream into the beginnings of a beard, Gen finally stopped at one of the few food carts still operating, both in winter and morning. But then, it was coffee. Between heat from the brew and proximity to the station, he would've been surprised if the owner ever had to worry about a lull in business.

He slugged the coffee down in one shot, bought another, then found a doorway to huddle in. Fortunately, between the walk and time spent haggling with the coffee vendor as to what constituted 'dangerous amounts', militsiya had already begun to straggle into work.

Though he kept his eyes peeled, he saw neither Kat nor her partner enter the building. Snow continued to fall in thick sheets. The coffee made him need to piss, and he unloaded his bladder in the alley, worry gnawing at him the entire time. When he came back, still no sign. Almost ready to give it up for a bad job, his luck broke.

The little brunette popped out of the building, pacing. She made circles in the snow, slowly packing it down. Something ate at her. Gen made his way over to the coffee vendor, bought a third cup, then waited, sipping it.

"A friend of yours?" the vendor asked.

"An acquaintance," Gen said.

"Ah, yeah. Hope she's not pregnant."

Gen looked at the man, who gave him a yellow-toothed grin. Rolling his eyes at the Kievan sense of humor, Gen walked away. Kat's partner finally emerged from the building, and they talked animatedly. Finally, she plucked a cigareta from his lips, tossed it into the snow, and stomped off. Her partner cast about, looking lost, then followed grimly.

Lover's spat?

Gen shrugged to himself and followed.

The Dripping Bucket. Of fucking course.

He spat a wad of snot in the snow. This would probably be his only chance to talk to her unless he stalked the woman home, a proposition that, no matter how slim, increased the likelihood he'd encounter Arkady on the way. Though, come to think of it, the man seemed to avoid daylight. Gen had never seen him outside nighttime, anyway. Then again, the same could be said of Gen. Third shift fucks with a man's sleep as surely as a dose of kroc.

He went around back of the building, traveling through the alley. Someone's woolen leggings were frozen to the ground, icy white lumps decorating them. Grimacing, Gen stepped over and deeper into the passage.

The Bucket provided rooms for itinerants and travelers, after a sort. Mostly they were for fucking. But if you'd seen the state of the rooms in the Bucket, you'd understand why people fucked in the alley instead.

Just under a minute, and he had the lock on the back door open.

Useful thing to know.

Poor kid from the Filth. Larceny was a hobby.

He stepped into the dark hall beyond the door, the mingled stink of dried cum, alcohol, moldy sheets, and the latrine hammering into his nose like a drunk with a grudge and a brick. He reeled for a moment, adjusting, then waited another as pins and needles chased new warmth through his extremities.

When he was sure it was safe to move, he crept nearer the bathrooms. Ugly in the daylight, the Bucket reminded Gen of a one-night stand you'd take home. Intriguing and arousing across the flickering glow of a candle. A shaved goat by dawn's light.. He spied Kat and her partner talking. The poor man looked hangdog. Whatever she might be, she was an expert ballbuster.

Abruptly, she stood, and Gen ducked back into the dark of the hall. She turned and stalked his way. His heart hammered. This was it. Eyes downcast, mind somewhere else, she slammed open the bathroom door and slipped inside.

Gen edged forward. Her partner's gaze was fixed on his drink. His fingers laced together, lips in a tight line. He looked like a man in love, and all the pain it carries.

Something distant pinged in sympathy, sending a shock of melancholy through Gen's heart. He shook it off in irritation, shooting a final look at Kat's partner. He hadn't moved.

Poor morose bastard.

One last glance around. No one was paying attention. Gen pushed the bathroom door opened and slipped inside.

"Back for more?" the woman at the counter asked, her tone mocking.

Gen froze. This wasn't the timid militsioner he'd threatened at the chandler's. This was the wildcat from the alley. She turned, face rippling through a tidal wave of emotion. Then she snarled and came at him.

Finally!

Fuck.

KATYUSHKA LEONOVA – CHAPTER TWENTY-SIX

A writer is dear and necessary for us only in the measure of which he reveals to us the inner workings of his very soul.

—Lev Nikolayevich Tolstoi

Kat entered the bathroom, stood staring at her jagged reflection in what remained of the mirror. At some point, long ago, it had been shattered. In the years since, Norylskans pried off corners and shards to bring home.

Because here, a bit of broken mirror is a fucking luxury.

Gods above she hated Norylska!

"The armpit of Kievan," she muttered. "The puckered shit-encrusted frozen sphincter of the entire world."

She remembered the first time Father took her to a Norylskan restaurant. They'd been here less than a week and were staying in the Hotel Profilaktoriy; he hadn't yet drunk his savings back then. She'd gone to the bathroom, only to discover there was no toilet paper in the stall. The locals, she learned, always carried at least a half dozen sheets folded in a pocket.

'A roll of toilet paper left in a public place,' her father said, already a little drunk, 'becomes public property and is redistributed as such.'

Looking back, he was probably quoting something he read.

Now, years later, she still carried folded squares of what passed for toilet paper. Waxy and slippery on one side, rough and sand-papery on the other. Each day a choice between useless and painful.

How very Norylskan.

The sagging timber floor of the Bucket groaned beyond the door. Had Maks followed her? Was he hoping for a quick bathroom fuck?

Nope. That smell. Raw animal musk. She knew it. The big mouth-breather who chased her through the Filth.

The door creaked as he pushed it open.

Run?

Where?

The only windows were small and painted shut with centuries of laziness.

Didn't matter. She didn't want to run. She wanted to vent her frustrations. Her father ruined her life. The militsiya ruined her life. Fyodor ruined her life. Maks ruined her life.

I ruined my life.

She turned as he entered. He stood there; back hunched, big cave bear brow thunderous. His face looked like the gods shaped it from soft iron with a crude ballpen hammer. He was still huge, still terrifying, but he looked different. A little broken. A little scared.

This was bad. So bad. Close quarters. No room to run. If he got those bearpaw hands on her, he'd pull her apart. But he was slow. Big, dumb, and slow.

"Back for more?" she asked, feeling her face pull tight in what was either a grin or a rabid snarl.

"Look," he said, raising his hands, palms out, "I need—"

Kat kicked in his right knee, drove her still swollen knuckles into his solar plexus, spun an elbow into his jaw, and kicked him in the balls.

Or tried to.

The first three blows landed clean and hard. His cave bear brain woke up in time to turn his hips and take the testicular attack on his thigh.

Snapping a fast kick to his other knee and driving three more lightning-fast punches into his gut, Kat retreated.

"Ow," he said, drooling blood from where she'd split his bottom lip wide. "That really fucking hurts."

Crouch low.

Small target.

Big, soft, terrified eyes.

Lure him in.

You're a helpless bunny.

"I'm not falling for that shit," he said. "I don't—"

Feint for the eyes, snap another kick at his balls.

He caught her hand, spun her hard, pulling her into a flawlessly executed choke hold.

Kat drove an elbow into his belly. It was like hitting rock.

He pulled her hard against him. Brute man stink, and blood and sweat. Arm under her chin, he closed her throat. She hammered panicked elbows into his gut over and over and he took them, unflinching.

"I could pull your fucking head off," he whispered into her ear. "And I will if you don't stop fucking hitting me."

She reached back, tried to claw his eyes out, and he tucked his head, protecting his face.

And squeezed.

Buzzing in her ears. Vision a collapsing tunnel.

"Stop," he growled into her ear.

She stomped on his foot, felt his big toe break beneath her heel.

He grunted in annoyed pain, said, "Fine."

The world fell away, swirled down a Norylskan toilet with all the other shit.

Kat woke on the bathroom floor. Limbs still attached. Clothes in place. Unmolested. Her skull throbbed.

The big mouth-breathing cave-bear bastard had retreated to the far side. "See?" he said. "Not dead."

Sitting, she rubbed at her throat.

"Would have been easy," he said.

Kat pushed to her feet.

"Fuck." He wiped at his bloody lip. "Let's not do that again. I was ugly enough to begin with."

The snarling spitting predator at the base of Kat's skull calmed like it recognized one of its own.

He made no threatening moves, but stood ready, studying her with surprisingly intelligent eyes. Maybe not kind, but not murderous.

"I could scream," Kat said. "Maks will come."

"Frankly," he said, leaning back against the door, "I'd rather fight him than you." He touched his ribs, wincing. "If you had twenty pounds of muscle, you'd have fucked me up good." He pulled a leather-bound book from a coat pocket, held it out in offering.

"What's that?" Kat asked, curious in spite of herself.

"Arkady's codebook."

She looked from the book to the man. "You're going to hand me another reason for him to want me dead? Fuck off."

"I think Arkady keeps track of what stones he gives to his people in here."

She didn't care. Having the book put a target on her.

"Not interested," she said.

"Apparently it's also got a listing of every militsioner and what stones they're wearing."

She remembered threatening to smash Penkin's teeth in against a desk. She remembered being desperate to please Fyodor, willing to do anything to keep him. She fought this monstrous lump in the Filth and fucked Maks in an alley.

Bite me. Bite me harder!

She came home stinking of cigareta and booze and cried herself to sleep for fear her life was falling apart. Then she went to work and got drunk and smoked all over again!

I don't drink. I don't smoke.

Proper young ladies didn't act like that.

Yet she'd already smoked at least two, and her second vodka of the morning was probably waiting on the bar.

You keep thinking you're two people.

Was her name in that book?

"What do you get out of this?" she asked.

Huge fists clenched and relaxed, and he bared his teeth at the floor. "I think he's poisoned me."

"No. I mean what *else* do you get out of this."

Hooded eyes studied her.

Gods above, she'd underestimated this man because of his build and smashed brick face.

"You want Arkady gone," she said, "You want to climb the ranks, be the next Shkut avtorityet."

He didn't blink. "The current one wants to kill you. Wouldn't you rather have one that is in your debt take his place?"

"Let me see the book."

Keeping his distance, ready in case she attacked, he handed it to her.

Opening to a random page she found the runic language of the Plemya tribes. She knew that writing, saw it on the shelf where her stones sat each night.

"Where did you get this?" she demanded.

"Stole it from Arkady."

"Where did he get it?"

"How would I know? Can you read it?"

She shook her head. "No."

Broad shoulders slumped in defeat.

Lazarev said the colours and types of stone meant something, were part of the code. She'd joked he used red for anger. He denied it but looked annoyed. At the least, she'd been close. Of course he'd use colours that made sense, if just so they were easier for him to remember.

"But I will," she added.

"How?"

"I know what language it's written in, and I have some ideas about the code used." She grinned at the hulking thug. "And I know where the library is."

"I don't have to tell you what will happen if you double-cross me on this, right?"

"You kind of just did."

He snorted a surprised laugh. "I guess so. You know…" he hesitated, looking from the book to her. "I didn't want to chase you. I didn't want to try and kill you in that alley."

"But you did chase me. You did try to kill me."

He sagged. "Yeah, I did." He sounded disappointed in himself. Turning away, he opened the door. "I'll find you later."

"You have a way of making everything sound like a threat."

"Sorry."

"What's your name?"

"Osip."

"The fuck it is. What's your name?"

"My friends call me Gen."

"You have friends?" she blurted before her brain caught up with her mouth.

"Used to."

"Oh. Sorry. Um. I'm Kat." She had no idea why she said that, felt like an idiot for sharing anything with this criminal.

He let himself out of the bathroom without another word.

Kat stared at the book in her hands. "Penkin," she said. The little svoloch had easy access to the elderly veneficum's messy office. No doubt he knew better than Lazarev did where everything was. Lazarev was a Master Veneficum who'd been working for the militsiya for half a century or longer; she doubted he needed to check his codebook to know what stone had which traits.

Brick face—Gen, she corrected, *thinks it has the names of militsioners and what they're wearing.*

That would change occasionally, have to be updated. She frowned at the book. Was it a painstakingly recreated copy? She could imagine Penkin being the type to carefully mimic everything down to the penmanship.

This time, she really was going to smash his teeth out against a desk corner. It was going to be beautiful.

Leaning out the bathroom door, she saw the big thug had gone out the rear exit. Maks still fidgeted at the bar, cigareta hanging forgotten from his bottom lip. Her coat, hung on the back of her chair, caught her eye. *Shit.* It would have been handy to have somewhere to hide the book. Tucking it under her arm, she returned to the bar.

Maks looked up, all puppy dog and hope, and immediately noticed the book. "What's that?"

"A book."

"I've heard of those. Nothing but trouble."

Taking her seat, she slipped it into her coat pocket, grabbed the lit cigareta from Maks' mouth, and shot back the vodka he ordered for her.

"You do know you're going to have to explain going to the bathroom with nothing, and coming back with a book, right?" said Maks.

She nodded. "Yeah."

He'd never believe she found it. Maybe if she'd thought of that in advance, she could have played this differently.

Dumbass.

"You remember the Shkut kryshas that chased me from that back alley veneficum?"

Leaving you alone with Arkady.

Maks nodded.

"He gave it to me."

"In the bathroom?" He stood, pulling on his knuckleduster.

"Cute," she said, "but you're too late for heroics." *Again.* "He's long gone."

"Why'd he give you a book?" demanded Maks.

"He wants help translating it."

"Translating? What language is it? I know Altin Ordu—had to learn it during the war. Let me see."

This felt all kinds of wrong. Fear festered in her gut. She had to move. She needed air and space.

Grabbing her coat, Kat stood.

"Translating what?" Maks repeated, reaching toward her.

"It's Lazarev's codebook."

"His what? Why would—"

"You were supposed to be there," she blurted. "You weren't! Where the fuck were you?"

"What? What are you—" Seeing her sling her coat on, he grabbed her wrist.

Kat twisted his arm and put him on the ground in one perfectly executed movement. He blinked up at her in surprise.

He'll follow.

She kicked him in the jaw, snapping his head back.

Maks slumped, unconscious.

The bartender nodded to her from the behind the bar. "Ma'am."

Nodding back, she bent to retrieve Mak's cigareta tin and helped herself to a smoke. She lit it from the previous smoke, pocketing the tin. Then, on a whim, she took his knuckleduster, slipping it into her own pocket.

Exiting the Dripping Bucket, she walked south, smoking and thinking.

Penkin stole Lazarev's veneficum codebook and sold it to the Shkuts. That much she was sure of. After that, everything was confusion.

Kill Penkin.

Yeah. That felt right.

First, however, she needed to read the book. She knew she wasn't herself.

I'm not me because I'm better than me.

She felt stronger, more secure and confident. She felt like a predator instead of prey.

"I've been prey my whole fucking life," she growled.

Seeing her militsioner greatcoat, people crossed the street to avoid her. That felt good. She laughed. Her grandmother once said it was better to be one of the people everyone is afraid of than to be afraid of them. Kat had been nine. Hadn't understood until now.

"I don't feel poisoned," she said to no one. "I feel *good*."

Lazarev was a Master Veneficum. He knew exactly what stones she needed to be better, and he gave them to her. He saw her weaknesses. He saw her doubts and fears. He saw her insecurity, and he fixed all of it. He cared. He listened. Even with a line of annoyed militsioners waiting to see him, he still had time for Kat. He was the father she never had.

'I think Arkady keeps track of what stones he gives to his people in here,' Gen said in the bathroom.

The man wasn't as dumb as she thought, but he wasn't a genius either. Why would Lazarev's codebook list what stones some Shkut avtorityet gave to his goons?

Gods above! She'd been an idiot!

If Penkin copied the book, anything could be written in there. Colonel Grinin would blame the old veneficum and have him shot.

Kat lit a fresh cigareta off the previous one and picked up her pace. There were books on the Plemya in the library. Their dead language was hardly a secret. She'd crack the code. Somehow, she'd prove Lazarev's innocence.

Then she'd kill that fucking weasel, Penkin.

GENNDY ANTONOV – CHAPTER TWENTY-SEVEN

Men and women, fire and water, truth and memory. None of these things interact well. But each is half of the whole of life, and without one, there is nothing.

—Yuliana Boleslava, Kievan Philosphic

His ribs hurt, and blood still coated the inside of his mouth like a copper blanket. Gen spat into the snow, a wad of red phlegm freezing as it hit the ice.

Gods, she packs a fuckin' punch.

If the woman had been manipulated as he had, her ferocity made sense. If not, she was a complete lunatic. Either way, it made her a lunatic temporarily on his side.

Your woman.

The words hammered into him with the weight of an avalanche. *Irina.* If Arkady learned of the book's theft, and Gen had no doubt he would, she needed to be warned.

Even if she doesn't love you?

Even then. He still loved her, after all.

Hell was built on kinder torture.

The fuckin' snow hadn't quit. Probably wouldn't for some time, now it had started. Still, the sootmen in the Filth fought it. Gen wondered if it was their Altin Ordu—an implacable invader, always pressing forward, always claiming

Kievan lives. He shook it off as laughable. No pile of snow had ever cut a man's guts out with a casual flick of the wrist.

Home.

It stood bright in the sooty drifts. As bright as any Filth home might. Light spilling from the windows. A band of mourning tied around the porch post.

That's it, then.

Gen climbed the stairs, fingers trailing the railing there. He'd built it himself, only a couple years back. In high summer.

He'd hammered the last nail home, feeling something new. Satisfaction? Pride? He'd created something, no matter how small and mean. After, he sat on the steps, hammer laid beside him, sweat rolling down his back.

The door opened behind him, soft steps across the boards of the porch. The clink of ice—where had she found ice in summer?—*in glasses. She sat beside him, and he caught the scent of her hair, the warm brush of her hip against his. She passed him a glass— sweet and tart, the colour of a dawn sunrise. The sugar burned his throat a little, but he sipped it contentedly all the same. She wrapped an arm around him, tilted her head onto his shoulder. They sat like that until the sun fell behind the city rooftops.*

It was the one memory he'd always considered his, like the core of a sun. In a lifetime of tearing down, just the once, he'd built up.

He reached the porch, and the door opened. Irina stood before him; shawl wrapped around her shoulders. Her eyes were chips of flint. She looked him up and down, then turned.

"Come in. And close the door. You're letting the cold in."

They sat at the kitchen table. The room smelled of cold stew and the tea Irina brewed with her back to him as he sat in his old spot at the table. He looked around the kitchen, feeling out of place in his own home. A home seemingly grown smaller since he'd left. Colder. When the kettle whistled, she poured a cup, turning back and taking her usual place beside him, mug clenched between her hands.

She'd offered him none.

Fuck, she does *hate you.*

Gen ignored Sobek.

"You're back," she said without preamble. "To apologize?"

Pride punched him in the chest, leaving a warm flare of anger. "To warn you," he said, trying to divert the flow of rage.

She sniffed, took a sip of tea. "Wouldn't need a warning if you hadn't insisted on this. 'I can make this work, Irina,' 'This is good for us, Irina.' *Chush—dumbshit."*

He opened his mouth, shut it. Looked down at his hands, fingers entangled, fumbling with one another. The stones around his neck clicked against together, chains jingling faintly.

"Stones?" she scoffed. "Do they make you wear those?"

The edge of old arguments crept into her tone. They'd fought about this in the past. When they were first together, and he could find no work aside from the plant, he wanted to use his pension for stones.

"They'll help me get ahead," he'd said. "I can be successful. We can live better than this."

Then too, her temper had flared at the idea.

"They'll make you someone else. Those things are poison."

"They tried," he hedged.

"So, you chose these? This? My Genndy wasn't good enough, for them or himself?"

"You don't understand-"

She held a hand up, shook her head. "You're right. I don't. Do you ever take them off? Do you see what they've—you've—done to our family? Do you even know who you are anymore?"

The question struck him in the heart like a harpoon. He hung his head again. He'd been right the entire time. He didn't deserve her. She'd been right.

"I'm a fuckup," he said.

Silence reigned for a long moment. "No," she said finally. "You are not a fuckup. But you did fuck up. Did you think of your child at all?"

The stones had nothing to say. What was it about this woman that utterly disarmed him? He looked at her, pleading.

"I did! I thought of our child and you and that the plant let me go and if I went to the mines, I would never see you, or I would die even sooner. But this was real money, Irina! This was security!"

"And yet you come to me with a warning! Is it the Shkut scum? Yeah? Is that it? Did they betray you as the Families do, and now no one is safe? You may have died in the mines, but now you've condemned me and your child as well! Which is worse, Genndy? Where is your security now?" she flung the cup against the wall and it shattered. She sat, staring at the dent it had made.

"I would never—" he began.

Her head turned slowly, and he imagined an old door, creaking open. Her eyes narrowed. "And yet you have. Go. Sit outside. I need to think."

He stood and left the house.

Night thickened around him. Cold coalesced into a fist, punched, squeezed at him in its delight at finding someone unprotected in the street. He huddled into his greatcoat, slipped his fingers into his armpits. He remembered long nights where the snow and wind howled and hammered at the eaves. Irina called them the Wolves of the North.

He'd wake from a night terror, gibbering about the cold and the teeth. She'd wrap her arms around him and promise as long as the fire burned in the hearth, it would keep the wolves at bay. It seemed the fire had been banked since then. Or perhaps he'd kicked dirt in the hearth.

A flood of memory.

The garden in the back he'd spent weeks saving for, scrounging boards from abandoned homes for the beds; the time the roof leaked and he'd spent a rainy week atop the shingles hammering scraps of tin and cloth wherever he could to help stem the flow; hauling huge fly-blown paracera carcasses from the wagons as they came into the plant, hunters standing by looking ragged and scarred; of making love in the rain in a city park; of strolling through the Norylska library, Irina's eyes alight in the echoing halls; a thousand other points of bright light.

And now this. The eclipse. The dark of the moon. The stink of the trench and the roar of artillery in the night. A raging inferno, and his life threatening to collapse into ash.

Arkady.

Burn it down.

Burn it all down.

The door opened, spilling light onto snow. Inside, the hearth roared. Irina sat beside him, handed him a cup of tea. They sat in silence for a while, Gen holding the cup, letting it warm his numb fingers.

"You're a fuckup," she said.

Told you.

"But you're my fuckup. The only question is what're you going to do to make it right?"

He opened his mouth, and she cut him off.

"It had better be good. And this better not happen again. Ever, Genndy."

He blinked. "Ever."

"There's a militsioner..." he began. She cut him off.

"Fuck me. Come inside, you idiot. I don't want to freeze out here. And stomp off your boots, or I swear to the gods, I'll remove your feet."

She walked into the house before him, and despite himself, he grinned.

"Come on, already, *chush*, I'm freezing!"

He followed her in, the door closing off night and cold behind him.

For a little while, at least.

KATYUSHKA LEONOVA – CHAPTER TWENTY-EIGHT

Ishcheglov was putting on his greatcoat, about to take leave of a lovely young lady.
"Aren't you forgetting about the money?" she asked.
Ishcheglov turned to her and said proudly, "Militsioners never take money!"

—Unknown Komik

Kat crossed the unimaginatively named Middle Street into Tikhonenko territory. Worshippers of Mokosh, the Great Mother, they ran the southern quarter with fingers into everything from prostitution to smuggling to politics and banking. Half the men of the Chernyshevsky Street Militsiya Bureau complained the better-dressed and better-equipped militioners in the southern precincts were on the Tikhonenko payroll. The other half joked they should go to the Shkuts to ask for a raise.

The difference one block made was stunning. In a few hundred strides the houses changed from wood and tin shacks to brick and stone. Roofs of cracked boards became rounded tiles of red clay imported from the west a great expense. It even stank a tiny bit less, though that might have been more of a masking effect from the many bakeries and sweets boutiques.

By the next block, the streets were near free of snow, shovelled down to the cobblestones. Even the alleys were cleared.

People in tailored jackets that couldn't possibly be as warm as the slovenly and much-patched attire of the north, looked fantastic. No doubt their brisk pace served not only to make them seem busy and important, but also warmed them somewhat.

A stunning blond in a tightly fitted waistcoat and hip-hugging skirt hurried past, the long heels of her boots clattering on stone, her lips blue.

"Pizda," Kat muttered under her breath.

Nothing said 'Norylskans have neither the time nor energy to read' quite like the city library.

The first time father brought her here, she'd stopped in the street, gawked at the colossal building. It looked like one of the great castles from the end of the tribal wars of the Norvezhskoye Plemya. A massive tower at every corner, crenellations bedecked fieldstone walls. Wrought iron bars guarded every window. Black as the darkest tower in any play, as a child she'd been awed and impressed. Later she learned it was simply filthy, stained by centuries of being in Norylska.

Climbing the long and shallow steps to the main entrance, she was winded by the time she reached the top.

"Business?" the guard demanded, stopping her with a raised hand. A retired militsioner, the man still wore his greatcoat.

"Militsioner Katyushka Leonova," she said. "CSMB."

He studied her own greatcoat, newer and better maintained than his, and shook his head. "Not right."

"What isn't?"

"Women. Working. You're taking a job from a man. How is he going to support his family now?"

"Maybe he can whore himself with the fucking silkies. You going to let me in, or do I need to tell Grinin you're interfering with an investigation?"

"I'm just saying it ain't fair some bloke has to be unemployed while you strut about in that too-large coat." He crossed his arms, blocking her path. "Ain't right."

Strutting? I don't even know how to strut.

"What's next?" he demanded. "Women in the factories? Women in banks? Lady soldiers?"

"All the crime families are run by women," said Kat. "Can you name a more successful business?"

"Different," he said with a huff. "That's a low sneaky kinda smart. Women are good at plotting and backstabbing."

"If you don't get your fat old ass out of my way, I'm going to show you how good I am at front stabbing."

Biting his upper lip, he stepped aside. "Yep," he said, "yer one of Grinin's."

The front desk sat empty, the librarian nowhere to be seen.

Kat stalked through cavernous rooms of empty shelves, her footsteps echoing down long halls. Passing an arched door with a massive hand-carved sign proclaiming it the Fiction Wing, she saw more rooms of vacant shelves. Cutting through the Political Sciences Wing, she found a single bookcase with eight copies of *A Time of Prosperity: The Ascension of the Khromov Family*. The economics wing had three books, all of them *A Treatise on the Failures of Altin Ordu Capitalism*. The Biology Wing was mostly books on the efficient harvesting of megafauna. It took half an hour of searching before she found a room labelled Languages. Inside, she found texts on Kievan grammatics, most of which she'd read in school, and several books on translating Altin Ordu. There was also a single dusty shelf stencilled with the words Historical Languages and no books.

"Fuck."

She turned in a helpless circle.

Should she go in search of a librarian? Was there one?

"Fuck!" she shouted, voice echoing down stone halls.

"Fucking be quiet!" someone shouted back. "This is a fucking library!"

Well, that probably answered the librarian question.

"Where are the fucking books on ruinic Plemya?" she screamed, voice raw from the cigareta.

"On the fucking Historical Languages shelf!" replied the distant, echoing voice.

"They're not fucking there!"

"Oh!" And then, after a score of heartbeats, "Try the History section!"

"Thanks!" she hollered down the hall.

"You're fucking welcome!"

Kat went in search of the History Wing.

Hours later, she sat smoking and flipping back and forth from the book on ruinic Plemya to Lazarev's code book. Her right foot tapped as she read, gathering speed until her leg vibrated. Stunned, she realized it was rather more than a simple list of men and stones. This was Lazarev's personal manual, his own notes taken over decades of study and experimentation. The earliest entries were over sixty years old. She couldn't imagine him as a young man.

Her stomach gurgled so loud she half-expected someone to yell at her. Vodka, cigareta, and a fistful of cold eggs, it said, is not a meal.

In some ways cracking the code was easier than she expected. Lazarev had relied almost entirely on the language barrier to stop people from understanding his manual. Translating a long dead language based on strange scratchings, however, was a challenge. To make matters worse, the veneficum often resorted to acronyms and shorthand.

The twitchy need to move, to act, grew.

Part of her wanted to hide here forever, lose herself in book after book. The Plemya were fascinating. For thousands of years, they warred across the steppes, nomadic tribes mounted on scruffy ponies. They hunted slower megafauna for food, used their monstrous bones as weapons, and worshipped towering obsidian obelisks from an even older age. The obelisks were said to be fallen gods stored in stone, though most scholars mocked the idea. Instead, they suggested the myths came from the early veneficum arts of enshrining traits and memories of the tribe's greatest warriors in stone. Such trinkets were highly valuable and passed down from generation to generation. Many young warriors, Kat read, wore stones of their fathers sunk into their flesh during ritualized scarification ceremonies.

She closed the book, brushing the cracked leather cover with her fingertips. This was the Kat she remembered. She used to spend entire days in the school library researching anything and everything that caught her interest. She'd go in wanting to learn something about the red-tailed hawk and come out knowing everything about the migratory routes of the deinotherium and how their spleens were valued as an aphrodisiac among Altin Ordu's inbred and syphilitic nobility.

Was that me?

For a moment, she wasn't sure. She had to close her eyes, imagine the Great Library in Kievan, and picture the young girl sitting tucked into a big, leather smoking chair in the lounge where her father left her. Even then, she wasn't sure. Sometimes it was a boy sitting there, and the library was smaller and in Yakutsk.

Focus!

She thought she had a reasonably solid grip on which stones the veneficum used for various traits, and the meaning of the colours chosen. In part, it was simple and rather predictable: The darker and richer the colour, the stronger the trait stored on that stone. Unfortunately, he seemed to have a fondness for stones in cooler colour range. He used a lot of sapphire, kyanite, lapis lazuli, zircon, and even lighter shades in topaz and aquamarine, and referred to them as green. Others, like tourmaline, chrome diopside, chrome tourmaline, peridot, chrysoprase, and jade, he labelled as blue. It became really confusing when she found the section on bluish-green stones.

Hoping she understood both enough Plemya to translate a few basics, and the code well enough not to be too far off, she hunted through Lazarev's book for her name.

She found a short list of militsioners at the end of the book. Either most only wore a memory stone, not needing the help of additional personality traits, or there was another list somewhere else.

Kat found her name.

Mixed feelings warred within. On one hand, she felt a strange gratitude to the veneficum. He put her in the book. The old man was probably the only person in the entire Chernyshevsky Street Militsiya Bureau who thought she was a militsioner.

Maks' friends, Prybilov, Maminov, and Tsukanov, were nice.

But they were dead. Murdered by the same Shkut enforcer who gave her this book. She wanted to hate Gen but couldn't dredge up the emotion. Their brutal deaths were too far away from her already considerable problems.

She remembered Gen hammering Maminov over and over with the submission stick, finally driving it through the militsioner's eye socket. She saw it stand there, quivering.

Kat blinked. *I don't care.*

She should though, shouldn't she? Shouldn't she, at the least, feel guilty about not caring?

Their deaths should have some impact. But she hadn't given them a thought. Instead of being horrified, she'd rushed off and fucked Maks behind the Bucket.

That's not me.

Or was it? It felt like many of her so-called normal emotional reactions were little more than acts, theatre of the expected. And not just for the benefit of others. Sometimes she was the sole audience. Fyodor got angry and stormed off. She worried and cried not because she cared, but because she was supposed to.

Is that true?

It felt true. At least now. Later, when the stones came off and she forgot this nightmare—or was shot by the state or skinned alive by the Shkuts—she suspected it might stop being true. Or at least she'd stop thinking it was true.

Was there a difference?

"All there is," she whispered, "is right now."

The Kat she was when the stones came off would wander into the Filth and give Arkady the memory stone and die a terrible death. Only this Kat, the Kat who drank and smoked and whose shoulder still ached from where Maks bit her, could save them. And all that was due to Lazarev. His stones were going to save her life. He was the only reason she could even begin to deal with this insane situation.

Lighting another cigareta, tucking it tight into the corner of her mouth, Kat got back to work.

The final piece was discovering the Plemyan number system and how Lazarev used it to grade the strength of the stones more accurately than relying on gradations in colour. The scale appeared to be out of five, though she saw reference to a stone labelled with an eight. She couldn't tell if she'd misunderstood, or if the aging veneficum made a mistake. The Plemyan four looked an awful lot like the eight.

In the end, she laid out what she could piece together of the stones she wore.

"Red agate," she read. "Grey striations. Saw-Scale. AGG four."

Pulling open her shirt, she checked the stones. One matched the description.

"What's a fucking saw-scale?" Kat shouted into the hall.

"It's a fucking snake!" the voice shouted back. "Mean as hell!"

A snake? Did that mean the personality trait was akin to a mean snake? Was it yet another layer of code?

She'd read of tribal shamans trapping the souls and aspects of various animals in stones to give to warriors, but those stories were ancient. Then again, there were always rumours the militsiya revived long forbidden veneficum practices during the war when it looked certain the Altin Ordu would win.

Had Lazarev given her a stone with traits taken from a snake?

Did it matter? She hadn't turned into a cold-blooded murderer, but she had been able to fight and flee Gen when he caught her in the alley.

Lazarev saved my life.

What was the AGG? Aggravated?

While worried—and it wasn't like she didn't have reason—she was hardly angry.

Aggressive?

You threatened to smash Penkin's face in.

Much as he deserved it, she had to admit that wasn't typical Kat behaviour.

AGG four. Four out of five levels of aggression? It seemed a bit much, but then she was so fucking timid to begin with, Lazarev probably thought she needed the boost to get her through the day and deal with the svoloch of the Filth.

"Blue Azurite. Mottled green and brown. Salt-water crocodile," she said, reading the next line. "IMP two."

She knew what a crocodile was, but what the hell was IMP?

Impishness?

She considered asking the echoing voice if crocodiles were impish, but it seemed like a stupid question.

"Come on, damn it. Personality traits." She smoked, ashed on the floor, itching to move on to the next line. "Impatience?"

What use would that be?

Did the veneficum think she was too patient to be an effective militsioner?

She thought about how Maks and the other reacted instantly in the back alley veneficum's when Arkady and his goons showed up. Was that the same?

It's only a two, she decided, moving on.

"Rhodolite Garnet. House cat, F. ESTR three."

She felt much faster than she had before, but was speed a personality trait? Or did it come from knowing, deep in her bones, what needed to happen?

"ESTR," she said. "What the fuck is ESTR?"

Estranged? Had Lazarev given her traits similar to that of an abandoned house cat?

No. If anything, she felt like she belonged more than ever before.

"Black melanite. Rat," she said, reading on. "INS/NRV three."

Gods above, this was frustrating! She felt nothing like a rat!

"Maybe I'm looking at it wrong."

She'd read about how no matter where you went in the world, you always found rats. They were an incredibly successful species.

She thought about those bright eyes and twitchy noses.

"They're alert."

It was damned near impossible to sneak up on a rat. That wasn't so bad.

Annoyed, she skipped to the next line. "Brown scapolite. Katina Sokolova, Kolyma-1428. FA/A five."

Each damned line was more incomprehensible than the last!

"Fine," she said, grinding her cigareta out into the brass ashtray at the corner of the table. "Katina Sokolova. That's a name. Obvious." Unfortunately, it wasn't one that meant anything. "Kolyma... That's the gulag in the Kolyma Mountains where Tsar Khromov sends all the worst dissidents." She wrinkled her nose in thought. "Fourteen twenty-eight."

If that was a date, it was over one hundred years ago. Could a trait be stored in stone for that long? She had no idea.

"Fuck," she whispered.

So either Lazarev gave her a bunch of stones with traits quite literally taken from animals—which she thought was forbidden practice, but then again this was the militsiya—or he'd named the traits after animals they reminded him of as part of his code.

Did it matter?

"Keep the memory stone but remove the personality stones."

Even as she said the words the idea terrified her.

"Isn't one of these stones supposed to be bravery?"

It appeared not to be the case, though perhaps she'd completely misread the code or her translation from ruinic Plemya was faulty. What if Lazarev didn't think she needed a stone for that? What if he knew she was brave enough?

She grinned at the crumpled butt of her cigareta, half wishing she'd used it to light another.

He believes in me.

Where no one else did, not her father, not Fyodor, not even Maks, Lazarev knew she wasn't a coward. He knew that when it mattered, she'd find her courage.

When I faced Gen in the bathroom, that wasn't the stones!

It was all her.

She wanted to cry for gratitude, to sprint back to the precinct and give the old man a hug.

"Penkin," she said, rising to her feet, collecting the leatherbound book. "Penkin stole or copied this and sold it to the Shkuts."

He was a worm, and she was going to stomp him flat.

GENNDY ANTONOV – CHAPTER TWENTY-NINE

Well, fuck. That could've gone better.

> —General Slava Grigori, at the Massacre of Tikhon Fields

"Let me get this straight," Irina said, rubbing her eyes with the heels of her hands, "Arkady—your boss—screwed you over with these stones, so you stole his codebook, and passed it off to this—this Kat, and now I have to hide because he's going to find out and probably try to kill me?"

Gen nodded; took another swig of the vodka she'd dug from behind a book in the living room.

"Fuck me, Gen," she said, and sighed heavily. "At least you don't do anything half-assed. I suppose I can stay with Mrs. Isay on the east side. I'll gath—"

She didn't get to finish the sentence. The front door—the door Gen had spent hours planning so it fit the frame just right—crumpled like an old man kicked in the stomach. It swung inward, slamming against the wall, one hinge loose. Boris stepped in, flicking a fat cigar into the hearth. A knot of Shkut men followed, spreading out.

Gen registered their faces, having met them at the party. Saveli, whip-thin and quick. Lavrenti, favoring a wide-bladed knife with a hooked end. Pankrati, big and stupid, holding an axe that looked like it'd been used for more than wood. Miroslav, more muscle than man. And Stinkteeth himself. Vicious. Fast. Scary.

Kill them all.

Gen stood, shoving Irina behind him. He flipped the table and ducked as a revolver thundered in the space. At least Boris wasn't wasting time. The round hammered into the thick wood of the table, splintering it but not penetrating.

Something in his head snarled, followed by the sound of scales cutting across ice. Gen welcomed them in.

Saveli and Pankrati try to come around the table, flanking. Gen's already on the floor, the table acting as cover from Boris' big bastard of a revolver. Kick across the polished wood toward the smaller of the two, sliding as he goes. Heel, out, driving into Saveli's ankle, snap the other leg up at the last second, catching the small man inside his knee. The joint pops like a gunshot and the ankle folds, Saveli going down in a heap of pained groans and misery.

Another shot from Boris' pistol, and Gen grabs the downed Saveli, rolling the man into a shield. The bullet catches him in the back, and Saveli looses a scream descending to a gurgle as a perforated lung fills with blood.

An impact snags Gen's attention, the edge of a blade shearing a chunk of skin off his still-bruised ribs. He flinches and rolls again, still holding the bleeding and choking Saveli. The man flings his arms up to ward the descending axe blow away. It catches him in the face and a shower of bone, blood, and brain cascade over Gen, detritus trickling into his mouth. He spits in disgust, and kicks Saveli's corpse off while Pankrati tries to loosen his axe from the man's head.

Another gunshot, and Gen ducks out of reflex.

Thank fuck Boris can't hit shit.

The bullet shatters a curio Gen bought Irina for their third anniversary. She shrieks in rage, and Lavrenti, who had been trying to press his attack, stiffens. Irina's massive butcher blade rips from the front of his throat, carrying a portion of his windpipe with it.

Another shot from Boris detonates the man's head, and a second on the heels of the first, punches into Irina's shoulder, folding her in on herself for a moment like crumpled paper. Gen doesn't see where, but she cries out and spins, a pirouette. The room slows. Time stops.

Her blood, an arc.

Her eyes, wide in terror.

Her mouth, set in determination.

Rage.

The world snaps to normal speed, and Pankrati comes at him, axe free of its bone prison. Miroslav's joined the fight, taking a different approach from the two dead men, and trying to trample Gen, relying on size and speed alone.

Pankrati's axe comes down.

Miroslav approaches, inevitable, deadly.

Gen sidesteps the clumsy overhand axe swipe, grabs Pankrati's wrists, and forces the axe into an upward arc, using its momentum against it. It finds a home in Pankrati's testicles, and Gen kicks the blunt head once, hard. It slams upward, tearing into his taint, cutting deep inside his pelvis. His guts drop out like a basket of fresh-caught fish on a trawler.

Gen dives to the side as Miroslav arrives, the man's momentum slamming him into Pankrati, sending the two tumbling. He snags Lavrenti's knife and rolls once, burying the hooked end in Miroslav's throat. He yanks, and the man's neck opens like a red zipper.

Boris' pistol roars once more, and Gen feels a chunk of meat from his already-damaged ribs disappear. Cursing, Stinkteeth throws the revolver away and shrugs off his coat. Tattoos cover every inch of his exposed arms.

I recognize that one.

He stands, tries to ignore the searing pain in his ribs. Tries to ignore the hole in his heart, Irina falling again and again.

Sucks in a breath, and the thing in his head builds a wall. He stands a little straighter. Tosses his coat in the corner as well, hefts Lavrenti's blade.

Gen nods toward a tattoo of Khagan spires with the number thirteen beneath them.

"You served."

"Aye," Boris says.

"Thirteenth Legion. Krupin's Irregulars."

"Aye."

They circle, each looking for the other's soft spot.

"Your bitch went down easy," Boris says.

"Aye," Gen replies, even though fire nearly consumes him from the inside.

Boris lunges, a knife in his hand where there had been none. Block. Parry. Retreat.

Bastard's fast.

"Krupin's," Gen says when they part. "Weren't they the ones at Red Pass?"

"Aye," Boris says, baring his teeth. They're black as night.

He lunges again, does something quick and complicated. The knife cuts Gen three times before he can disengage.

Can't afford to lose more blood.

"Gonna eat your woman when we're done here. Might even leave you alive. Might even let you watch," Boris says, trying to bait him in again.

It's not that Gen disbelieves it. It's that he can't afford to get caught off guard. The man is walking murder.

"If," Gen says instead.

Boris stops, cocks his head to the side in amusement. "If?"

Gen darts forward. Boris sees it coming, dances out of the way, knife lashing out. It catches Gen, leaves a long cut on his forearm.

Fuck.

Done with words, the Skhut assassin moves in, fast and low. He lands a score of hits. Gen's bleeding from a dozen places, the knife in his hand in turns sticky and slippery. His vision doubles.

Sheathe the blade.

Was hoping it wouldn't come to that.

Do it, or he'll do it for you.

Gen disengages, watches the other man's feet, hips. Can't watch the hands. Can't watch the eyes. A good fighter never telegraphs. Shift of stance. Subtle, weight moved to back leg to launch weight forward.

Gen drops his guard—not too obvious—blade not up quick enough, reaction time a second too slow. Boris lunges for the kill. Reflex kicks in, and Gen turns slightly, lets the knife pierce him. It rips into the muscle over his hip, snags.

Pain, ice-cold, fire-hot. It's an iron poker in his side. Surprise registers on Boris' face.

Don't kill him.

What?

We need him.

Gen reverses the killing stroke at the last second, hammering the hilt of his knife between Boris' eyes. The man roars in pain, releases his own weapon, and staggers back. Gen lets the fury come then and presses the attack.

He crushes the man's eye socket with a roundhouse. Hard kick to the inside of the knee. Boris skips back, but it's still enough to dislocate, if not break. He stumbles, throws something at Gen.

Fuck!

The needle misses by an inch, but Gen can hear it sizzling where it struck wood behind him.

Nasty fucking things. Thought only OSD had those.

The passenger in his head is quiet. Gen redoubles his efforts. Straight kick to the point of a hip sends Boris spinning. The man lands face down, and Gen jumps on his back, smashing his skull into the floor. Teeth and snot and blood form a chunky puddle. Gen doesn't stop until the man stops struggling. He checks, once, to make sure he still has a pulse, then rolls off him.

Deep breaths. Control the pain. Control the adrenaline.

The world forces itself back into focus.

Irina. Somewhere in the wreckage of their kitchen. Spotting her, Gen crawled over. She'd propped herself up against the cabinets, fingering a hole in her blouse. Only a small amount of blood marked the tear. Grazed, then.

"Couldn't shoot for shit," she said, half to herself, half to him.

"Yeah," Gen agreed.

He joined her at the cabinet, resting his back against it. They sat in silence for a minute.

"Mrs. Isay?" he asks. "Is she the one who always smells like cabbage?"

Irina shook her head. That's Mrs. Isaev. Mrs. Isay is the one who looks like a wrinkled toe."

Gen made a face.

"Oh, this you're okay with, but a toe?" she gestured at the catastrophe surrounding them.

Another stretch of silence.

"What're you gonna do, Gen?" she asked.

"Question him."

"And then?"

"Kill him."

"And then? The militsiya? You're going to let them handle it?"

Gen shook his head. "I have to be sure the job's done. That they can't ever come after us. No bribes, no lenient sentences."

She made a sound of disapproval, then looked at him. Seemed about to say something, then changed her mind. Her eyes held his.

"And you can do that? Make them leave us alone?"

"I can make them leave you alone, yeah."

"And what about us?"

He didn't answer. When he did, it was to change the subject. "Get your things. Go sit with toe lady. I'll send word when it's safe. And if I don't..."

"You will."

"If I don't, get out of Norylska. Find a militsioner. Find anyone. Leave."

One more long silence. Finally, she found her feet and picked her way over the wreckage and down the hall to their room. After a time, she returned, bag in hand. She looked around their house. Sorrow writ itself large on her face. And fury. Gen didn't know for who. Wasn't sure he wanted to. She looked at him and smiled.

"I was just thinking. Of Sochi in the summer."

"Yeah?"

"Yeah," she said.

They'd always talked about moving there. They'd had a chance to go, just the once. Being newlyweds, they'd seen little of the countryside, and even less of the city.

She gave their home a long look then, a sigh escaping her, then left the back way.

His body reminded him he was fucked up. Between Kat and Boris and the entire shitshow this week had been, he felt like a prolapsed asshole. He looked down. Blood pooled in his lap.

Fuck, that's a lot. What's good to stop bleeding? Oh, yeah.

He cut strips of cloth from the nearest corpse—Lavrenti? Saveli? Didn't matter. They were dead. Wouldn't miss the shirt. Taking his time, he carefully packed each wound with ash from the bucket by the fireplace, binding them with a strip of cloth. Assuming he lived through this, he'd see a chiurgeon. The best chiurgeon. Not a Family chiurgeon.

Gen laughed aloud.

Fuckin' blood loss.

At least he didn't have to worry about Boris. Someone loses consciousness like that, they rarely wake right up. And even if they do, they ain't right. He used the cabinets to lever himself up, fumbled through the kitchen until he found kvass and bread. Ate 'til he felt a little better.

Stomach full, head centered, he proceeded to cut strips from the dead mens' shirts until he had several lengths. Then, he made his way over to Boris. He flipped the man with some difficulty. Boris' face reminded him of a paracera flank he'd botched once. Flat and mangled, mostly toothless now, it resembled nothing more than a bruised hunk of meat.

Gen cast about, looking for something to secure the man to. Finally, he settled on his old chair. With a great deal of pain and some struggle, he managed to get the limp seated. It took two tries, and a pause to catch his breath, but he did it.

Then, one by one, he tied the man's limbs down. Legs to the legs of the chair. Straps around the chest and neck. Around the forehead. Finally, the arms to the arms, taking care to strap forearm and wrists separate. Satisfied, he made his way back to the kitchen and out the back door.

The snow molded Irina's passage like a sentence trailing off. He stood there, the reality of the situation hitting him like a brick to the skull. For a moment, the world wavered. Then the stink of copper carried from the heat of the hearth inside, and he scooped a bucket of snow.

He sat the snow beside the fire, waiting for it to melt.

Krupin's.

He'd heard of Red Pass. Osip's dossier on Sobek confirmed it. The man's own memories confirmed it. If even half of it wasn't myth, made up, or misremembered, Boris would be a hard one to crack. The men of Krupin's Irregulars had been trapped in that pass for three months, cut off from supply lines. By the time the OSD found them, only half their battalion remained. The other half were bones, picked clean.

Gen glanced at the bucket. The snow had melted. He stood, picked it up, and dumped it over Boris' head. The Shkut assassin woke, sputtering in surprise and rage, a litany of curses on his lips. He struggled to free himself, but only succeeded in making the band at his throat tighter.

Gen turned Irina's chair from the fire and sat on the edge, Lavrenti's blade in his fist. He tapped the flat against Boris' knee.

"I'm going to ask you some questions. You're going to give me some answers."

Boris struggled again, and Gen cut off one of his fingers to make a point. The man clamped his lips tight, screaming in his throat.

"Do we understand each other?"

No reply. Gen sighed.

"Then I hope you're ready for a long day, tovarich."

KATYUSHKA LEONOVA – CHAPTER THIRTY

In Kievan, it takes more courage to retreat than advance.

—Tsar Besarionis dze Jughashvili

There was still no one at the front desk when Kat exited the library. The fat old retired militsioner on guard shot her a dirty look as she passed. On a whim, she stopped halfway down the steps and marched back up to face him.

"Yellow fingers," she said.

"What?" He looked at his stained fingers.

"You smoke."

"Think yourself a first-class detective, eh?"

"So you have matches," she said.

"I do."

"Let me see them."

She waited as he fumbled, fat fingered, through the inner pockets of his greatcoat.

"You're right-handed," she said, "Your matches are in the left side breast-pocket."

He retrieved a slim cardboard box of wooden matches. Snatching them from his grip, she spun on a heel and walked away.

"Worth it," he called after her, "to watch that victorious strut."

How the fuck can he see anything in this stupid greatcoat?

Men. Most of what they thought they saw was in their imagination. How many times had she seen guys ogle a woman who was six hundred strides away and swaddled in a floor-length parka?

She walked north, suddenly aware of the swing of her hips. Did she walk differently with the stones on?

Can't blame Kostas for this.

She felt better, fearless. Not a big surprise if that manifested in a more confident stride.

Why is it called strutting when women are confident but for men it's just walking?

Lighting a cigareta, she inhaled hard and deep, holding the heat in her lungs. Gods a pivo would go down well right now. And food!

The sun sat low in the west, a sanguine smear of pollution and swollen storm clouds. An icy wind blew in from the north, tugging at her coat and hair. Her face and ears burned with the cold. The whole world felt *crunchy*, like compacted snow.

Taking a different route back to the Filth, she passed by the hut she and Fyodor shared. After the massive stone homes of the south, chimneys belching smoke from roaring fires, it looked small and sad. The eastern wall leaned in, bowed by the weight of the snow-covered woodpile. Decades of soot stained the windows grey. No smoke wafted from the chimney, a rusting tin pipe jutting and an awkward angle through the roof.

He hasn't come home.

It was kind of disappointing. She'd looked forward to his reaction when he climbed into bed and discovered she puked all over his side.

It would be cold in there, the drinking water crusted over with ice.

Everything still, a mausoleum of broken dreams.

They were shitty dreams anyway. What was so great about being the pretty and well-behaved housewife of a lawyer who drank and whored with the partners? What was so fucking fantastic about living in fear of his anger, worrying each day what his mood would be like when he finally came home?

'Are you so perfect that you should never change and grow?' Lazarev asked on that first day.

Only now he'd worked his veneficum magic, helped her change and grow into a stronger, more confident woman, did she realize how good a question it was.

I thought I was happy.

Living in that shitty shack, chopping wood and slogging groceries from the poor northern market every day, she thought she had everything.

Resisting the urge to douse the shack in oil and set it afire, she continued north.

Never going back there again.

She didn't know where she was going, where she'd stay, but she'd figure it out. She had a job. Soon, if she wasn't shot or skinned, she'd have money.

Maybe I can stay with Maks.

She laughed at the thought. It turned into a broken sob of pain. Once his memory stone came off, he wouldn't know her at all. And at the end of the day, when she handed in her stones, she'd forget all this. She'd forget the strength. She'd forget the confidence. She'd return home to that fucking shack and wait for Fyodor like a puppy, tail wagging, desperate to please.

She wanted to carve a note to herself into her arm.

Don't go home, you stupid pizda.

Snorting an unladylike laugh, she wiped her tears on the sleeve of her coat.

Still blocks from the precinct, Kat tuned onto Chernyshevsky Street. The setting sun and centuries of filth turned the precinct red like blood.

A figure waved at her from across the street, jogging to intercept.

Maks.

Shit.

Rubbing his bruised jaw, he slowed to a stop several strides distant.

"You kicked me. In the face!" He looked more upset by the last part than physically injured, as if he wouldn't have minded so much if she'd kicked him somewhere else.

"Sorry," she said, not at all sorry.

If he doesn't get out of the way, I will kick him somewhere else.

"Where were you?" he demanded. "I've been searching the Filth for hours! I was worried!"

He was? Concern and anger warred across his face. But was he worried about her, or that she was getting close to cracking this foul business wide open?

She loved and desperately wanted to trust him.

That's Kostas, not me!

Something lurked behind his caring eyes. Suspicion? Anger? Whatever it was, he was trying to hide it.

Maks made a placating gesture with his hands. "Everything is going to be all right. I talked to Penkin."

Kat froze. "Are you fucking stupid? It was Penkin who stole it in the first place."

"He did?" Maks blinked in confusion. "That makes no sense. He's Lazarev's apprentice, a veneficum-in-training."

He's Lazarev's apprentice?

Kat's mind raced, putting the scattered pieces of the puzzle together. Penkin had access to the vault and the stones, many of which hadn't been touched since the war. Where the assistant was fastidiously neat, Lazarev was scattered and messy. It would be easy for Penkin to take some of those long-unused military stones and sell them to the Shkuts. That was probably where Arkady got the ones he gave to Gen.

And Maks ran straight to him.

He held out a demanding hand. "Give me the book. We can still fix this."

Fix this. Penkin would get the book back and they'd kill her like they did Kostas and yeah, everything would be fucking fixed.

"I can't," she said. "As long as I have the book, I have *something*. You'll give it to Penkin."

He blinked in confusion. "Penkin? I'll give it to—" He cut himself off, started again. "Look, Kat, I just want what's best for you." He stepped closer. "We're partners. We're in this together."

He's lying.

"You think I'm stupid," she snapped. "You think I don't remember. You weren't there."

"There?"

"You were supposed to meet me. They fucking skinned me alive and I held out knowing you'd come because even if you can't love me the way I love you, we're still fucking friends!"

"You love—" Understanding and pain lit his face. "Kostas? You can't be."

"You betrayed us! Me! Him!"

"Fucking gods no." His eyes widened in horror. "They tortured him for hours! Stones with that kind of pain aren't supposed to stay in rotation."

"And then at that veneficum, just you and Arkady alone, and you saunter out like nothing happened."

"I didn't saunter—"

"If I give you the book, I'm a dead man." She twitched. "A dead woman."

"Gods above," growled Maks. "You're as crazy as a cat in heat."

"You have to back off," said Kat.

He moved closer. "You know I can't do that."

"Please."

He barked a laugh of derision. "You think I'm an idiot. You think you can play me. Smoking and drinking with me, chatting me up." He looked away. "Dragging me behind the Bucket to fuck me." She tried to argue, and he talked over her, not listening. "You're trying to get in my head. Well, I've been a militsioner a long time, and maybe I'm not the best, but I'm not dumb. Let's see how this looks from an actual sane point of view."

"I'm not crazy." The armour of the stones cracked and for a heartbeat she felt like the old Kat, facing Fyodor's quiet anger.

Again, he ignored her. "You left the veneficum with that huge Shkut kryshas chasing you. You admitted he caught you, yet wandered out of the Filth with nothing but a few scuffs. And then later he corners you in the bathroom and instead of killing you, he gives you Lazarev's book. For reasons I can't even begin to comprehend."

"He thinks Arkady—"

"I'm not fucking done!" He stepped closer, got bigger. "I saw the way you held the book when you came out of the bathroom. If I hadn't said anything, you'd have happily tucked it into your coat without a word." He squared his shoulders. "You're not leaving with that book."

"You're not taking it."

"No?" His hand slid into his coat pocket and he frowned in confusion.

"Looking for these?" she asked, brandishing his knuckleduster. The deadly weight was a comfort.

He didn't move, didn't retreat. "I was looking for my cigareta."

"You're a shitty liar."

"I'm a shitty liar? Penkin told me you stole the book. Lazarev told him that—"

"Of course he did."

Maks reached for her. Not fast, not threatening, but she slapped his hand aside. Never let a bigger opponent get hold of you, a lesson hammered into the slim Kostas over and over in bootcamp before the war.

"You can't run from this," said Maks. "Lazarev knows everything. He said you're a Shkut infiltrator. He said you stole the book."

Real fear. "He said that?"

Maks nodded. "He told Penkin."

"Penkin? Did you actually see Lazarev?" she demanded.

Maks hesitated. "He was in the back, in the vault. Penkin told me everything."

Lies. This was all lies, his story changing as she picked holes in it.

Surprise and momentum were the weapons of the smaller opponent. A good fight was one that ended before the bigger man knew it started. A fair fight, the drill sergeant said, was an idiot's fight.

Kat glanced over Maks' left shoulder with a confused frown. When he turned to look, she punched him in the throat with the knuckle-duster on her right hand. In her head she'd seen his throat crushed flat, him falling back gagging and helpless. Instead, he managed to take most of the impact on a raised shoulder.

Coughing, Maks retreated, hands up and ready for a fight.

It was always going to come to this.

The way he kept trying to get closer. That bullshit puppy dog act. Penkin sent him to kill her and retrieve Kostas' stone. It all made sense. Lazarev might not notice a few missing stones no one had used in years, but he'd know if the stone of a murdered militsioner disappeared.

Stones with that kind of pain aren't supposed to be in rotation. The one thing Maks said that sounded true.

I bet Penkin swapped the one Lazarev meant to give me for Kostas'.

It made sense. If the assistant could copy Lazarev's writing so perfectly, he could easily make changes to the stones worn by various militioners. The veneficum had no idea who she wore; not once had he mentioned Kostas by name. Gods above, had Penkin tried to poison him against her, breathed lies into his ear?

"If you're really Kostas," said Maks, "then you know we sparred many times. I always won."

A weak distraction and a lie.

Kat ducked under his lunge, hammered an iron punch into his ribs.

Mak grunted in pain.

Two could play at the mental game.

"He loved you," she said.

"No, he didn't." Hurt doubt.

"Not this you, the *real* you."

Maks was too easy. She read the instant his thoughts turned inward.

Kneeing him in the groin, she snapped an elbow up into his chin. Knees buckling, he crumpled. She followed him down, hammering him with punches.

Betrayal.

Murderous rage slithered in her gut.

They loved him. They hated him. Every fucking night the Shkuts skinned them alive and they waited for him. Every night he failed to come.

He lied.

He left her to die.

He was supposed to be there! He was supposed to save them.

Kat hit him again, felt the crunch of bone.

He flailed at her, disjointed pawing. Brushing aside his arm, she hammered iron punches into his face.

Wet choking.

Silence it.

He was trying to turn Lazarev against her. Her only hope, the one man who believed in her. Silence him forever so he couldn't spew his poisonous lies.

White teeth.

Break them.

"I loved you!" Kat screamed into the shattered ruin of his face.

He lay limp, unmoving, beneath her.

She stood.

Penkin. This was all Penkin's fault.

GENNDY ANTONOV – CHAPTER THIRTY-ONE

If intellectuals in the plays, who spent all their time guessing what might happen in the next decades, were told prisoners would have their skulls squeezed with iron rings; lowered into acid baths; trussed up naked to be bitten by ants and bedbugs; a ramrod heated over a stove thrust up their anal canal; a man's genitals slowly crushed beneath the toe of a jackboot; and, in the luckiest possible circumstances, prisoners tortured by being kept from sleeping for a week, by thirst, and by being beaten to a bloody pulp, not one of the plays would have reached the end because all the heroes would have gone off to insane asylums.

—A.S., *Islands in Sibesk*

Gen let Boris scream while he heated the flat of the knife in the hearth. When the iron glowed red-hot, he pressed it against the stump of the man's severed finger. The flow of blood slowed to a trickle in a geyser of stinking steam, meat surrounding the wound blistering and boiling, smelling like so much cooked pork.

Gen's stomach rumbled in contrast to disgust welling up at the sudden hunger pangs. He wondered when he'd last had a decent meal. A moment of understanding for Boris and the Khagan Thirteenth, the men trapped at Red Pass, passed through him.

Was that how it started? Had one of their own grown weak and fallen into the fire? Had they perhaps tried burning a body for fuel and instead wakened their own appetites? Or had they simply fallen on the dying like wolves, only to discover later, as all men raised from animals did, that meat tasted better roasted?

Gen's mouth watered, and he pushed the thoughts away.

These damn stones.

The task.

He regarded Boris. To the man's credit, he hadn't shed a single tear, though pain lined his face, as if spiteful fingers pinched the folds around his eyes and mouth. He'd shut his eyes tight, perhaps to retreat to a safe place.

You know what to do.

Gen shied from the thought. A litany of horrors wormed its way across his mind, each more terrible than the last, and he knew this was the least of where this might go. He tapped the freshly-cauterized stump of Boris' finger, making the Shkut assassin jump in surprise. Boris opened his eyes, fixating on Gen with hate.

Better if he'd left them closed.

Self-loathing rippled through Gen as he imagined Irina's reaction to the scene. Better she had gone. Had never known the man he'd become. The man he'd been. It's the way with all people who entwine in another's life, though. They only get glimpses through a dirty window into who the other truly is. Sometimes the window breaks, however, and the things they see beyond leave shards of glass in their heart. Gen was sure Irina had one lodged in hers now, cutting away at the ties that had bound them for so long as easily as it might shred heart and artery.

"Genndy Antonov," Boris said, words coming out like meat from a grinder. They cut into Gen's reflection, bringing him back to the now. "Lieutenant, Ninth Division. Irkysk. Bronze Cross. Commendation for Gallantry Under Fire. Commendation for Exceptional Service."

How-

OSD. The man was part of the Thirteenth. They'd know. We always knew.

A small piece clicked into place in Gen's head. Boris' hate, disdain for him from day one.

"Hero," Boris spat. The word an indictment. Gen knew what came next. Made his face a mask. "The Altin Ordu have another word for you. As did your own men. Butcher. Thresher. The Red Death.

"They watched at Veliky. After taking the town, you slaughtered anyone who'd raised a hand in defense. Down to the animals. Root and branch, isn't that what you called it? Rooting out the poison?

"At Kazan, you had your men nail the huts shut, and set fire to the homes until they told you where the Altin Ordu had gone. Forty-four corpses, we'd recovered, working cleanup. It smelled... delicious.

"And in Irkysk. Oh, Irksyk, the brave Gen. The gallant Gen. When they stopped you murdering, they found nearly as many of your own men heaped among the Altin Ordu.

"Then you come home, and pretend you were never a monster."

Lies. Half-truths.

"The war made me a monster. It made beasts of us all. In some it slumbers, and they fight to keep it chained in the dark. Others wear its skin proudly," Gen said.

He removed another of Boris' fingers, sawing slowly through the bone. The man did scream then, and thrash in the chair. Gen waited until the bleeding slowed, then cauterized the wound, smoke trailing from the stump.

Sobek stirred in his head, and he felt movement. Ice dropping over emotion, freezing it in place. Purpose replaced it. Cold logic.

"You know what the problem is with a knife like this?" he asked by way of conversation. "It's clumsy. Good for chopping and stabbing, but not enough finesse to it."

He tossed the weapon aside and made his way to the kitchen. Taking his time, he picked a knife from the butcher block. The blade was long and thin, and like all of Gen's knives, sharp enough to peel air.

Good sharp knife. Means the pain will build, hit him in waves.

He took his place across from Boris again, and laid the new tool on his knee.

"Where is Arkady?" Gen asked.

Boris closed his eyes, clamped his lips shut. Gen cut into the man's trousers, exposing his testicles. A threat. He could no more unman someone than he could kill a child. Boris clenched his thighs in anticipation.

"Fine. Let's have another conversation, before that one. You came to kill me. My family."

Boris nodded, eyes flickering open again. Gen leaned in and snipped the man's ear off. It came away easily, blade parting it from the side of the man's head like a leaf pruned from a flower. Boris moaned, and tried to tip his head as blood flowed down the side of his neck, pooling in his collarbone, dribbling down his chest.

Gen cut the man's shirt open.

"My wife?"

Boris nodded. Gen took a nipple, slicing it free as easily as a man snips the end from a sausage. More blood, fat and muscle exposed beneath. Another groan of misery.

"What proof does Arkady have?"

Despite the pain, Boris sneered. "He found what you'd stolen. What you'd done to Artyom."

"The snake."

"The snake. Idiot."

"Ah-ah. Language."

Gen set to with the knife, cutting a circle around Boris' pinky finger, Sobek guiding him, whispering technique like poison. With practiced movement, he ripped the meat off, leaving bone and vein exposed like a diagram laid out in a chiurgeon's textbook.

Agony struck the man, and Boris vomited, chunks of meat mixed with watery bile cascading down his chest. The mixture hit the wound where his nipple had been and he let a squeal of pain as the acid got to work. The remainder coated his exposed testicles as it flowed to his lap.

Gen slammed the knife into the wood beside Boris' genitals. The assassin flinched for the first time.

"Some people think torture is pain," he said. "It's not. It's time. Knowing your time is up, and just... waiting. You have family, Boris?"

The man didn't answer him.

"Ah, of course you do. The Shkuts. Champions of the everyman. Dashing knights-errant."

A flick of the blade upward, close enough to Boris' testicles for him to feel the cold passage of steel. The Shkut enforcer squeaked, a mouselike sound. It was all Gen could do not to laugh.

"Root and branch. Funny you should bring that up. You know why I used that tactic, Boris? Because we'd found in the past that leaving the families of dissidents alive just created more dissidents. But slaughtering them to a person, salting the earth where they lived? Effective in stomping out future pain and sending a message to witnesses.

"For coming after my family, I'm going to exterminate yours, like the cockroaches they are. The only question is, do you help willingly and find yourself a quick grave, or do I make this last?"

Boris set his jaw, glared daggers at Gen.

"Fuck, I was hoping you'd say that. When I'm finished, the Hell I send you to will seem like Heaven," Gen said.

He stood and grabbed Boris' forehead. The man tried to thrash, tried to turn his head, but Gen had tied him too securely for that. When that didn't work, Boris shut his eyes tight, forehead furrowed. A temporary display of defiance. Gen prised first one eyelid up, then the other. He removed the lids with surgical precision.

Is this me, or Sobek? Am I the snake or the fang?

He mentally shrugged, casting the folds of skin into the fire, then sat.

A constant stream of tears flowed from Boris's naked eyes, mingling with blood from the severed eyelids. He made wounded animal sounds in his throat.

"Want to blink, don't you?"

Boris grunted.

Fuckin' hope I didn't break him yet.

"They're going to dry and start to itch. In all likelihood, it'll drive you mad before I can kill you. You should think about that. Take your time."

Gen stood, stepped through the back door into the icy early day. The cold was bracing, a sharp counterpoint to the stifling heat of the living room. He took a breath, two.

We could walk away. Killing Boris would send a message.

He glanced over, saw Irina's footprints still outlined in ice.

Not until she's safe.

Another deep breath. He walked back inside.

Boris was a horror show. A staring mannequin of a man strapped to a chair, covered in blood and vomit. The constant stream of tears had dried, and the whites of his eyes grew a web of red veins.

Gen sat across from him again.

"They say you can find the measure of a man in what secrets he keeps. I wonder what secrets your blood and bones hold? Your lips, your toes?" he hovered the blade over the man's testicles. "Your future children? Where is Arkady?"

Boris remained resolute. Gen grabbed his hair, forcing the man's gaze down. With the other hand, he parted the flesh of the man's thigh, laying it bare as he had so many Paracera hides in the factory. Peeled the skin to the sides, opening it like a book. Red striations of muscle, white lumps of fat, yellowed tendon peeking out from the carmine forest.

Boris keened, a mournful sound, and Gen severed a thick bundle of muscle. Boris cried out as it peeled back.

"Where." He cut another. "Is." Another. "Arkady?"

Muscle shriveled away from bone, exposing purple vein, throbbing in time to a panicked heart. The keening reached a new pitch, fresh tears flowing from exposed ducts. Had Boris eyelids, his eyes might have rolled wildly. Instead, they flicked around the room in panic. Still, he kept his secret.

Gen rammed the flaying blade into the tendons keeping his leg whole. Severed the limb from its moorings. They snapped with a wet twang. Boris screamed, voice cracking. Gen didn't wait, beginning to peel the other leg.

"Gods and devils below!" Boris finally bellowed, voice cracking on the syllables. "He has a safehouse beneath the Square of the Patriots! A monster you've made me a monster you've ruined me, my beautiful flesh, you've ruined me!"

Sanity departed, filled the air with imprecation, pleading, and babble. Finally, it returned. Boris snapped his mouth shut. Glared balefully. As if he could anything else. "You'll never survive. Never. When they find what you've done, the Family will kill you and all you love. Root and branch. Root and branch."

He resumed babbling, a litany of nonsense. Gen sighed, stood. Yanked the tongue from the man's mouth as one might rip bread from a loaf. Blood rushed from between Boris' lips even as he continued to gabble nonsense. Gen sat down once more.

He retrieved the snake's fangs from a pocket and pressed them one at a time into Boris' naked orbs. The poison inside the hollow needles had lost no potency, and sizzled as it ate at them. His eyes deflated slowly, running and dripping like wax down his cheeks.

He'd ceased to scream at some point, the noise in his throat little more than scraping and clicking.

Gen rammed the flaying blade into an empty socket, the knife sinking hilt-deep, scraping the back of the skull. One last thrash, a final cough of gore from a ruined throat. The man died as he'd lived. Hard and Ugly.

Gen leaned back, wounds throbbing. He felt the beginning of a fever coming on. He didn't doubt the Shkut were careless with their weapons. Exhaustion threatened to overwhelm him.

How did I miss you?

Sobek's voice cut into the lethargy.

You weren't looking. You didn't want 'honorable' men. You wanted killers.

An oversight. A shame, you would have been an asset to the OSD.

I have enough horror to account for without it sanctioned by the state.

Yet, somehow you still cling to what you call morals. You only think they stand because you attach them to a cause.

Gen ignored the rest. There was still work to do. He stood and found the last of the liquor in the house. His bottle of brandy, stashed in the bookcase. He held it for a moment. Irina had gifted it to him on their first anniversary. Possibly the only thing in the Filth that didn't taste of turpentine and ash.

He emptied the bottle over Boris' corpse, then threw it to the side. Stooping with a grunt, Gen retrieved the man's knife, kicked the body and chair toward the hearth. He waited until it caught, then retreated to the kitchen, waiting a little longer still until the room was ablaze.

Heat singed his eyebrows, made the hairs on his arms curl. When he could stand it no longer, he swept on his coat and stepped out the back, halting in the yard. Smoke rolled from the doors of his home.

He needn't worry about the fire spreading far in this weather, nor the militsiya showing any time before tomorrow. Filth problems. And it was often said, Filth problems required Filth solutions.

Gen turned, scanning the snow. Irina's footprints trailing to the east. He gave the house one last look. Flames licked from the windows, between cracks in the slats.

A lifetime, gone in a moment.

He knew he should feel something more. Sorrow, perhaps. Only vague nostalgia and a driving sense of urgency pushing him onward filled the places where it might have sat.

He headed west, hopping a neighbor's rickety fence, then down a narrow alley separating homes so close they might be syphilitic lovers. On the street, one last look back. The sun hid behind a haze of cloud, as if even it were ashamed of what it found below. Smoke from the fire joined that from the factory, an incestuous blending of life and death.

Come, there is blood to shed yet.

Gen moved south, toward Arkady.

KATYUSHKA LEONOVA – CHAPTER THIRTY-TWO

The poet's soul could not stand the shame of petty insults.

—Mikhail Lermontov

Kat stood over Maks, searching herself for some feeling, some emotion. Regret? Rage? Vindication?

The blood of the setting sun succumbed to grey as ashen cloud devoured the sky. Wet snow fell hard, blanketing her partner. It gathered in his lashes and hair, turned red where he bled. The red faded to pink as more fell, disappeared beneath pristine white.

The war with Altin Ordu ended with the worst winter Kievan had seen in centuries, both armies caught unprepared. Men froze to death at their posts, rigid sentries who wouldn't sleep until the thaw. The priests proclaimed Marzanna, goddess of winter, seeing the imminent fall of Khagan, stepped in to save her people.

As ever, the gods had little regard for the cost.

'*Though Mazanna hides away our sins*' the priests said, '*each spring Rudjevid reveals our guilt.*'

Only the distant groan and growl of the forges and reducing factories broke the perfect silence.

Maks didn't move, didn't twitch.

"You betrayed Kostas," she told him. "Ushakov skinned him alive and he never spoke because he knew you'd come; he knew you'd save him."

She remembered it so clearly, the ice-feel of razor-sharp steel slipping through flesh. At first, as if stunned, the body felt no pain. It crept in, cold turning to fire. Snake-souled Ushakov, tongue flicking, reptilian twitch. The pain of the blade was nothing compared to the peeling.

"I'm going to kill him," she told Maks.

She doubted there was enough man left in the Shkut torturer to notice or care.

"I'm going to kill Arkady, too."

There could be no peace. Giving him the stones solved nothing. Surrendering them to Grinin solved nothing.

"I'm going to kill everyone involved. Anyone who would hurt me."

Kat understood men now. Kostas fought in the war. He was infantry. He fought in the trenches, walked endless alleys of mud and frost-encrusted corpses. She remembered fixing a bayonet to her empty rifle, screaming as she charged the Altin Ordu lines. The hot steam hiss of bullets, men crumpling like abandoned marionettes as if Mokosh cut the strings of their life. She knew what it felt like to push steel into a man's chest. Kostas hadn't worn the stone back then, but he thought about it so often the memories were there for her.

"Men are terrible creatures of fear and insecurity," she told Maks. "You hide everything you could be."

Snow gathered in sightless eyes.

"Women fight different," she said. "Slow. Subtle. We win by changing you, though not the brutal and clumsy way a man seeks to change a woman. We win by changing what you want to be."

Is that why woman run the crime families?

The streets were empty. Maybe because of the coming storm. Maybe because two militsioners just fought a bloody battle.

"In the vocabulary of a soldier, I suppose we're sappers."

The precinct waited at the far end of Chernyshevsky Street. Grey stone, cold and threatening.

She prayed Lazarev was safe. Had Pekin panicked, worried Kat was getting close, and killed him? The assistant didn't seem the type to keep a level head if stressed. If only Maks hadn't run straight to him, told him everything.

Another betrayal.

"I don't have time to war the way a woman would," she told her partner. "So, I fight the way men do. And you know how that ends."

Death.

Bloody hands tucked into the pockets of her greatcoat, Maks' knuckle-duster still in place, Kat entered the precinct. The old man with a single eye at the front desk—*Gregor!* she suddenly remembered—didn't stop digging behind the frayed eyepatch as she strolled past.

Everyone noticed her and no one saw her.

It reminded her of the way Maks moved through the Dripping Bucket on that first day, oblivious to the anger.

They hate me.

She saw it now in the set of their shoulders, the way they pretended to ignore her. The coded language of men she only understood because she was secretly one of them.

They resented her presence, the fact she took what should have been a man's job. As if there were a limited number of employment options and that one man who would have been a militsioner now starved on the street with his family.

She'd been so caught up in how they were all trying to ogle her tits and ass she hadn't noticed. They still did that—men were entirely capable of lusting after something they loathed—but that desire only contributed to the hate.

Not yet end of shift, no militsioners lined up at the Veneficum's office.

Kat entered without knocking.

Startled, Penkin, looked up from his desk, frowning at the intrusion. "Miss Leonova." He looked past her. "Where is Maksim?"

"Don't pretend to be surprised," she said, locking the office door behind her.

"What, *exactly*, do you think you're doing?"

"What I should have done a long time ago."

She strode toward his desk.

Penkin shuffled back in his seat but didn't rise. "Much as it seems an eternity, at least to me, you've only been here three days."

Kat barked a harsh laugh. "Yeah, forgot. I guess Kostas always hated you too."

"Kostas?" he asked, brow furrowing in confusion. "Maksim's old partner? I didn't think you'd met."

"Stop pretending you don't know," she said.

Kat stood over the assistant. He sat, lips pursed in annoyance, as if daring her to touch him. As if the very thought she could be a threat was inconceivable.

"Maksim said you had Veneficum Lazarev's book," he accused. "Lazarev was enraged. I've never seen him so angry."

A sick twisting she hadn't felt since her father got angry with her as a child coiled in her gut.

Penkin tried to turn him against me.

"Where is he?" she asked.

"In the vault."

Seeing the closed vault door, fear tightened her chest. Was she too late? Had he already murdered the old man?

"I think it would be best if you handed over your stones now," Penkin continued. "*And* the book you stole."

Take off my stones?

She'd forget everything. Helpless and weak, she'd be at Penkin's mercy. She remembered flinching from his dislike when they first met. He'd walk over her like everyone else. And she would let him.

He'll blame me for everything.

"I bet you'd like that," said Kat.

Dragging the assistant from his chair, she smashed his nose with an elbow.

It felt good. Much better than beating Maks.

She hit him with a knuckleduster still dripping her partner's blood.

Making wet *smurk* noises, Penkin pawed at her.

Pathetic.

"You thought you could use me," she growled.

She hit him again, shattering teeth.

"You thought I wouldn't figure it out."

Frantic clawing. Manicured fingernails raked her arm and she hit him again.

Penkin folded, curled up on the floor.

"So fucking smug."

Grabbing the nearest chair, heavy oak with the blunt simplicity of all militsioner furniture, she hit him with it.

Blink.

Kat leaned forward, both hands resting on the back of a chair. Breathing hard, sweat plastered her hair to her brow. Loose paper and writing utensils littered the floor.

Where am I?

She wore a rusted and bloody pair of those knuckle-things gangsters wore on her right hand. She couldn't remember where it came from.

Someone knocked on the door and she froze in fear.

"Everything all right in there?" a muffled voice asked.

Still leaning on the chair, she swept her gaze across the office. A young man in an expensive suit lay on the floor. Face bloody and broken, his skull was distorted. One eye a gory ruin. The other stared white and wide at the ceiling. One of his arms bent the wrong way, forearm turned at a sick angle in the middle.

Penkin.

Someone had beaten him to death.

Looking down, she saw blood painting the legs of the chair she leaned against. Bits of hair clung to the gore.

Again, the knock and the voice.

This chair.

Someone killed the veneficum's assistant with the chair she held.

Demons below, no.

Had she walked into the scene of a murder?

Nothing made sense!

Kat tried to piece together her memories.

I came to work. I was talking with Lazarev.

She put on the necklaces, and then here she was.

Am I still wearing it?

Still bent over, her shirt hanging open, she looked in. The stones were still there. In this position, they no longer made contact with flesh.

Take them off. Go home.

Home. Fyodor.

That bad man had come to their home, threatened them. He said if she didn't bring him the stones, he'd skin her alive. How long had it been? It felt like a heartbeat had passed since Lazarev gave her the stones, but everything hurt now. Knuckles bruised and swelling, her hands ached. She felt like she'd chopped wood for hours.

Penkin dripped blood.

Fresh. Someone murdered him right here in his office. Were they still here?

No. It was just the two of them. Whoever it was must have fled when she arrived.

She looked at the bloody brass knuckles on her right fist, the shattered ruin of Penkin's face.

No.

She flinched from the terrible sight.

Take the stones off. Give them to Lazarev.

She and Fyodor would find somewhere to hide until all this passed.

Kat pushed herself upright. The stones rested against her chest.

Penkin, that weaselly little fuck, lay on the floor where she left him. Hefting the chair, she found it undamaged.

"Good chair."

The militsioners made things to last.

"Penkin," said the muffled voice from beyond his office door. "You all right in there?"

"He's fine," she said. "Fuck off."

Whoever was out there grumbled and fucked off.

Realizing how close she'd come to removing the stones and leaving herself utterly helpless, Kat heaved a sigh of relief. She didn't dare take them off until all this was over. Reaching back, she tied a knot in the slack of the chain, making sure she wouldn't lose contact with the stones again.

Releasing the chair, Kat surveyed the room. Penkin's fastidious office was a disaster, blood-spattered papers littering the floor. She'd silenced him quickly enough he hadn't been able to call for help or make too much noise.

Lucky.

Lazarev.

Penkin said he was in the vault. Was he dead?

"If you hurt him..." Kat warned Penkin's corpse.

The vault door swung open, and Lazarev exited. Slowing to a stop he looked from Penkin to Kat.

"I can explain," she said.

"I certainly hope so. Because right now, it looks like you beat my assistant to death."

Kat winced. "Yeah. Well. I suppose I did."

Showing no hint of fear, Lazarev raised an eyebrow, waiting.

"He works for the Shkuts," she said. "I think he's been stealing military stones."

"You think?"

She withdrew the book from her greatcoat pocket.

"Where did you get that?" asked Lazarev.

"A Shkut kryshas by the name of Gen. He stole it from Arkady, a Shkut avtorityet."

"I see." Brow furrowed; he rubbed his chin in thought. "This is worse than I realized."

"You knew?"

Ignoring her question, he said, "Your partner was here. I heard him talking with Penkin. Did he find you?"

Kat nodded. "I think I hurt him."

"But he's still alive?"

She shrugged, uncertain.

"We'll deal with that later."

"Should we take this to Grinin?"

Lazarev shook his head. "You've killed at least one militsioner and possibly two. The Colonel will never believe you unless we have proof they were dirty."

"I have the book."

"But we can't prove where it came from. It's just as likely Grinin will think I sold it to them and then we'll both be shot."

He looked lost, scared.

"I wouldn't let anyone hurt you," she swore.

Flashing a look of gratitude, he said, "I have an idea. But first, we need to get out of here before someone finds young Penkin." He turned a dazed circle, taking in the state of disarray. "One moment."

Ducking back into the vault, he returned a moment later, slinging on a new necklace of stones and tucking it under his shirt. Shrewd eyes surveyed the room.

"We'll put him in the vault," said Lazarev. He stood straight; the stooped slope of his shoulders gone. He sounded commanding, certain. "A quick tidying will have to do." He turned on Kat. "You did well. I'm proud of you." Her heart soared and she wanted to scream with joy. "We have to work fast."

GENNDY ANTONOV — CHAPTER THIRTY-THREE

If only it were all so simple! If only there were evil people insidiously committing evil deeds, and it were necessary only to separate them from the rest of us and destroy them. But the line dividing good and evil cuts through the heart of every human being. And who is willing to destroy a piece of his own heart?

—A.S., *Islands in Sibesk*

Beneath the Square, Boris had said.

Gen stood on the outskirts of Patriot's Square, a cigareta clenched between his lips. He'd never smoked before, wasn't sure why he'd started. The craving had crept into his skull like a sneak thief, and by the time he was three streets from home, he'd had to stop at a newsstand for a package of tobacco and a box of matches. He'd stood outside, rolling the things like he'd done it a hundred, thousand, times before, fingers numb and shaking.

The first drag made him cough. The second clung to his lips and throat like a lover's juices. It made him dizzy and lightheaded, and he savoured the sensation.

People trundled through the cleared cobbles of the square, breath pluming. Clouds loured overhead, lightning turning near-black to purple. The storm rolled in, thick and angry, cold racing ahead like a herald, a promise of ice.

Beneath the square. He knew it was more complicated than that. Had it been easy to find, anyone seeking a warm stable home away from Norylskan winters would crowd the tunnels. Until the militsiya found them, anyway. Nothing pissed the state off more than someone living in unearned comfort.

The Bucket stood on the far side of the crowd like a malevolent sentinel. Gen let his eyes roam over people and shops, and plucked a memory from Sobek.

Not hard, he'd found, the longer you shared space with another. The walls became less solid, blurry. The hard part was enforcing boundaries threatening to erode like sand in a windstorm.

Rude.

Gen laughed. He let his eyes fall on the statue of Solynska. The old man stood stern and proud, rifle clutched in one fist, the other upraised in a gesture of defiance. At its back, a door, cleverly concealed from passing eyes. Behind the door, a sloping tunnel. Maintenance shaft for the thermals. If Kievan engineers could be counted on for one thing, it was the application of subterfuge in civic planning.

He made his way casually to the statue, isolated near a sickly clump of birch trees fighting for survival. Bare white branches raked black sky. Once in the shadow of the revolutionary, Gen worked quickly, popping the door and slipping inside.

The dark swallowed him.

The wall of the tunnel was damp, but not frozen, air thick with humidity this close to the geothermals. He fumbled in the dark, looking for a light source. Fingers finding the cold iron of a lantern, he lit a match, the wick sputtering to life.

Thank the gods for small miracles.

He crept down the tunnel. It descended for some way, deeper than he'd expected. As he went, Gen became aware of the weight of the city above him. Not just stone and flesh, but emotion, memory, and misery. It felt like a ten-ton hammer waiting to drop. Then, descending, deeper and deeper, his thoughts turned to below. In the stories, Hell lay just beneath the surface, waiting for its due of souls, and more than one Plemyan hero had taken the wrong path and ended up a devil's feast.

The passage levelled out, giving way to a proper maintenance shaft. Pipes ran the length, branching off into the darkness. Gen squatted, set the lantern on the floor, and lowered himself beside it with a grunt of pain.

They'd sent three of them below in Veliky. The Altin Ordu had dug tunnels beneath the village. Killed entire households, replaced them with their own and dumped bodies in the fields, among the stalks of winter wheat. Some little guy, Kuzma, found an opening on patrol. Gen had rerouted the entire company, camped only a mile or so outside.

They'd gone in, just the three of them—Gen, Kuzma, and Bronislav. They were about three hundred yards into the tunnel, crawling on their bellies, when the first trap went off. Bronislav's head vaporized with a muffled thump.

They'd had to drag the corpse out and start over. Four hundred yards the second time. The Altin Ordu had buried a knife-spring in the floor of the tunnel. Kuzma dragged his guts another ten yards before he bled out. Gen towed the soldier out himself.

He picked two more, and they went in, Gen at the lead this time. The tripwires were clever: gossamer-thin strings stretched across the tunnel. He took his time, paused at each hint of resistance, each glimmer of silk in the light.

What felt like hours later, they came up in the first hut. Gen slaughtered everyone in it. And the next. And the next. By the time morning rolled around, Veliky had been liberated, Altin Ordu bodies hung from the branches of oaks outside town.

They'd given him a medal for that.

And still OSD labelled him a monster.

The memory faded. The glimmer of tripwires criss-crossed the tunnel. Gen unsheathed Boris' blade and got to work. One by one, the strings fell free. One by one, the memory of dead comrades came to him.

Kuzma's face flashed by again—wide smile, face like putty. Small and ugly, but funny. Gen's hand slipped, and he tripped the wire he'd been working on.

A metallic twang.

He threw himself to the ground, a bolt tearing through the air where he'd been. It clattered harmlessly against the wall behind him. Gen lay on the stone of the floor, breathing damp air in great gasps. His side hurt still. Fuck, his entire body hurt. His heart, like a thousand needles worming their way into his veins.

Irina, walking out. A smile on her lips, eyes like open wounds.

He closed his eyes.

So easy to rest here. Boris is gone. Irina is gone. My home, ash. I could turn around. Find Irina. Flee for Khagan.

You think he'd let you rest? You think he'd let you just vanish, that he'd buy that? And even if he did, would Lia?

Sobek raised a good point. Had Arkady told anyone other than Boris? Was he playing his cards close, in case this went south for him? When it was over, and he'd won, what was his move?

Your disgrace, your utter downfall. Irina and your child, in their graves.

No.

He levered himself up, limbs shaking. A deep breath. He drew on the strength in the stones, steadied himself.

No.

Step.

Step.

One foot in front of the other, and he was moving again. The pain hadn't faded, the fever remained. But he had work to do. He could die later. Probably would.

The lines came down, one by one. Veliky was the past. Irina and his child, the future. He cut until his shoulder ached and his eyes throbbed in their sockets.

Arkady had to be the most paranoid bastard in Kievan, which was saying something.

Finally, he cut the last line. The ends drifted to the floor like spiderweb. On the other side, an iron door, a keyhole cut into the metal. Gen knelt beside it, listened. Nothing, just the gentle susurrus of air. He dug into the pockets of his coat, found the picks there. Slipped the torsion bar in, the hook against the tumblers.

He'd done this a hundred times before as a kid. Sometimes it was the only way to get the bread you needed to live. Sometimes you just wanted some candy. Sometimes you pretended to have a wealthy friend, snuck into his house with your wife, and fucked on his billiards table. Gen's hands shook, slipping off the tumblers.

Fuck!

Closed his eyes, worked the pick by feel. It came easier the second time, tumblers aligning. The lock gave with a gentle *click*, door easing open. Gen checked the threshold, set the lantern down, and hefted Boris' blade. If Arkady was in there, he'd have to hit the place fast and quiet.

He slipped into the crack between door and frame. Froze.

Light flooded the room. Gas lanterns hung on the walls, hiss of flames a constant counterpoint to the soft breathing of the bodies in beds arrayed in a wide grid. Gen blinked. Thirty? Forty? Every person sleeping. Not even the mutter of dream or a wayward snore broke the quiet.

What the fuck is this?

He padded around the room cautiously. If one woke, they would likely raise the alarm for all. He came across a row of women and paused. This one, he recognized. The Shkut silky, pert breasts tenting the gauzy blouse she wore. A frown furrowed his forehead. He moved to his left, and found another row—

men in good suits and perfect hair. He recognized one: The banker who'd originally paid out his pension after the war.

Gen's stomach clenched. Something like fear crept into his guts, an icy fist squeezing his bowels. He was suddenly seized by the urge to shit. Ignored it until the cramps in his pelvis passed, the aftershocks traveling up into his wounded ribs and side. He leaned against a bed until he could move again.

Another row—Mrs. Fedya, the woman who ran the Filth farmer's market. Mr. Oleg, his old landlord. Gen moved through row after row, seeing more faces he recognized, or thought he did, panic threatening to flood him. Finally, in the centre, he halted. Arkady lay on a bed, dark skin in contrast to the white sheets. He breathed evenly, looked at peace.

Kill him, be done with it.

Gen sat on the edge of the bed. He would. But first he had questions. He slapped the man lightly on the cheek. Then, when he got no response, harder. Again, harder than before. Arkady did not stir. On a hunch, Gen moved to the next body, a young woman in her prime, breasts partially exposed, legs long and lithe. He pinched a nipple until colour bled from it. She too ignored him.

Or couldn't respond.

He moved through the rows once more, slapping, pinching, leaving little cuts on each body with the knife as he passed. Not one woke. When that failed, he yelled. Loud enough to wake a sleeper at first. Then louder, what Irina called his 'command voice'. Finally, screaming at the top of his lungs. First to wake them. And when they didn't wake, to loose the things built up in his chest. He screamed from frustration. Fury. From wrath and loss and hate and pain. He screamed until his throat was raw and his voice threatened to fade into silence.

Gen stood beside Arkady again, echoes dying down. He leaned in, opened the man's shirt. No stones hung around his neck or adorned his fingers.

More questions, more puzzles.

He slapped Arkady out of contempt. Out of anger. The man's head rocked to the side, and still he continued to breath steadily. Gen grabbed the man's hand and snapped three fingers, the sound of breaking bone like pistol shots in the room.

Nothing.

He did the same to two more bodies, breaking and cutting.

These are the living dead. Shells.

A veneficum did this.

Rage again, white-hot and blazing. He started in one corner. When you've got a difficult task, sometimes it's easier to approach from a mathematical angle. Disassociate, become mechanical. A machine built for harvesting.

Irina's garden, corn straggling toward the sun, stalks withered with the changing of the seasons. She'd laughed when he tried to slash them down and they wobbled, bouncing back up.

"There's a trick to it," she said, bunching them in a fist then hacking into the bundle. They came away clean. "There's always a trick to reaping."

He slit a throat. The first spray of blood from an artery surprised him. Always did. It coated his face and neck, soaked the front of his shirt, mingled with his wound dressings. Dead beasts had no pressure left in their veins. Gen had cut hundreds open, their lifeblood drooling from the incisions. Living bodies, however, even devoid of spirit, still had hearts pumping in ribcages, fluttering like red birds.

Blood welled, spilled over, a broken fountain. It stained the sheets, pattered on the floor, formed rivulets. He moved on. Slit the next throat, and the next. Rivulets became a river, the river a flood.

Gen paused halfway through. Not so different from harvesting paracera. Cut the arteries, bleed it so the meat doesn't spoil. The only thing missing from this slaughterhouse were hooks to hang the carcasses.

He flexed his wrist, rolling it until the bones popped.

Back to work.

Cut, cut, cut. Sever the ties that bind. Rip the throat and spill the life. Gore, so thick it clotted as it dried. Clung to the cuffs of his pants. The stink of copper and iron, and shit and piss became another entity in the room, a haze built from the memory of life. It embraced each snuffed soul, smothered the spark from them.

Finally, he came to the centre. Arkady still lay in repose, an ocean of blood around him. Gen waded it, crawled atop the body, straddling the man's hips. He leaned in, Arkady's sleeping breath soft against his cheeks.

"My only wish is that you were awake so I might savour this," he whispered in the man's ear. "When you get to Hell, tell them I'll be close behind. Maybe they'll give you a running start."

He raised himself up and brought Boris' knife to bear. Hammered it into Arkady's chest. The Shkut's breathing hitched, burbled. A gurgle of air erupted from his lips, chased by a crimson bubble. It clung there for a moment, then burst, spattering the Solostian's face in a smattering of carmine freckles.

Gen pulled the blade toward him, heaving backward until the sternum cracked and split. Arkady's ribs released, his chest deformed, the wound tearing open. The heart inside still beat feebly.

Gen reached in and ripped it free. Hot and slick in his hand.

Hunger, deep and abiding, stomach clenching in desire.

He bit into the thick muscle, tearing a chunk free. He chewed, savouring the flavour, then cast the rest to the pool beneath the dead Shkut.

The door opened behind him, and Gen, still crouched over Arkady's corpse, turned.

KATYUSHKA LEONOVA – CHAPTER THIRTY-FOUR

The Altin Ordu call their veneficum 'büyücü. Culturally-driven differences in their approach to the art are worthy of further study. Due to unfortunate choices of wording early on, we have blinded ourselves to certain possibilities. The typical Kievan practices a physical skill—be it a music instrument or a martial art—over and over until the moves become rote. Rather inaccurately, we call that 'muscle memory.' Muscle, it turns out, is wholly incapable of storing memory. Rather, the repetition of physical actions creates new pathways in the subject's brain. Muscle memory' is entirely neuronal in nature, meaning it is something that can be captured by a sufficiently skilled veneficum.

We have long been impressed by the seemingly impossible skill of the Altin Ordu fencing masters. Now we understand its source.

—Iskusstvo Veneficum

After hiding Penkin's body in the vault and neatening his office enough to pass a quick inspection, Kat followed Lazarev from the precinct. Militioners nodded to the veneficum as he passed, but no one commented or said anything.

He walked like a different man, stride purposeful. He had none of his typical forgetful hesitancy. His entire bearing changed. Previously, she couldn't imagine him in the war.

He uses his own arts.

The real Lazarev was a peaceful old man. But he knew when that version of him wasn't up to the challenges it faced. Kat understood all too well. If anything, she felt closer to him.

We're the same.

Together there was nothing they couldn't do.

Late in the evening, the western horizon showed only the faintest bloody blush. Sootmen hustled their carts from lamp post to lamp post, scampering up their stepladders to fill and light the lanterns. Others worked the streets, shoveling snow into waiting wagons. For now, they'd achieved a stalemate, but it was a war they were doomed to lose. After years in Norylska, Kat knew storm clouds when she saw them.

"It's going to be a bad one," she said, strolling at Lazarev's side.

He didn't answer.

Instead of heading south, to where she'd assumed all the ranked militioner officers lived, the veneficum veered north, heading deeper into the Filth.

"Where are we going?" she asked.

A strange thrill chased through her veins at the thought she might see Lazarev's home.

Of course *he lives in the north.* A man like Lazarev had no interests in the comforts of wealth.

This new Lazarev intrigued her. He wore his body differently from the man she knew. This wasn't the first time he changed, she realized. There was the Lazarev that Home Kat—as she'd begun to think of her other self—knew, and then there was the man he became once she donned her stones. Home Kat had none of her respect for the veneficum. He always seemed like a kindly old man, but her appreciation for him grew when she wore the stones.

It's because Home Kat doesn't see how he changed us, how he made us better.

Less afraid.

The weight on her right hand caught her attention; she still wore Maks' knuckleduster, now damp with the blood of two men. She recalled Home Kat's horror when she saw Penkin.

She's weak.

Walking at Lazarev's side, Kat stole a look from the corner of her eye.

'Some people are what they are,' Arkady had said in her kitchen. 'One layer. No matter what you're wearing.'

She understood now. It wasn't Lazarev that changed, it was the way she saw him.

The stones make me more perceptive, allow me to see more of the man he really is.

"We live surrounded by walls," Kat said, lost in thought. "Most of them we build ourselves."

"How so?" he snapped the question the way Kostas' drill sergeant used to bark orders.

"Walls to protect us from hurt. Walls to keep us distanced from others." She thought about Maks, hiding at home with his books and then coming to work to drink and fuck at the Dripping Bucket. "They're prisons."

"Morals," said Lazarev. "Ethics. Proper behavior. Right and wrong. All cages. As if anything in life is so black and white. Murder is bad unless you're at war. Torture is bad unless getting that information will save lives. Stealing is bad yet who wouldn't take a loaf of bread to feed their starving child."

Kat blinked and a tear fell. She couldn't help it. All her life her father pushed these ideas into her, made her feel guilty about everything from wanting a doll to being angry he ripped her from her life in Khagan.

Lazarev's stones opened the door to her cage.

She owed him everything.

"Thank you," she said. "You freed me from the prison I made for myself." She wanted to tell him she loved him, that he was the father her father should have been. She couldn't speak the words.

"Some people are what they are," she said, struggling to express her appreciation for this multi-layered man. "But you are someone entirely new."

Lazarev darted her a startled look.

Flickering lightning lit the clouds from above, turned them into hollowed ghosts, the translucent bones of gods.

"Gen is dangerous," said Lazarev.

"You know him?" she asked, surprised.

"You said he was a kyrshas. That type of enforcer are known for their cunning brutality. Why did he give you, of all people, the book?"

Of all people?

"He thinks Arkady gave him poisoned stones. That's how I figured it all out," she said. "He brought me the book and I was immediately suspicious of Penkin. When Maks told me Penkin was an apprentice veneficum, I realized it had to be him. He had the access and the knowledge."

Lazarev's laughed, a strange, humorless sound. "Sad to say, I never suspected my assistant. I suppose that explains why he was so willing to work late, after I'd gone home. You did good."

How long had she waited for those words from her father? Long enough she gave up, stopped waiting.

Kat hurried to match Lazarev's long-legged stride.

A gust of wind, hard and cold from the north, snuffed most of the street lanterns, undoing the work of the sootmen. Tonight, it seemed, they were losing a war on two fronts.

"For a moment," she admitted, "after I killed Penkin, I was horrified at what I'd done."

"You did what you had to do." He sounded distracted.

"I was standing there locked in fear, someone banging on the door. All I wanted was to run back to Fyodor."

"As if that cowardly lawyer could protect you."

He was right. When Arkady came to their home, Fyodor didn't even put up a fight. They could have raped and murdered her right in front of him and he would have done nothing.

Well, he'd have been quietly angry.

Mostly at all the time he wasted trying to turn her into the woman he thought she was supposed to be.

"It was the stones," she explained.

"What?" Lazarev asked.

"The way I was standing. The memory stone was no longer touching me. For those few moments I was *her* again."

"The best place to keep stones is on the inside."

"Swallowing them?"

Grunting a laugh, he said, "Pebbles tucked into incisions made in the flesh. The savage tribes still practice this as a form of scarification, but there's no reason such things need be visible."

He led her through a twisted maze of streets and quiet homes, many little more than sheds. They crunched through shin-deep snow. Pristine white, the filth of Norylska had yet to stain it.

Norylska fouls everything.

The city was strangely quiet, as if the white blanket devoured all sound.

Only the oldest buildings were stone. Most were wood and tin and mud. Windows lit by sputtering auroch-fat candles, stained by the stinking smoke.

Kostas recognized the neighborhood.

"Do you live near Patriot's Square?"

"We should be safe enough," Lazarev said. "Gen—the Shkuts—don't know about this place." He said something under his breath. "We'll figure out what to do with you."

What to do with me?

She realized she'd been so rushed to explain Penkin, she hadn't told him everything.

"I'm wearing Kostas' memory stone."

He grunted again, slowing to study the square ahead. Attention flicking from shadow to shadow, he finally nodded. Entering the Square of Patriots, he stayed close to the walls, away from the streetlamps.

Kat followed.

It's so cold it doesn't stink any more.

"Arkady wants the stone because he tortured Kostas to death," she explained. "He wants to destroy the evidence."

Again that distracted grunt.

He isn't surprised.

Hadn't Maks said something about such stones being removed from rotation? Or was he lying about that too?

She'd expected some reaction at the revelation Penkin gave her the memory stone of a militsioner who'd been tortured to death, but he simply nodded and kept walking.

Or maybe he wasn't listening. To be fair, she'd murdered his assistant and told him the Filth's biggest crime Family had their fingers in the militsioners. He could be forgiven for having a lot on his mind.

No. He knew.

'Different,' Arkady, had said, studying her. 'Sometimes it's like that, you know? Some people are what they are. One layer. Like Anitpov here. Antipov is always Antipov. No matter what you're wearing.'

She remembered being ashamed of the sad shack she and Fyodor shared. Now, the idea of caring what some Filth criminal thought seemed foolish.

What you're wearing. He meant stones, not clothes.

'But you, my dear, Arkady continued. 'You are someone entirely new.'

I wasn't what he expected, because I wasn't wearing my stones.

No. That wasn't right. When he said *no matter what you're wearing*, he referred to himself. She looked different to him.

She understood. Antipov was always Antipov, no matter what stones Arkady wore. But she seemed different.

Like the way she saw Lazarev differently when she wasn't wearing her stones.

But that only makes sense if he knows me.

Lazarev cut through the shadow of an ancient church, heading toward the statue of Solynska.

At the base of the statue he slowed, again taking a moment to study the silent streets.

Snow fell hard, coming down thick and heavy, cutting vision to a score of knee-deep strides. With half the streetlamps blown out, you'd be practically on top of someone before you had a chance of seeing them.

More than anything, she wanted to share a drink and a cigareta in the Dripping Bucket with Maks.

You can't. You killed him.

Lazarev waited, gaze sliding across the square, head cocked slightly as he listened.

It wasn't my fault; he tried to take the book.

"The storm is a bit of luck," Lazarev said. "It'll hide our tracks."

Nodding to himself, he pushed through the snow to the rear of the statue.

He slowed at he reached a squat maintenance door set in the base. "Fuck."

It was the first time she heard him swear.

"What's wrong?"

Pulling the door open, he said, "Someone has been here."

"You live under the statue of Solynska?"

"Quiet," he whispered. "The snow covered their tracks so we can't tell if they've left or await us inside."

"Should we go somewhere else?"

Lazarev gestured at the door. "Dig."

It took several minutes of shoveling snow with her bare hands before they could lever the door open wide enough to enter.

"Follow," he said, slipping into the dark. "Close the door behind you."

Kat did as instructed.

The old man she'd known tottered about his messy office with a look of lost perplexity. This Lazarev prowled like a cat. He was directed purpose, carved free of hesitation and doubt.

Down, into the bowels of Norylska, into the hellish realm of Vyraj where the gods sent all the worst traitors and sinners.

A dim shape, Lazarev moved through the darkness with utter confidence. She followed him down a long hall.

Crouching, he said over his shoulder, "They disarmed my traps."

A long knife appearing in his hand as if by magic, he slid forward, a ghost.

Kat's fist clenched around the comforting weight of Maks' knuckleduster.

The long tunnel ended at a door. Slightly ajar, light showed through the cracks.

"If it's Gen," said Lazarev, "kill him fast." Bright eyes, glistening shards of obsidian, studied her in the dark. "I need you to protect me."

"I will." She would allow no harm to befall him. "Get behind me," she said, approaching the door.

Lazarev did as instructed.

Peering through the crack, she saw a well-lit room beyond. A dozen or more cots sat in neat rows, upon each a butchered body.

She had to protect Lazarev at all cost.

Kat pushed the door open, saw Gen standing over Arkady's sundered corpse, bloody face stretched in a savage grin. He held a dripping machete in his fist.

He's dead. Arkady is dead.

With the Shkut avtorityet gone, she might yet survive this.

But the scene looked wrong. These people lay motionless as Gen slaughtered them. Kostas knew defensive wounds, and not a single person here bore one. Gen had moved from cot to cot, killing, and no one had woke to resist him.

Impossible. It wouldn't have been quiet.

Lazarev entered behind her. "I've changed my mind," he whispered, voice choked with rage. "Hurt him. Break him."

'I have no desire to hurt you,' Arkady had said in her kitchen. *'Though your quietly angry boyfriend over there, him I'd like to break.'*

My quietly angry boyfriend.

She'd heard that phrase more than once.

"Who the fuck is the old man?" demanded Gen. He winced in pain, one hand clutching a bloody wound in his gut.

He's been in a fight.

But that fight didn't happen here.

Lazarev knew Fyodor was a lawyer and a coward. She'd never mentioned that.

'Some people are what they are. No matter what you're wearing. But you, my dear, are someone entirely new.'

The betrayal shattered her heart. A thousand times worse than any hurt Fyodor could ever cause.

"This," said Kat, stepping aside, "is Arkady."

GENNDY ANTONOV – CHAPTER THIRTY-FIVE

All violence and politics consists of some people forcing others, under threat of suffering or death, to do what they do not want to do.

—D Puskyn, *Exile*

Someone's here.

A moment later, another presence in his head confirmed the thought, the scent of aftershave carrying on an ice-cold draft cutting through the heat haze of the room. Gen turned, found Kat standing in the entrance, an old man, though stiff-backed, trailing at her heels. His eyes glinted like polished stone.

Veneficum.

Sobek snarled the word, though in recognition or contempt, Gen couldn't be sure.

"Who the fuck is the old man?" demanded Gen.

He climbed off Arkady's bed, pain knifing into his gut like a Kievan acrobat, and he winced, hand going to his side in reflex.

"This," said Kat, stepping aside, "is Arkady."

Gen flicked a glance at the bodies in the room, at the corpse of his former employer cooling on its slab. Puzzle pieces slammed into place in his mind, urged on by Sobek. He flicked blood from Boris' blade and took a fighting stance, lowering his center of gravity, legs wide. The old man did the same.

Militsiya training.

"Kat, stay back," the old man shot over his shoulder. "I'll deal with you later. But for now, stay safe, my dear."

They closed the distance. A grin spread across Arkady/Not Arkady's face. Gen had seen that grin a thousand times before. Altin Ordu men, confident in their ability to murder. Arkady had grown the same grin when presented with a particularly tempting morsel of violence. The old man roared, the sound carrying war with it. Death rode the wave.

Gen would be the shoal it broke on.

The old man came faster than Gen expected. He feinted once, laid a hot line across Gen's bicep, then retreated.

Old. Slow.

And yet, he stabbed you a little.

Shut up.

They circled, Gen favoring his wounded side, trying to keep it away from the old man. Arkady did the same. Stooped a little, steps halting despite obvious eagerness to bleed Gen. They eyed one another like predators in the taiga.

"This is the kryshas from the Bucket?" Arkady mocked. "Little more than a broken hunk of meat."

Gen snorted, snapped his blade forward. Pain flared, a fresh trickle of blood from the wound filling his waistband. He winced, his strike falling short, only scoring a nick against Arkady's wrist. The old man turned the blade with his own and cut into the back of Gen's hand, trying to force him to drop the knife.

Clutch it tighter, ignore the ache.

Watch the blood-that'll get slippery.

"And you? The *avtorityet*—great and powerful Shkut. Little more than a walking corpse," Gen said. "Your man, Boris. He died screaming."

"You know what's interesting about owls?" Arkady asked.

"No. Enlighten me," Gen said.

"They call twice when they're hunting—first time loud, second time soft. Prey lowers its guard. Sounds like they're leaving, then they drop out of the sky and put claws through your eyes."

"The 'you' in this conversation being prey," Gen said. I don't find it easy to identify with meat. It's interesting you do."

Arkady sneered and lunged again. A quick exchange, wrists and knives like quicksilver. Gen came away a little worse for it. The old man had snagged his forearm twice. Probably cut a nerve. His fingers slipped from cold to hot, hot to cold, pins and needles running under the flesh like a stream.

The wound in Gen's side opened a little more. Flowing in a sticky wave, blood overwhelmed the dam of his trousers, spilling inside and out, leaving a trail of heat on the inside of his thigh, curling rivulets around his calf like a lover's fingers. He scurried back to buy time, feet slipping in the gore coating the floor. He leaned against the nearest bed, watching the old man do the same. Their breathing came in heaving sighs.

Fuckin' tired. So fuckin' tired.

Arkady took another breath, straightened with it. He waved the blade in his hand. A thin thing, wicked sharp. Like a splinter carved from ice.

"A waste, talent like yours. You could've been *somebody*. Instead, I'm going to end you. First you. Then your fucking pathetic bitch and your crotch fruit." He made a motion with his free hand, like pulling an apple from a tree. "Right from the vine."

He came on with new fury, and Gen backed off, panting in pain and exhaustion. Gen slipped, small of his back slamming into a bed.

Fuck, that hurt.

Arkady ripped his shoulder open with that blade—that *fucking* Altin Ordu blade—then his ribs. The world threatened to go black. Gen staggered, and the old man backed off. Pain etched itself in stark lines on his face. The last assault had cost him something. Still, he wasn't bleeding half his life onto the floor.

Arkady took his rest again.

Now!

I can't—nothing left.

"This is my fault, really," Arkady said. "Should've given you something more. Something to shore up your loyalty. Man like you—too strong in the heart. Too stupid in the head. Boris was right. You're a wild dog. Snapping at anyone passing. Probably your father's fault."

Gen snapped his head up at that. Arkady pushed himself off the bed he'd been leaning against. Staggered once, corrected. He'd flipped the blade back against his wrist, hilt held tight in his fist.

Solostian.

He attacked again, the blade never where Gen expected it. It cut into shoulder and cheek, nearly took an eye. He tried to move into the man's guard, stab into his guts. Landed only blows against something hard beneath the man's shirt, the edge bouncing off.

Arkady's blade came down, meaning to pierce behind his collarbone and sever the artery there, bleed him quick; end it. Gen dropped his own knife and grabbed the man's wrists with both hands, staving off the attack. The old man was shockingly strong. Or he'd simply grown that weak.

You're fucking up, fuckup. Gonna die here.

Too soon. Not ready.

Your child is next. Your wife. All because of pride. Because you wouldn't dig in the earth. They're gonna cut your baby from her guts. Leave her womb a bleeding wound.

No.

Then let me in. You know me. I kill for pleasure. I kill for curiosity. I cut myself in the small hours, just to feel something. I will bleed this man in a blink, drain him dry.

Gen opened himself to the voice in his head.

KAYUSHKA LEONOVA – CHAPTER THIRTY-SIX

Luck would not have happened without misfortune's help.

—Kievan Proverb

While the men fought, a war waged inside Kat's head.

Lazarev was in danger! She should help him. It would be easy. Once Gen's back was turned, step in and punch him in the base of the skull with the knuckledusters. She knew how to pivot so her entire body weight was behind the blow.

But it wasn't Lazarev.

Or was it?

Was he Lazarev pretending to be Arkady, or Arkady pretending to be Lazarev?

One was the only man who genuinely seemed to care for her, who gave her these stones and made her strong and confident. The other threatened to kill her.

Gen screamed, staggering away as the veneficum followed, effortless slipping between fighting styles that took decades to master.

Implacable. Eternal. Lazarev was iron will.

More than anything, she wanted to fight at his side, to make him proud.

He threatened to skin me.

But that didn't mean he would.

Why put all the effort into *making* her, if he planned on killing her?

No, that made no sense. His plans went deeper. It was her lack she couldn't understand them.

He used you to get Kostas' stone out of the precinct.

She remembered him watching as Ushakov peeled the flesh from her.

'How did you know who the leak was?' Arkady demanded. *'Were we sloppy?'*

Because he knew who the leak was. It was him. He referred to himself as we.

He was trying to figure out how Kostas had figured out that Lazarev was the leak in the Chernyshevsky Street Militsiya Bureau.

She wanted to laugh. Kostas hadn't known.

Gen and Lazarev talked as they fought, the former growling ever weaker threats and taunts, the latter starting to wheeze.

He's tiring.

No quantity of stones, no combination of traits and skills, could change the fact that Lazarev was an old man. If she didn't come to his aid soon, Gen might kill him.

Lazarev hissed in rage and retreated as the kyrshas cut him.

No, no, no, no.

Gen brought her the book, but he'd already tried to kill her in an alley. She had to trust that Lazarev had plans beyond merely getting Kostas's stone out of the precinct. She was too valuable to him. He made her. The stones. The way he listened when they talked. No one ever did that.

Father, with his bottle, never needed her. Couldn't hear a word she said.

Fyodor, with his plans and his bright future, didn't need her, couldn't imagine her being useful beyond her ability to look pretty and make children. He needed the quiet and proper wife she could never be.

Lazarev needed her like no one ever had.

Was that it? Was being needed worth so much?

"I see the spark there now," said Lazarev. "A complex, rooted deep. It's so much easier to own a man who needs fatherly approval."

Listed among the stones Kat wore: Katina Sokolova, Kolyma-1428. FA/A. The only entry not pertaining to an animal. A woman's name, and Kolyma gulag, a labour camp famous for breaking people.

She saw it in herself with dreadful clarity, a desperate need for validation. When Lazarev said he was proud of her, she'd wanted to scream with joy.

That's not me.

Father was furious when she told him she was moving in with Fyodor even though they weren't married, and yet she'd done it anyway. Fyodor had been ready to leave her when she told him she was taking a secretarial job with the militsioners, and it hadn't stopped her.

But one word from Lazarev and she'd have done anything for him, been willing to kill to protect him.

FA/A. The strength of the trait was listed as five.

A powerful need for Fatherly Approval and Authority.

The men fought, slashing and cursing. They moved slower and slower, Gen, weak from blood loss, Lazarev gasping, moving like a man his age.

It's so much easier to own a man who needs fatherly approval.

FA/A five. The simple brown stone.

Kat touched the necklace of personality traits within her shirt. The chain was too thick to break easily, the veneficum made sure of that. To remove one, she'd have to remove them all. She'd still have Kostas' memories, but she'd be helpless, terrified Home Kat. She hated that Kat, loathed her weakness.

I need these stones.

How could she fight without them?

Lazarev followed Gen around the bed where Arkady's slaughtered body lay. She loved him. He was the father she'd never had, never deserved. To remove these stones was to betray him, betray his trust. She'd lose him. Forever.

Remove the stones and she'd lose everything. She'd lose her rage and bravery. She'd cower in the corner sobbing, waiting for someone to come save her just like Kostas had.

But Maks never came.

And he wouldn't this time either.

Lazarev is manipulating you.

He tinkered with her emotions, adding stones to alter her personality to his need. He wanted her malleable and obedient, like a dog.

She trusted him and he betrayed her.

Grabbing the necklace, she hesitated. *Home Kat, you're not as weak as you think. You can do this.* Lifting off the chain of traits, she tossed it aside. Her crushing need to please Lazarev, her desperate hunger for his approval, faded.

Kat found a new rage, one deeper than any trait stored on stone.

GENNDY ANTONOV – CHAPTER THIRTY-SEVEN

"Change can be as complex as a butterfly emerging from its cocoon, or as simple as a blade ending a life. The world is not biased."

-Visjnic Russ, Khagan Street Philosphic

When Gen was a child, they'd attended the orthodox ceremonies, as all good Norylskans did. He recalled endless hours of sitting in the pews, listening to the priest drone on about salvation, legs aching to run, head full of summer chaff and sunlight. When winter closed in, the sermons turned as dark as the weather. The verses became things of blood and horror, of damnation.

Gen thought he'd seen the worst of humanity in the war. Knew what Hell on Earth looked like. Sobek's thoughts were vile, putting the lie to Gen's knowledge. Thick and putrescent, rotting and black. For all the calm on the surface, the man was a roiling cloud of raw fury.

Arkady's stinking breath in his face.

The knife, descending.

"I see the spark there now. A complex, rooted deep. Again, my mistake. It's so much easier to own a man who needs fatherly approval. But you hated yours. Not enough affection? Did he beat you? Did he sneak into your room while you slept, and touch you in your soft places? Or did he simply not love you?" Arkady asked.

He leaned in, and the blade dropped another couple inches.

"Doesn't matter. If he doesn't love you now, he never will," Arkady said.

Sobek milled like a cancer in Gen's mind. Ice-cold, spiked and needling. The feeling flooded his limbs, seized muscle as one might overpower the driver of a carriage.

"Lazarev," he said, taking control of Gen's mouth, contorting the vocal cords, voice taking on the quality of metal dragged over stone. "You puling fuck."

The old man blinked as if slapped, then something the size of a small and furious beast slammed into Lazarev's spine and he went sprawling. Gen slid to the side in time to avoid going down as well. Arkady's hand jerked open, blade skittering across the floor. Kat straddled Arkady's back, her diminutive form landing punch after punch into his kidneys. He grunted at first, then screamed as it went on.

"I loved you! I trusted you! I would have done anything for you!" she screamed as she beat the man into a pulp, bloody brass knuckles flashing on her hand with each blow. "Betrayer!"

Sobek watched for a moment, then called her name in that same grating voice.

"Katyusha!"

She paused long enough to look up.

"A man like this—he deserves so much worse."

He knelt beside the old man, lifting Lazarev's head by the hair. One eye had already begun to swell from impact with the floor, lips split and oozing a thin red trickle, nose bent awkwardly to the side.

"You, of all people, should know you cannot bury your sins. In the gulag, do you know what I dreamt of? A snail crawling along the edge of a straight razor. My dream, every night; my nightmare. Crawling, slithering, along the edge of a straight razor... and surviving. I will enjoy every moment of this," Sobek said, then spat into his face.

Lazarev flinched once more, and Sobek slammed his skull into the floor. He stood back and leaned against one of the beds, swaying slightly.

"This body is fucked up," he said conversationally to Kat. "Gen should take better care of us."

She stared at him.

"Well?" Sobek asked her. "You going to finish the job?"

He leaned down with a pained grunt and tossed her the knife Gen had been carrying. She caught it neatly, inspecting the edge.

She cut the old man, talking as she worked, whispering. Apologies. Begging forgiveness. A stream of endless malice.

"Tsst," Sobek hissed through his teeth. She paused in her work. "Slow. Slower than that. You want him to last."

Kat hesitated, knife making shallow cuts.

"Here, let me show you," Sobek said.

He knelt beside her, took the knife at an oblique angle, hooked the tip into the flesh. Pushed it slowly forward. Lazarev moaned.

"Shh. Shh now. Plenty of time for misery. Right now, this young lady needs an education."

Sobek worked the blade until it was sheathed in Lazarev's flesh. He brought it up, expertly severing the subcutaneous layer. When he pulled the knife free, the skin of the old man's back billowed up, bruising and swelling as the edema beneath grew.

Lazarev wept in misery. Sobek leaned over, close to the man's ear, Kat's eyes on him.

Poor girl. Poor misguided girl. Well, we'll set her right.

"Quiet now," he tapped Lazarev's cheek with the knife. "Or I'll have your tongue before its time."

He moved back into position, slapped the loose skin of Lazarev's back. It jiggled and sloshed, and where he'd made the incision, blood oozed from the wound like animals fleeing a forest ablaze.

"Now you," he said, flipping the knife handle-first.

She took it tentatively, made another incision beside the first. Lazarev grunted in agony as the knife went in. Too deep, too acute an angle. Likely to sever too much muscle, possibly puncture a lung.

"Tsst. Careful," he admonished.

She paused again.

"You don't want to cut too deep. Sever an artery and your prey escapes." He entwined his thumbs, flapped his hands like a bird leaving the nest, making a fluttering noise to accompany it.

She looked unsure of herself.

"It's fine," he said. "We have a long time. Besides, everyone has to start somewhere."

She pulled the blade free, Lazarev gasping with pain. The man shit himself at some point. Kat didn't seem to notice, or care. She slipped the knife into his back again, at a better angle, cut the skin free in a wide swathe.

Sobek looked on, nodded in approval when she glanced to him.

"You're doing fine. I just need to rest a little."

He wanted to hold on. Wanted to watch every moment of this man being flayed alive. But this body—gods, the man who owned it had been careless. He sank to the floor, back against a nearby bed, and stayed there.

Closed his eyes.

KATYUSHKA LEONOVA — CHAPTER THIRTY-EIGHT

As children we strive to be who our parents want us to be. As youths we strive to be who our peers want us to be. As adults we strive to be who the state thinks we should be. As parents we strive to be who our children need us to be.

In the end we are nothing, hollow echoes of need built on the perceptions of others.

—D Puskyn, *Exile*

Lazarev lay still. His chest didn't move, no rise and fall of breath.

He's gone.

He was a flayed ruin, dissected.

I did that. Me.

Home Kat. No trait stones. Only Kostas' memories, and he seemed at peace with the horror.

You're a monster.

The admission was oddly unmoving. Had she always been a monster? Had she simply needed a push to set herself free?

Wiping her bloody hands on Lazarev's greatcoat, Kat rose to her feet. "I suppose I owe you my thanks," she said to the veneficum's corpse.

She felt numb, gutted like what the reducing factories did to paraceratherium.

What should she do?

Dead men everywhere, most of them by her hand.

No going back to Fyodor now.

She laughed, a cracked broken sound echoing through the stone hall beneath the statue. They'd come for her. They'd find her. She killed Maks and she killed Penkin. Grinin would put a bullet in her head and be glad to be rid of her. A woman in the militsioners was insanity. He'd report the failure to his superiors in Khagan and never give her a second thought.

The only women with jobs were those running the crime families.

The necklace of traits caught her eye. She collected it, careful not to touch the stones.

Gen thought Arkady poisoned him. Had he, as Lazarev, poisoned her? Saw scale snake. Crocodile. Rat. A fucking house cat. Hadn't she thought something about feeling like a cat in heat after fucking Maks behind the Dripping Bucket. 'House cat, F. ESTR,' Lazarev's book said. Estrus? Had the fucker literally given her a stone with a trait lifted from a horny female housecat?

She kicked his corpse.

And some woman they'd cracked in a gulag with a desperate worship of father figures.

Did they do it to her on purpose?

It made sense. Why wait for traits to happen naturally when you could shape them by shattering people's lives in exactly the right way.

Like a master gem cutter shaping a diamond.

Scanning the floor, she found Gen's knife with the heavy pommel. Grabbing it, she used the blunt end to smash the brown stone to dust. Loyalty to the undeserving was useless.

Kat touched the other stones, one by one, feeling their traits whisper through her like passing ghosts. She liked the woman they made her. Kat the saw scale viper was capable of anything, and she'd need that if she was going to survive the next couple of days.

What a laughable thought.

Donning the necklace, tucking it into her shirt, she immediately felt better. What had been a stray thought gelled into what was probably an insane and doomed plan.

"The only women with jobs," she told the veneficum, "are those running the crime families."

She couldn't return to Fyodor, and her position with the militsioners wouldn't last past the moment they found Penkin. She'd need some way to support herself.

Kat touched Lazarev's book in her pocket. She hadn't entirely cracked the code yet but knew she could.

Blood leaked from the veneficum, pooled thick and black.

And there's a vault full of stones, many dating back to the war.

If she was fast, she could saunter in and fill her pockets.

Could she do this alone?

Gen groaned, coughed a weak sputter of blood bubbles.

Maybe I won't have to.

The man was dangerous, murderously violent. But there were uses for that.

Why would he be loyal to me?

She glanced at the dust of the brown stone. She had the book. She'd find the stones she needed in the vault.

I could make him loyal.

At least, if he didn't bleed to death first.

A moment's indecision as she realized she had no idea how to stanch even a small wound—never mind a perforated gut—before she remembered Kostas knew an unlicensed back alley healer.

Grabbing his ankle, Kat dragged Gen to the base of the stairs. Big as he was, he was heavier than she expected.

"With all the fucking blood you lost," she told him, "you should weigh less."

The storm above continued, unabated. Snow had pushed the door open, powdered the top steps. The world beyond was a flurry of white.

Once again grabbing him by the ankles, she said, "This is going to hurt," and hauled him up the stairs.

His head bounced off each step with a hollow *thonk*, and she muttered curses and apologies.

Hopefully his brain won't be porridge by the time I get him to the top.

"Would anyone even be able to tell?" she asked.

He said some woman's name, and Kat knew she'd have to replace that love and loyalty with something more useful.

Kat dragged him through thigh-deep snow, leaving a long trail of blood. Everything hurt. Her arms ached. Her legs shook from the effort. Heart slamming in her chest, lungs labouring desperately to draw each breath, she pulled him deeper into the Filth.

Get Gen to the healer.

Get the stones from Lazarev's vault.

Understand enough of the veneficum's book to know which stones the Shkut kyrshas needed.

"You're not a Shkut enforcer anymore," she told him as she pulled him around another corner. "You're a Leonova avorityet. You've been promoted!"

Where was I?

Get the stones from the vault, as many as she could cram into her pockets. Stealing from the militsiya seemed a good start to a life of crime.

Learn what she needed from the book, return to the healer, give them to the big stupid dead weight who'd better not be fucking dead already.

Give?

What if he didn't want them?

She remembered the way she lost contact with the stones when she bent over that chair after killing Penkin. That was dangerous. If Gen was going to be her brigadier, she needed to *own* him.

He'll be at the healer's.

And he already had a good number of handy holes in him.

Yeah, she liked it. Make sure he was loyal and stayed that way forever. Loyal like he was to that Irina woman—whoever she was.

No, *more* loyal.

Kat pulled Gen through the snow, dragging him into a narrow alley Kostas recognized.

"It's going to be a busy night," she told him.

GENNDY ANTONOV – CHAPTER THIRTY-NINE

There can be only one permanent revolution—a moral one: regeneration of the inner man. How is this revolution to take place? No one knows how it will take place in humanity, but every man feels it clearly in himself. Yet in our world everyone thinks of changing humanity, and no one thinks of changing himself.

—D Puskyn, Exile

Light and dark, light and dark. Something rough and cold against his spine, soaking through his clothing. He'd complain—thought to—but it felt good on his aching fevered skin. A sense of movement—halting, vomitous. His guts threatened to spill, first from the inside, then through the holes cut in him. But somehow, he held together. He always did. Good old Gen. Solid Gen.

The world faded for a time.

Warmth. The sharp scent of alcohol, cold metal against his back. Was he on the table at the plant? Would they butcher him as well, now? No part wasted, fuel and food alike.

Voices at the periphery of awareness. One, low, basso. The other a strong alto. The alto gave orders, the basso rumbled in reply. Like Solynstyn's *Concerto in E.*

The thought brought Irina to mind. Of the time they'd snuck over a wall in the south. Grass! Hedges! They huddled in the foliage and listened to the strains of music filter from the Tchaichov Opera House.

They were nearly caught that time, and they tumbled over the wall in flight, laughing as they went, the homeowner threatening to call the militsiya.

"Call my ass as well!" Irina shouted back, and Gen had to pull her into an alley, muffling her hysterical giggling.

They'd stood against the bricks, and looking into her eyes in the moonlight...

She is water, and I am dying. The depths of her crushing me with the weight of her regard.

Pain flared in his chest, and he opened his mouth to call her name. Only a dry rasp came, lips chapped from thirst, tongue tacked to the palate.

Water. Water.

And on the heels of that, the cut-flower scent of decay.

The light retreated again.

Another flash of light.

Irina, wrapped in sheets and sweat, breasts free from the fabric, nipples erect. Her breathing sounded like the sigh of wind through trees, while his more like a forge bellows. They laid beside each other, naked and cooling, Gen going soft, their fingers entwined.

"Lilia," she said into the aftermath of lust.

Gen blinked sleepiness away, turned his head. Licked his lips. He swore the woman had drained him of every drop of moisture.

"Sorry, what?" he asked.

"Lilia," she said.

"For?"

She turned her head to meet his gaze, a slight smile on her lips. Curls played in a chaotic storm across her pillow.

"A girl. Lilia for a girl and Yuri for a boy."

Gen made a face. Irina's eyebrows came up.

"You don't like Yuri?"

"I like Yuri for a child that gets beat often."

"Hm. Pavel?"

He hesitated.

"You hesitated," she said.

He laughed. "I like Artyom."

She pursed her lips, considered. "Artyom," she said, tasting it, rolling the name across her tongue. Finally, she nodded. "Artyom. Or Kiska."

Gen gasped in mock outrage and narrowed his eyes. "You wouldn't!"

She rolled on top of him, wearing nothing but a wicked grin. "Stop me."

Her lips were fire.

The light faded again, a rage of memory dying.

He woke to cool sheets, bright light. The bed he lay in was clean and comfortable, as things go in Norylska. Outside, the storm had abated. Inside, a man in a white coat sat at a nearby desk, making a flurry of marks in a ledger.

Gen cleared his throat and winced, needles tearing at the lining. The man looked up, nodded to Gen's right. A small table beside the bed held a tumbler of water and bowl of thin broth. The smell of the broth turned his stomach, but he drank the water down greedily.

Melted snow.

It was cold as a Norylskan whore's nipples, and probably the best thing he'd ever drunk. He placed the empty glass on the table, took a breath to belch. Something stopped him from inhaling fully, and he looked down. Gauze wrapped the majority of his torso, backed by thicker pads where the wounds were worse. An extra-heavy pad covered the spot over his heart, and he frowned.

I don't remember being stabbed there.

Yeah, but did he remember much of anything from that day? He'd been fighting Arkady—Lazarev—and then he blacked out and woke up here.

What day is it, anyway?

As if anticipating the question, the man at the desk answered. "Thirdday. You've been unconscious for two. Your little friend was worried. Didn't think you'd survive. But I know better. I see when a man walks the line, and you were not ready to cross it yet."

"My little friend?" Gen rasped.

"The... brunette. Tough bitch. Dragged you in here herself. Not happy about it, though. Muttering and cursing the entire time. Had to get her to calm down so I could see what was wrong. Didn't want to give you up right away."

Angry?

Not for you. Not at you.

Ah, yeah. Lazarev. He'd made some comment about fathers. And then— another blank in his head. Gen muttered in frustration.

The man in the desk crossed the distance while Gen was lost in his head. He inspected the bandages, alternatively making tutting noises and scratching notes on a pad as he went.

"You were pretty mangled when she brought you in. Said you'd been in some sort of industrial accident."

He narrowed his eyes, as if expecting Gen to spill the truth. Wasn't going to happen. The doctor snorted in amusement and changed the subject. He tapped the pad over Gen's heart with the end of his pencil.

"Had to pull some heroic measures. But your friend assured me you wouldn't mind."

Gen nodded, forced a smile. "Well, thank you, doctor."

The man turned to go.

"Say, can you do me a favor?"

The doc turned back. "For a koyln, sure."

"My friend will have it. Find a woman named Irina Antonov on the east side of the Filth. Tell her... tell her..."

Words failed him. He wasn't sure what to tell her.

He'd survived? Would she care? Would that just alert Lia and Dmitry they had loose ends to clip?

He loved her? She knew that.

He was sorry? No, words rarely patched wounds cut by action. Only more action might heal those.

Nothing seemed adequate, and he shook his head, giving the man another sad smile. "Nothing. I'll tell her myself. But thank you."

Gen knew it for a lie, but let it sit anyway. What were lies between strangers, after all?

Matveev, The Tsar's Heart. Irina loved that one.

Fitting, he thought, to bury that part of his life as surely as he'd buried any other enemy he'd made.

Love, an enemy?

A stranger at the least.

The doctor looked disappointed at losing out on a koyln but nodded all the same. "Not a problem. I'll be out for lunch. You can make do here? The pot's in the corner—it would do you good to move around. More water in the pitcher, over there. And your friend should be back before I am."

"Thank you," Gen said.

The doctor nodded in acknowledgement once more and left. Gen sat in silence for a while, staring out the window. Snow lay in an ashen blanket across the city. Where the sootmen managed to clear it, rough paths wended their way across the street. In rare cases—under eaves and awnings—where ash had not fallen, snow sparkled like diamonds.

An intense craving for the past, for the days before death and war and betrayal, rolled over him, nearly pulling tears free in its passage.

You can never unmake a virgin. Another old Norylskan saying. He laughed bitterly, and pain spiked near his heart.

The chest. Did he stab you in the chest?

Why was this bothering him?

Gen peeled back the corner of the dressing above his heart. The skin beneath was sutured, angry red where thread forced the edges of the wound into a ridge. It didn't stink, and that was a relief. One thing any soldier learns to fear early on is infection. Gangrene is a killer and an eater of limbs, but any number of illnesses could fell or break him.

He tugged on the corner of the bandage again, and it peeled away easier. Beneath it, a flat plane of obsidian. Surrounding it, smaller stones, a constellation of traits embedded in his flesh.

Gen laid his head back, sighed. Closed his eyes. He knew his reaction should be horror, should be rage. Instead, he only felt... relieved. Resigned. He'd fought so long, and so hard. He'd done his best. Maybe this time he'd be stronger.

When the war ended, the state had told the soldiers they'd served with distinction, had earned their rest. War was war, service guaranteed citizenship, and now they stood as true men of the nation, exemplars of the Kievan peoples.

What no one tells you is the truth.

War haunts.

It's a ghost in the room, sitting quietly in the corner. It watches. Your meals, your leisure, your work, your fucking. It watches, and for the most part, is content. It's a phantom, after all. A thing that *had been*.

But now and then, by way of some eddy, some whirl of the aether, some twist of metaphysics and memory, it became *discontent*, for lack of a better word. It raged at the walls of its cage, because it could only go where you went, only experience the things you did. Your life was its framework and its tether, and in those moments of raw fury, it beat fists of pain and loathing against your brain. You had forced it into visions of horror it could not let go, could not forget or misremember.

You knew to do either was betrayal of the ordeal, so you keep it shackled. Because this is *important*. You don't tread the paths of Hell and pretend you hadn't. War is a crucible. The ones who come out the other side are flawed steel, cracks patched with glass. The specter is a frail shell of ice holding the whole brittle mess together. You could no more ignore it than a length of steel in your guts.

As for those who hadn't made it, you carried their ghosts as well.

Haunted. He'd always be haunted.

But not Irina. And not Kat. They need not be. He could spare them that. He was vast and could hold many horrors.

He placed a hand on the stones in his chest, felt their facets against his palm. Cool, reassuring. If Kat had done this, she had good reasons. To protect him. Make him stronger, smarter. Ready. She had carried him all this way! Gods, what he'd give for a woman so loyal, so strong. If he'd had a hundred such as her, the Altin Ordu would have fled the steppes the moment they stepped into the sun.

Anything. You'd give anything.

His lips pursed in thought, and he tapped the obsidian, feeling it vibrate in his flesh.

The Shkuts were still out there. He had gone to war once; he would do it again. For better reasons this time.

War it is, then, tovarich.

KATYUSHKA LEONOVA – CHAPTER FORTY

All Kievan's greatest philosophers are from Norylska because Norylska teaches us the one truth: Life is grey.

There are moments of black, when the dust from the smelting furnaces blanket the city in soot.

There are moments of white, after a fresh snow fall.

But they are moments.

Grey is the natural state.

—Viilash Abumkov, Norylskan Philosopher

After selling one of the military stones she stole from Lazarev's vault, Kat had enough set aside to keep her and Gen in some style. At least until he recovered. Moving every few days so as not to draw attention, they now stayed at the Talnakh Hotel in a small but well-appointed suite. Every meal was room service, their bar restocked daily, all laundry seen to by attentive staff. Compared to the shack she shared with Fyodor, this was unbelievable luxury.

Fyodor. Strange how the man, who had once meant so much, ceased to mean anything. She could have done nothing. She could have lived out the rest of her life without ever thinking about the man again. She could have left him be, let him get on with his pathetic cowardly existence. No doubt he would have replaced her within the year. Even that wouldn't have bothered her.

She could have done nothing.

Instead, she sent Genn over with rather vague instructions: Break him. Don't kill him.

She never asked for details.

Her new dresses, made by a tailor who came to the hotel, were the finest cotton she'd felt since leaving Kievan. Simple, yet elegant. They even hid the Altin Ordu Galand double-action revolver she now wore in her lower back, though the tailor had grumbled about the modifications. Her stones, with the exception of the housecat, had been polished and set in a tight choker necklace that would never break contact with her skin. Not quite valuable gems, they passed for inexpensive jewellery.

Nice as all this was, it couldn't last. For one thing, staying in Norylska's finest hotels for too long would draw attention. There weren't many of them.

They needed a home. They needed somewhere safe, somewhere they could control. She wanted thick walls and guard towers. She wanted big men with guns and submission sticks. If she sold all the stones, she could probably live in comfort for the rest of her life. Kat didn't want comfort. Or not *just* comfort.

Gen knocked, letting himself into the suite. Recovered enough to be out and about, he spent his days scouting talent and making quiet inquiries.

Shedding his new greatcoat, brushing off the worst of the snow, he hung it on the oak coatrack. Improving quickly, he still moved tentatively, afraid to open his wounds.

Two more weeks, and he'll be an unholy terror once again.

Which was good. She had need of an unholy terror.

Kicking his boots off like a little kid, he collapsed into the sofa across from her. Arms and legs thrown wide, he took up most of it. He was, she decided, handsome enough, if you liked your men blunt and hard.

He's a cross between a shovel, a hammer, and a slab of stone.

Several beatings and a couple of knife fights hadn't done his face any favours in terms of classical beauty, but then that had never been one of his strengths. Still, it gave him a kind of brutal edge she rather liked. And when they walked together, men got the fuck out of her way instead of trying to ogle her.

"How'd it go?" she asked, heading to the bar and pouring two large cognacs.

Gen waited until she'd handed him his and taken her seat before answering. "No problems. I talked to some people who know people. The militsioners found Lazarev in a room full of dead Shkuts. All those corpses were employees one way or another. From Arkady, right to the silky."

He looked decidedly ill about that last bit. Kat didn't ask.

"They found Penkin and that pretty boy who was your partner," he added.

"Maks."

That still hurt. Lazarev had inadvertently taught her some valuable lessons. The stones were valuable, but each had a time and a place. Walking the streets seething with coiled viper violence might feel good, but sometimes clear thought was more important. Having spent the last week with Lazarev's manual, she worked to fine tune what stones she wore, and when. Veneficum, she'd realized, were a blend of doctor, scientist, and artist. Lazarev had been a master of the first two aspects, but rather crude in the last. He painted with broad strokes, lacking subtlety.

"Yeah," grunted Gen. "And, of course, they noticed their vault had been emptied."

"Of course," she said, sipping cognac. "What's their working theory?"

"Well, they have a murdered veneficum's assistant, a dead militsioner, and their veneficum was found in a Shkut hideaway with a dead avtoriyet. They're thinking he stole the stones, got caught in the act by Penkin, and had to murder him. With everyone dead, it looks like maybe the Gruzdev Family caught them unawares. Tensions have been high between the four families as of late."

Gen flashed a bent grin. Once he felt good enough to walk, he'd demanded something to do to help pass the time. Arming him with a selection of revolvers, she sent him to work the families, killing shestyorka, the street-level associates.

"They're still struggling with the Maks angle," Gen said. "He was, by all accounts, a good militsioner. With you missing and assumed dead, it throws some suspicion his way. Maybe he was working with the veneficum. Or maybe Maks was onto Lazarev and died trying to stop him."

"They think I'm dead?"

Gen downed his drink, glanced at Kat. When she nodded, he rose and gestured toward her cup.

"No thanks," she said.

Fetching himself another cognac, he returned to the couch, did that leonine sprawl thing she decided was rather fetching.

"No one suspects you survived. Too many dead men for a little girl to walk out of all that unscathed."

That was good. It meant no one would be looking for her.

"Oh yeah," said Gen. "The new militsioner veneficum arrives next week from Khagan. Apparently, he's young, fresh from the akademiya. Rumour has it Colonel Grinin didn't want someone with 'history.'"

A young man. Perhaps not a Master Veneficum like Lazarev, he'd still know more than Kat. She'd been studying the manual as Gen recuperated, but there were terms and ideas she needed help with. She'd considered going to a street veneficum, but hesitated. For the most part they were self-taught, dangerously ignorant.

"It would be handy to have a fully trained veneficum in our pocket. Handier to have a militsioner veneficum."

"Dangerous," said Gen, fetching a bright brass cigareta tin from his breast pocket. He frowned at the dark smokes within. "Never get used to not rolling my own." Standing, he crossed to where she sat, offered her one, lit it with a crisp wooden match.

Kat shrugged, inhaling smoke and letting it coil from her nose. "Less dangerous once we get our stones into him."

Lighting his own, he returned to the sofa. "Have you thought about a name?"

Wanting to distance herself from her past, she'd decided to shed her family name. No one would quake in fear because the Leonovas were coming.

Lazarev thought to poison her with his stones and misjudged. He made her stronger, more dangerous than she ever could have been without them. The saw-scale stone planted the idea.

"What do you think of Gadyuka?" she asked.

"Viper." Cigareta pinched between thumb and forefinger, he inhaled hard, held the smoke in as he thought. "I like it."

GLOSSARY OF TERMS

Avtorityet – Brigadier in a crime Family. A ranked member.

Blood and bones – Expletive. Like saying "bloody hell" or "Jesus Christ!"

Boyevik – Literally 'warrior' works for a Brigadier. Is in charge of finding new guys and paying tribute up to his Brigadier. Boyevik is also the main strike force of a brigade (bratva).

Byki – Crime Family bodyguards (literally: bulls)

Gods above and demons below – A particularly crude expression of rage and anger.

Gods and demons below – corruption of the former, used primarily by veterans and Family members who believe the heavens are empty.

Goluboi – slang for homosexual

Iskusstvo Veneficum – *The Art of the Veneficum*. The unofficial text on the art and practices and laws governing the veneficum.

Krysa – Street slang for a rat or snitch, someone who reports to the state/militsioners.

Kryshas – An enforcer in a crime Family. Particularly, a clever or brutal one.

Kvass – low alcohol drink brewed from rye bread, Common as a refreshment/with meals

Metka: Mark, or victim. Family slang for someone who's not gonna make it.

Militsioner – Policeman. A cop.

Militsiya – The Police. Law-enforcement is a branch of the military. Most cops are veterans from the war.

Novogodnyaya: New Years

Otdelyeniye – A large/major police station

Pivo – beer

Pizda: Cunt

Plemya – Viking tribes. Ruled the lands of Kievan before the rise of the Tsars.

Ponchiki – donut balls

Pustyak – Pushover

Sekretnaya Sluzhba Ubiystv (SSU) – Secret Assassination Service

Shestyorka – An "associate" to the crime Family. Errand boys, lookouts, and informers, they mostly stay out of the real action, work to earn their way in to the Family.

Sootmen – Responsible for sweeping the streets of coal dust during the warm months and shovelling the coal-stained snows during the winter.

Svoloch – Slang for street scum, dirtbags, criminals

Tantsor – Male ballerina (ballerino)

Tovarisch – Comrade. Somewhat formal, used among police officers. "Tovarisch Colonel."

Ublyudok – bastard

Uchastok – A local police station

Ura! - Cheers!

Vyraj - Kievan heaven and hell. Heaven, in the sky, is where the birds go during the winter. Hell, below ground, is a place of snakes and dragons, land of sinners and traitors.

Yuryev Industrial: Military manufacturer. Kat's father was Secretary of Finance before being sent north.

CLAYTON - ACKNOWLEDGEMENTS

No book is written in a vacuum, and I'd like to thank a few people for making this possible. First of all, Mike, for taking a shot in the dark on someone who may or may not be him anyway. He says he lives in Canada, but have you ever seen the two of us in a room together? Regardless, I've somehow learned something here, despite myself. Second, Krystle. God damn it, woman, stop being so brilliant. You're making my inferiority complex flare up. All the same, thank you for your insight, even if I have thus far resisted every effort to insert more smooching. Thank you, Carrie, for your relentless cheerleading. You shouted encouragement every step of the way, making even the tough parts not so tough. Finally, thanks to Sarah, our brilliant editor, for making this thing shine. Oh, and thanks to the community. As always, you are kind, welcoming, and just the best. Now get off my lawn, the lot of you.

PS: Krystle, you were completely wrong about breaking that last chapter up, and we definitely didn't do it after all.

MIKE - ACKNOWLEDGEMENTS

First, a huge thank you to Clayton for jumping into this insane project with both feet and for tolerating the ranting emails at four in the morning. This was fun to write, and I'm amazed we managed to train wreck those two story lines so beautifully.

Carrie Chi Lough and Krystle Matar beta read this thing several times. This novel is much improved for their feedback and suggestions. Except for that suggestion to break up the last chapter. Pfft! That was crap. You're crazy. We totally ignored you and no there isn't an extra chapter now in this version. That aside…thank you! And if you haven't read Krystle's *Legacy of the Brightwash*, go do so now. It's crazy good.

As always, I am endlessly grateful to you, the reader. Having people to share my little brain movies with makes it worth taking the time to two-finger type the damned things.

Cheers!